MR. TEXAS

MR. TEXAS

Lawrence Wright

ALFRED A. KNOPF New York 2023

THIS IS A BORZOI BOOK
PUBLISHED BY ALFRED A. KNOPF

Copyright © 2023 by Lawrence Wright

All rights reserved. Published in the United States by Alfred A. Knopf,
a division of Penguin Random House LLC, New York, and distributed
in Canada by Penguin Random House Canada Limited, Toronto.

www.aaknopf.com

Knopf, Borzoi Books, and the colophon are registered trademarks
of Penguin Random House LLC.

Library of Congress Cataloging-in-Publication Data
Names: Wright, Lawrence, [date] author.
Title: Mr. Texas : a novel / Lawrence Wright.
Description: New York : Alfred A. Knopf, 2023. |
Identifiers: LCCN 2022057285 | ISBN 9780593537374 (hardcover) |
ISBN 9780593537381 (ebook)
Classification: LCC PS3573.R53685 M77 2023 |
DDC 813/.54—dc23/eng/20221202
LC record available at https://lccn.loc.gov/2022057285

Jacket art by Barry Blitt
Jacket design by Chip Kidd

Manufactured in the United States of America
First Edition

To Ann Close
That's a wrap

MR. TEXAS

A long cloud of dust trailed the black sedan racing down a caliche road toward the Walter Dunne spread. The horizon was dark and the mesquite trees bent in the north wind, waving at Mexico. A few idle pump jacks were rusting amid the creosote bushes. A slight rise lay just ahead, revealing a low-slung adobe wall encompassing the graveyard.

The land was hard, dry, used up. The people who lived in these parts were also hard. Their ancestors settled on giant claims back when there was grass enough for cattle, but generation after generation had seen it wither away. Those who remained on the land were marooned by history. There were no cities within hundreds of miles. The remaining towns were little more than hamlets with half the buildings evacuated like old movie sets. An occasional gas station marked the intersection of county roads, but it was likely abandoned so long ago that the company it represented was extinct as well. You could go for days without seeing another human being, or even hearing your own voice until you had reason to speak. Airliners streaked across the high sky, and from that distant vantage passengers enjoying their cocktails might look down and think, *Jeez, what a huge, empty, totally worthless country.* And they'd go back to their crossword. You could almost hear the shades snapping shut as they jetted by.

The service was already under way when L. D. Sparks parked his Lincoln at the end of a line of pickups and slipped into the crowd of mourners—a respectable turnout, befitting the prominence of the decedent. Some men were in suits but most wore dress jeans and shirts with pearl snap buttons, the women in somber dresses, purchased from catalogs, that reached to their Sunday boots. Their faces were lean and leathery and strongly formed, marked by the sun, faces you rarely saw in the soft suburbs, more like old family photographs, ancestral in nature, plain and unprettified and not to be trifled with. It was the hands that you finally noticed, chapped and red and laced with veins like braided rope, palms as hard as oak, some men could barely make a fist, and when you shook it was like grasping a brick. They were scarred from accidents and animal bites, knuckles broken by obstreperous equipment, some were missing digits. You couldn't live in these parts without getting hurt. Compared to a lot of folks, Walter Dunne passed into the next world with enviable ease, his heart having failed to keep the beat.

The tent over the grave bucked and billowed in the wind. Anywhere else you'd think it was about to rain, but there was no water in the approaching storm, a blue norther, bringing nothing but cold and trouble. The pastor, gray-bearded with the eyes of a benevolent fanatic, was leading a hymn, and because nearly everybody went to the same Church of Christ in Fort Davis, they joined expertly in the a cappella singing:

> *Yonder, yonder! Yonder in the great beyond*
> *Peace and love await*
> *Beyond the pearly gate*
> *Over yonder in the great beyond!*

L.D. hadn't been to church since the Nixon administration, but the song found its way back into his mouth as easily as if he had been singing it that very morning. The familiar harmonies awakened memories, not altogether unpleasant, of his long-forsaken youthful piety, enforced by family and community and really everyone he knew. But look at him now, the silver-haired cynic in a gray western-cut suit and handmade boots, tall, slender, suave, part of the scene and apart from it, a man who knew exactly where he ought to be, on top of the world and in control.

Governor Abbott was there and said a few kind words of the sort that might be said of anyone not convicted of a felony. The deceased and the governor represented different parties, but L.D. thought it a smart move on Abbott's part to plant a flag in the district, which had been solidly Democratic since the Civil War, but after Trump the chickens were out of the coop. At least, L.D. hoped so. The governor slyly called Walter a "friend and occasional ally," overlooking votes that might be inconvenient to recall in the face of the fierce widow in the front row with the folded flag of Texas in her lap. Walter might be dead, but his influence lingered.

After the eulogies—there must have been seven or eight of them, all on the same themes, good family man, selfless public servant, little truth in any of it—L.D. got in line to toss a few desiccated clods into Walter's grave. He noticed old Ben Fortson hobbling in his direction so he moved off a bit to avoid him, but Ben would not be dodged.

"My oh my oh my, looky who's here," Ben said, his eyes alight with deviltry.

"Good day to you, Judge."

"You come all this way for Walter Dunne?"

"He was a good man."

"True or not, he's no use to you now," Ben observed.

"You're a harsh old bastard, Ben."

Ben's laugh detoured into a dry cough. "I seen you casting your eyes over this lot," he said when he recovered.

"I mighta been," L.D. allowed. "What's it to you?"

"Walter's not even in the ground and you're shopping for his replacement."

"Not shopping. Poking around, like."

"Waste of your time." Ben spat into the dust, the only moisture the soil had experienced in months. "You oughter run over to Alpine, talk to the mayor, he's got an appetite for higher office, they tell me. Sees hisself as governor one day."

"He's about as likely to get a blow job from the Queen of England." L.D. indicated a portly man with slicked-back hair, dyed black, and jowls like a Great Dane. "What about Morales? Big family, Chamber of Commerce . . ."

"Cartel money," Ben said under his breath.

A prosperous-looking figure was shaking hands with everybody in reach. "That would be who?" L.D. asked.

"Charlie Ford. Owns the bank in Marfa. Beats his wife."

L.D. sighed. He had never expected this to be easy, especially out here in ground zero of nowhere. These people didn't seem entirely real to him, more like actors with strong features, rounded up and dressed appropriately for a scene in which L.D. discovers the next Ronald Reagan. How likely was that? And they certainly felt the same about him, a stock character from the Big City in a gray Italian suit who happens to drop in, a visit to the zoo. He even had the pocket square, a true dude.

"A female would be nice," he said. "Keep up with the times."

"Valerie Nightingale!" Ben said, practically dancing a jig. "County commissioner. Veteran. Helicopter pilot in Afghanistan. Tough, smart, everything you dream of."

"You're making me hard," said L.D.

"Only one problem."

"What's that?"

"She's not of your tribe. And she's gonna announce next week."

L.D. nodded as if he knew all about Valerie Nightingale. He didn't like to lag behind the rumor mill, especially when it was bad news. He didn't like it at all. "Nobody's unbeatable," he said irritably. "Just need the right candidate. Someone young, popular, and smart."

"Smart enough to let you do his thinking for him."

"Merely helping the democratic process along," said L.D., studying his nails, which were perfect.

"Raping virgins, more like it," said Ben. "And at a funeral to boot."

Just then the norther hit with a wallop of wind, blowing hats off half the men, who chased through the gravestones after their tumbling Stetsons.

★

The same wind coursed through the parking lot of the auction house in Fort Stockton as Sonny Lamb unloaded fifteen heifers into the livestock pens. They were polled Herefords, a breed valued for its toughness, fertility, and ability to survive on native grasses. But they were also, in Sonny's opinion, supremely handsome animals, with immense, soulful eyes and sweet dispositions, slow moving and unrufflable, as if the minute hand and the hour hand had changed places on their inner timepieces—a calming influence, in other words. The truth is Sonny didn't have the emotional distance to be a cowman. He named all his animals and could easily distinguish them. Sometimes when he walked the pasture he felt like a teacher entering the classroom and saying hello to the children. He might have fared better in a less intimate profession. At least the teacher didn't have to sell off his students to make a buck.

He looked the part of a cowboy, though—tall and broad shouldered, with a tan line on his forehead where his hat came to a stop. When he smiled, a network of sunbaked wrinkles went to work, crinkling his eyes and dimpling his cheeks. His nose inclined a bit toward his left shoulder, the result of a foul ball on the high school baseball field. His stance was a little swaybacked, and his Adam's apple raced up and down, especially when he sang. He was a darn good singer. If you were next to him in church, you'd notice him harmonizing. But his speaking voice was subdued, like a lot of folks out here, contrary to what you might think of a country so unbounded that you'd want to shout for attention. No. Their voices echoed the hush of the place, distant bird calls, whispers, hums, mumbled confessions, rustling leaves, the creaking of the windmill, all so subdued that a forceful sneeze would startle the dead.

In this underpopulated part of the world, where everybody knew everybody, reputations formed in grade school shadowed a person all the way to the grave. Sonny was widely known as a good-hearted loser, friendly, never met a stranger, fun to chew the fat with, smart enough but you wouldn't mistake him for Einstein. He'd had a rough go of it, the war and all, but he married above himself and settled into the modest life that was offered out here.

He knew what they thought. Now, with the drought, Sonny was bumping close to the bottom, facing a diminishing future in the ranching business, but hardly alone in that. The prospect of failure sharpened his ambition to do something, be somebody, but those blanks had yet to be filled in. Life hadn't turned out the way he had hoped. Like a lot of wounded people in this part of the world he parked his failed dreams in a mental corral.

The auction manager tallied the cattle emerging from the trailer. "Fifteen heifers," he noted. He pasted tags on each.

"And the bull," Sonny remarked.

The auction manager recognized Sonny. They had played ball together at Sul Ross State University. Joe Frank Schotz. His father owned the sale house. "Splendid animal. Sure you want to sell?"

"Want has nothing to do with it."

"I hear that." Joe Frank took a closer look at the bull: reddish-brown saddle and pure white face with curls from his nose to his horns. You'd want to kiss him, but you'd have to respect the raw power in the animal, the mass of muscle that makes a man feel mouse-like by comparison. "He's a beast," Joe Frank said. "Awful pretty. Got nuts like soccer balls. Registered, I'll bet."

"I brought the papers."

"Sonny, I gotta tell you this ain't the best time to go to market with an animal like this. What's his name?"

"Joaquin."

"Joaquin. Goddamn. What a sweetheart." Joe Frank tore off the tally sheet and handed it to Sonny. "Hope you get what you came for."

Sonny hosed down Joaquin and gave him a thorough shampoo, followed by a blow dry and a light buzz with a beard trimmer to even out the pelt. Normally, Joaquin liked primping for a show, he was quite the vain creature, but Sonny felt him trembling. "Settle down, buddy," he whispered as Joaquin's ear bent toward him. "You'll have a whole new harem. One day you're gonna thank me."

The auctioneer stood on a podium over the sawdust arena, spitting out numbers in a cascade of sixteenth notes as the ring manager paraded an emaciated steer in front of a couple dozen ranchers, who were more likely to be sellers than buyers. The animal and the audience shared a sleepy acceptance regarding their destiny, accounting for the submerged quality of the proceedings. Too many folks like Sonny had made the mistake of waiting for rain that never came. Now they were unloading their herds in a hurry, capsizing the market. The land wasn't the only thing that had dried up; money had moved on, followed by hope. West Texas waged eternal war on optimists.

Powdery motes swam in the air. Sonny spotted Doris at the top of the bleachers, so he hiked himself up the stairs. She had lines in her face that would do the Marlboro Man proud. Used to being the object of gossip just short of scandal, Doris surrounded herself with a harsh sense of humor like an electric fence, which kept the critics at a respectful distance. She ran the café in Alpine. She was a character. She was also Sonny's mother.

"What are you doing here?" Doris asked as Sonny sat down.

"I might ask the same of you."

"I just came to ogle the boys," Doris said, flicking the ash off her cigarette. "Look at the ass on that one."

Sonny didn't respond to that. It could be a joke or she could be dead serious.

"You got any stock left?" Doris asked.

"We're hanging on to the calves. Hope for better next year."

"Ed put down three heifers," Doris said. "Right out in the field. Too weak to get in the trailer."

"Really, Mom, why are you here?"

"I'm seeing Bud Schotz," she said, indicating the auctioneer, Joe Frank's dad. Buddy Holly glasses and a jaw like a doorknob.

"Is that really true?"

"We're an item," she declared. "We've been seen together."

"Well, I guess that's good news."

"You guess right. He's a man of means, and, you know, still functioning below the belt buckle."

"Mom, stop."

"Tender little ears you got."

Sonny had a kid sister, Marlene, who had long since packed up and moved off to Bangor, Maine, which if you look at the map is about the farthest point in the continental United States from Presidio County. So the parenting duties, in the sense of taking care of Doris, not the other way around, rested entirely on Sonny.

"Any buyers here?"

"Mostly the slaughterhouse. Fatso in the flat-brim buckaroo." Doris indicated a corpulent individual down front.

"Keep your voice down, Mom. He's looking at you."

"Horrors."

Bud Schotz slammed his gavel down as the slaughterhouse man took a pencil off his ear and made another mark on his tablet. It was painful to watch. Even Doris was respectfully silent as, one by one, the slaughterhouse man with his scarcely perceptible nod bought the entire lot. There was an air of stultifying indifference about him that wafted through the auditorium like anesthesia.

Half an hour later, the first of Sonny's heifers came up. They were all fine breeding stock, but that didn't matter now, they were destined for hamburger. In an hour or so they would crowd into a semi and journey to a feedlot in the Panhandle, camp out there about five months, but more likely seven or eight months considering the shape these cows were in, until they reached their ideal weight, around 1,200 to 1,400 pounds. Eat and shit, it wasn't much different from life on the ranch, except rudely concentrated, just a trough of water and bins of grain, no wandering around the pasture looking for Mom or nosing about with siblings. The smell is worse than anything you've ever encountered, which is why the feedlots are set as far as possible from human habitation, God help anyone within a mile of the place. Then it's off to the packing plant, a polite term for the execution chamber. The cows arrive already washed, as if they're going on a date, and unfed, to minimize contamination. They smell death ahead as they're goaded into the chute, which curves to blind them from seeing what's about to happen, but they know. They moan and weep. And then blackness as a bolt slams square in the middle of the forehead and interrupts their consciousness, a humane gesture that is also thought to enhance the flavor of the meat. A chain grabs hold of the left hind leg, and up they go onto the rail. Throat quickly cut, the bleeding begins, followed by skinning, splitting of the carcass, cooling, then the butcher gets to work. Today a cow; tomorrow, a T-bone. Civilization is built on such.

Suddenly the atmosphere in the auction house quickened. "Sonny, is that Joaquin?" Doris asked when the bull charged into the arena as if it belonged to him. It was like seeing a heavyweight champ burst into a club gym. The crowd sat up, abuzz, studying Joaquin's stats on a screen above the auctioneer's podium.

"All right, all right, very fine bull, two years old, got his papers right here," Bud said, waving the registration certificate in the air. "This is a foundation animal. Put him in your front pasture and folks will take notice. Start the bidding at ten thousand. TEN-TEN-TEN GIMME TEN-TEN-ten-ten . . ."

Some sales start slow. Bud knew the proper value of every animal that came into the ring. Even with a modest opening bid, you sometimes got a little resistance. Still, he was puzzled by the immobilized bidders before him, given the charismatic animal in the ring. "TEN-TEN-TEN." Bud never liked to drop a bid because it reflected on his own estimation of the bottom line, but there was no reserve on the sale, so he forged ahead. "NINE-NINE-NINE DO I HEAR NINE-NINE-NINE-nine . . . EIGHT!" Again Bud paused, which he never did, and surveyed the sparse crowd imploringly. An auctioneer can sense when the audience digs in its heels. He knows that the sellers have placed their trust in his ability to charm the dollars out of those pockets, and if he fails, mortgages don't get paid, hay doesn't get bought, careers end. So do marriages. In a good year—back when there were good years—ranchers would bring stock to auction and walk away with what might be the only check they got until the following spring. Many were now living month to month. It was a heavy load to carry, and Bud did so nobly. "You wanna improve your breeding program, this bull is for you!" Bud said. "C'mon folks, don't let this opportunity pass you by. I know there's hard times out there but this is a once-in-a-lifetime bargain. Let's start again, at SEVEN-SEVEN-SEVEN . . ."

People were dead still, some actually sitting on their hands, fighting the urge. Sonny could see they were embarrassed for him. Meantime, Joaquin pranced around and pawed the sawdust, like the only living creature on the planet, his hot breath clouding the chill air.

"FIVE!" Bud cried. "Folks, I've never done this before, but if I don't hear five I'm gonna stop the auction. There's no way this fine animal should sell for less than half his worth. So there you have it. Five or we bring in the next animal."

Bud's gavel was in midair when the slaughterhouse man tipped his buckaroo.

"FIVE-FIVE GIMME SIX, NOW FIVE, GIMME SIX-SIX-SIX," pause, then less forcefully, "Six, six, I have five, do I hear five and a half?" Bud's eyes scanned the crowd, pleadingly, looking for anyone who would spare Joaquin the indignity of the slaughterhouse. Surely, as cattlemen, they must perceive the absence of justice, the offense against nature.

Doris raised her hand. Bud gave her a look and pointedly ignored her bid. "FIVE-FIVE, GOING ONCE, GOING—."

"SIX!" Doris called out so the whole world could hear. Bud rolled his eyes. "Six from the cowgirl in back," he said, "who ain't got her head screwed on today."

"Mom, what are you doing?" Sonny demanded.

"I need a new pet," she said. "I'm lonely."

"What are you gonna do, sell the café?"

Fortunately, the slaughterhouse man bid six and a half.

"Seven!" said Doris.

"Mom, you don't have seven thousand dollars," Sonny said under his breath. "Please stop."

"Let's get some other bidders in here," Bud pleaded. "This is the finest animal we've had in here all week. SEVEN, I GOT SEVEN, NOW HALF, GIMME HALF—"

The slaughterhouse man nodded. You could see he was feeling competitive, perhaps a little jealous of his privilege to buy any damn animal he wanted. Maybe he had also heard Doris's remark about his portliness and thought he'd give her something to think about. By now everyone in the bleachers was watching Doris. Bud also looked reluctantly in her direction. "Who'll give me eight?" he said.

Doris was very still, then said, "I'm sorry, Sonny."

"I know. Thanks, that meant a lot to me."

"SEVEN AND A HALF, GOING ONCE, GOING TWICE—"

Sonny tipped his hat.

"EIGHT THOUSAND in back," Bud said. "I'VE GOT EIGHT, GIMME NINE, EIGHT NOW NINE-NINE-NINE . . ."

Doris squeezed Sonny's hand. Then the slaughterhouse man upped the bid, who knows why, maybe out of spite. It was far beyond a bargain for the purposes he had in mind.

"Nine thousand! Nine from the gentleman in front," Bud cried. "Now we're talking folks. This is one splendid animal, certainly worth more than that. Who'll give me ten? TEN-TEN-TEN."

Sonny nodded.

"Ten thousand dollars! Someone make it eleven, do I hear eleven?" Bud said, looking at the slaughterhouse man. But the slaughterhouse man shook his head, having made his point, and awarded Sonny a pitying smile.

"Sold!" Bud said, "to Sonny Lamb, his own damn bull!"

★

Sonny drove through the gate of the Apache Springs Ranch around sunset. They were on nine thousand acres an hour south of Marfa and sixty miles from the Mexican border, about as isolated as anybody on the whole continent. Land out here went for a thousand dollars an acre, but it was hardscrabble and in a good season could support only one cow per fifty acres. Lately, it'd been hard to make a go of it with a hundred acres per cow. It wasn't just the grass dying in the drought, the water was drying up everywhere, stock ponds were shrinking, the earth was beginning to crack into jigsaw pieces.

The sky was still light but the valley between the red mesas was soaking in the evening penumbra under a new moon. Had he thought it through, Sonny might have waited another hour till it was dark enough to unload Joaquin without Lola noticing. That would give him time to think up a plausible explanation. But there she was, standing on the porch. Sonny gave her a cheery-looking wave as he passed on his way to the pasture.

Lola tracked him down as he was prodding Joaquin out of the trailer. "You bought your own bull?" she said.

Sonny hated to disappoint Lola for a million reasons, one of which was that she could make him feel like a total fuck-up. Which he was not.

"How'd you know?"

"It was on the radio."

The full measure of Sonny's disgrace was becoming apparent. "They were gonna turn him into dog food," he explained. But Lola turned on her heel and marched back into the house.

"We're in trouble now," Sonny confided, as he fed Joaquin a peanut butter cookie, his favorite. But he couldn't help feeling relieved as he watched Joaquin gambol off and take possession of his pasture. The place where he belonged. Joaquin represented the future, if there was a future to be had.

Vistas in this part of the country are so immense you can see storms a hundred miles away. The norther was bringing heavy weather—lowering clouds and lightning over the mountains, thunder grumbling like timpani and the wind whipping up dust devils on the parched prairie. Over dinner, Sonny bet Lola five dollars it would finally rain. "You've lost enough money already today," she observed. Sonny looked into his bowl of chili as if it might contain a reply to that observation, but there was none.

Lola of course was well acquainted with Sonny's shortcomings. Had she been at the auction she could have sized it up before he

unloaded the trailer. He certainly knew how much they were counting on that money. There wasn't much left to sell, except the ranch
itself, which had belonged to her mother. All they really had in the
world. It wouldn't do any good to make him feel worse than he
already did, but she couldn't stop herself.

"Ten thousand dollars!" Lola said for about the twentieth time.

"It's not like I had to pay all that," he said. "It was just the auction fee, like two hundred bucks."

"Ten thousand we would have had if you'd just kept your hands
in your lap."

"I know. It's all my fault. I'm really sorry."

Lola wasn't finished but she could see that nothing she said
was going to make the money magically reappear. "Oh, don't go
so hangdog," she said. "It's just, I'm so sick of pinching pennies. I
know you're working hard, but we're on the brink of disaster here."
And then, under her breath, one last time, "Ten thousand dollars!"

There was nothing soft about Lola's life. Compared to city
girls she was sparely constructed, with long, ropy muscles. She
didn't consider herself attractive, but she was certainly arresting,
with unflinching blue eyes and a scar on her right cheek that came
from a tumble in her barrel-racing days. Except for that and one
ill-considered tattoo she was flawless. She often wore her honey-
colored hair in a ponytail to keep from having to fuss with it, braid-
ing it through the back of a trucker hat, where it bobbed about like
the tail of a palomino. Anyone with experience in the West would
instantly recognize her as a cowgirl.

Lola loved the land but also felt chained to it. She subscribed
to certain magazines—*The New Yorker*, *National Geographic*,
Architectural Digest—that kept her up to date while at the same
time feeding her shyness about stepping out of her zone. Her accent
confined her like an invisible fence to this vast, unpeopled region.
She harbored fantasies of jettisoning the ranch for someplace she'd
only heard of—Cape Cod, for instance, or Vancouver. Even Houston would be a dazzling alternative. Who would she be if she wasn't
who she was? She felt her life speeding by, rendering such existential

questions purely hypothetical. It was too late to make a change; it was too late the moment she was born.

Lola had known Sonny almost her entire life. She had been friends with his sister, Marlene, from first grade on, and long before they ever dated she was set on marrying him. He was the most attractive boy in his age group, never gawky even in his teens when he was the quarterback of the chronically losing team and sang in a country cover band. With only seven thousand people in the entire county, there weren't a whole lot of boys to compare. Back then, Sonny was the object of a lot of female projection, with those deep-set scuppernong eyes and Elvisy hair. The eyes hadn't changed but the hair was thinning and the bald spot on the dome was claiming more territory. Tell the truth, he was forty years old with little to show for himself. Lola's family always thought she sold short, and sometimes she wondered if she would have made the same choice had her world had been a little wider.

They went to bed listening to the grumbling of the approaching storm and gnawing on the uncertainty of three months from now when they wouldn't be able to afford hay for the cows they still had. Lola forced herself to stop talking about the money, although the issue was on both their minds. They should start making contingency plans, but all alternatives led to uncertain places, and it wasn't entirely clear they would continue on the same road together. This is something they didn't talk about.

In the middle of the night the storm was on top of them, like war. Sonny was still awake, fondling his regrets, when a lightning bolt exploded nearby. Their dog, Bandit, a bull terrier with a patch surrounding one eye, leapt into bed and burrowed under the sheet.

"He's a little scaredy cat, aren't you, Bandit?" Lola said.

Another lightning strike sounded like it was in the next room. This time everybody jumped. Bandit moaned and trembled.

"Wow, that was close," Lola said.

Sonny got up and walked out onto the porch. No rain, he would have lost the bet. A narrow slice of night sky separated the blackness of the earth and the blackness of the clouds like a window closing on creation. Flashes of lighting illuminated the silhouette of the Davis Mountains and formed cobwebs on the dome of the sky like a cracked China bowl. *No telling how big this storm is*, Sonny thought, *all the way to New Mexico at least.*

In this darkness, something caught his eye, a brightness where there hadn't been brightness before, a speck of orange and yellow across the floor of the high desert at the base of the opposing mesa, and then Sonny realized what he was looking at.

"Fire! Across the valley," he told Lola. "Must be the Miller place."

While Sonny loaded the truck with shovels and gunny sacks, along with gloves, jackets, and helmets—the basics—Lola phoned the other members of the local volunteer fire department. They were already awake because of the storm. With no other fire department to call on out here, neighbors had to take care of each other. Grass was money, especially now, but in this drought it was also explosively combustible. The month before there had been a fire on the other side of the mountains that shot up a plume like a hydrogen bomb. Wildfires were finishing off the West.

It took half an hour to get to the Miller place, even with Sonny driving at high speed, and by that time the wind had blown the blaze across the prairie, the shriveled yellow grass gulping the flames and creosote bushes feeding sparks to the wind. The earth glowed in an awful majesty so bright it illuminated the clouds, which seemed almost in reach.

A Ford 350 with a water pump in the bed served as the nearest fire engine. It was already at the Miller place, along with a couple dozen overwhelmed volunteers. Some had never fought a fire before, at least not one this big and hungry, and amplified by lightning strikes that kept everyone off guard. Lola passed out gunny sacks to those who didn't have them, which they soaked in the stock tank and used to bat out the flames, trying to keep the inferno away from the house and the barn directly downwind.

As chief of the volunteer force, Sonny raced his pickup across the field to intercept the pump truck, which was doing no good by spraying the back of the fire. Sonny honked until he got the attention of the driver, Frank Acosta, who looked at Sonny as if he had no idea where he was. Lightning danced all around, landing like mortar shells, reminding Sonny of Iraq, but he couldn't think about that now. He had learned that much from war, you set some thoughts aside to be pondered when you were alone and safe. Or maybe you never revisited those thoughts at all, you just put them in a casket and buried them, along with friends now gone. The job was to live.

He motioned Frank to follow, directing him toward the front of the blaze. It had crept within a hundred yards of the house. You could watch it move from clump to clump through the yellow grass and then suddenly jump ten feet in the air.

George Miller was standing by the house, stupefied by the scope of the disaster that was ripping his life apart. "Is your family safe?" Sonny asked.

"Jeannette's getting the kids in the truck," George said robotically. He was carrying a television. The older Miller boy was loading the back of a Suburban with silverware and photographs and whatever else the family could manage to save. "We're gonna lose it all," George said. "The whole damn thing." His family had been on this land for a century.

"No we're not," Sonny said. "We're ahead of this. Just take care of your folks and we'll take care of the fire."

Fear was the main problem here, Sonny figured. People couldn't think straight, even those who'd been trained and done this before. The volunteers were making feckless random attempts to quell the sparks with the gunny sacks. "Francisco!" Sonny called out to his assistant chief. "Make a line!" Francisco Saenz knew what he was supposed to do, all right, and he suddenly snapped to and organized the others in formation, delegating one of them to refresh the dampened gunny sacks. The air was hot and painful to breathe, the grass as dry as newspaper.

Sonny barely registered the bolt of lightning that struck the barn, but he did notice that a television news truck had shown up. One of the stations in Midland kept a roving truck in Marfa, and somehow it had gotten notified of the fire and was already here. Why the actual fire department couldn't send one of those pump and roll engines in the same amount of time was a mystery. The marauding fire leapt onto a grove of dead cedar and rose up in an immense red wall. Some of the volunteers froze in awe. "Don't look!" Sonny shouted. "Keep your head down! Do your job!"

The task was to starve the fire quickly, before the blaze outflanked them. With the beaters and the pump truck now in front of the flames, Sonny organized the remaining volunteers to make a fire break with shovels and hoes, scraping away everything but the dirt. Sparks flew up like rockets. The firefighters could easily be surrounded and trapped by the blaze; it had happened before in this country, a dozen killed at a time. There was no one else who could help them now.

Lola was in charge of the bucket brigade. There was practically no pressure in the hose, so they fetched water from the stock tank, but the water was no match for the wind, which had lost direction and had begun to whirl, the heat having created its own atmosphere. Everyone was moving fast but the fire was faster, vaulting over the heads of the beaters, who had to re-form and stamp out the fresh blazes before they gained some measure of control. Lola could hear excited voices rising in volume, but she was so intent on filling the buckets that it wasn't until the scream that she turned around.

The barn was ablaze. Flames gushed from the eaves. For a moment, Lola was frozen in place, wonderstruck by the hellish glory of a force so mighty, a force that threatened even the will to survive. Into her consciousness came a sound—high, keening, hysterical—it was Mary Lou Miller, the ten-year-old.

"Coco! Coco!" Mary Lou cried. "Momma, Coco's in there!"

Jeannette was struggling to get the toddler into the car seat while holding on to Mary Lou.

"Let me go!" Mary Lou screamed, writhing in her mother's grasp.

"Mary Lou, the barn's full of hay, it'll go up in a minute," Jeannette said, forcing herself to be calm and firm. "There's nothing to be done. Now get in the truck, we gotta save ourselves!"

As Lola watched, Mary Lou broke away and ran into the burning barn.

"Mary Lou! Mary Lou!" Jeannette cried, and then she rushed after her daughter, still carrying the baby. Without a second to think, Lola raced after Jeannette and blocked her. Fires are made even more dangerous by the panic they spread, and running after one child with another on her shoulder could only magnify the tragedy. Jeannette knew this. The horror was written on her face as she sank into Lola's iron embrace. A blast of heat surrounded them like a furnace and the flames painted them in a brilliant orange glow. The hay in the barn suddenly ignited and the bales exploded. Jeannette sank to her knees.

It was then that Lola saw Sonny run into the barn. His silhouette was black against the flames and then he disappeared right through them.

The air itself seemed to be ablaze. Sonny could barely breathe there was so little oxygen left in the barn. He heard the girl on the other side of the fire before he saw her. She wasn't screaming now. She was trying to calm a horse that was making sounds that Sonny had never heard a horse make. An Appaloosa mare. She spun about and pawed the air, bucking frantically, dangerously close to Mary Lou.

"Coco, Coco, stop, I'm here!" Mary Lou cried in an oxygen-starved whisper. "I'll save you!"

The girl had gotten the stall door open, but the mare was berserk, seeing nothing but fire everywhere. Her whinnying turned into an eerie wail. In her frenzy, Coco kicked in the gate of the stall, then spun about and came down hard on Mary Lou.

Sonny waited until the horse reared again then grabbed Mary Lou before the hooves landed on her. She was barely conscious and didn't have any struggle left. Sonny tucked her face into his fire jacket and ran through the flames with his eyes closed and his head down. A timber crashed behind them, drawing another deathly scream from Coco.

Sonny gasped and drank in the air the moment he got out of the barn. He saw Lola holding Jeannette and the look on their faces. When Mary Lou got her breath, she began sobbing, her face wrenched in agony. It wasn't pain, it was grief. "Coco! Coco!" she cried.

Jeannette reached for her daughter, but Mary Lou wouldn't let go of Sonny. She pounded his chest despairingly, her blows weak and hopeless.

Everyone could hear Coco's tormented screams.

"Coco's dying!" Mary Lou cried.

Sonny found himself saying, "Don't worry, honey. I'll get her."

Lola heard this. "Sonny, don't!" she said. "What are you thinking?"

"I gotta at least try," he said.

Lola took Mary Lou in her arms. There was no point trying to stop Sonny. He grabbed a wet gunny sack and covered his face as he ran back into the inferno.

No other sounds arose other than Coco's wails and the crackling of fire as it ate the hay and chewed the walls of the barn, belching out cascades of sparks. Flames had broken through the roof. It wouldn't be long before the entire structure collapsed into a smoldering mound of ash.

Mary Lou cried into Lola's shoulder, unable to look. The heat was unimaginable. Lola felt like her face was burning. And Sonny was in there.

Jeannette took Lola's hand.

★

The barn was so bright that Sonny could see through the gunny sack, like looking at the sun through darkened glass. The dampness of the sack preserved his eyes, so they didn't melt out of their sockets, and his helmet kept his hair from catching fire.

The flames didn't care that he was being the hero. Although he had known mortal fear, Sonny had never experienced anything like this heat. In some suppressed region of his brain, he registered the spectacle of his own probable death and the final seconds of his life. His actions were spastic and confused. He was helpless. He had to turn around. There was still a chance to save himself.

Then he glimpsed a huge figure rearing off to the side of him where he wasn't expecting the horse to be.

Coco had found a narrow unburned spot. She didn't register Sonny's presence. Weakened by the depleted oxygen in this furnace, she was pawing the air, her nostrils flaring, her eyes yellow in the flames and full of horror. There was no second chance with this animal. Sonny stood directly in front of Coco. He put his hand on her neck, which was ready to burst into flames.

"Whoa, whoa, I got you," Sonny said. Then he threw the gunny sack over her head and held it tight.

Coco started to buck, but she recognized that the cool of the gunny sack was her only salvation. She kept turning around, trying to edge away from the heat, but there was no escape now, the fire was everywhere. Sonny kept his eyes closed as much as possible. He was going to have to mount her if they had any chance, but she wouldn't hold still. Both their lives depended on it.

A rafter fell and Coco reared.

"Now, now," Sonny said, "calm down, girl." The sound of his voice seemed to reach her. Then he suddenly grabbed hold of Coco's mane and pulled himself onto her back. She spun around in blind confusion. He tugged on her mane until she was pointed toward the flames blocking the door, then he spurred her. "Go! Go!" he yelled.

Coco leapt into the fire.

★ **2** ★

Although he might don the garments of a country squire, via Orvis and L.L. Bean, and could speak the lingo with native ease, L.D. didn't care for the territory out here. Some summer days you could set a pot of beans in the noonday sun and they'd be cooked by suppertime. Then winter came and you felt the breath of Manitoba crawl down your neck. L.D. had seen blizzards that buried cattle alive. It was a mystery to him why people would spend their lives in such a forlorn and godforsaken place, unless there were fortunes to be made, but that prospect had long since passed on.

He spent the night at the Hampton Inn in Alpine, passing up the faux Old West lodges with the wagon-wheel bedsteads and shiplap walls of reclaimed wood. He detested nostalgia, especially when enlisted in the service of commerce. He recognized that the Hampton Inn was a culturally destructive force, along with Motel 6s and Quality Inns and Dairy Queens and Whataburgers, homogenizing every little hamlet. Fine. He didn't care. Wipe the slate clean and reset the history clock, starting with the invention of personal-size toiletries in the bathrooms and food that tastes exactly the same anywhere you go. When you delve into the boonies you want to avoid novelty. On the other hand, if a man needed information that might not be found on the side of U.S. 90 in a motel that, by evidence of the parking lot, favored long-haul truckers, that man would have to venture beyond the franchises. One would have to meet the natives on their own turf.

"Waffles up," the fry cook called out as L.D. entered the Texas Moon Café. It was, L.D. noted sadly, truly authentic. Booths and barstools. A signed black-and-white Willie Nelson headshot. Plus Rick Perry and Vince Young and minor celebrities he didn't recognize. The first dollar earned taped to the cash register. A jukebox that had been here since the last world war, with satellite jukes in the booths, the kind where you put the quarter in and flipped the pages with the songs listed. "San Antonio Rose" by Bob Wills would be there. Patsy Cline. Marty Robbins. Moon Mullican. "Sixteen Tons." "The Wayward Wind." Frozen in time.

"Chet, your order's ready," the woman behind the counter said.

"Well, Doris, ain't you gonna bring it to me?"

"We're understaffed around here," Doris observed, "and you could use the exercise."

Chet, who did need the exercise, grudgingly extracted himself from the booth and collected his stack of waffles, which was capped with a scoop of butter melting over the edges like a lava flow. L.D. calculated the calories as about a quadrillion. He settled onto a barstool at the counter.

"Coffee, mister?" Doris said. She was in a category that L.D. would define as tough old broad, but with a speck of whimsy in her eyes. The pot was already in her hand.

"Whatever you can spare," L.D. replied.

"Where're you from?" Doris asked as she filled his cup.

"How'd you know I'm not from here?"

" 'Cause I know everybody here and you ain't one of them. You look like a tourist, which can't be possible, so I'm supposing you have other business."

L.D. could take a lesson from her in prying into other people's affairs. "And what do you suppose that to be?" he asked.

"If we were anyplace else in Texas, I'd say landman."

"A fine line of work."

"But not yours, I'm takin' it."

"Is there much oil and gas in these parts?"

"Does it look like we're rolling in royalty payments? Which is

why I ask, since it's sorta surprising to see a gentleman such as yourself, wearing pressed jeans and thousand-dollar boots stroll in like
he's in Big D or whatnot."

" 'Doris,' it says on your nametag."

"You're evading the subject."

"I think you're flirting with me."

"So what if I am. I've already run through every available suspect
in three counties."

"I'm mighty flattered."

"But you'd like some breakfast."

"Now that you mention it, what's the *spécialité de la maison?*"

"I'd recommend the steak and eggs with hash browns, unless
you're worried about your figure."

Steak here meant chicken-fried. Why, in cattle country, must fine
meat be treated in such a barbarous manner, L.D. wanted to know.
On the other hand, chicken-fried steak had an appealingly corrupt
taste, with all the worst qualities—fat, salt, red meat—and L.D. surrendered to the fact that he was going to die somewhat sooner than
he might have and in a more awful manner than he hoped for.

Since he was on a mission, L.D. scouted the room, but there
were no obvious candidates in view. Four heavy guys in overalls and
MAGA hats, obviously they'd been breakfasting here for decades,
their butt prints preserved in the plastic upholstery. Maybe worth
chatting them up. There were haircuts he hadn't seen in a while,
flattops and crew cuts, an elderly couple sitting with their pigtailed
granddaughter, and several cowboys devouring mountains of car-
bohydrates who hadn't seen a barber since before the pandemic. A
handful of other folks were too old to invest in, but you never know,
you just never know. The important thing was to be alert. Whatever
you're looking for is also looking for you, the poet said.

L.D. turned his attention to the television mounted on the wall.
There was news coverage of Walter Dunne's funeral. L.D. did not
see his own face in the crowd of mourners, which was a disappointment, since he had hoped to catch a glimpse of himself in his new
powder-gray Italian suit. And then the massive breakfast arrived and

he forgot himself, distracted by the sheer volume of nourishment before him. The toast alone was enough to sustain him through a week, thickly cut and grilled, "Texas toast," it was called on the menu. The steak lapped the edges of the platter. L.D. held up his empty cup, and Doris grabbed the pot.

"Hey, Doris, ain't that your boy?" Chet called out from the booth. "On the TV?"

"Dear Lord!" Doris cried. "It's Sonny!"

The fry cook grabbed the remote and turned up the volume. It was some story about a brush fire in Presidio County. Happens all the time. Neighbors helping neighbors, which is "heartwarming," according to the reporter. L.D. glanced impatiently at the hovering coffee pot. Then he scanned the room again and saw the rapt faces. He turned to the television.

"And a team of volunteer firemen showed up, with gunny sacks and shovels and one old pump truck, and somehow they put out the blaze. But the real heroics came when lightning struck the barn and caught the hayloft on fire. One of the firemen, rancher Sonny Lamb, rushed into the flames to rescue ten-year-old Mary Lou Miller, who was trying to save her mare, Coco, who was trapped inside. Then—Molly, you won't believe this part—Lamb ran back into the barn and saved the horse as well."

There was a shot of a crazed horse leaping out of the flames of a burning barn, and holding on to its mane was some wild cowboy identified on the screen as "SONNY LAMB, VOLUNTEER FIRE-MAN." It was hard to tell what he looked like with his face covered in soot, but he was clearly one of those brawny cowboys you see out here, common as fence posts. He looked a little abashed to be on camera. "It was a tricky blaze, but we were fortunate," the cowboy was saying, when suddenly the adorable horse-owning ten-year-old jumped into the frame and hugged him. "Weren't we, Little Bit?" the cowboy said, unveiling a smile through the soot that L.D. would have paid a million bucks for.

Somehow his coffee cup got filled, but L.D. was already on the move.

★

Midday Sunday dinners after church were mandatory in the Sharp family. Instituted by Lola's mother years before she passed away, the tradition was kept alive by her children, mainly to prevent Ed Sharp from unraveling. Ornery and gruff but secretly sentimental, Ed was known to walk out on movies if there was a hazard that he might cry. Hazel's death had left him so desolate that his sons took his guns away. The firearms had long since been restored, but the place Hazel occupied in Ed's heart never would be.

The ranch house was tucked under a hundred-year-old stand of cottonwood trees. Shade was a precious commodity, made possible on Ed's place by the remnants of Cibolo Creek. When Lola was a girl, it was still deep enough to swim in, but the drought had reduced it to a pitiable dribble, home to crawfish and little else.

As soon as Lola and Sonny entered, Marta, the housekeeper, swept up to them, full of welcoming exclamations as she unburdened them of their offerings. Sonny had brought a bottle of the tequila that Ed particularly favored, and Lola had cut some cosmos and beebalm from her garden.

"Hidey, Ed," Sonny said cautiously, judging the old man's mood.

" 'Bout damn time," Ed grumbled. They must have been all of ten minutes late.

The room was full of Lola's family. There was Ed Jr., a banker in Marfa, and his wife, Toni, a full-time mother and teacher's aide; Chuck and Jenny, who together operated a small ranch about fifty miles north; Buster, with the Border Patrol, and his wife, Pauline, who had a nail salon in Valentine, an unlikely business in this country, although she supplemented her income selling CBD products. The Sharps were all amazingly fertile people, as evidenced by the battalion of children streaming in for dinner. Lola and Sonny were the only childless couple of the lot.

Sonny knew very well what the family thought of him. He wouldn't say that any of them were thunderous successes or pillars of the community, but they all carried themselves with an air of importance that Sonny could never hope to achieve. His own parents divorced when his father went to prison. Sonny himself was a bust as a rancher and had failed to take care of Lola in the fashion she deserved. What's more, he was obviously no stud. Whenever Sonny walked in an air of judgment filled the room like a massive fart.

"Hey, Uncle Sonny!" one of Ed Jr.'s boys cried. "We saw you on TV!"

"You did?"

The other kids nodded eagerly. "Yeah, that was exciting!" one of them said. At least the kids loved Sonny, they always had. Some generational thing, he supposed.

"Yeah, we also heard you bought a very fine bull the other day," Chuck remarked, surveying his kinfolk for the rewarding chuckles he received in return for his wit.

"I guess everybody's heard about that," said Sonny.

"Now why wasn't that on the TV?" Chuck demanded, pressing his advantage.

"Well, I don't know, Chuck," said Sonny. "Maybe nobody else gives a shit."

"Marta, where the hell's dinner?" Ed growled. He didn't like contention in the family, and there had been ever since Sonny came into it. "What're we waitin' around for?"

"El monstruo," Lola whispered to Marta.

"Siempre así," she replied.

"Quit that Mexican talk and let's eat," Ed demanded.

The baronial dining table was set for the adults; the children were in the kitchen. Lola loved the big dining room, with the pottery her mother had brought from Oaxaca displayed on the sideboard alongside Ed's collection of arrowheads and fossils, and the view through the picture window of the little creek winding through the cottonwoods resembled an illustration in a children's book. Hummingbirds by the dozen came to the feeders that Hazel had set out so many years ago.

Ed had diminished from his former state, when he was as rawboned and gristly as they came, but you could see him in his sons, with their long faces, thin lips, ears larger than nature required; they were beefy men with shoulders like plow horses, distinctive without being handsome, but not ugly by any means, just plain and solid, born to work. Lola was her mom all over, with her fine features and skin somehow not turned to leather like her siblings. And yet there were daddy genes at work in her as well, the narrow nostrils, the cornflower-blue eyes.

"One good rain," Ed said. "If there is a God who loves us, he could damn well show us a little affection."

"We're just a big tinderbox," Chuck observed.

"You should have seen the fire at the Miller place," Lola said. "It could happen to any of us." She was cutting Ed's meat for him. He had suffered a small stroke several months before. "I can do that," Ed protested, although he couldn't, really.

The drought was on everyone's minds. Ed Jr., the banker, reported on foreclosures in the area. It seemed like half the county was belly-up. All the names he mentioned had faces to them. Buster said the Border Patrol had recovered the bodies of three migrants over in Pecos County, about as far from water as you could be.

"Climate is changing," Sonny ventured. "We gotta face it."

Lola kicked him under the table, but it was too late. "The climate is always changing," Jenny said sharply. She was the chair of the Presidio County Tea Party, about five people. This argument could go on for hours. "Think of the Ice Age."

Her husband, Chuck, pitched in. "We've had worse droughts before, right, Pop?"

"Nineteen fifty-six," Ed recalled. "Wiped out pretty near every rancher in the West. Daddy had a rainmaker come out on the place. Or said he was. Set a couple cannons on the ridge and shot holes in the clouds. That was the idea, anyway. Scared the crap out of the livestock."

"There's just nothing you can do, that's the frustration," Buster observed.

"The governor has set aside a day for prayer," Jenny said brightly.

When Ed chuckled, she added, "Well, I don't see any other ideas being put forward."

"I'm telling you, desalination," said Sonny. "It's the future."

"Here we go again," said Chuck.

"There's an ocean right under our feet, an aquifer *eight hundred feet deep*," Sonny said, lingering in sheer astonishment at that figure. "We're talking over five billion acre-feet in the brackish layer. Just imagine what we could do with all that water. Irrigate our crops. Swimming pools. Goldfish ponds. Anything you can imagine."

"You learned this on the internet," Buster concluded.

"He went to a conference in Lubbock and came back all starry-eyed," Lola said. "Ever since he's been obsessed with this,"

"Good water's all gone," Ed said. "It's turned to salt. Wonderful for shrimp farming."

"It's just so simple!" Sonny said. "You use renewable energy resources. Wind draws the water to storage tanks, and solar cells power the desalination plant through a process called reverse osmosis." He stared at the blank faces. "It's really kinda neat."

"Maybe ask the governor to pray on it," Ed said, stabbing a morsel of ham.

"I don't see anything wrong with that!" Jenny cried out.

"Honey . . ." Chuck gave her a silencing look that had no effect. Jenny got wound up talking about miracles and the power of prayer. Everyone glumly ate the tapioca pudding Marta put out.

★

"They don't hate you," Lola said as they rode back to their ranch. "They just don't get you."

By now the sun was almost down and the sky had softened. Pillowy clouds absorbed pink rays and would soon turn into an epic sunset. Sonny's jaw was working. Finally, he spit out, "It's just—what am I supposed to do?"

"Not anything. It's not your fault."

"It *is* my fault."

"I don't see how you come up with that."

"Everything I touch turns to crap."

"That's not true!"

"Name me one success. One thing I've done that I can look on as—yeah, I did it, I set out to accomplish something and I by-God did it."

Lola was quiet.

"No wonder they don't respect me."

"Sonny, I love my family, but they're not setting the world on fire, either. They all had advantages you never did." When Sonny didn't respond, she added, "It's not just us. Everybody's struggling, even them. You know that, don't you?"

Sonny nodded.

"Well, then, stop feeling sorry for yourself." She was driving, figuring Sonny was too morose to pay sufficient attention to the road. Plus, he might not hear what she had to say.

"You should give yourself a little credit," she said. "You came back from Iraq in pieces. None of my brothers, or their wives, for that matter, ever served anything or anybody other than themselves. Nothing wrong with that, it's just not in them. But you did. And it cost you. I don't think either of us thought you'd be as pulled together as you are now. We had our troubles, not saying they're all behind us, but where would we be if you were still on those painkillers? That took a lot for you to get past, where many have not. That took grit, Sonny."

"I couldn't have done it without you."

"That's true. You needed me. That's what marriage is about. Standing together. Although you nearly blew it with the women."

They rarely talked about that. There was a time when women brought him consolation, or what passed for it. Sonny wasn't sure if Lola wanted him to open up about it, or if she was still nursing a wound that had never fully healed.

"Not excusing it, but that was part of the music life, playing the clubs, taking drugs and whatever else was offered," he said. The memory of those nights rolled in afresh, unending pleasures it seemed at the time, but all the while he was swimming out to sea, farther and farther from the shore. "I wanted us to get back together, but that didn't seem possible then."

"I bear some of the blame for giving up on you," Lola said.

"I'd given up on myself, so why would you think any different?" Sonny said.

He didn't want to revisit this period of his life. There was a mixture of shame and pleasure that still warred in his memory. He turned his attention to a herd of pronghorn cantering at forty miles an hour along the fence line, easily keeping up with Lola. It was a game with them, the fastest land animals in North America. If Lola sped up, they would, too, but Lola wasn't playing that game.

"I never really understood what caused you to change," she said, unwilling to let the matter drop. "Not the drugs and stuff, I can see how that would happen with the pain you were in. You must have gotten something out of that experience or you would never have wandered down that road. But you had the willpower to set all that aside. It cost you, I know."

"I was looking for something," he said. "Turned out I was looking in the wrong direction."

It was almost dark now. Lola turned into their road and passed the pasture where Joaquin stood like a god from some ancient culture. They bumped through the road ruts toward the house, which was just a dark shadow, but in the shadow was a darker shape, a big, black Lincoln, and a man in a suit was sitting on their porch, shielding his eyes from the glare of the headlights. "Who in the world?" Lola exclaimed.

"Consultant?" Lola asked. They were sitting in the living room, L.D. on the couch below the longhorn skull, as Lola examined the man's business card.

"You could think of me as a kind of scout." His baritone voice was whiskey smooth, familiar and confiding. He might have been an old friend just checking in, so happy to see them again.

"Like a Boy Scout?" she said as the teapot screamed.

"Like a talent scout."

"I gave up my singing career a long time ago," Sonny said.

L.D. smiled apologetically. "Tell the truth, I'm in politics."

That brought the conversation to a stop. Lola returned from the kitchen offering a McDonald Observatory cup that had the solar system splayed across it. L.D. stirred his tea in silence as if he had nothing much on his mind. As if they were supposed to do the talking.

"You live in Austin?" Sonny asked to break the quiet.

L.D. nodded.

"Well, you came a long way," Sonny said, leaving off the "for what?" that was the rest of the thought.

"True, true, true," L.D. replied, as if that were a thoroughly original observation. "You ever notice whenever something happens in some broken country like Afghanistan or Ukraine they always compare it to Texas? Just a little smaller, they'll say, every damn time. Than Texas. You know France is also a little smaller, but nobody says Texas is bigger than France, do they? Though it surely is, and you'd think occasionally somebody would notice. You could pass through half a dozen European countries in the amount of time it takes to cross the Lone Star State."

Lola and Sonny nodded. The size of Texas was something everyone could agree on. Although they had never been to Europe, they did know that Marfa was about halfway between Beaumont and Los Angeles. It was a matter of pride, as if sheer size were some kind of wonderful accomplishment instead of a considerable impediment. It took Lola forty-five minutes to get to the Dollar General in Marfa. One way. Seventy miles an hour on the paved part.

L.D. set his cup on the coffee table with the apparent intention of getting down to business, but he eased into it. "You may have heard about the recent passing of Walter Dunne, the state rep from District 74?" he said, looking directly at Sonny. "Your district."

"Everybody knew Walter," Sonny said.

"A dear, dear friend," L.D. said.

"Oh, sorry for your loss," Lola said.

"Hard to believe he's really gone. Lot of us down in Austin thought he was irreplaceable."

"So are you taking a poll?" Lola asked.

L.D. looked at her for a second or two, then began to laugh, so hard he could barely speak. "A . . . poll? No . . . not . . . not a poll!" he said, dabbing merry tears. "Drive near five hundred miles for a poll?" He shook his head in wonder, as Sonny and Lola gaped at him. It occurred to Lola that this man might not be entirely sane, in which case what a mistake to have let him in the house. Bandit strolled in to see what the uproar was. He immediately went to L.D. and began to lick his hand. Bandit would be no use if this got out of control.

"Actually, I'm in the market for a candidate."

"What does that have to do with us, Mr. Sparks?" Lola asked.

"Please, call me L.D. Everybody does."

"We're kinda isolated out here," said Lola. "We don't really mix with people like that. Political types, I mean." She might have added that the nearest other human being was twenty miles away.

"I don't suppose you do," said L.D. "That's why I'm here. Governor has called a special election. This district needs a new representative, pronto. Someone who stands for good, conservative values. Someone who commands the respect of all who know him. Someone with ideas. A patriot. A hero. A Republican."

Sonny looked at Lola. "Honey, do we know anybody like that?"

L.D. said, "I got a fair idea it'd be you."

"Me?" Sonny said, totally dumbfounded.

"This is a joke?" Lola said in the same instant.

"I'm as serious as an undertaker," said L.D.

"What in the world makes you think I'd want to go into politics?" Sonny asked.

"That's what I'm here to find out. Whether you'd be willing to make the sacrifice to represent your neighbors in the capitol of Texas."

By now Bandit had made a place for himself in L.D.'s lap. L.D. was scratching him behind the ear in exactly the right spot. The dog's eyes rolled in pleasure. There was not a doubt in Lola's mind that L.D. could have scooped up their dog and raced off in his Lincoln with nary a forlorn glance from Bandit, the little traitor terrier.

"What do you know about us?" Lola asked. "Did you just pick us out of the phone book or what?"

"I know you were the Rodeo Queen at the Fort Worth Stock Show a few years back. I know Sonny played ball at Sul Ross. He came within an inch of getting a recording contract with RCA, and it's a damn shame he didn't. I know you and Sonny missed two mortgage payments and you've been selling off your herd because of the drought. Hard times, nothing to be ashamed of."

Lola and Sonny were astounded that anybody outside of Presidio County knew or cared the least bit about them. That this crazy man would pop in—all the way from Austin—with encyclopedic knowledge of their backgrounds, even embarrassing details of their financial life, this was just too much. Lola had to remember to close her mouth.

"How in the hell do you know all this?" Sonny demanded.

"I been asking around. Small town. Met your mom, she's a fine woman."

That explained a lot.

"As a matter of fact, there's one other thing I know. I can get you elected if you want to run."

"How's that?"

"Funny how a person can live his whole life being good or bad but there's nothing on the record, nothing that you can hold in your hand and say, here, take a look, this is who I really am. But that little bit of video of your heroics at the fire the other night—pure political gold. Put that in a campaign ad and you'll have folks jumping out of trees to vote for you."

"You haven't even asked what my political views are," Sonny said.

"Far as I can tell, you've never voted."

"That's right," Sonny said.

"We're not political," Lola said, as if that settled the matter.

L.D. grinned. "I can't tell you what a huge advantage that is. Gives us a chance to write your own script. You can be anybody."

"Sonny doesn't even know if he's a Republican or a Democrat," Lola said.

"I'm a Republican," Sonny said.

"When did that happen?"

"I've always been. You just never asked."

This whole conversation was making Lola crazy. It was like some game show where they come to your house with a bag full of surprises and you're supposed to jump up and down for joy. But that was not what she felt. "Obviously, you know our financial situation," she said to L.D. "There's no way on God's green earth we can afford for Sonny to go into politics. Even if he was at all interested, which he's not."

Sonny gave her a look.

"It's a part-time job," L.D. said soothingly. "A hundred and forty days, every other year. Goes by like a freight train in the middle of the night."

"How much does it pay?" Lola asked.

"Six hundred bucks a month, when the legislature is in session. I'm just talking about the salary, you understand. There are other benefits. Pension, health care, per diem. And certain intangibles."

"But he has to campaign and all that. We're not rich."

"The money part will take care of itself," L.D. said. "Trust me. There are people who want to see a bright young man such as your husband representing this district. People who want to invest in his career."

"Now we're talking about a career?"

"I feel a little like . . . *whoa!*" Sonny said.

"Quite natural," L.D. said. "Man comes out of nowhere and says he can change your life. How often does that happen, right?" He tucked Bandit under his arm and walked over to examine the photos on the mantle. "This is you in Iraq," he observed.

"Yep."

L.D. took a closer look. "Rangers."

"Don't make me out to be more than I am."

"I bet you signed up right after 9/11."

"That's a period of my life I'd just as soon forget."

"Mr. Sparks," said Lola.

"Call me L.D."

"We need Sonny here on the ranch."

"It's a sacrifice, I know. Public service. It's hard, hard. Takes a kind of nobility—"

"I thought we were talking about politicians," Lola said.

L.D. chuckled. "I see where you're coming from. But the kind of person who would do this work has to have balls, if you don't mind my saying. He's got to want to serve. He's got to have ambition, but also be willing to humble himself. I think Sonny Lamb may have those qualities. 'Course, I may be wrong. You know best." He paused. "I understand that you need a little time to think it over."

"Right," said Sonny.

"We do?" said Lola.

"I'm at the Hampton Inn," L.D. said, as he set Bandit on the rug. "You got my card."

★

"'Think it over'?" Lola exclaimed as the dust from the departing Lincoln shrouded the night air. "What do you mean?"

"I don't know why I said that. I'm a little weirded out." Sonny felt dizzy and exhilarated at the same time.

"But you're not seriously considering this," she declared flatly. Then in the silence, "Are you?"

"Of course not. But still."

"Na-uh. 'Still' nothing. Forget it."

"Lola, c'mon, I'm just thinking it over, like he said. What's wrong with considering the man's offer?"

"I don't want to talk about it."

"Lola!"

She turned her back and washed out the teacups. Sonny knew enough not to push the matter. He walked outside, down to the turn-off to the highway, stars lighting the way. Better to let some of the steam out of Lola's mood. Truth was, his feelings were hurt that she wouldn't even consider the idea. Maybe it wouldn't have seemed so crazy if one of her half-assed brothers had announced his candidacy. And how is it that anybody steps up and says he's running for office, he's the man for the job, who thinks like that? But once the idea has crept into your mind, then why not? Who else? People emerge. Ordinary citizens, something triggers them to stand in front of the pack and say, *It's me*. And then people say yes to you, or no to you, but how can you know who you are in their eyes unless you stand up? You don't even know yourself if you don't try. Abraham Lincoln would still be splitting logs. Ronald Reagan would be making B movies. But something had stirred inside them and they had taken that step. It wasn't like Walter Dunne had been any great shakes.

Once again, the stars mocked him. Out here you were fully aware

of the speckness of your existence in the universe, the majesty of
eternal creation compared with the swift and insignificant transit of
one such as yourself. Nothing in your life made any difference in the
countenance of the heavens bearing down on you, no more than
the mountains and the cows and the rattlesnakes. After considering
the vanity of ambition, especially in one so unaccomplished, Sonny
recollected that he had only one life, and where was that headed?
Was he always going to be standing alone in the night begging the
stars for answers while never living fully, never testing the limits of
who he might be? Why else were we born? For the longest time—he
couldn't date when it started, but maybe in the Army field hospital
in Iraq—he had detected a vacancy inside himself, probably it was
always there but when you're young it was different. When you're
young the world is spilling over with possibilities, and you're out
there shopping for your future, maybe this, maybe that, trying on
destinies to see which one fits. So you choose or you just let life
happen; either way you might become aware some night when you
should be prancing through dreamland that there's a hole in the
place where there should be the fully realized you. You missed a turn
back there. Night after night the hollowness expands as you watch
the possible destinies take their leave. Nobody's coming to your rescue. And then the truth rolls in like a giant wave that drowns your
spirit and you realize that you're nothing more than what the stars
see, that pitiable speck in the universe.

Sonny worked himself into quite a state, which he then had to
walk off again so he wouldn't start another fight he was unlikely to
win and wasn't worth having. But it gnawed at him that Lola missed
the whole point—the whole point being *Why not me?* At least she
could have given it some respectful consideration.

On the other hand, he thought, *she's right. The idea is totally
ludicrous.*

Or maybe not. Maybe it was a sign, and Lola just hasn't seen
it. Yet.

★

Lola was watching Ted Cruz on Fox News. She gave Sonny a look like a dagger in his eye. "Politics," she said. Obviously, she hadn't cooled down.

Sonny took a book to bed and waited. It didn't take long.

"You're actually thinking about this?" Lola demanded. She stood there with a toothbrush in her hand and her teeth half brushed.

"Why shouldn't I?"

"Suppose he said you should be a brain surgeon or the ambassador to Timbuktu? It's crazy."

"Okay, suppose it was you he was asking," he said. " 'Lola Lamb, we sized you up and think you've got real potential. We see you as a leader in your community, someone your neighbors love and trust'— all true, by the way—wouldn't you at least chew it over? I mean, this is the opinion of an expert."

"How do you know he's an expert? He just dropped out of the sky like Mary Poppins and all of a sudden you think you can fly."

"Maybe he sees me in a way that folks around here don't appreciate. Your family, for one. My whole life, folks have been running me down. Loser this, loser that. Nothing I ever wanted for myself has panned out. You might not realize it, but I'd still like to be somebody. I mean really be *somebody*. And you heard him, he says he can get me elected."

Lola softened, a bit. She knew how sensitive Sonny could be on the subject of his success, or lack thereof. But she did feel alarmed. "Can you actually see yourself going house to house asking people to vote for you? Is that really you? Shaking hands, making speeches?"

"You don't think I can do that?"

"I'm not saying you can't, just that in our entire life together I never saw you express the least bit of interest in glad-handing and backslapping and all that kind of crap." Lola went back to the bathroom and finished brushing her teeth.

When Lola put it like that, it didn't sound very manly or sincere or modest, the Gary Cooperish qualities that Sonny privately associated with himself. He imagined the scene Lola had just described. It was not appealing. Doors slammed in your face. Kissing babies that spit up on you. As a matter of fact, he had never been particularly patient with the politicians he had encountered—such as Walter Dunne, a total phony. Is that who I want to be? These thoughts were still tugging at him as he drifted into a restless sleep. And then he woke up moments later, remembering being onstage. He knew what it was to stand in front of a crowd. Truth was, he missed being the center of attention. He also had ideas—big ideas—and one other thing: he didn't have much to lose. Except the ranch and Lola.

When he felt Lola rustle the sheets, he figured she was still awake. "I think I might be good at this," he said in a low voice.

Lola opened her eyes. Her face was somber but she was no longer mad. "Tell me why you think so," she said. "Convince me."

"I look around, I see everybody stuck in the same place, all of us scratchin' bottom, and nobody has any plans for change."

"And you do?"

"Well, yeah. Like my desalination idea."

"If it's such a great plan, why hasn't somebody said something already?"

"It's not a bad idea just because it's my idea."

"I never said any such thing. It's just—you don't know how these things work."

"I'd learn! I already signed up for an online course in hydrology."

"You're just full of surprises today."

"You don't think I can do it, do you?"

Lola was quiet for a moment, which suggested that was exactly what she thought, but what she said was, "You don't have to raise your voice."

Sonny was surprised at himself. He was getting worked up. A couple hours ago, he would never have considered running for office, it would have been like joining the circus. But the idea had been presented as perfectly reasonable. A sure thing, more or less.

"Don't you want our life to change?" Sonny asked. "I do! I want to count for something."

"I'm not saying you're not capable of doing the job," Lola amended. "God knows, you'd be better than Walter Dunne. You're a quick study. You've got a good mind. I always thought you were a frustrated engineer. And people respect you, even if you don't see it. Look at how they depended on you at the fire. You took charge. You knew what to do when others didn't. I'm so proud of you for that."

"Wouldn't you be proud of me if I got elected?"

"I'm proud of you when you act from your heart, not when some huckster comes around selling other people's dreams. I need you here, Sonny. It's not like we can afford another hand."

Lola rolled over in her I'm-done-with-this-I'm-going-to-sleep position, leaving Sonny to stew. She was right. She was always right. It was pointless to debate her. Even if in a single instance such as this one she happened to be wrong, everybody would agree with her anyway. That was the dynamic of their relationship. Lola was the one who ought to be running for office. People would just bow down. Sonny was a good-hearted fuckup who bought his own bull, et cetera, et cetera. That hollowness inside him ballooned to the point he thought he would burst wide open.

"Just never mind," he said. "I'm not gonna do it. You're totally right about me."

"What does that mean?"

"I should settle for what I've got and be happy. I don't want to lose sight of the most precious things in my life. I almost lost them once. And if this puts all that in jeopardy, it sure ain't worth it." He sighed. "Good night."

"Good night," Lola said.

She couldn't leave it at that. To surrender like that, it wasn't like him, especially since he was clearly tormented over this bizarre offer that had flown in the window like a disoriented grackle and couldn't find its way out of the house. "There's something going on with you," she observed. "You were stirred up even before that politics fella wound up on our porch."

"I guess."

"C'mon, Sonny, be real with me. This whole episode is turning our marriage upside down. I need to know what's really going on with you."

He didn't respond. She waited. It was pitch black and quiet except for Sonny's breathing. "Something happened to me when I was in that burning barn," he confided in a tentative, faraway voice. "I didn't think I was gonna get out alive. And I wondered if it mattered—to me, to anybody. Maybe everybody would be better off if I weren't around."

"Do you really think that you don't matter to me?" she said, her voice breaking.

"No, no, I know you love me. But I've failed you, I haven't given you the life you deserve. I don't have the life I want, either. Just look at where we are, practically broke, watching the land die all around us. I've struggled to figure out how to break through, but I never did. I thought, *If I get out of this barn alive, I've gotta change. I gotta be somebody, I gotta ride outta here into a new life, be the man I oughta be.* These were not like regular thoughts. They were commands, like somebody telling me get on the damn horse and take charge! And then, like an answered prayer, this guy shows up and says, 'Sign here for that new life of yours.' How am I supposed to say no to that? So far the only thing I ever accomplished that amounts to anything is marrying you, and I can't see why you ever agreed to that."

Lola turned over. Her cheeks were wet. "There is a reason," she said quietly.

"What?"

"You're a good man. And I'd take that over you having some high-powered job or being a famous country singer or whatever dream you have cookin' in that kitchen of yours."

Sonny put his hand on her shoulder and rested his head against hers, their breathing synchronized, her body so warm. Lola said, "Maybe it's time you asked me what I want, for a change."

Sonny was shocked that Lola would open negotiations. "Okay, what do you want?"

"I want a family."

"Well, I want that, too."

"The full thing. Babies, car seats, homework, soccer games."

"Well, yeah. We've tried."

"Maybe not hard enough. I've talked to the doc and she's got a program she's maybe gonna put me on. But you'd have to be a part of it, obviously."

"Sure, I'll do whatever might help."

"It's lonely out here. I want to hear their little voices. I dream about them. But time's running out. How are we gonna pull off having kids if you're off in Austin and I'm here running the ranch?"

"I haven't got elected yet."

"Answer the question."

"We'd just have to find time to be together."

"I still think it's a crazy idea."

"I prob'ly won't do it," Sonny said.

Lola pressed her lips together in an odd, only Lola expression. Sonny knew it well. It preceded the well-thought-out bottom line, the court of no appeal. "If you want me to agree to this," she said, "we'll need to establish a breeding schedule."

"Breeding schedule?"

"Timed exactly to my fertility windows."

That was a term Sonny had never heard before.

"And this time you're coming with me to the clinic," she said. "I'm serious."

"I know."

"I don't hear you saying yes."

"Yes."

"Okay, then, let's get started right now."

★ 4 ★

The director was a twentysomething with a nose ring and half her head shaved, the other half dyed purple. Chaya was her name—just Chaya, like Beyoncé or Cher, so certain was she of her future renown. She had caught L.D.'s attention with a splashy ad for Toyota. The Sonny Lamb campaign was one more opportunity to display her artistry before she started shooting a feature for Netflix. L.D. and his staff gathered in the ad agency's intimate theater on Sixth Street in Austin. The lights dimmed and the screen lit up with a supersaturated shot of the Alamo, the most sacred site in the state.

"His family has been in Texas for six generations," the announcer said, "going back to Isaac Lamb, who fell at the Alamo." Next there was a shot of Sonny in his Army uniform, looking like a movie star, the photo having been fiddled with. "Sonny also fought for liberty, in Iraq. He returned to work the land." This was over Sonny riding a horse and cutting out cows. Chaya had to rent a horse for the shot because Sonny's aging quarter horses weren't "star quality." She found a white gelding at a ranch outside Fort Stockton—a nod toward Ronald Reagan's noble Arabian mount, El Alamein—and had Sonny dress up in a matching white hat as he roped a heifer that had been chased into the shot. Sonny was good at that stuff.

"He became a volunteer fireman," the announcer continued, approaching the climax of the ad, "protecting the lives and property of his neighbors." Here was the money shot of Sonny on Coco, bursting through the flames of the burning barn, although it had been entirely re-created and filmed against a green screen to get the pyro-technics right. "Soldier, patriot, rancher, fireman, Texan—Sonny Lamb is one of us." Once again, Mary Lou Miller hugged him (L.D. had to pay the Millers handsomely to pose for that shot), followed by Sonny's million-dollar smile. "I'm Sonny Lamb," he said at the end, still on his horse, "and I approve this message." The horse reared and Sonny rode into the sunset, followed by a drone.

"Beautiful," L.D. said gleefully. "One for the ages."

"I had a vision," Chaya said proudly. Although she was raised in Plano she spoke with a kind of Middle European accent that you might hear at Cannes or Davos. "We ask ourselves, 'Who is this man?' And we imagine that he is a legend, a myth, like a god among us. Strong. Beautiful. Brave. Man against nature. These are the qual-ities we award him—Texas qualities. So we title this reel 'Mr. Texas.' This is the image we convey to your voters."

★

After a congratulatory lunch at the Headliners Club, L.D. returned to his office on Congress Avenue, the Capitol gleaming in the sun just outside his window. His personal domain. If you wanted some-thing done in Texas, you didn't go to the governor. You didn't go to your state representative or senator. No. There was a hierarchy that had to be preserved. Hundreds of lobbyists clustered in the high-rise rookeries around the pink granite Capitol dome, but only a handful were real players, the people who handled the money, who made the deals, who kept the chits, who wrote the bills and placed them in the hands of the lawmakers. L.D. was the pinnacle, dominating the political landscape as no other lobbyist ever had. He was a Texas maharajah.

But as central as L.D. was to what is playfully called the "demo-cratic process," he had a problem. The Texas House contains 150 members, but even with the new legislators L.D. had only 75 votes he could count on. One more and he would rule the world. Now, with the killer ad in the can, L.D. was certain that he had his seventy-sixth vote. He could almost float out of his chair. He looked around the room at his staff. Their eyes were shining like kids in front of the ice cream truck.

What they saw in Sonny were the essential qualities L.D. sought in a candidate—youth, looks, good teeth, and naïveté. He was presentable enough but maybe could use some work on the nose. He could belt out a tune, which might be an asset. Pappy Lee O'Daniel, one of the legends of Texas politics, was a singing flour salesman on the radio, dominating state politics for years despite being a total ignoramus. He'd roll into town with the Light Crust Doughboys backing him up and you couldn't keep the women away. That could be a problem with Sonny, L.D. thought. Lots of men go into politics for the sexual favors that come their way.

On the other hand, that Lola. She was a tough one, he assessed. The political wife was a role undergoing renovation, old-fashioned homemakers no longer fit the narrative, and Lola could certainly be an asset. A real rancher. A link to the hallowed pioneer women of yore. Power couples, that's where the play was. Lola and Sonny, ranching elite—at least, they could be made to look that way—it would sell. Magazine spreads, morning television shows, the camera would lap them up. Who knew how far Sonny Lamb could rise? Governor? Senator? And L.D. would be in the driver's seat, all the way.

He had to stop, this was getting out of hand.

"So, Hector, what do you think?" he asked Hector Valdez, the campaign manager L.D. had selected for Sonny. Hector was in his mid-forties. A slender, black bandito mustache provided the villainous look he cultivated. Somewhere along in his childhood, all sentiment had been surgically removed from his soul. He was a brilliant gamesman at the summit of his infamous career. He knew the moves. He would work for anybody who could pay his tab. And he never lost.

"Is that really true about the Alamo?" Hector asked.

"It checked out," said L.D.

Hector shook his head. How often do you get that lucky? The staff just chuckled and looked at each other, dizzied by their good fortune. They were all talking about "Mr. Texas" as if that were a real person and not some gaudy conceit cooked up by a high-end ad agency.

"Don't get me wrong," said L.D., trying to mute the giddy vibe. "This kid is raw. He needs guidance. We'll have to gently break him to the saddle. And that Valerie Nightingale, she's a hot ticket. Experienced. Well known and liked. Widely respected."

"She is now," said Hector laconically.

Everyone laughed. L.D. loved that about Hector, how professional he was, like a butcher whacking off the head of a chicken. Then the plucking began. It was a process.

"Tell you what," L.D. said. "Hurry on out there, get him some press. Nothing too challenging. Get his tootsies wet."

On his way out, Hector grabbed a box of brochures that were "Paid for by Citizens for Sonny Lamb"—the newly formed political action committee that was funding the campaign.

★

They all drive Lincolns, Sonny thought, as he and Hector rode into Marfa for his first radio show. Along the way, Hector coached him on the essential issues.

"Immigration," said Hector.

"Texas is a land of immigrants, and we honor that," Sonny said, "but we can't control our destiny if we don't control our borders."

"It's a matter of . . ."

"It's a matter of *national security*."

"Health care," said Hector.

"We can't have the federal government imposing huge deficits on our state budget. Texans deserve the chance to choose their own doctors and insurance."

"Don't forget to call it Obamacare," Hector said. "But as much as possible, you want to steer clear of issues. Our people don't care about those things. They care about values."

"Values like what?"

"Small-town values."

"That's like a code?"

"It's an incantation. Doesn't mean anything, just makes people feel good about themselves."

They were just rolling into Marfa, the existence of which complicated the small-town-values formula that Hector was advocating. Marfa was a watering hole for sophisticates. Like a lot of county seats in Texas, it was built around a central square, with a Disney-esque wedding-cake courthouse that was still the tallest structure in town, and the most charming. On the weekends, the hedge fund billionaires flew in, buying up shabby adobe cottages for ungodly sums and dressing like ranch hands. It was a mystery to Sonny. Some decades ago, a high school shop teacher turned artist from New York City named Donald Judd had bought an old military facility on the edge of town and turned it into a museum filled with the gargantuan aluminum boxes he fabricated—glorified ice chests, in Sonny's opinion. Lola loved the stuff. There were vintage pickups driving around with WWDJD bumper stickers. What Would Donald Judd Do. It's a weird country we live in. Meantime, all over the state other small towns were drying up and blowing away. Why Marfa and not Big Spring?

Marfa Public Radio was inside a repurposed gas station with a herd of rental bikes and electric scooters parked in front, typical hipster scene. Sonny had never been inside a radio station, even during his singing days. Not much to it, he now saw. A newsroom with two reporters, one speaking Spanish on the phone, the other staring into space—the act of creation, Sonny supposed. He was given a cup of burned coffee and ushered into the studio—a former garage where they used to do lube jobs, now fitted out with a round table and microphones on spring-loaded swing-arm stands, sound baffles on the walls, and a picture window onto San Antonio Street. You could barely see the producer behind tinted glass who was running the equipment. The whole operation was crammed into a space about the size of Sonny and Lola's breakfast room. Sonny eased himself into an empty seat.

The hosts were a middle-aged married couple, the Martindales, Pat and Pat, famous in these parts.

"Pat," said Pat the husband, "we got ourselves a special election coming up."

"That's right, Pat," Pat the wife said. "Poor old Walter Dunne passed away."

"What a loss."

"We knew him well, didn't we?"

"On the show—what?"

"Maybe fifty times."

"Do you remember the story he told about his momma . . . ?"

"Oh, he could tell a story, all right!"

"We do miss him, don't we."

"Fine man, yes, indeed."

Sonny watched them gab. He was sitting right in front of them, invisible, wearing the earphones they'd given him, but why he needed earphones was a puzzle. Then he heard the producer behind the tinted window say there was a commercial break coming up in ten seconds. Pat the husband took off his earphones and stretched, then scratched his armpit. "Of course he was a lyin' son of a bitch who had his dick in every stray piece of snatch he could round up."

"Pat," said the producer, "that went on the air."

"What the fuck? You said we were going to a commercial break!"

"In ten seconds. You jumped the gun."

"You really screwed the pooch," wife Pat observed.

As it happened, the commercial was an ad for Valerie Nightingale. "For the last ten years on the county commission, I've made budgets, sat in planning meetings, overseen county roadwork, allocated our precious resources—serving our citizens by doing the nitty-gritty work of government," she was telling the world. "My opponent has no relevant experience whatsoever. I hope when you go to the ballot box you'll choose the candidate who cares about the issues and knows how to make government work for all of us."

Sonny listened to the ad with a fixed grin on his face. She sure sounded smart and experienced. He had never run for office before, that's true. Never made a budget, also true. Valerie Nightingale was right about him. What was he doing here? Who did he think he was?

The producer was saying, "Back to you in three, two, one . . ."

"And here we are, back again, after a little radio interference," wife Pat said cheerily. "I couldn't quite make out what it was."

"Aliens," said husband Pat, without remorse.

"Well, that might be so, Pat, some foul-mouthed alien who can't count. Now, back to the election." She turned to Sonny. "We have ourselves a bona fide candidate sitting right here."

"This is the Republican."

"That's right. Sonny Lamb, from Presidio County, who's taken it into his head to run for Walter's seat. Sonny, welcome to the Pats."

"Thank you, Pat," said Sonny. "Thank you, Pat."

"Sonny," said the wife, "folks round here have known you forever, since that epic losing football season at Jack Hays Consolidated High School, but this turn toward politics has caught some of us by surprise."

"This is something I've wanted to do all my life," Sonny said. "Representing my neighbors, serving our community, standing up for Texas—it's been a dream of mine since boyhood." He could say this without a flutter because it was in some way true, at least the part about wanting something.

"We had Valerie Nightingale on the show last week," wife Pat said. "She's a very impressive candidate—"

"A hot little number," husband Pat interjected.

"—*highly experienced* and well qualified."

"How long have you folks been doing this show?" Sonny asked in a friendly tone, hoping to change the subject.

"We ask the questions around here," wife Pat said pertly. "So we get to the important stuff in the brief time we have with our listeners."

"Speaking of that, we have our first caller," husband Pat said, pushing a flashing button on the speakerphone. "Good morning."

"Hi, Pat. This is Doug over in Fort Davis. We sure love your show, but Pat, you gotta watch your language."

"Have you got a question for Sonny Lamb?"

"Yeah. Ain't you the same guy who bought his own bull?"

"Good question, Doug. What about that, Sonny?"

"Ha. Yeah, I guess I am."

"He did what?" wife Pat asked.

"He took his bull to auction and bought him back," Doug explained.

Wife Pat scrutinized Sonny with new interest. "How much does a bull cost?"

"Let's just say it was less than he's worth, at least to me."

"I think that's sweet."

"Caller number two is on the line."

Sonny noticed some kids peering into the picture window. As a matter of fact, a small crowd was gathering and some of the cars were slowing down on San Antonio Street as the drivers cast glances into the studio. One caller wanted Sonny to stop a pipeline. Another demanded an ice rink in Alpine. Finish the border wall. A new ballpark. Life in politics was beginning to seem like Santa's lap, where every heart's desire gets pronounced.

"We get politicians in here all the time telling us how they're gonna make things better, and as far as I can tell the whole damn kit and caboodle are a bunch of lying thieves," an elderly gentleman from Marathon offered, evidently expecting Sonny to agree. "They don't give a country crap about folks like us. I don't know if you can say 'crap' on the radio. They're all in the pockets of So-and-So."

"Well, I'm sure there are some good folks in the legislature," Sonny said. "I'd like to think that I'd be one of them. My goal is to help my friends and neighbors realize their dreams. Some of those dreams might need a little government assistance, some of them might need government to get out of the way. Either way, I'll be there to help you. We share those same small-town values—"

"What about health care?" some lady on line two interjected.

"You mean *Obamacare*?" said Sonny, casting a knowing look at Hector, standing behind the producer.

"I mean *health care*," the woman said firmly. "Texas has the highest number of uninsured people in the whole country. Just what do you intend to do about that?"

"Well, obviously *Obamacare* is not the solution," Sonny said, sticking to the script. "Texans need to be guaranteed access to their own doctors—"

"Valerie Nightingale told us she would gladly accept federal dollars to offset state Medicaid expenses," the woman said, cutting Sonny off before he could get "creeping socialism" out of his mouth. She had the authority of a federal prosecutor, which, who knew, she might well be. "Valerie's proposal would contribute over five billion dollars every year to the state and billions more to the health care system. What's your argument against it?"

Sonny was at a loss. "I gotta level with y'all," he finally said. "I really don't know a lot about the Medicaid issue. Why don't you tell me about it?"

"We got nearly five million Texans without insurance," the prosecutor said. "Highest in the nation. Do you know how many deaths could be avoided in Texas if we accept the Medicaid funds? More than seven hundred. Every year! Seven hundred Texans killed by politicians!"

"But it raises our federal taxes," Sonny said, remembering one of Hector's dictums. "I'm for cutting taxes and relieving the burden on homeowners. There's no such thing as a free lunch."

"We've already paid our federal taxes, and it's going to those thirty-six other states that accept Medicaid subsidies," the prosecutor said. "Counties in Texas are forced to pay for indigent care, and that raises our property taxes, so we get it coming and going."

"Well, darn," said Sonny. "You make an awful good argument. I gotta learn more about this."

"You do that."

Next caller: "Mr. Lamb, where do you stand on the Second Amendment?"

"I'm a proud gun owner, if that's what you mean."

"Are you carrying a gun right now?"

"Well, no."

"Then what good can you be if some lunatic comes bustin' through the door and assassinates one and all?"

"Don't worry, caller," said husband Pat. "We got that covered."

"This is Pastor Frank from Candelaria. I'd just like to ask the candidate what he stands for. Like, his core values. We don't need another slimeball in Austin, we got enough of that sort already."

"Pastor, I want you to know that I stand foursquare behind small-town values."

"And what would small-town values be?" the man said in a voice that wasn't going to accept the velvet palaver.

"Oh, you know. Friendliness, for instance. Being good neighbors."

"Empty words," the pastor observed. "Those aren't things you can pass a law about."

"What laws are you thinking about?"

"Like that gay marriage thing. What in the world were they thinking when they said a man could marry a man? The Bible's very clear on this."

"Uh-huh."

"And guns, Second Amendment. Don't go tryin' to take away a person's firearms."

"I sure wouldn't do that."

"Abortion."

"The Supreme Court has spoken on this," Sonny said. "And Texas has about the strictest laws in the country against abortion. You think we need something more?"

"Start with banning contraception. It's anti-life, just like abortion. 'Fruits of the same tree,' one of the popes said. People get accustomed to sex without consequences. If the law says abortion's a crime, where's the punishment? Some girl gets knocked up and decides to kill her baby, she should pay for that. I say it's a capital offense. Murder in the first degree. A few exemplary executions would do a world of good."

"What about the man in the picture?" Sonny said. "Are you for executing the father as well?"

The pastor paused and took a breath. "We've been praying over this very question," he said. "It's a theological debate that's still unresolved. But it's the mothers who are the real killers."

"Let's have the next caller on line three."

"Hi, Pat. Hi, Pat. This is Doris over at the Texas Moon Café."

"Hey, Doris! We sure love your chicken-fried steak."

"I have a question for the candidate," Doris said. "Why didn't you consult your mother before you made this decision?"

"Mom, can we talk about this maybe not on the air?"

"But that's a really interesting question," wife Pat said.

"Don't just assume you've got my vote," Doris said. "And since when did you become a Republican?"

"Mom, really?"

"That Valerie Nightingale is the real deal."

"We were impressed," wife Pat said. "Super smart."

"And very nicely packaged," her husband added.

"Doris," the wife said, "are you still going with Bud Schotz over at the auction barn?"

"It's off and on, Pat."

"Well, these things . . ."

"Exactly."

★ 5 ★

"This ain't near as easy as you said it was gonna be," Sonny complained to L.D. and Hector at his campaign headquarters in Alpine. Several morose staffers sat around rented desks, waiting for their phones to ring. The place had the atmosphere of a locker room at halftime when you're behind fifty touchdowns. Smeared. Slaughtered. Why go back out there, it's hopeless. You might die.

"I never said it was going to be easy," said L.D. "I just said I'd get you elected."

"I don't see how," Sonny said. "Valerie Nightingale is like twenty points ahead."

"She's got the Dems, the Mexicans, the women. Not many beans left in the pot," said Hector, the man who never lost. "Folks have been voting for Walter Dunne for years and years, why are they going to switch parties now just because he's kicked the bucket? We have to give them a good reason."

For the past month, as Sonny had been knocking on doors and visiting garden clubs and junior colleges and chambers of commerce, it seemed like every yard in Alpine, Fort Stockton, Marfa, and even Valentine sported a "Nightingale for Texas" sign. Half the pickups in Presidio County had her bumper stickers. There were T-shirts, hats, pins, a whole Valerie Nightingale swag industry.

"How's she tracking?" asked L.D.

"Sixty to our thirty-five. Even with the *pinche* Alamo in our ad."

L.D. gave Sonny a hard look. "You prepared?"

"Prepared for what?"

"The unexpected," said L.D.

"Like what?"

"Suppose someone—a private detective, let's say—dug into your background, what would he find?"

"Is that going to happen?"

"As I say, you gotta be prepared," said L.D. "And the first step is letting your campaign manager know what secrets might be hidden in your closet."

"Think of us like priests," Hector added. "Whatever you say goes no further." He made a gesture sewing up his lips.

"If there's dirt to be dug," said L.D., "we need to know."

Sonny could see they were both dead serious. "I'm a child molester," he said.

"Any convictions?" Hector asked blandly.

"That was a joke!" Sonny said. "And you were still going to try to elect me? Is there anybody you wouldn't campaign for on principle?"

"We've had a fair number of perverts in office," said L.D. "Some of them did a pretty decent job."

Sonny had off and on been toying with the thought that this whole campaign was some kind of prank that L.D. was playing on him. Concealed cameras were following his stumbling efforts at campaigning. It was streaming on Facebook. Theatergoers were watching him, cracking up, spilling popcorn, everybody loves to laugh at a loser.

Another possibility: L.D. was actually working for Valerie Nightingale. She hired him to recruit an opponent with no chance in hell. Both of those theories were more plausible than the one that L.D. claimed was the truth: that Sonny Lamb was going to be the next state representative from District 74.

"Women?" L.D. asked. "Drugs? Bankruptcies?"

"Yes."

"Which ones?"

"All of them."

"Uh-huh," said Hector, as if Sonny had been hiding this.

"Well, nobody asked me till now," Sonny said. "I was really messed up when I came back from Iraq. I did a lot of things I regret."

"Anything else we should know?"

"My dad is serving time." Sonny could read the expression on their faces. "I guess it was stupid of me to think I'd ever get away with this."

L.D. shook his head. "There ain't no saints in politics, Sonny. It's all a matter of how you tell the story. Your dad in prison is not bad or good, it's just a fact, but facts are not the story. The story is how you deal with it. The story is what you learned from it. But you gotta control the narrative of your life. Don't let your opponents tell your story. You bust out there and claim it. Now, it might be a story people don't want to hear, that's true. But you'd be surprised how much people want to welcome the sinner home. You agree, Hector?"

Hector nodded. "At this point, he's got nothing to lose." He added that they should head on over to the high school to size up the gym, but Sonny's phone buzzed. It was Lola summoning him home at once. They had a deal, after all.

"I'll see you at the debate," Sonny said as he rushed out the door.

★

Lola had calculated her fertility window, six days during which Sonny had agreed to have sex twelve times. Sex twice a day was a dream come true—at first—but it began to get in the way of his campaign and it was awkward to explain his abrupt absences. He began to feel like a cow that had been taken to the barn for milking, and the milking was nice but no more than what was expected. On the whole the cow wanted to be milked because of the relief that followed, a sensation like nothing else in the world. But there was a diminishment of delight. One began to be aware of the machinery of the act, the stimulus-response of it, the biological plumbing required, the comedy of desire, et cetera.

Lola insisted on an early-afternoon/nighttime schedule because mornings on the ranch were the busiest time. She had stopped even pretending to be enjoying herself. Sonny would rush back from a Lions Club luncheon or a wine-and-cheese meet-and-greet to find Lola pointing at her watch. In bed. Naked with her knees in the air. Let's get this over with, quicker the better. Sonny already had his shirt off by the time he hit the porch. He felt sympathy for Joaquin, who had a whole herd to service.

It did occur to him that Lola was quite a thrilling sight. And yet . . .

"What's wrong?" Lola asked.

Sonny stared down at his unresponsive organ. "I dunno," he said. "This has never happened before." Normally he was as reliable as a pop-up toaster.

"Too much sex?" Lola asked. "I know it's a really demanding schedule."

That was no doubt true, but inadmissible in the court of male self-esteem. "It can't be that. I think I'm just, you know, worried about getting to the debate on time."

"You feel rushed," Lola said helpfully.

"I guess I do."

"It seems mechanical, not romantic."

"A little bit."

"I don't think that's really it," Lola said. She was sitting up now, her luminous breasts hovering above him, unofficially off-limits because of his hard-to-explain lack of interest. "There's something else going on with you. Ever since you got in this race you've been distracted. Not yourself. Are you scared, Sonny? Is that what's going on?"

It was like she had an X-ray of his psyche. Of course he was scared. He was about to debate Valerie Nightingale in the high school gym. She was going to expose him, destroy him, eat him alive—and he was supposed to have sex?

"I'm a little anxious, sure. Maybe my mind is somewhere else."

"You don't think you can beat her, do you?"

"It's not a matter of think. I *know* I can't."

"You underestimate yourself," Lola said. "You can be very persuasive when you have your heart in it. You convinced me, for instance."

"Yeah, but I should have listened to you. You were right about this all along."

When Sonny got vulnerable it was hard to argue with him. And strange, Lola thought, that we're finding ourselves on opposite sides of where we used to be. Maybe not all the way, but they were each seeing something they had been avoiding, swinging around to the conclusion that they were both right and both wrong, but right and wrong in different ways than they were before. "I don't know about that," Lola said. "I can see this race really means something to you. It's been a long time since you got this passionate about anything. Just having a talk like this, it's been a while. What matters is that you've come out of that shell you had around you the past few years. I thought you were back after the war, but you weren't, you were locked away somewhere inside yourself. And when you got off the drugs you still weren't really Sonny, or what I remembered was Sonny. After that, I kinda forgot about ever seeing that person again. We all get older. We all change. But now, it's like I was living with your identical twin and suddenly the real you comes knocking on the door, and I realize that I missed you, the real you. That other guy was fine but not quite the man I married."

"You're right," he said, "it has been a long time. But it all feels temporary. I got my hopes up and placed a bet on my future. But if I don't win, I don't know, I just don't know how I'm gonna be after this. If I could only hold on to that feeling that I am somebody! Boy, where did that go?"

"Sonny, you're talking about the election, but it doesn't matter. Win or lose, you've made a change."

"A colossal loss sure ain't gonna help my self-respect. Oh, well. At least I gave it a shot. I'm doing everything I'm supposed to, whatever they tell me to do. These guys are professionals. They've coached me, done what they can. But I'm out there talking about stuff I don't really understand. Working really hard, trying to learn, but it's like I'll be standing there, making my speech, and at the same time watching myself from across the room and thinking, *Who's that phony?*" He sighed. "I sure wouldn't vote for me."

"Well, if you don't believe in who you are, how do you expect other people to?"

"Exactly my point," Sonny said.

"Why can't you just say what you truly believe?"

"I don't always know what that is," he admitted. "They gave me this book full of positions that I'm supposed to take about stuff I've never thought about. The more I learn, the more I wonder whether I can be the person they want me to be. Would I be a coward if I just decided to quit?"

"Not if that's what you really want. But Sonny, remember what you said. You always wanted to be somebody, to make a mark in the world, and out of the blue, this man comes along and offers you that chance. But you don't have to be his robot. He took his chances when he picked you. Just try being yourself. If you lose, well, that's fine, you come back to the ranch and we move on with our lives. At least you'll lose knowing that it was really you out there asking for people to believe in you. What's the point if you win and it turns out people were voting for somebody who doesn't exist? Somebody who's a bunch of words in a briefing book? Be yourself, Sonny. Let everybody see you for the man you are. Maybe they'll love you. I sure do."

Somehow during this talk, Sonny came back to life. "We'll have to make this quick," he said.

★

"Each candidate will have two minutes to tell us about themselves, followed by questions from our panel," said Helen Bobbitt, the longtime speech teacher and debate coach at Jack Hays Consolidated High School. Other than her white hair, which was teased into a museum-quality beehive, she was just as Sonny remembered, formidable and judgmental—Miss B, they called her. A withering look from Miss B could still raise the blood pressure of practically anyone in Presidio County, since everyone who went to Jack Hays Consolidated would have gone through her classes. She sat at a table under the basketball goal, flanked by a pair of reporters on either side. There were maybe fifty people in the bleachers. People didn't take politics very seriously around here, except for having a general loathing for government as a concept, although a good portion of the population was living on Social Security and food stamps, and the very school they were in wouldn't exist without state and local taxes. Folks would far rather take in a minor league game at Koker-not Field in Alpine, a scaled-down replica of Wrigley Field—scaled down like their lives, which replicated lives lived larger elsewhere.

"The toss of a coin has determined that Valerie Nightingale will go first," Miss B said.

Sonny took a peek at his opponent. They were standing behind lecterns in mid-court. He vaguely remembered her. She was a couple years behind him at Jack Hays. Maybe she had been on the drill team. Trim, poised, she carried herself with that old military rod up her back. Built-in precision. Just the way she held herself com-manded respect. Sonny straightened his shoulders. He almost felt the need to salute. She returned Sonny's glance and gave him a wan smile, the message being: *Sorry I have to do this to you.*

"Thanks, Miss B," Valerie said. She had a clear, strong voice, probably sings alto in her church choir, Sonny guessed. "I fondly remember those trips you took us on with the debate team. One of my proudest moments was when we went to the state tournament in Austin. The big city! I imagined that one day I would come back there to represent my friends and neighbors in the Capitol. That was quite an ambitious dream for a young woman from West Texas." She had the gift of taking in everyone in the audience as if she were talk-ing directly to them. Folks were leaning in her direction, elbow on knee and chin on fist, intently studying her. Captivated. Every word out of her mouth was perfectly crafted. She was the type who never made mistakes, a machine-tooled exemplar of competence.

"After I got out of the Navy, I couldn't wait to get back to Texas,"

Valerie continued. It was always a good idea to apologize for leaving Texas, even when you were serving your country. A little contrition was called for, and she delivered it nicely. It went down like buttered toast. "I've devoted myself to attending the needs of my constituents, both on the planning board and the county commission. I've made budgets, overseen county roadwork, allocated our precious resources—doing the hard work of government. I'm a member of the state bar, and I'm on the boards of a number of local civic organizations, including 4-A, Beautify Texas, and the Girl Scouts. Now I'm asking you to make my young girl's dream come true. Let me take all that experience to Austin and be the best state representative that District 74 has ever had. Give me that opportunity, and I'll make you proud. Thank you, and God bless Texas."

Valerie's life flashed through Sonny's mind. Tenth grade, teacher's pet, perfect in every way. Naval Academy, breaking barriers. Warrior. County commissioner while studying for her law degree. Slender, clear-eyed, nice bones. Well turned out in a dark blazer that subtly quoted the Navy dress blues she used to wear. The Fitbit on her wrist: she probably ran five miles a day. People like her naturally got ahead—because they deserved it. They're better. They're smarter. They have immaculate values. They manage their money. They watch their diet. They've never been convicted of a criminal offense. There was a trajectory to her life, a lighted path. He wouldn't be surprised if one day she was president. Sonny would answer a knock on the door, and there would be her biographer . . .

"Thank you, Valerie," Helen Bobbitt was saying. "Mr. Lamb?"

"Hi, Miss B," Sonny said. "I also remember the time spent in your class. The D you gave me. That was an act of mercy. At the time, my parents were divorcing and my dad was on trial for cattle rustling. Most of you already know that, so there's no reason to pretend it didn't happen. You may not know that I went through drug rehab when I came back from Iraq. My marriage was tested."

Sonny noticed Lola trying to shrink into her seat. No doubt she was thinking she had given him too much encouragement to be himself. Well, here he was, letting it all hang out. Lola's whole family was there. They had come to watch him fail. Hector was not making eye contact. Neither was L.D. There was no way out but forward.

"Lots of soldiers had problems, so I wasn't any different," Sonny continued. "I wish I had handled it better. There was a lot of growing up I had to do. But I found myself, with the help of my wife, Lola, who's put up with more than she should have. So I'm saying, I've got experience, too. I've been down. I know what it's like to struggle. I'll represent people who've been through hard times, not just the fat cats, but people who only want a chance to prove themselves. Folks oughta know who they're voting for. If you choose me, you'll find a friend in Austin who will fight for you every step of the way. Thank you." Then he suddenly remembered: "Oh, and God bless Texas."

Miss B was looking at him strangely, the way she did when she wanted you to crawl into a roach hotel. "The first question is from Bill Brands with the *Alpine Avalanche*."

Brands was a skinny scholarly type who wrote haiku on the side. "Ms. Nightingale, the next session of the legislature is likely to be dominated by very conservative values. I am wondering if your personal values as a liberal Democrat might stand in your way."

"Thank you for your question, Bill," Valerie said, with what appeared to be genuine enthusiasm. "First, I take issue with the word *liberal*. I'm a Democrat in the mold of Walter Dunne, who so many of us knew and loved. My values are the same as the good folks I grew up with—love of family, church, and our great state. That's not going to change when I get to Austin."

"Mr. Lamb, same question for you," Brands said. "You just made some rather surprising admissions about your background. Do you think you can represent the small-town values of your constituents?"

"One thing I can say, Bill, is that my values have been tested. I know how to lead, and I know how to fight—" He was just about to deliver one of the boffo lines Hector had given him when Valerie cut in. "May I follow up on that?" she said sharply. "Mr. Lamb, nobody doubts that you served your country and you love your state. But if I were on your football team and I never played before, would you give me the ball? If I were in Iraq with you and had never trained in the military, would you trust me to take care of your soldiers? Okay, you say you know how to lead and how to fight, but do you know how to legislate? That's what the people of this district need."

Sonny heard the sound of a toilet flushing as his dreams went down the drain.

★ **6** ★

"I guess it's time Sonny became a real politician," L.D. said in the dispirited campaign headquarters the next morning. A couple desks were vacant with no fare-thee-well from the rats who had abandoned ship. Whatever support Sonny had before the debate was gone. Someone had returned a yard sign.

"What's that supposed to mean?" Sonny asked.

"It's all about winning, Sonny," said L.D.

"Whatever it takes," Hector added.

"But you've gotta show us you really want it. You can't accomplish a thing if you occupy the high ground while your opponent runs circles around you."

Sonny didn't realize he was occupying the high ground, or really any ground at all. The part about watching Valerie Nightingale lap him again and again was sure true.

"What L.D. is saying is that there's been a change in tactics," Hector said, in a voice that indicated the time had come to drown the puppies.

"If you want to walk away, just head for the door and don't waste our time," said L.D. "But tell us now, are you in or are you out? If you're in, you gotta be all the way in, not just a little bit. Because from here on out, it's gonna get nasty."

Sonny had certainly thought about throwing up his hands and surrendering to the unstoppable force of Valerie Nightingale. He wondered why he hadn't already done so. Shame was a big part of it. He'd look like such a fool if he backed out now, but he looked like a fool already, getting his ass kicked in each of the dozen counties that made up District 74, from Del Rio and up along the Mexican border to the edge of El Paso, an immense swath of land, containing about 160,000 people. Consider what he was asking those few who might actually cast a ballot in a special election, the ranchers who would have to drive to Marfa or Valentine or Fort Davis or Del Rio or Van Horn or Eagle Pass and hunt down the polling places in the school or local library, an investment of at least an hour maybe two getting there and back. Those diehard, responsible voters weren't buying what Sonny was selling. The only thing that kept him in the race was his desire to be the kind of person that good, responsible people would actually vote for. Someone they trusted and admired enough to surrender a precious morning of their lives to register their choice in a contest most people didn't care about. Someone like Valerie Nightingale. But every day on the campaign trail was a measure of how far he was from attaining that goal.

"I want this more than anything I've ever wanted, aside from Lola," Sonny found himself saying. "I want to prove to everybody that I can do this. I know it in my heart. I just need the chance, and honestly, this might be the only chance I ever get."

L.D. and Hector looked like they were going to induct him into some mystic order, there was that air of seriousness. *Everything will be revealed, and if you ever tell, we'll have to strangle you.* Sonny tried to wedge his mood into the mood of the moment, but looking into their faces he drifted into an ironic, distant place. This whole experience was beginning to feel like a giant comedy. He only wished it were happening to somebody else.

L.D. reached into an old-fashioned leather briefcase, respectably weathered, with his initials, L.D.S., embossed in gold. He handed Sonny a manila folder. "Cast your eye on this," he said. "Some research we did on your saintly opponent."

Sonny's eyes seemed to bounce off the page. It was hard to take it all in. "Hmm," he said. "Wow." Then, "I don't know if I can say these things."

"You don't have to say a thing," said L.D. "Leave it to the CGG."

"Citizens for Good Government," Hector explained.

"I don't know," said Sonny again. "I don't like winning this way."

"I hate to break it to you, Sonny, it's not all about what you want," L.D. said, in a harder voice than Sonny had heard him use. "This rope-a-dope strategy ain't working. You gotta push back, put her on the defensive, give your campaign a chance to breathe. She may seem like a giant, but it's up to you to cut down the beanstalk. We're just giving you the tools to do that."

"I'll think it over."

"Do that," said L.D. tersely. "But know this. I've got an investment to protect. There's only one path to victory. This is it. You turn away now and it's over."

★

Sonny saddled up Rosebud and rode off without a word to Lola. He followed a dry creek bed where he sometimes hunted fossils. Dinosaur bones and ammonites were easy to find if you had an eye for them, especially during the brief rainy season, they just popped to the surface after a hundred million years. Much of the earth here was Cretaceous limestone, and it was porous. Over the eons water percolated deep underground into the capacious aquifer below the parched surface—a massive hoard of wealth, a liquid Fort Knox, just underfoot, the salvation of the West Texas way of life. Why couldn't anybody else see that?

He nudged the reins and Rosebud turned onto a scratchy trail that wandered through the sagebrush, scarcely visible and seemingly aimless at first, like a child's scribble, then gradually rising toward the red-faced mesa that curtained off the ranch in the east. A chill breeze caused Sonny to tip his hat low on his forehead. Had he given it some thought, he would have brought a jacket. With each twist in the trail the ranch house he had shared with Lola for twelve years receded further from view—like Sonny's old life, the one that frustrated him with its limitations, but also rewarded him with semi-happy normality. The higher he climbed, the more out of reach that existence felt to him.

He came into a low-growing forest of piñon pines clutching the edge of the slope. You had to admire their tenacity. They covered the flatlands during the Ice Age and then climbed the mountains as the glaciers receded, chasing the narrow temperate zone, surviving drought, fire, and blistering heat, individual trees living for hundreds of years. Here the footing was steep and rugged, so Sonny left Rosebud to graze on the pine nuts while he bushwhacked up the side of the mesa another two hundred feet.

He was climbing the rim of an ancient volcano. The land around here was full of eroded craters from another era. A team of geology graduate students from Texas Tech once passed through, and the professor told Sonny that his ranch was a lot like the surface of Mars. Sonny didn't know what to do with that information, but he liked the idea of being connected to the heavens. The geologists found rocks on Sonny and Lola's place that were 3 billion years old, about the oldest rocks in the world. They came by for lunch one afternoon and presented him with one of those rocks, which was still on the porch. Sonny loved looking at the land through the professor's eyes. He told Sonny that these dry high plains were once covered by an inland sea and fetid, fern-lined marshes, chockful of reptiles and giant insects. When the sea retreated, some of it got stuck in what became known as the Permian Basin, and the life-forms, mainly plants and plankton, died off and were buried by sediment, like a layer cake, which went into the oven of Earth's creation and became oil. One little geological anomaly produced so much wealth. The Permian was two hundred miles north of where Sonny stood or he'd be a rich man now. The first human to walk into Texas arrived twenty thousand years ago, which was about one two-hundred-thousandth of the geological history of the state. The professor said that, if the history of the Earth were represented as a single year, humans appeared on the planet only in the last hour of creation, and humans didn't arrive in Texas until the last minute of the last hour.

Sonny clambered over a stretch of loose shale and came to a place where the boulders loomed in soft, voluptuous forms, casting purple shadows in the late-afternoon light. He was searching for the cave he and Lola had discovered the year after moving here. As far as he could tell they were the only living people who knew about it. Somewhere in the shadows was the opening. Although it was probably too late in the year for rattlesnakes, this was their native terrain, so Sonny was careful where he stepped or put his hands when he crawled over the boulders. He could just see the chimney of his ranch house and the barn beyond. His life.

And there it was, a dark seam between two rocks that was like a gateway into the heart of the mountain, into prehistory. The entry was a narrow tunnel about four feet high, you wouldn't notice it right away, it looked like just another shadow, but you felt its cool breath. Sonny bent down and took off his hat and crept through, watching for bats overhead. It was clammy like a marble tomb and reeking of ammonia. When the tunnel opened up a bit, Sonny turned on the flashlight on his iPhone. Sure enough, there was a colony of Mexican free-tailed bats hanging from the ceiling, tens of thousands of them, hibernating with their wings drawn around them like Count Dracula's cape. The bats had led Sonny and Lola to this spot in the first place, streaming out of the cave in a great smoky cloud at sunset.

The tunnel veered left and down into total darkness. Some charred rocks marked the entrance of a cavern, where icicle stalactites dripped into shallow cisterns—feeders for the aquifer—and blind catfish darted about in the pristine pools. Who knows how deep the cave reached into the mountain. Sonny had only explored a few of the branches. If he wanted to go farther he'd need better equipment than an iPhone and cowboy boots.

He came to a place where the walls slanted down to a clear stream of water. The footing was slippery, so he put his phone in his pocket to keep it from getting wet, in which case he'd be a goner—without the light, the cave was totally black, blacker than anything, the color of death, he would never find his way out. He sat down and inched along on his butt to a ledge twenty feet away, although the ledge seemed to recede as he advanced. He finally bumped into the place where the rock rose up and became dry again, and he turned the phone light back on. The cavern was the kind of place you might expect to run into trolls or elves. The formations were soft-edged like melting ice cream, resembling ghostly palm trees or church organs or Volkswagens. An ascending passageway led to another chamber. It was dry here, free of formations, the ceiling lost in the gloom.

The petroglyphs were on the face of one immense wall. The colors had faded but were still discernible—red, orange, yellow, brown, and black, earth hues. Sonny had pieced together some of the story in the imagery: a buffalo hunt, the great horned beasts studded with arrows, all overseen by a feathered figure at least twelve feet tall that Sonny assumed was a medicine man, maybe a self-portrait. Some rock paintings in the Lower Pecos region went back ten thousand years, but this was not that old. Among the images on this wall were three horsemen with hats, which had to have been Spaniards passing through in the sixteenth century. Some folks said Cabeza de Vaca came this way. *So many lives have been lived here,* Sonny thought, *years and decades and centuries and millennia. Even if it is the last minute of the last hour of creation, it's my turn.*

Centuries ago, some Indigenous person, probably a Mescalero Apache, had a vision and put it on this wall. He had to do it. There was nothing idle about this work. It was an act of devotion. He had traversed the country searching for a place. Or maybe he was harvesting pine nuts and just stumbled on it and was inspired. Possibly the bats gave it away, as they had for Sonny and Lola. The Apache would have carried a flaming torch, dipped in animal fat, into the tunnel, taking the same cautious steps as Sonny. When he found this place, he would have built a fire—right here, the charcoal marks were still on the wall—and lashed piñon limbs into a scaffold with twine made of buffalo hide. Using the pigments he had gathered from the earth, hematite and calcite, he mixed them with mud, spit, blood, burned animal bones, and feces. And then the artist began his work. He may have sought inspiration in peyote as he stared at the

blank limestone, waiting for his vision to reveal itself. The fire and
the low levels of oxygen in the cave created hallucinations, accom-
panying his own shadow dancing on the wall as he labored. The artist would have shuttled back and forth to the front of the cavern to
gather his breath, returning again and again to finish what was the
only evidence of his existence that would survive him.

Why hide it? Maybe it was like a message in a bottle, waiting to
be discovered. Sonny wished he understood what the message was.
He could invite some scholar to help him, but then it would no longer be a secret. It would be studied, a subject of debate. The aura
of holiness and yearning and mystery on the wall would be drained
away. Kids would sneak onto the property and smoke dope and try
to commune with some made-up spirit. Sonny felt obliged to protect
the intention of the artist, whatever that was.

At the bottom of the painting, there was an outline of a hand.
The artist had spray-painted it with red ochre pigment that he had
blown through a hollow reed, so the hand was perfectly represented,
this little shadow of a long-dead human, with the fingers spread in
a kind of Vulcan salute. Sonny placed his own hand on top of it.
He wondered if in some cosmology he and the artist were the same
spirit, reincarnated into Sonny Lamb, and that he had been destined
to discover this place, to rendezvous with his former self, who had
something to tell him, a message only for him.

Perhaps the message in the painting was that a way of life was
coming to an end. Sonny felt a connection with that. The buffalo
hunters gave way to the Conquistadors. The Spanish were gone,
with few traces. One day, so soon in the ambit of history, Sonny and
Lola and everyone they knew would also be gone. The ranch house
would be a ruin, and the ruins would turn to dust and blow away.
Seas would rise and mountains would fall. Sonny had never felt so
strongly that his life was ebbing, inevitably, pointlessly. He had—
maybe—a chance to make his mark, like the ancient artist in the
cave. He could leave something behind. But it would come at a cost.

★

Lola suspected that Sonny had gone off to the cave when she saw Rosebud's stall was empty. She was picking vegetables for dinner when she heard the horse clopping through the gloaming to the barn, and then Sonny emerged from the dark.

"That was a long ride," Lola observed. She held half a dozen tomatoes in her skirt. The first frost was yet to come.

"Lot to think about."

"Listen, Sonny, you shouldn't brood about this election. Whatever happens, folks got to see the Sonny Lamb I know. He's a caring, intelligent, and decent man."

"Lola . . ."

"Let me finish. There's something I've been meaning to tell you but for some reason I held back. It's this: I'm proud of you, Sonny. I'm proud that you want to be somebody. Maybe the odds are just too great this time around. It always was a long shot. You gave it all you got, and that's who you are. We've got a pretty good life. I know we've got challenges, but everybody does. If you lose, it's okay."

"I'm not gonna lose."

Lola looked at him with a poker face. She knew the odds. "Well, you've certainly got a good attitude. Let's go in and I'll make us a pitcher of daiquiris. Lencho went to Ojinaga and got the good stuff." Lencho was the only hand who still lived on the place. He had worked for Lola's mom.

But Sonny didn't move. The collision of emotions had him tongue-tied. Standing in front of him was the most precious person in his life, the person who defined him. They lived on Lola's ranch, they socialized with her family; people thought of Sonny—if they ever did—mainly as Lola's husband. He was desperate to become his own man. And here was the opportunity at last. It would never come again. This was it, a one-of-a-kind miracle. "If I had known what it was gonna take to win, I would never have gotten into this in the first place," he confessed. "I just don't want you to be ashamed of me."

"Politics is a dirty business, Sonny. I know that, but I hope you won't do anything you regret."

"The only thing I'll regret is if you wind up hating me."

"Sonny, if you think you're putting our relationship on the line, don't do it."

Sonny walked toward the house. When he got on the porch, he turned and said, "I'm gonna win, Lola. That's the deal. That's what it's all about."

7

"Pat, I guess you read the news in the *Big Bend Sentinel* this morning," Pat Martindale said on *The Pat and Pat Show* the next morning.

"I certainly did," Pat said, her voice painted in colors of outrage and titillation. "'Nightingale Charged with Neglect.'"

"Well, we happen to have Valerie Nightingale sitting right here. She rushed right over to explain herself."

"Good morning, Pat. Good morning, Pat."

Valerie was in the familiar hot seat facing the homologous Pats, who even looked alike—beakish, with low foreheads and close-set eyes full of spiteful glee. "First of all, thank you for giving me the chance to respond," she said patiently. "I'm not here to make excuses or 'explain myself.' I'm here to tell you my side of the story. And it has the benefit of being true, unlike what you might have read in the newspaper."

"Are you saying this is *fake news*?" Pat said.

"It's slanted news. It comes from some phony organization backing my opponent, who I never thought would stoop to this kind of thing."

"Well, last time you were on the show, you said you shared the values of the people you'd be representing in District 74," said Pat. "You didn't say you were on the board of Planned Parenthood."

"The baby-killer factory," Pat added for clarification.

"That was in the past," said Valerie. "But I'm proud to have served the organization that provides vital health care to indigent women in Texas. It's not just abortion, which is what politicians are always saying. It's breast cancer, it's—"

"Charged with neglect, the paper says," Pat interjected.

"It also mentions that the charge was dropped," said Valerie.

"Neglecting your *children*," said Pat. "You didn't tell us you had children when you were on before."

"Those charges were all part of an ugly divorce. I don't know how it got in the paper, but I've got my suspicions."

"Maybe somebody thought voters should know."

Valerie tried to hold on to the in-control ex-military officer she was and assume command over these flesh-eating miscreants while still sounding nice about it, nice in the way people listening on the radio would relate to, firm but appealing, wronged but not a victim.

"Have you ever been accused of something you didn't do?" Valerie asked.

"No," said Pat. "I got away with most of that."

"It's true I had a hard time balancing my life as a single mother with the work I was doing on behalf of my constituents. And today we have a wonderful relationship, we—"

"They don't live with you, your daughters?"

"They live with my ex in California."

"*California!*" the Pats exclaimed simultaneously.

"We see each other frequently. Vacations and Christmas. We went to Vancouver and spent the best—"

But the Pats weren't having it. There was a clear narrative in their minds and it didn't need to get conflated with the distracting verities of real life. "How are you going to take care of the people of this district if you can't take care of your own children?"

The question was a garrote around Valerie's neck. The Pats would tighten their grip until her life in politics was extinguished. And all for the entertainment of their listeners, not because they really cared. About anything. It was good fun.

"Listen, Pat," Valerie said, her teeth clenched, "Both of you. I don't think the voters of this district care about mudslinging. They want the best representation in Austin they can get. My opponent is bought and paid for by the energy lobby. Is that who—"

"Let's go back to the part about your children, neglecting your children."

"I never neglected my girls!" Valerie cried, losing the composure that had always marked her as a creature of destiny. "What was going on in my personal life, my marriage . . ." She took a breath. "It was all a long time ago and totally irrelevant to this campaign. Can we talk about the issues?"

But the vultures continued tearing off strips of flesh. "How many daughters are we talking about?" Pat asked.

"Three lovely daughters."

"In *California*, you said . . . ?"

"I'm not going to talk about this anymore," Valerie said, taking off the earphones and walking out into the blinding sunlight.

★

One look at Mary Margaret McAllister and you knew she was ready for anything. Tall, sardonic, and world-weary, she had just clocked her fortieth year on Earth, and yet she still commanded the attention of just about any man in the room. It's not that she was so beautiful or sexually appealing, although she was attractive enough to merit notice. No. What got to men was the instinctive sense that she was an infiltrator, a woman who had too much inside knowledge of the opposite sex. It was spooky how well she understood the hormonal mischief that animated the male of the species, almost as if she were really a man in a woman suit. Politicians feared her wit and no-bullshit demeanor, amplified by a husky voice that sounded like a million cigarettes although she'd never smoked. She knew the lingo, told the jokes, slapped the backs—one of the guys but also one of the enemy, sultry and dangerous, difficult to trust but impossible to resist. Naturally she had a reputation. She had been through many men. She liked to drink. Even if she was a little careless with her personal life, she never played favorites professionally. Everybody was fair game for Mary Margaret. She was a force.

She had been reporting on Texas politics for more than a decade and watched the political map of Texas go from being solid red to having blue measles. The demographic shift in the state was making itself felt politically as the suburbs along the I-35 corridor from Laredo to Denton filled up with Hispanics and liberals. Houston was the most diverse big city in America. Even the Dallas–Fort Worth Metroplex was unrecognizably moderate. Californians were pouring into the state, most of them tax refugees, but they were complicating the political scene with their well-funded, high-tech left-libertarianism. Everybody knew what a shift in Texas meant for national politics: Republicans would have no viable route to the White House. Most of the old warhorses in the GOP would live to ride again if they resided in the rural heartland, but they were washed out of the cities almost entirely. The revolution was coming, it was just over the horizon.

On the other hand, Mary Margaret reminded herself, this was Texas, so don't get your hopes up.

"There's another story we've been following out in District 74," she told her viewers. "Longtime legislator Walter Dunne passed away in September, and the closely watched race to succeed him has turned into an ugly brawl between Democratic stalwart Valerie Nightingale and Republican newcomer Sonny Lamb. This was a bitter race, with a lot of bad feelings on both sides. All evening Valerie Nightingale has enjoyed a narrow lead, but we just got the final tally from Del Rio, and it appears that Lamb has squeaked by with a margin of twenty-seven votes. Not exactly a landslide, is it, Representative Lamb?"

Sonny was in the ballroom of the Hotel Paisano in Marfa, along with a couple dozen supporters. He stared into the camera with a sickly grin. "Well, it was a victory, Mary Margaret, and I'll take it."

"A lot of mud got thrown around in this race, and it was mostly coming from your side."

"Mary Margaret, I'm new to this business," said Sonny. "You'll have to tell me if throwing mud means telling the truth about your opponent's background. I was open about mine. This was a tough race, but it was fair. When people went to vote, they knew who they were voting for."

"Can we expect to see the same divisive politics on your part in the Texas House?"

"I like getting along as much as the next guy, but when it comes to serving my constituents, I will fight for what I believe in."

Standing on the edge of the small crowd in the ballroom, L.D. whispered to Hector, "Our boy's a quick learner."

"Like he's been doing this all his life."

Lola's reaction was more tempered. Something had shifted in their life together, but it was too early and maybe too big to assess. What was simple—their life—had become complex, and not just a little but unendingly more complicated, requiring adjustments yet to be made.

"Well, you did it," she said when the camera went off.

"You don't sound too happy about it."

"I'm not unhappy," she said. "I'm just thinking our life is going to change from this very moment, and I've got no idea what's on the other side of the mountain."

"Me neither."

"I am worried about being apart from you so much. When you were deployed, that was hard on both of us, maybe harder on me than I ever let on. But it was for a specified period of time, and this is different."

"It's not going to be my whole life," Sonny said. "Sure, I'll be in Austin a lot, but I'll be home a lot, too. And you can come visit. Lencho can watch over the spread. Just think of this as a new chapter in our lives. We still have all the old ones, but now we have this, too."

Sonny had an annoying new habit of spinning the future to point in the direction he was already headed. It was the kind of thing politicians did.

L.D. interrupted. "Sonny, you've got a call," he said, holding out his cell phone.

"Tell 'em I'll call right back—"

"Sonny," L.D. said meaningfully. "This is a call you gotta take."

"I just called to say congratulations," Valerie Nightingale said. "You won. That's what we say when we lose."

"Valerie," he said, then paused, because he really didn't know what to say next. He was suddenly a little choked up.

"Are you okay?" she asked. "Sounds like you didn't expect me to call."

"Honestly, everything about this experience has been unexpected," Sonny said. "Some things happened in this campaign that I'm not proud of. You're a fine person. The people of District 74 would have been lucky to have you."

"Yeah, well." She sighed. "I was fooling myself that folks would look at my service and pay no attention to my personal life."

"My life hasn't been so spotless."

"It's different for women."

"Evidently." Sonny was about to sign off, awkwardly, but he couldn't help himself. "Maybe this is inappropriate, but can I ask you something? Do you think I'm a bad person? Do you hate me? Do I deserve your hatred?"

Valerie was quiet and Sonny was about to say sorry and goodbye when she began to speak again. "That night in the gym, our debate, you said some things that surprised me. Made me think there was more to you than I expected. Honestly, I thought I was going to be running against some good ol' boy with zero intellect and a heart like a prune, which is pretty much the usual. I know you regretted being so open about yourself, but to me you came across as somebody I could respect."

"Tell the truth, I'm still trying to figure myself out," said Sonny.

"Politics is a rough game. Good sportsmanship is not a part of it and there's no prize for losing. It's really a moral tug-of-war between the ends and the means. Lots of great leaders fought dirty to get where they were. I would have done more myself in that department if you hadn't pre-empted the whole campaign we had to paint you as a drugged-out loser."

Few words in Sonny's life had ever made him happier. "I'll make you this promise, Valerie. I may not do things the way you would have, but every day I'm in that seat, I'll think about how hard you would have worked, and I'll try to work harder. I've got a lot of catching up to do."

"Good luck, Sonny. I do kinda hate you, though."

★

The next Sunday at Ed Sharp's, a new mood occupied the dinner table. It wasn't respect, exactly—more like bewilderment. There was dismay that the butt of family jokes was no longer pathetic, coupled with the realization that he could be useful. Ed Jr., the banker, told Sonny he needed to do something about negotiating the dates a state examiner can audit banks. "Last summer, Toni and I had tickets to Rome, and all of a sudden they walk in the door, and we've got them all week. We had to eat the damn airfare."

"That must have cost a lot," Sonny said.

Toni nodded vigorously.

"It's an infringement of my rights, way I see it," said Ed Jr.

Sonny tried to sound sympathetic while straining to remember the last time he and Lola could afford to leave the state. "But aren't they supposed to surprise you?" he asked. "Like, if you've got a bunch of cash you're laundering for some drug lord, they'd catch you in the act? Not saying that would ever be you."

"Here's the thing, Sonny. Who do I see to get that money back? Who's going to give us that two weeks we were going to spend in Italy? You get me? Essentially, I was robbed in my own damn bank."

Pauline pitched in about the burdensome regulation of nail salons. "It's not just sterilized instruments, I'm okay with that," she said. "They just get into everything."

"Like what?" Sonny asked. Until this moment, he never knew that nail salons were regulated.

"You have to wear shoes," Pauline said, with an air of disbelief.

"You don't wear shoes?"

"I *have* to wear shoes! That's the point! What if I don't? Does the state of Texas have to care if I'm barefoot?"

"Pauline never wears shoes around the house," Buster informed the table.

Then Marta appeared, trailed by the children, carrying a red velvet cake with cream cheese frosting, which Lola had confided was Sonny's favorite. They came in singing "Happy Birthday," in the glow of the candles. The grownups joined in, somewhat less grudgingly than in the past, another signal of Sonny's changed status and the prospect of getting something out of the relationship. The old man held up his ice tea for a toast. "Give 'em hell," Ed said, and seemed to mean it.

"Will do, sir."

The kids had drawn pictures and cards for him. And Lola had a gift: a leather Samsonite backpack with a laptop slot that looked very professional.

By the end of dinner, Sonny had acquired a list of demands. "This is going to be my life, I guess," he said to Lola on the way home. "Everybody thinks they can just tell me what they want and I better get it for them."

"Isn't that the way politics is supposed to work?"

Sonny rarely took a stab at philosophy, but he cogitated on this for a bit. "I think everybody has an idea of a perfect world," he said finally. "It's like, things would be great if the government never looked over our shoulders and we could smoke grass and carry our guns and walk around without shoes. Or, rich people should be locked up and then the government could pay for all your needs. The weird thing is, everybody's perfect world is different. I think politics is about trying to make the world a little more perfect for most of us."

Lola was looking at him strangely.

"What?" he said.

"I don't know. You're just different."

"In a good way?"

"That's yet to be decided."

Sonny wasn't sure himself what to think. People came to him now. Lola's own family lobbied him. They looked up to him, or pretended to, but he was the same-sized person. It was a little like wearing boots with extra-high heels. In any case, for the first time in his life he wasn't a loser. He was a winner. By twenty-seven votes.

After all her doubts, Lola had to admit that she hadn't fully measured who Sonny was capable of being. She didn't approve of politics in principle, but the race had made her more aware of social issues. She had always thought of herself as entirely self-sufficient, and of government as an intrusive annoyance, certainly not worth the expense. Lola did understand that there were people less advantaged than she, but she had her own struggles and nobody from the government ever knocked on her door and said help was on the way. Sonny's race made her understand that government could be a tool to better people's lives instead of simply serving as a box to put half your money in. All that said, what really mattered to Lola was that the election made Sonny a more interesting person—larger, tougher, more serious and more confident, quicker on the uptake. He had a self-deprecating humor, and people liked that. Windows had been opened on Sonny. But Lola nurtured a private concern that he was in some vital ways less hers.

8

Jupiter was still in the sky when Lola walked with Sonny across the pasture, just before dawn, to the dirt airstrip where their little Cessna 180 was parked in a prefab hanger. It was an old taildragger manufactured in 1955. Everything on the plane except the body itself had been replaced many times. It was admittedly a shaky contraption and Sonny had painted a four-leaf clover on the door for luck. Most ranchers in this part of the country had a similar setup; spreads were too large to patrol by horse or jeep alone. Plus, it was nice to take the occasional trip to Dallas or Midland to see a movie and get a real meal. Sonny loved to fly; it gave him the chance to ruminate, chewing his cud like some cow contemplating the nature of the universe as she saw it.

Sonny carried a couple of suitcases and his new backpack, bulging with books about legislation and Texas history and legal stuff that Sonny felt he had to know. Lola could see he was taking this really seriously.

"I'm gonna miss you," she said.

"Me, too."

"Are you nervous?"

"Why would I be nervous?" he asked.

"You've never even been in the Capitol building, have you? I guess I'd be a little on edge if I were in your place."

"I'm excited," he said. "I think something good might happen."

Lola couldn't help but say it. "Be careful, Sonny. I hear all sorts of things about what they do in that city."

Sonny had heard about Austin as well, but he wasn't interested in drugs anymore, and frankly he was a little tired of sex. They had just passed through another Olympian fertility window and Sonny didn't mind having a break. "Don't worry," he assured Lola. Then he added, "I'm gonna make you proud of me."

"I was proud of you before any of this happened."

"I know. But really proud."

Lola kissed him, then gave him a look. "Just watch yourself, that's all."

Sonny loaded his suitcases and climbed into the cabin. He cranked the ignition but nothing happened. He waited a second, primed the engine again, and cranked. The little craft sputtered to life. It always made a racket, as if it were going to sling bushings and pistons in every direction. Sonny eased it out onto the airstrip and waved to Lola, then took off to the north just as the sky began to brighten and another day was born into the world.

Sonny and Lola's ranch shrank into perspective, a shadowed patch on the vast high plains. There was the Miller place, still blackened by the fire. Ahead were the Davis Mountains. From the air, they looked like wadded-up wrapping paper, green and crumpled, rising out of the khaki plains of the Chihuahuan desert. As he got closer to Fort Davis, he spotted the ranchettes with outbuildings sporting retractable roofs. This area was filling up with amateur astronomers, drawn to the dark sky and the nearby McDonald Observatory. They were probably just headed to bed.

He banked east into the rising sun, which purpled the stratocumulus clouds cloaking the horizon. To his right was the Rio Grande, a thin silver ribbon in the morning light, and beyond that, Mexico. On his left, he could see I-10, which he followed as far as Junction, where the Hill Country began. Here the land was gentle and interlaced with rivers, and the dawning sun spread the shadows of live oaks across the pastures. There were glints of stock ponds—this was cattle and goat country—and newly planted vineyards amid the old German and Czech stone cottages. Buzzards rode the updrafts in wide, lazy circles.

He was leaving his old life for a new one, its shape yet to be discovered. There were those moments where life takes a turn. Marrying Lola. Joining the Army. He wouldn't be who he was if he hadn't made those choices, the good ones. He'd made bad choices as well, although most of them didn't feel like choices so much as drifting wherever the current took him. He now saw that the solution to his problems was action. Taking charge of his life rather than letting it happen. He cogitated on how his new responsibilities would change him. This was his chance to start again, in a place where nobody knew him and expectations didn't exist, except for whatever L.D. had in mind. Sonny realized there was a tab to pay, but it was too late now to ask what it was.

As he flew, Sonny listened to an old Tony Robbins motivational tape. "Everything on Earth has a purpose, and you do, too," Tony was saying. "Once you declare your intention you will find your life's true meaning." And so it was to his life's true purpose that Sonny flew, across the ranches and farms and the increasingly networked lattice of highways, until Austin appeared, gold and silver in the morning sun. Nesting among the brightly illuminated skyscrapers was the pink granite Capitol, where destiny awaited him.

★

Much to do: find a place to rent during the session, buy a second-hand pickup, set up his office, and hire a staff. Everything needed to be in place before the session started in January, a month away. Sonny spent a week shopping for furnishings and dishware and bought a serviceable ten-year-old Ford 150. L.D. had promised that all his living expenses would be taken care of, but frugality was so much a part of Sonny's mind-frame that the thought of renting a condo in the Four Seasons or something like that never occurred to him. In any case he had yet to see any of that money.

Because he'd been elected at the last minute, Sonny had missed the orientation. Nor had he had much time to study the rules and procedures. Was there ever a legislator as green as he? Everybody else in this giant building was ready to go. They had been trained, hired staff, picked out furniture, joined caucuses, made friends, and forged themselves into a freshman class that would always have that special tie. Sonny stood outside that circle, a nobody from nowhere.

He entered the Capitol grounds and strolled up the wide walk-way past the Confederate monuments. Although the Capitol was only four stories tall, it appeared immense and muscular. Everything about the building, its formality, its grandeur, its symmetry, made it clear that this was where power resided. And now a fractional por-tion of that power was in Sonny's hands.

He waited at the back of a line of tourists to be scanned, then passed the marble statues of Stephen F. Austin and Sam Houston into the great rotunda. Sonny could not clearly separate the visitors from the probable staffers, members, and lobbyists who circulated this busy intersection, some bustling, others loitering, gabbing, or taking notes (must be reporters). A rowdy group of fourth graders were horsing around atop the gleaming terrazzo floors inset with the seals of the six nations that once governed Texas—France, Spain, Mexico, the Confederacy, the United States, and, in the center, the Republic of Texas, an entity that lasted only a decade but loomed over the history of the state like the pharaohs of Egypt or the impe-rial dynasties of China.

"Children, can I have your attention!" the teacher nominally in control of the kids cried, to little effect. Then: "EXCUSE ME!" Her voice ricocheted in the marbled chamber, bringing the room to a halt and attracting the attention of the Capitol Police. Tourists peeked over the ascending balconies to see what was up. The fourth grad-ers subsided sufficiently for the teacher to resume her instruction. "Okay, where are we now?"

"The Capitol!"

"McDonald's!"

"The girls' bathroom!"

"Very amusing," the teacher said. She reminded Sonny of a brittle geometry teacher at Jack Hays Consolidated who had a nervous breakdown the second semester of his sophomore year. The kids reminded him of himself.

"This is the Capitol of the state of Texas," the teacher said. "This is where the laws are made. Brandon, leave Kneesha alone. Look straight up at the inner dome, and what do you see spelled out around the golden star?"

"Texas!"

"It looks like the inside of a boobie," Brandon observed.

"You'll see 'Texas' written all over the place," the teacher said. "Some kind of fetish for ego gratification," she muttered to herself.

"Miss O'Toole, what's a fetish?" a girl next to her asked.

"Moving on." The teacher turned her attention to the portraits of the mostly dead former governors lining the walls—the greats, the near-greats, the crooks, the idealists, the woefully incompetent—spiraling from one floor to the floor above it and the floor above that, dizzyingly, through the generations backward into time. "Note the total absence of ethnic diversity," the teacher said of the portraits. "And only two women, one for each century since statehood."

Sonny had no idea where else to go, so he trailed behind the kids as the teacher led them down the marbled halls and the colonnaded foyers, the grandeur pressing down on him with gravitational weight. Inscribed in the floor mosaics were twelve hallowed battles of Texas independence. It was good that the kids were there, making Sonny feel less of an intruder. He had just come to size things up before getting down to whatever work was going to be like, so sneaking into a pack of fourth graders led by a flinty feminist was good cover for his aimlessness. All those fortifying Tony Robbins admonitions dissipated in his mind, along with his confidence, and he surrendered to being a tourist, or at least thought of as one.

The kids clambered noisily up a flight of stairs and suddenly they were in the House of Representatives. Sonny hadn't quite prepared himself for this, like when the gate in the rodeo snaps open and you haven't yet got your grip on the reins but the bull is already in the arena. First of all, it was the largest room he had ever been in. He took in the coffered ceiling, like a grand checkerboard way up high, and the galleries on three sides that one day would be filled with spectators. The room streamed with slanted light from the wooden shutters masking the giant windows. Once again he had that eerie sense of being watched, as if he were in a movie, and being in a movie was more real than real life. Maybe the audience understood him better than he did himself. His breath was getting shallow and quick. He felt a little wobbly in the presence of so much history, of which he was now a part in some meager fashion.

"Each desk seats two representatives," the teacher told the students. "And in the back of the room, you see that elevated space, it's called the speaker's rostrum. That's where the person with the gavel stands. Notice that flag behind the rostrum? That's the actual flag they carried at the Battle of San Jacinto, where the Texans massacred the Mexican Army, what today we'd call a war crime."

Sonny's head spun around. "What about the Alamo?" he interjected. "Wasn't that a war crime?"

"Sir, you're interrupting a class tour," the teacher said irritably.

"Just want them to hear both sides," Sonny said. "It's my history, too."

"And who are you?"

"Name's Sonny Lamb."

"Well, Mr. Lamb, are you a tourist or do you just stand here and offer jingoistic historical pablum?"

"I wouldn't know what that is. But no, I'm not a tourist. Actually, I just got elected."

"See, class," the teacher said, "this is what I've been telling you. One more white man to run the state. I get so tired." She asked Sonny, "Aren't there any qualified women in your district?"

"As a matter of fact, the lady I beat was a lot more qualified."

The teacher nodded, reaffirmed in her beliefs. The encounter fit nicely with her lesson plan, that the patriarchy was in charge and women were subjugated and not given the opportunities to flourish because of people just like him, and this was doubly true in Texas. "Well, welcome to Austin," she said from a towering moral height.

"Please do as little harm as possible. All right, students, how many times do you see the word *Texas*?"

"It's on the desks."

"It's on the chairs."

"The glass doors!"

"Yeah, and the lights."

"There's a million of them!"

Sonny went off to find his desk. He heard one of the students asking about the two large boards on either side of the speaker's rostrum with little light bulbs beside each name. "Those are the voting boards," the teacher explained. "When the speaker calls a vote, the yes or no votes light up beside each representative's name. Can you kids find the name of your representative on the board?"

Sonny looked, and there it was. His name. And he fell to the ground.

★

He had been in this place before, quiet and peaceful unconsciousness, closer to death than sleep. The untroubled land of bygones bygone, a place you never want to leave, like your mother's breast, soft and warm and exactly what you need. But then something drags you back to the unwelcome reality of the present. In Iraq, it was pain, merciless, ceaseless, the only truth in the universe. Except for the sky, which was like any sky, and the earth, the undistinguished stretch of dirt where he was lying, and the smell of kerosene from the Humvee that had been blown off the road scattering helmets and rifles and soldiers, and everything was leaking, including him. At a level below the god-awful pain he could sense that he was being drained, his blood spilling into the dirt. That's how they all died, 90 percent of them, they just bled out, such a quiet way to pass. The only thing that broke the silence was the gasping sound from Sonny's chest as he tried to breathe.

It was night, and the stars looked down on him pitilessly, his death being a matter of indifference to the universe. At that moment it hurt too much for him to think he was dying for a mistake, but that had been on his mind ever since he had arrived in that country, ostensibly to root out terrorists and confiscate weapons of mass destruction, which didn't exist, but that didn't matter, the Americans were here and they weren't going to say oops and go home. Now Sonny Lamb was on the side of a cruddy dirt road just outside Fallujah. Lola would get the news, the death detail would drive out to the ranch in their dress uniforms, wondering who the hell would live so far away from anything at all, to tell her that her hubby was KIA. Then they'd walk off the porch and get in their car and drive away. And everyone would know that it was for nothing, for a lie. For politics.

But he didn't die. Private First Class Pinkerton, a farmboy from rural Mississippi, around Tupelo, ripped open Sonny's uniform and pressed his hand on the wound and held it there. Pinkerton was maybe nineteen. They were all kids or little more than that. He knelt beside Sonny and sang to him, probably some song from the Baptist hymnal, a tune not familiar but comforting. When Sonny stopped breathing, Pinkerton put his lips on his and blew life back into his lungs. Sonny closed his eyes and went back to that sleep that is more than sleep, the promise of eternal rest.

The shrapnel took out a kidney, he learned when he swam into consciousness in the field hospital. He remembered the Pakistani doctor who brought him the news that he was going to be sort of fine, and congratulations you're going home. So actually this made twice that he went to death's edge and somehow got summoned back.

It was Brandon who noticed. "Miss O'Toole, what happened to that man?" he asked.

"Who?"

"Mr. Lamb."

Miss O'Toole looked around but didn't see him.

"He fell down," said Brandon. "I think he died."

"Oh, my God," the teacher said when she spotted Sonny stretched out on the carpet. She gestured frantically to a state trooper. By now the curious children were swarming around. "Don't touch him," the teacher warned. "He may have some disease."

"This is so awesome," said Brandon.

★

Sonny felt a sharp pain in his chest. He was aware that he was making a big scene and that he would probably die in public, in front of children. Their mouths were shaped like Cheerios. The teacher's face loomed over him, her blond hair encompassing her pale face, moonlike, her large eyes both stern and troubled. Sonny started to get up, but the teacher gently pushed him back on the carpet. "Don't try it yet, give yourself a minute," she said. "The nurse is on the way."

"I'm fine," Sonny gasped.

"You just passed out in front of a dozen fourth graders."

"I did not pass out," Sonny tried to say. He wanted that on the record. But he didn't have enough breath to speak. Also, consciousness was a scratchy signal that kept going in and out. The margins of his vision were fuzzy and his hands tingled. Sweat poured off him as if he was standing in the rain.

The nurse, a skinny guy with tattoos, popped an ammonia capsule under Sonny's nose, startling him into total, unwelcome clarity. Tourists and troopers had joined the schoolchildren to gawk at the dying cowboy on the carpet.

"Take a deep breath," the nurse said. "You're hyperventilating." He put a steadying hand on Sonny's head, which was surprisingly calming, like Pinkerton's had been back then. "Now take another breath and hold it." Sonny did so. "Now slowly let it out." After four of these, the nurse was able to put a blood pressure cuff around Sonny's arm.

"Is the pain better?"

Sonny nodded.

"Was it a stabbing pain or did you feel like your heart was being squeezed?"

"More like a knife."

"Any pain elsewhere? Your arm or your shoulder?"

Sonny shook his head.

"Have you fainted before?" the nurse asked.

"I did not faint. I'm having a heart attack." This had become a matter of pride.

"Tell me what happened."

"I don't know. I was just standing here, and I saw my name on the voting board—"

"You're a member?"

"Newly elected."

"Oh," the nurse said, nodding in recognition. "No wonder. I see this a lot with new members."

"They have heart attacks and die?"

"They panic," said the nurse, instinctively turning to the teacher. "You don't happen to have a Prozac, do you?"

"I've got Xanax and Paxil," she said.

"Maybe one of each," said the nurse.

The teacher gave Sonny a reappraising look. "He's actually kinda vulnerable," she observed.

★

"All the new members have been randomly assigned offices and parking spaces, and because you have zero seniority, I'm sorry to say, you're literally at the bottom," Victoria Haney, the chief clerk of the House, said cheerfully. Prim and brisk, she led Sonny down the long, subterranean halls with an air of ownership, her heels clicking, hips turning this way and that. Sonny wasn't sure he would ever find his way through the basement addition by himself. "You get the worst parking spot. And wait till you see your office." It sounded like she was sharing a joke, but she wasn't the type.

"I thought I was going to get Walter's old office," Sonny said.

Victoria looked at him sadly. "That only comes with seniority. Like everything around here. And you've got less than anyone. Your office allowance is $13,500 a month. It's not enough. Out of that you pay your staff, your travel, and rent for your district office. I can tell you it goes really quickly. You can of course supplement it with your own money or campaign funds."

Clickity-click went Victoria's heels as she smartly rounded yet another corner in the endless marble labyrinth. "I don't suppose anyone gave you guidance about setting up your office and your staff?" she asked without waiting for an answer. "First order of business is to hire a legislative director. That's essential. You'll need the guidance, although frankly freshmen never pass their bills. A little tip: Make sure that all the Eagle Scouts in your district get a Texas flag, a lot of newcomers forget that one." She handed him a spiral-bound copy of *Rules of the House*. "Everything you need to know is in here. Commit it to memory."

At the end of the windowless hall was a door with a sign saying:

SONNY LAMB

DISTRICT 74

Sonny felt a little light-headed.

"You're not going to faint again, are you?"

"I didn't faint," said Sonny.

"Well, here's your key. Welcome to the Texas Legislature, Representative Lamb." *Clickity-click, clickity-click*, she marched away.

Sonny opened the door and turned on the light. There was a tiny reception area with a couch and a lamp, and what looked like a student carrel behind a bookshelf. His personal office opened onto a dank light well. No rugs. No pictures. No reading chair. He needed almost everything. He couldn't imagine how he was going to pay for it and get everything ready by the start of the session.

Still, look at this. Here he was with an office in the Capitol, or under it, to be precise. Half an hour ago he was dying and now he felt oddly relaxed, despite the gloomy surroundings. He had arrived. But he had no idea what to do next.

★

When members spoke of wanting a seat at the table, they were talking about the domino table in the speaker's quarters on Monday night. Carl Kimbell would be there, a red-faced catfish farmer from Mineola and Tea Party primitive—glib, stupid, and corrupt, but a lot of fun. He was reputed to be the brains behind the QAnon caucus. Gilbert Delgado, who owned a Ford dealership in Three Rivers, was the Democratic entrant in the domino game. Carl and Gilbert couldn't have been further apart politically, but they got along just fine outside of public view, the trick being that each of them knew the other didn't believe what he was saying. They were pols, not ideologues. The game was overseen by Big Bob Bigbee, the tortured, noble individual who loomed over the Texas political landscape like a colossus on the prairie.

"Your pockets look a little heavy tonight," Big Bob said as L.D. eased himself into the fourth chair. Big Bob had the grumbling voice of a Mafia don mixed with a West Texas accent. His great, ruined face was a roadmap of all the battles he had fought, the divorces, the trials, the illnesses, the humiliations, and the triumphs. L.D. adored him, but warily, knowing how explosive he could be when some cog slipped in his machinery and everybody had to run for cover.

"Thank you for noticing," L.D. said cheerfully.

"What this time?" Carl asked. He hated the thought that money was being made without him.

"Liquor dealers' account," L.D. said.

"What the hell did you do to deserve that?" asked Gilbert, who also had unsatisfied financial aspirations.

"Nobody said I *deserved* it," L.D. said, waving at the ceiling. "It just appeared, like manna from heaven. A blessing. Dropped from the sky."

"Hell, he already has the tort lawyers and the insurance companies," Carl complained, "not to mention Mr. Peeples."

"You're getting greedy, L.D.," Big Bob agreed. "It's unseemly."

"Bob, what was I to do? They came begging, I'm supposed to turn them away? The poor suffering liquor dealers?"

"He's getting rich, and we're doing all the work." Carl was working himself into a snit. The others nodded.

"Matter of fact, I've been tilling the fields," L.D. said. "While you gentlemen have been warming your backsides, I've been meeting some of our newcomers."

That got Big Bob's attention. "Any keepers in this new bunch?" he asked hopefully. Like a coach, he was always hoping that the next draft would produce a few stars. Lately, the talent on the floor was awfully thin.

"There's a few you might keep your eyes on," said L.D. "Jack Small from Beaumont."

"Giant Jack?" said Carl.

"Giant Jack Small, yeah, the former Aggie fullback."

"'Give the ball to Small,'" Big Bob said, reciting a well-known mantra from Aggieland. "I'll find a place for that old boy."

"Back to the boneyard," Carl grumbled, picking up another tile.

"There's that teacher from San Antone," said Gilbert, on behalf of his party. "Angela Martinez."

"Holy jalapeño," said Carl, nearly jumping out of his chair, "she's a hot mamacita."

"So many women," Big Bob observed.

"So many—or too many?"

"They're takin' over," Gilbert declared, assured of agreement at this table of fossilized pols.

"Boys, there ain't but one thing a man can do that a woman can't," Big Bob said. "Pee standing up. And there's glory in it. Hell, I used to could knock a can of corn off a fence post."

No one doubted Big Bob's prodigious capacity in that department.

"I hear she's ambitious," said L.D., "this Martinez woman."

"She related to Leticia Martinez?" Big Bob asked, referring to the former mayor of San Antonio, a legendary figure in that city.

"Daughter," said Gilbert.

"If she's anything like her mother, we're in trouble," Carl said.

"Already filed a bill," said Big Bob.

"What's that?" L.D. asked.

"Some pretend it's not a pro-choice bill."

"Better step on it before it begins to crawl," Carl advised.

"She'll be lucky if we don't enact a death penalty for mothers before the end of the session," said L.D.

"I wouldn't count her out," Gilbert said. "She's the pick of the litter in my camp."

"I've never seen so many pre-files," said L.D. "Clean air, utility dereg . . ."

"Creation science, Carl?" Big Bob said.

"You don't believe in the Bible?"

"It's either catfish or creation with you."

"I'm a simple man, Big Bob."

"I think we'd all agree on that."

"And a shitload of new voting restrictions," said Gilbert. "When are you guys gonna start believing in democracy?"

"Democracy is fine, as long as the right people vote," said Carl.

"Did you say 'the white people'?" said Gilbert.

"Not out loud, and don't quote me."

"You guys never stop, do you?"

The players studied the shape of the game. It was never the same, a provisional art, like a sandcastle that will soon be washed away.

"Domino," said Gilbert.

"You lucky son of a bitch!" Carl said in disgust.

"I got a knack," Gilbert explained.

"A fella I want you to keep your eye on," said L.D., casual as could be, as Gilbert shuffled the tiles. "Sonny Lamb, District 74."

"Your new pet vote?"

"He's a talented young man, Carl. I'm bringing him along."

"Walter Dunne's old seat," Gilbert said mournfully. Walter had been the rare white male Democrat, an endangered species. Walter had held the seat at the domino table that Gilbert now occupied.

"And you'd like to have me put him on . . . let me guess," said Big Bob. "Energy Resources."

"That'd be very farsighted of you," L.D. said gratefully. It was shaping up to be an excellent session.

9

There were half a dozen very attractive young women sitting in Sonny's outer office when he arrived at nine in the morning, carrying a portrait of Sam Houston he'd bought on eBay to hang over his desk. Sonny nodded at them and went into his office, to find L.D. standing next to the window, the only place he could get cell service.

"What are all those pretty girls here for?" Sonny asked when L.D. finished his call.

"Applicants for your chief of staff and legislative director."

"Where'd you find them? At the Pi Phi house or the Yellow Rose?"

"One of the perks of the job, Sonny. Plus they act as bait, bringing in members and lobbyists who might enjoy the view while they do a little business with you."

"L.D., I need somebody with experience, not just, you know."

"Our office provides all the guidance you need. We write the bills, suggest how to vote, anything you desire. That's what lobbyists do. We've got a special interest in you, so we'll help in any way we can. We're not gonna let you fail."

That sounded okay, but as green as Sonny was, he still recognized trouble. Ever since the election he had been expecting something like this—the unspoken assumption that L.D. owned him. And why wouldn't he think that? He had recruited Sonny, raised money for the campaign, crafted the talking points, and, of course, smeared Sonny's opponent and cleared the path to victory. "Look, L.D., I'm grateful for what you and Hector have done, I really am, but I can't just sit here like a caged canary. I need help. A lot of help. My own staff kind of help."

"If you insist. But in terms of qualified, experienced legislative draftsmen, there's not a lot left to choose from. There's been a fight for talent for months. Hmm." L.D. appeared to be giving the matter some thought.

"There's gotta be somebody," Sonny said impatiently, "considering the fact that I'm totally new and have no idea what I'm doing."

"Well, there's Wanda Stringfellow."

"And this person's experienced?" Sonny asked.

"Very."

"Also, I'm a little confused about what I'm supposed to do here. Like now. The session hasn't started, but I see all these other reps in their offices, and they seem busy. So what are they busy with? Shouldn't I be busy with what they're busy with?"

"The good news is, you don't have to do a damn thing," L.D. said. "The session begins in a couple days, but the first couple months are really slow. There only have to be enough members present to make a quorum. Otherwise, you could just as well be back at the ranch until March."

"Are you kidding? There are only a hundred and forty days in the session and you're telling me to take the first couple months off? Sounds like you're saying don't do anything. Put my feet up. Break out the sunscreen."

"The state constitution doesn't allow bills to be introduced for the first sixty days. Every session is like a roller coaster: the first bit is the long climb up, and then all hell breaks loose. So you can use this time to meet your colleagues. My fellow lobbyists will come by to advertise their agendas. All that said, you're mainly here to collect money before the session starts."

"Really? People are just going to give me money?"

"Lots," L.D. said, as if that were the most normal thing imaginable. "What else did you think the event this evening is for?"

★

The Austin Club inhabited a late-nineteenth-century opera house, built of limestone blocks twenty-four inches thick to protect against the heat. The façade, a two-story wooden gallery, reproduced what the building looked like back in the day when Lily Langtry sang and John Philip Sousa's band played and Edwin Booth was Hamlet. The interior had the slumped, handmade, shabby-chic quality that old buildings naturally acquire; furnished in period style, it evoked what the citizens of a frontier town would have thought was the pinnacle of elegance. Now it was the domain of power brokers, who came for the cigars, the whiskey nights, and the sense that history had awarded them custody of the future.

Sonny followed L.D. past the dining room up the creaky stairs to a private room on the third floor. "Ordinarily, there would be eight or ten of your colleagues here collecting donations, but everyone else has already filled their bucket," L.D. said on the way. "Because you're a last-minute addition, the speaker made a special allowance for you to receive contributions beyond the deadline. After today, no more donations till the end of the session. What you get tonight has to last."

A long line of lobbyists awaited Sonny's arrival, scores of them, maybe as many as a hundred, and more arriving. "Are you kidding?" Sonny said under his breath, as he smiled and nodded. "These people actually came to meet me?"

"We're just getting started," L.D. promised.

Sonny got the sense that most of them were here because of L.D. Everybody knew him. They regarded him with respect bordering on awe, and the fact that Sonny was tucked under his wing clearly made an impression. The room was economically suited for its purpose, with a desk and chair facing the door, and a settee in the back, where L.D. situated himself, scrolling through his email and feigning disinterest. As his colleagues entered the room one by one, they glanced first at L.D. to make sure he registered their presence. L.D. would nod, break out a perfunctory smile, and go back to his phone, whereupon the lobbyist finally glanced down at Sonny, who was, after all, sitting right in front, waiting politely, like a puppy waiting for a treat, which was the envelope in the lobbyist's hand. There was a brief introduction. "Brian Massingill from AEP," or was it AEG, Sonny wasn't clear what either of them was. "Just wanted to say hello." And the envelope would be handed over, Sonny would thank the person, then put the envelope in a drawer with the others because L.D. said it was bad form to pile them on the desk, much less open one in front of the donor and comment on the amount.

Concrete contractors, private pilots, affordable-housing advocates, property appraisers, broadcasters, city and county officials, Goodwill, health care providers, otolaryngologists (whatever that was), REALTORS (who wanted it written into Texas law that they would always be all caps), sports psychologists, automobile dealers, bitcoin miners, cattle feeders, Catholic bishops, cotton ginners, craft brewers, railroads, the Coalition for Affordable Power, the Campaign to Prevent Teen Pregnancy, the Texas Dental Association, the Texas Deer Association—an endless procession of worthy and not-so-worthy causes presented themselves, personified by the man or woman who handed over the check.

Thirty minutes into this, Sonny declared that he needed a bathroom break and signaled to L.D. to follow him to the men's room. The line now stretched down the hall and part of the way down the stairs. "Is this even legal?" Sonny said to the tile wall behind the urinal.

"They're exercising their First Amendment privilege to support you," said L.D., who was shoulder to shoulder performing the same. "You could be a little more gracious about taking their money."

"What do they expect in return?"

"They want your vote."

"That's what I'm afraid of."

"Look, Sonny, this is how democracy gets paid for. They know you've got hundreds of contributors, or will have by the end of the evening, and there will be conflicts. Good manners will tell you to return a check if you know you're going to vote against them. For instance, you got the Texas Homeschool Coalition and the Texas Teachers Association. They're both going to be angling for your support, but they're in a battle over tax money, which is as dirty a fight as you can get into. If you feel strongly about public education, you might tell the homeschoolers not to waste their wad. Mainly, though, they want to be able to walk through your door and feel welcome, that you'll offer them a soft drink and listen as they plead their case. After all, they're charging billable hours, and the longer they sit on your couch, the more money in their pockets, whatever you choose to do. You don't need to feel excessively obligated." L.D. concluded his business and zipped up. "Except to me."

★

The next morning Wanda Stringfellow arrived, pushing a walker and huffing from the long hike to Sonny's office. She was maybe seventy, overweight, and formidable. She reminded Sonny of Winston Churchill.

"I have a few rules," Wanda said, not even bothering to ask for the job. "One is, keep your hands to yourself. Every man who comes here wants a sex kitten to manage his calendar and give him blow jobs. Go elsewhere for that."

"Yes, ma'am."

"Say again?"

"Yes, ma'am!"

"Second is, you gotta speak up when you're talking to me. I'm a little deaf. I do have hearing aids, but they tend to whistle, so I don't like to wear them. I hope you're not carrying a bill."

"Actually, I am! It's for using renewable energy to desalinate—"

"Freshmen never get their bills passed," Wanda said, cutting him off.

"Why not?"

"Nobody is afraid of them. They've got no power. They've got nothing to offer. They don't understand the process. It's like teaching algebra to kindergarteners."

"I came here to do something!" Sonny said. "Not just be a part of the furniture!"

"I assume you're an attorney. What is your area of expertise?"

Boy, this is getting ugly, Sonny thought. "Look, I don't have a law degree! I don't have an area of expertise! Except maybe cows, I know a lot about cows."

"I didn't get the last part," Wanda said.

"Cows!"

"You'll be a project, for sure. Let me do the staffing. They should have given you a class on this like everybody else, but picking the right people is the key to success. I know who they are. You don't."

"Agreed!" Sonny said, realizing that he was surrendering a considerable amount of power to a woman he just met. He had fallen for the Winston Churchill aura. Wanda Stringfellow was going to lead him to victory.

"So show me the money," Wanda said. "Let's see what we got to work with."

He handed Wanda the cardboard box full of checks from the lobbyists. Wanda was unsurprised, obviously used to transactions where people just give you dough, like wedding gifts without the wedding. "First thing we do is make a ledger of contributions, and that will allow us to draw up a budget for the session."

Sonny was still troubled by the morality, if not the legality, of the transactions. "Wanda, exactly why would they give me money?"

"Access," she said. "At least, that's what they say."

"And that's different from a bribe?"

"Call it what you will," she said unhelpfully as she went back to her desk. Five minutes later, she returned, waving a check. "Sonny, most of your donations are three or four figures, what you'd expect, and there are a lot of those. But this one"—she dangled it in the air like a rat by the tail—"it's for a hundred thousand dollars."

Hearing that all his troubles were over, Sonny jumped to his feet. "Good God! Who's it from?"

"Odell Peeples." Wanda glared at him. "You never told me that you were one of Mr. Peeples's hirelings," she said, her voice quivering with indignation.

"Okay, that's a bad thing! Up until recently, I didn't rightly know who he was!" Sonny said. "I've never even listened to his show! I've seen the billboards and stuff but it's not like I'm a believer! Or a 'hireling'! *A hundred thousand dollars?*"

Wanda's expression slowly shifted from suspicion to pity, allowing for the fact that he simply might be naive and incompetent rather than purely wicked. "Sonny, sit down," she commanded. "I'm going to lay this all out for you so you don't get confused."

Sonny sat down.

"First of all, there's a hierarchy of fools who run this place," she said. "You're just the fool on the bottom of the totem pole. Above you, you have your liberals, who occupied the bottom of the pole until you came along. They've got a boatload of causes but zero power. They sit in the back of the chamber in a place we call Red Square. Just above them in fecklessness are the frat boys. They're here for the sense of entitlement that being in office gives them. They're about as useless as the liberals because they believe in nothing except having fun. Then you have your religious zealots. They're stuck halfway up the pole because until last session they only cared about waging war on abortion. They won, so now they're just hunting around for any old witch to burn. To their credit, they can't be bought off, at least not completely. Lurleen Klump is their main champion.

"Above them, you'll find the Freedom Caucus, Carl Kimball and those folks, not a majority but a considerable bloc who will run riot if they get out of the cage. Trumpsters before there was Trump. As far as they're concerned he's still president and will be until he breathes his last. Some were in Washington for the insurrection at the Capitol, or claim they were. They bought the whole package. Eliminate taxes, public schools, gay marriage. Arm teachers. Arm children. Arm everybody.

"Then we come to the real horses in the House, the ones with actual power. There are about a dozen of them, all white Republican men except for Ernestine Smallwood, the Democratic rep from South Oak Cliff, who has served in this House longer than most of these characters have been alive. She's chair of Calendars. You can't catch a cold if she hasn't put it on the schedule. You'll soon learn which committees matter and which ones you might have a chance to be assigned. The committee chairs sit at the knee of Big Bob, who makes all the assignments personally, so there's never any question who's the boss. But even Big Bob is not at the top of the totem pole, because that's just the House.

"Then there's the chamber on the east side of the Capitol, and in the House we never call it the Senate."

"What do you call it!?"

"We call it 'The Other Place.' It's inhabited by political zombies whose minds have been taken over by the Dark Lord. All the lieutenant governor cares about is waging culture wars. He sabotages the useful legislation we pass in the House by simply not bringing it up in The Other Place. Dan Patrick has done more harm to Texas than any politician in modern times. I have to admit, part of me admires his skill. But that's why the politics in our state went so berserk."

"What about the governor?"

"Feckless. Texas is a weak-governor state. His only powers are to veto bills, make appointments, and call a special session. Other than that, it's a ceremonial office. He spends his days dreaming up theatrical stunts to keep his name in the news. Because he's constantly frightened of being primaried by the Dark Lord, he pretends to be more extreme, but everybody knows it's an act. If he were something other than a politician, he might have been a perfectly nice man, but nice men don't hold the reins of power in Texas. The higher they go up the totem pole in Texas, the more they are stripped of humanity and compassion."

Wanda's assessment was sobering, but Sonny had long suspected as much of the state's leaders. He started to thank her for the lesson, but she wasn't finished. "And we haven't even gotten to the top of the pole," she said. "The penultimate character is your buddy L. D. Sparks, he and a handful of key lobbyists. They run the show in the legislature. And you're not going to hear me say they're all bad. So many people come into office with no idea what's important or even what they want to do. The lobbyists fill in the blanks for them. They're essential to the process. They also represent the people, even if they're not elected. If you're in a union, if you've got a business, if you want to change the laws, you have lobbyists working for you. The system is too complicated for ordinary people to thread the needle. Lobbyists are paid to tell your story to the people who matter. They also hold way too much power and are constantly corrupting the members. Although it goes the other way, too—members bilking the lobbyists, blatantly putting their votes up for sale to the highest bidder.

"That brings me to the top of the totem pole. Odell Peeples is the devil."

"By which you mean what?" Sonny asked. "That he's a bad man or he's like the actual Satan-type deal?"

"It's not for us to know such things," Wanda said. "However." She cleared her throat for the important bit. "If the devil is a real creature living amongst us, then he would be rich and powerful and a force for evil. He would be arrayed in the garments of righteousness. That is exactly who Odell Peeples is. He owns the legislature, at least a working majority."

The whole picture was in view now. Sonny replayed the track of his life from the moment he saw L.D. sitting on his porch, like Beelzebub, the prince of demons, Satan's favorite fallen angel, looking for another soul to steal. Sonny had long since walked away from the literalism of his church teachings, but there remained in the deep recesses of his unconscious the archetypes he heard preached Sunday after Sunday, haunting his childhood imagination like Disney villains, unreal but unforgettable. Shaking off the superstitions of his environment was challenging, and he was never entirely shed of them. Moreover, what Wanda was saying made sense, theologically.

"Are you suggesting that the Texas Legislature is all a bunch of devil worshippers?"

Wanda thought for a moment. "Maybe not all of them."

Sonny took a breath. "Don't deposit that check!" he said, adding, "at least, not yet!"

★

Sonny picked up Lola at the airport in his new used pickup and escorted her to the Pecan Grove Trailer Park, which was like a museum of recreational vehicles. He parked in front of a mildewed Airstream, scarcely bigger than a VW bus. There was a picnic table in front. Vines twined around the towering winter-bare pecans. It looked like a place where hobbits lived.

"Whaddaya think?" Sonny asked, ducking his head upon entry. He set Lola's overnight bag on the little breakfast nook table, which was already piled with books and papers.

"You're gonna live here?"

"For a hundred and forty days, yeah, it's home sweet home. It's got all the essentials. And you can't argue with the price."

Lola looked around. There was a stove and a sink. A narrow door that must lead to the shower and toilet, and another that would be the closet. A settee in the back. "It folds into a bed," Sonny explained. His guitar rested against the wall. Just going from one end of the Airstream to the other required one of them to turn aside. "Cute," Lola said. "Where'd you get the dish towels?"

"The Martha Stewart Collection at Kmart. Bedsheets, too. You're impressed, aren't you? C'mon, you can admit it."

"I'm seeing a whole new Sonny Lamb."

"You know, I am, too," Sonny said. "I'm a different me. Not like I'm on top of the world or anything like that. I'm scared to death. I'm up most of the night studying, trying to figure out the rules, which are so intricate you wouldn't believe, and there's nothing to be done but to learn 'em all the way down or you'll never get anywhere, especially if you're starting from nowhere like me. There are folks here from every place in Texas, different races, different ideas, the whole state poured into one big room. And I'm just a shitkicker from Boogaloo."

"Quit running down where you're from," Lola said sternly. "There's nothing wrong with who you are."

Those words went deep. Lola could be hard—a subset of her West Texas stoicism—but when the chips were down you could count on her to tell you the truth. There was nothing false or contrived about Lola. And nothing set her off more than other folks thinking they were better than she was, because of birth, or education, or looks, or celebrity. You had to earn your place with her, it didn't come free.

"It is weird to be living in a real city," Sonny said. "Seeing people everywhere. Thousands of folks, every day, in the Capitol, on the streets, in the grocery store. There are all kinds of churches, schools, teams. And people dress different, which is interesting, not every guy in jeans, for instance. When was the last time you saw a man in shorts?"

"They do that in Marfa."

"I started thinking about how many choices people have to make about how they're gonna look, what movie they're gonna see, who they're gonna invite, where they're gonna go for dinner, what they're gonna believe, every single morning figuring out who they're gonna be that day—can you imagine making that many decisions before breakfast? Made me think how uncomplicated our life is on the ranch. Like, when was the last time we went out to lunch?"

"Do you mean uncomplicated or uninteresting?"

That was certainly a question. "There is something pure about our life, and I love that," he said cautiously. "But all these choices, it's stimulating. Some weeks on the ranch we only see each other, at all, the whole week. Maybe Lencho and some cowboys. I'm not saying it's boring, but you know . . ." He realized that he was painting a picture of a life that no one would want to live, and that wasn't fair. "I just wish you could spend more time here. We could do things. Movies, theater, lots and lots of music. It's not as much fun without you."

He pulled her to him and she yielded to his embrace. "It's a nice dream," she said. "Maybe one day." He drank in her buttered-toast smell, his hands on her strong, lean back. He was proud of her strength, which set her apart from most women he knew, even other ranch women didn't have Lola's muscles, but there were also the soft parts, which were all the more glorious on that firm frame.

"We better get dressed," Sonny said. "Don't want to miss the swearing-in."

He was buttoning his best white shirt when Lola emerged from the bathroom with her thermometer. "I just ovulated," she announced.

"Oh gosh. Can't this wait?"

"You know the deal."

★

They raced up the steps of the Capitol, right into a queue of spectators snaking through the metal detectors. Lola urged him to jump the line, but Sonny was too much of a populist to flout his newly acquired authority. Fortunately, the trooper who had observed him fainting recognized him and motioned him aside. "You're late," the trooper informed him. Sonny and Lola took the stairs two at a time. Standing in front of the entrance to the House chamber was the sergeant-at-arms, gesturing at his watch. "You're late," he said, as if everybody didn't already know. "Let him through," he told the trooper at the door. "Hurry!"

There they all were, Sonny's punctual colleagues, in place for the ceremony that takes place every other year on the second Tuesday of January, the opening day of the Texas Legislature. For this one moment, family members were allowed on the floor. The magnificent House chamber was packed, the gallery filled, the afternoon sun streaking through the slots of the wooden plantation shutters. Sonny negotiated a path to his desk. His seatmate, Harold Morton Jr., nodded as Sonny slipped in beside him. "You're late," Harold whispered.

"District 149, Joseph Tran," the chief clerk, Victoria Haney, was saying.

"Present!" Tran called out. His family had fled Vietnam after the fall of Saigon in the massive exodus of boat people. They were attacked by pirates; they were fired upon by naval vessels; several people on the overcrowded ship died of starvation. Perhaps as many as 400,000 refugees perished in that historic migration. But the Tran family wound up in Galveston, where his father became a shrimper and his mother worked as a domestic. They managed to put Joe through law school. Now here he was, representing his community in the legislature.

"District 150, Jack Small."

The hulking figure at the desk in front of Sonny stood and declared himself present. Heisman Trophy winner. Sonny was amazed by all the stories that brought these people to the statehouse. Of course, they weren't all heroes, by any means.

"All members present and accounted for," Victoria intoned, "except District 74."

"Madam Clerk, District 74 has arrived!" Sonny hollered, as everyone in the room turned to take in the miscreant who was late for his own swearing-in.

Victoria shot him a chastising look. "We will now administer the oath," she said. "Members, please stand and raise your right hand and repeat after me: 'I, state your name.'"

"I, Sonny Lamb, do solemnly swear or affirm that I will faithfully execute the duties of the office of a member of the House of Representatives of the state of Texas, and will to the best of my ability preserve, protect, and defend the Constitution and laws of the United States and of this state, so help me God." That was it. He was officially a member. A representative. A legislator. A lawmaker.

Lola watched as Sonny recited the oath. Nothing in their marriage had surprised her so much as this new turn in their life. Sonny was suddenly somebody. More than that, he had a future. Yes, there was financial sacrifice involved. Lola would definitely need to hire another hand. But she was beginning to realize that her own status had also changed. She was married to an important man. He wasn't just a dead-end cowboy, as some had thought—even in her own family. He had power. Sonny wanted her to be proud, and she was proud. Another less welcome emotion arose, which was envy. Not a lot, but it was there. Suppose it was Lola rather than Sonny with her hand raised, entering a new life. Sonny would agree that she would have been the better candidate, beloved in her community, someone people naturally turned to. She didn't want the job, so why was she even thinking this? Privately, she had always harbored the belief that she was the main partner in their marriage, boss of the ranch, keeper of accounts, the hirer and firer of cowboy labor, the one with the big family with modest wealth behind her. All that made Sonny's accomplishment even more impressive. He had none of that, and look where he was now.

Lola followed the other family members to the gallery as the secretary of state presided over the first order of business, the election of the speaker, the merest formality. Everybody knew that Big Bob had the pledges. He was sitting behind the rostrum almost out of view from the floor, jiggling his foot, ready to leap into action as soon as this ritual was concluded. Two members, a Republican and a Democrat, provided nominating speeches, a little more relaxed and jokey than they might have been in the case of a serious contender. A white-haired Republican, Kent Maxwell of Harris County, offered a stream of insider wisecracks about Big Bob's "sober assessments" and "devotion to the institution of marriage"—remarks that drew on a history well known to members of this body and really to any Texan who followed politics. Bob Bigbee's personal life was an ongoing train wreck, and yet he persevered, through his drinking, his divorces, the occasional jail term, and somehow he survived, hypnotizing his constituents with his astonishing immunity to disgrace, even now evoking tears from Representative Maxwell as he summarized the great man's devotion to the state, an attachment so fierce and obvious that members could find no better leader if they searched the pages of history, yea even Sam Houston or Stephen F. Austin would bow in the direction of the Titan of Texas, Robert Keenan Bigbee. Gilbert Delgado, the Democrat, was barely more circumspect in his praise, saying that this, the fifth term of Bigbee's service as speaker, would be the greatest of them all, because of the unity of the House—meaning the absence of credible opposition. "My momma told me it's sometimes better to stick with what you know," Gilbert said. "And we all know Big Bob."

★

It was a time to be nice to each other before the knives came out. Asleep at the Wheel played "Miles and Miles of Texas" and some classic Bob Wills tunes on the Capitol grounds. The weather was ideal, as it often is in Central Texas in January, a blessed month with soft light and cool evenings, although in Texas the elements can suddenly reverse course and castigate the mighty and the fallen alike. But this was one of the perfect nights. The unmistakable, salvation-eliciting odor of barbeque suffused the nostrils of legislators and their families, fetid, musky, a primitive perfume redolent of sex and war, rousing the ancient savage lust for meat.

Eyes peeled, Lurleen Klump wandered through the crowd with a glass of pinot grigio. This was the sixth term for the sharp-featured Tea Party doyen. She was a particular type of society lady. She had found the Lord as a teenager in Corsicana, graduated from Baylor University, married an oilman, and discovered politics with the same zeal she brought to religion. To her, faith and politics were the same.

Stylish, her bright white hair roped into a severe bun with a buzzard feather added as a fascinator, everything about her was essential and carefully constructed—her outfits (western cut, even though she came from deep East Texas), her jewels (turquoise and silver, she could be a Navajo), her religion (Southern Baptist)—everything except her politics, which resided in a gray area between nihilism and libertarianism. She attended high-dollar, invitation-only conferences with speakers who proclaimed inside knowledge, the kind of stuff the mainstream press has been hiding from you. Her philosophy wandered near the shores of conspiracy thinking and the dark web without ever falling into the déclassé black hole of QAnon. She was a theocrat, like many on the fringy right, but not a white nationalist, like the Tucker Carlson acolytes among the frat boys. But she was a friend to such movements, believing that America should return to its roots as a Christian nation. When Donald Trump was elected, Lurleen thought salvation was at hand, but along came the devil and you know what happened.

Finally she spotted her quarry in the dining queue. "When they said there was a Black Republican, I just had to see it with my own eyes," Lurleen said as she approached Harold Morton. She didn't bother to introduce herself. Everybody knew Lurleen.

Harold was expecting this moment. He was always having

to explain himself, especially to white Republicans (that is to say, nearly all Republicans), who couldn't believe that he agreed with them. He was a medical man, wealthy, fastidious in dress and habit, a prudent investor. Take away race and he was almost a poster boy for conservatism. But his fellow Republicans still looked at him as a refugee from the ghetto, just as the Democrats tended to view him as a traitor to his race. "I embrace conservative values just like you, Lurleen," he said, as he accepted a generous slice of brisket. (Lurleen chose the Elgin sausage links.) "I don't see that the color of my skin has anything to do with fiscal responsibility."

"Where do you stand on affirmative action?" Lurleen asked, a show-me-your-papers question that allowed only one response.

"You mean, reverse discrimination?" said Harold.

A joyful quiver ran down Lurleen's spine and her eyes brightened as if an emotional rheostat had just been turned up. "I've been preaching this for decades!"

"Listen, Lurleen, all I want is a level playing field," Harold said, as he took a scoop of potato salad. "I have no use for critical race theory or postmodern economics. I believe in reason and opportunity. Enough with this government assistance! You're helping my community to death!" Red beans and slaw finished the buffet, along with a dollop of red sauce and a dash of Tabasco on the beans.

Lurleen froze in place, blocking the line as she declared to anyone in hearing, "I have met the future of the conservative movement."

Harold readily agreed. "If the message doesn't reach minority voters, there won't be a conservative movement in this country. That's what makes the messenger important." He nodded and started off to a likely spot, but Lurleen caught the sleeve of his jacket before he escaped and whispered in his ear, "Black lives matter."

"It's okay, Lurleen, I already know that," Harold said. "But thank you."

★

Carl Kimbell, the catfish farmer from Mineola, wandered over to meet Sonny and Lola, who were standing somewhat awkwardly by themselves. "L.D. told me all about you," Carl said. "You took Walter Dunne's seat. Turned District 74 red. Walter and me, we were buds, despite the difference in affiliation. Shared a few honeys on occasion."

"Uh, Carl, this is my wife, Lola."

"Evenin' ma'am, you gotta forgive me. I'm just a country boy. I love the three Bs—the Bible, boobs, and barbeque." For this last point, he held up the beef rib he was gnawing on. "Tell me something, Sonny. You think there was anything funny 'bout the way Walter went out?"

"Funny?"

"Like funny business," Carl explained. "Assassination, for example. Maybe antifa. Walter was a bear on that subject. Maybe they took him down."

"Where'd you hear that?"

"Mr. Peeples," said Carl, as if that settled the matter.

"The guy on the radio?" Sonny asked. "The 'Me the Peeples' Mr. Peeples?"

"He's pretty much got it figured out," said Carl. "You wouldn't be a part of it, by any chance?"

"I don't think there was anything to be a part of," said Sonny. "By all accounts, Walter died of a heart attack."

Carl looked at Sonny through squinty eyes. "Which side are you on, partner?"

Sonny took a second. "Are you saying you actually believe this?" he asked.

"Maybe not 'believe' it, but entertaining the idea. Curious, you know. Man had a lot of enemies. Draggin' him into court, that kind of thing."

"I didn't know Walter was in legal trouble."

"Child support. He was a little behind."

"Doesn't seem like a reason to murder him."

"But see, you never know, do you?" said Carl. " 'Specially when children are involved, the weirdest stuff happens. Sexual stuff, you know, don't even wanna talk about it in front of the missus." Carl nudged his eyebrows in Lola's direction and took another bite of the rib. "Give it some thought. I could be wrong. But I could be right. See, that's the thing. Depends on what kind of world you live in, what you believe. You maybe have a different conception of the universe, for instance. Than I do. But if you think about it, I mean really, deep down think, you'll see angles you didn't see before. And then you look behind them angles, and *whoa*. You know what I mean?"

"Not at all."

"It may come to you. In the middle of the night, of a sudden. The truth, like, Hello! There it is, why didn't I see it before? And I don't fault you for being, you know, conventional on this stuff. I was like that. It took me years. Keep an open mind. Things may be revealed to you."

"Thanks, Carl. Will do."

"Okay, then," said Carl. "I need another cerveza."

"Are they all that crazy?" Lola asked when Carl was out of range.

A smoky female voice responded, "Rest assured, Carl is in a class by himself. The man has the mental carrying capacity of a soup spoon."

It was Mary Margaret McAllister, the newscaster. Somehow she rated an invitation to this members-only picnic. "Sonny Lamb, the great come-from-behind story," she said in an ironic, unfriendly manner. "Welcome to the Lege, cowboy."

"It was hard fought, that's for sure," Sonny said warily.

"I hope you think it was worth it."

"I never said a word against her, if that's what you mean."

"No, you let someone else do that for you," Mary Margaret said. "I've been covering this hellhole for a long time. I know how it happens. Some guy walks in and throws pixie dust in your eyes, saying you're the next LBJ. Then you get to Austin and find out that you're just some boy carrying water for the lobby."

"I'm not anybody's boy."

Mary Margaret wasn't as tall as Sonny, but she was up there, even without her boots. Yes she was physically formidable, but her mind is what made her really dangerous. You wouldn't know from her accent that she had been educated at Princeton and taken a degree in international relations at Sciences Po in Paris. Many a self-regarding politician learned to his regret that it was a mistake to test her. "I don't know if you're fooling yourself, but you're sure not fooling anybody else around here," she said. "Somebody made an investment in you. I think I know that somebody. He's gonna expect a return. That's the way it works for guys like you."

"Are you harassing our new members, Mary Margaret?" It was Big Bob.

"Yes, I am," said Mary Margaret. "What's it to you?"

"Don't pay her too much mind," Big Bob told Sonny. "We've been married on at least two occasions that I remember, is that right, Mary Margaret? Or was it three?"

"No, Bob, just the two."

"Feels like three. And I survived. More or less. Now scoot, M.M. I gotta talk to these folks."

Mary Margaret kissed him playfully on the cheek. "Love you, Bob."

"Don't make a habit of broadcasting it to the world," he muttered, as Mary Margaret strode off. He stuck out his hand for Lola. "Hidey, ma'am, Bob Bigbee."

"Yes, Mr. Speaker. Lola Lamb. I'm—"

"Ed Sharp's little girl."

"You know him?" Lola was shocked. Her father had never said a word.

"Knew your momma, too. She was a truly lovely lady. Sure was sorry when she passed."

"Thank you," Lola sputtered, awed by the fact that the speaker had—somewhere in his long career—bumped into her parents, and years later was able to retrieve their names like a magic trick. Maybe at the Rotary Club or the Cattlemen's Ball. An incident no doubt long forgotten by her father, but not by Big Bob Bigbee. Did he know everybody in the state?

"Sonny," he began, "you're taking the place of a man who was eighteen years in this House. I'll be frank with you. Walter was a lot of fun but he never accomplished anything that was worth a jigger of horse piss."

"That sure as hell ain't gonna be me," Sonny said.

Big Bob smiled at the presumption. "Freshmen don't have seniority," he warned. "You're the lowest of the low. You get dibs on nothin'—office space, committee assignments, parking spots, not a damn thing. But remember, you do have one little item everybody wants. Your vote. There are a hundred and fifty members here, and the ones who succeed are those who can count to seventy-six. You're gonna feel a lot of love, but it's all bullshit. They don't love you, they love your vote."

"I'll take that to heart, sir."

"Behave yourself. Pay attention. And don't believe in fairies. Good things only come to those who earn them. I'm not saying it's a meritocracy. It's a Bob-ocracy. And I keep my eyes open. Let me offer you a word of advice, something a wise man said. 'In politics, some folks grow, others swell.' Learn to tell the difference and you'll be all right."

Big Bob clapped Sonny on the shoulder and headed off.

"Wow," said Lola.

★ **10** ★

They're called lobbyists because they wait in the lobby. Just outside the doors of the House chamber you can usually spot six or eight of them, sometimes many more, standing around, pacing, sitting on the stairs, trying to get a signal on their cell phones. There's a similar scene on the Senate side of the legislature. Anyone earning more than $1,620 in a calendar quarter or accumulating more than $810 in expenses or spending more than forty hours as a lobbyist is required to register with the state and pay the annual $750 fee. Private citizens working for causes lobby as well. Every session Willie Nelson shows up to plead for marijuana legalization. Even his clothes are made of hemp.

When a member of the legislature passes through the lobby, he or she may expect to be mobbed by advocates for anything from sales tax relief to making the Branch Davidian compound a state park. The causes are diverse but the motives are the same: they all want something, and they want it enough to trudge down to the Capitol or pay somebody to do it for them. The successful lobbyists have something to offer in return, usually in the form of campaign contributions or votes. Parties and free meals, step this way. Friendship and sex, also on offer, the advantage being that neither has to be declared.

To see a member, a lobbyist drops in at the sergeant-at-arms office, just outside the door to the chamber. He fills out a note and hands it to a page, and the page enters the chamber, stepping past the brass rail enclosure and into the members-only sanctuary. Many elected officials served as pages or interns or staffers when they were young. Some would say that's when the fire was lit.

For instance: when L.D. was at the University of Texas, he got a job as night watchman at the Capitol. From eight p.m. till four a.m., he had the place entirely to himself. He would patrol the halls and check the doors and every hour he would insert the key hanging around his neck into a time clock to indicate that all was well. Otherwise, he was free to wander. He loved to race his three-speed Schwinn down the marbled corridors, marked at the intersections by cast-iron columns forged by inmates in the Texas prisons. The grandeur of the place stirred dreams. It was also a great place to bring dates for a private midnight tour.

In the summers, he would go home to Port Arthur, and those dreams would cloud over, so distant was he from the locus of power. The weather was humid and miserable, like living in a sponge. Hurricanes struck nearly every year. His father worked at the refinery, the largest in the U.S. (now owned by the Saudis). It was a big smelly armpit of a place, the air a stew of sulfur dioxide, benzene, chloroform, and other toxins that produced the rotten cabbage odor that so characterized L.D.'s childhood memories, and which might account for his obsessive cleanliness.

When L.D. was in high school, his dad died of brain cancer, a disease that affected an uncommonly high number of refinery workers. The town itself had been dying for decades. The most famous refugee from Port Arthur was Janis Joplin, who was scarred by the narrow-minded conformity that threatened any trace of original thinking, and she left Texas bursting with the anger and insecurity that fueled her music. For kids just younger than Janis, such as L.D., her escape showed the way.

The Capitol was the great magnet that drew him again and again to Austin. In law school, he worked on the Senate side, as an aide to A. R. "Babe" Schwartz, who represented Galveston and was a master of the legislative arts. In those days, all the power was in the hands of the Democrats, many of whom were more reactionary than the few Republicans who had just begun to crack the monopoly. No one could rival Babe's oratory when he got wound up. L.D.'s only aspiration was to be as talented and righteous and relentless as Babe in his fights for coastal protection and anticorruption. L.D. also stayed close to some of the very rich constituents who backed his boss.

What L.D. learned from Babe was the use of power. He saw that power was a river—one that could flow in either direction, but always toward one group or individual and away from another. Sometimes the river was a trickle and sometimes a flood, but it was here, in the legislature, that power was directed. The people in those seats under the Capitol dome, the 150 representatives and the 31 senators, along with the governor and lieutenant governor, operated the controls. Power was win-lose. People were taxed or they received benefits; they got jobs or lost them; they were elected or defeated; they gained influence or became superfluous; they rose high or plummeted, like dear old Babe did in 1980, when he lost to Buster Brown, one of Karl Rove's early victories in his successful campaign to turn Texas from blue to solid red. That was real power. But it was Babe who inspired L.D. to run for the House. He got elected and served two terms as a Democrat before dropping out, under circumstances he preferred not to talk about.

Many of the old members remembered L.D. from those days. Even now, they would stop and chat with him about characters from that era, the heroes, the crooks, the wizards, the idiots, all of them woven into a mythological narrative called "Back Then." Everyone was tougher, more enlightened, crazier, dumber, hornier, greedier, and a lot funnier Back Then. The battles were more epic. The fights were bloodier. Money flowed more abundantly. Rules were more relaxed. The whores were more accommodating. Issues were more existential. Good and evil were always and entirely at war. L.D. was a reliable historian in that he knew how to paint the stories in colors more vivid than they might have merited. Anecdotes were polished. Punch lines were sharpened on jokes made thirty years ago, which could still bring a nostalgic chuckle from the graybeards or an appreciative titter from the newcomers who sought to drink in the lore. They would be part of that lore one day. Stories would be told about them that were slightly more than true.

On principle, a handful of liberals still refused to talk to L.D.—in public, at least—because he was a traitor to the party, having been a Democrat in the days when Rick Perry was as well, but most members who returned for this session had learned their lesson. Just now, for instance, Lloyd Johnson, a stalwart leftover from the Ann Richards era, waded into the lobby scrum, shaking hands and clapping backs. Lloyd was a great drinker, and he paid for it with liver disease and heart problems and a nose that could light the way for Santa's sleigh. He was still hanging in there, though, one of the last raging libs in the House, proudly occupying a chair in Red Square. Now here he was gabbing with the lobbyist for AARP, Melissa Richardson, who was revered among her colleagues for expensing her breast implants. Oh yes, a few members like Lloyd might turn their back on L.D. in front of their constituents, but Lloyd's eyes blew him kisses as Melissa ran through her talking points about prescription drug prices.

To those who knew L.D.'s past, his present was not a mystery. Countless former members trod the path from the Capitol to the lobby, selling their former influence—including Babe, for one. They financed the campaigns and wrote the bills. The skillful lobbyist must have a working knowledge of the committees in both the House and the Senate and be welcome in the offices of the current but constantly shifting membership. Officeholders were just pieces on the chessboard, to be moved in the direction most likely to benefit the client. Most of the pieces were pawns, but a first-class lobbyist—one with experience on the floor—knew which pieces had crowns on their heads.

L.D. was no different in that respect. What caused him to stand out is that he tracked the river of power to its source. That source was money. Other lobbyists were looking for clients; L.D. looked for money. When a wildcatter brought in his first big well, L.D. was there to instruct him how government could aid him or destroy him.

When the tech giants considered moving to the robust Texas suburbs, they needed a player to negotiate the tax breaks. L.D. would show the way. When mayors caught the state intruding on their tax base, L.D. taught them how to keep the legislature out of their pockets. Gradually, the money people and the power people began to look on L.D. as an all-purpose friend. If a rich man wanted to buy a sports team, he knew who to call. When the director of prisons was found to be serving dog food to inmates, L.D. helped him explain to the press how nutritious—and tasty!—Alpo was, as the director would personally demonstrate. When the attorney general, a pious crook, was caught fixing up a girlfriend with a well-paying job with a real estate developer in exchange for settling a damaging lawsuit, L.D. not only managed to quash the whistleblower complaint, he got the AG's wife elected to the Texas Senate. Yes, L.D. was a first-class fixer—historic, really, in the lobby world—but it was all because he had gotten upstream of the power and put his hands on the money.

"You wanted to see me, Mr. Sparks?"

Standing before him was the bellwether of Hispanic hopes, Angela Martinez. Right off the bat he could tell she had an edge on her, a little of the AOC cockiness befitting the bright promise she portended. In the whole long history of Texas politics there has never been a broadly popular Hispanic candidate who could take the next step to statewide office—save for Ted Cruz, who was palpably more Canadian than Cuban. Henry Cisneros, the Castro twins, none of them stepped into the ring to run for governor or lieutenant governor. But hope, like a mirage in the desert, forever floated on the horizon. That hope was invested now in a freshman House rep from San Antonio, who was a long way from delivering on that promise. Still, Angela Martinez bore watching. L.D. knew she had an agenda, along with a bill that had about as much chance of getting through committee as an Oreo in a frat house.

"I've heard all about you," Angela said before L.D. even got his hand back.

"Nice to know I'm being talked about."

"Not much of it is nice."

L.D. grinned. He relished the repartee that comes with being the bad guy everybody needs, the one people hate because he holds the kitty, the power broker whose agenda comes first before you get the goodies. L.D. could afford to be genial and gracious-seeming; his reputation did the dirty work for him.

"That's the price we pay for being effective," he said. "We're in the same game, Representative Martinez. I have clients, you have constituents. We both want to please our customers." Angela didn't bother to hit the ball back. She waited for him to get down to business. "I just wanted to welcome you," he said, "see if there's anything you might need."

"Like tickets to the Super Bowl?"

"Information. How the system works. What it takes to get that bill you filed out of committee."

"It's already been assigned?"

"Will be. The Select Committee on Health Care Reform."

"How do you know that?"

"Information is power. Happens to be my line of work."

"You're telling me it will be a problem getting it to the floor, but you haven't read it, you don't know who supports it, you don't have any idea how many Texans want some trace of humanity and good sense in dealing with women's health issues."

"Miss Martinez, even if you had all the support you dream of, there are a million ways for a bill to die. Especially one that comes with the pro-choice baggage you're carrying."

Angela chewed on this for a moment. People called her a progressive, but she saw herself as a pragmatist. She knew that her bill, Health Protection for Texas Women, was considered largely symbolic, a gesture toward the coalition that funded her campaign. She might be green, but she wasn't naive and she wasn't here to fight ideological battles. She wanted actual victories.

"So you help me," she said, "what do I do for you?"

"Whatever's in your heart."

"Right. Said the devil, 'Sign here.'"

"All I ask is that you open your door to me," L.D. continued, in a voice that poured honey on a biscuit. "Over ten thousand bills will come up this session. You care about maybe a dozen. My clients care for a few. Most of the rest nobody gives a country crap about. You hunt?"

"I've been told I should," Angela replied.

"I'm putting together a little group for the speaker, going down to Refugio next week to let the air out of some wild hogs. I can put you on the bus."

"I don't have a gun."

"Good God, Miss Martinez!" L.D. exclaimed. "Don't tell anyone else that!"

When Angela returned to the chamber, her desk mate, Ernestine Smallwood, gave her a big-momma sizing-up look. "What?" Angela asked, laughing at the expression.

"I've been working in this hellhole since Adam bit the apple," Ernestine said. "I know what goes on here."

"Uh-oh, did I do something wrong?"

"No, baby, not yet. But I see trouble in your future. Maybe some good trouble."

"I have no idea what you're talking about."

"Little birdy told me you just got invited on L.D.'s fabled pig hunt. Only a select few are chosen, and now you're one of them."

"Are you going?" Angela asked.

"Oh, good Lord, no. I'm an indoor woman. Besides, some of these members might like to train their guns on me."

"I really don't know why I got invited."

"You *really* don't know? You might should take another look in the mirror. You'd see what everybody else sees. 'Specially them cats in the frat boy corner."

Angela flushed. She was used to being noticed, but this frank appraisal by the legendary Ernestine Smallwood, the lion of South Oak Cliff, unnerved her. "I don't think my . . . *appearance*"—saying the word under her breath—"at least, I hope that doesn't have anything to do with it."

"Oh, c'mon, girl," Ernestine said, rearing back to take in the full view of Angela Martinez. "Don't you tell me you don't know how to use all those outrageous assets. You wouldn't be here otherwise. The question is, what are you gonna use them *for*?"

★

That was a question that had been in Angela's mind since she was a teenager. She was the oldest of three daughters in a family of activists. Her mother had come from Crystal City, which was famous for two things: the Popeye statue downtown, symbolizing the spinach fields where Angela's grandparents labored most of their lives; and the activism that was born out of those same fields. Her mother, whose maiden name was Leticia Gutiérrez, was a student at Crystal City High School when the school board ruled that only one cheerleader could be Hispanic, all the rest Anglo. At the time the city was 80 percent Mexican American. When two cheerleader spots came open and the school board refused to appoint a Hispanic to one of the slots, the students walked out. Leticia, sixteen years old, had been a cheerleader aspirant. Now she was one of the protest leaders. When they formed a picket line around the high school it made national news. Film crews swarmed around Leticia, who was smart and charismatic and would have been a terrific cheerleader.

The federal government got involved, mainly in trying to coax the students back to school, but by now Leticia had found her voice. She wasn't intimidated by the spotlight. The strikers presented a list of demands, including more Hispanic teachers, bilingual education, and more challenging course work. Eventually, the school board caved, and the following year Mexican American candidates swept the elections for school board and the city council. That victory led to the formation of La Raza Unida and the birth of the Chicano movement.

By that time, Leticia had graduated valedictorian and entered Trinity University in San Antonio. Overnight she became a powerful force in Texas politics, especially in San Antonio. Propelled by her compassion but also by resentment of the obstacles that had blocked opportunities for Mexican Americans, she got elected to the city council and then spent two terms as mayor. When she retired, she organized a group of Hispanic women who met for breakfast each Tuesday in Mi Tierra, a landmark restaurant downtown, where political candidates auditioned for their approval. Las Mamas, as they were called, had their eyes on Leticia's beautiful and talented daughter, surely destined to be first Hispanic governor of Texas, or senator, or who knows. She had the chance to live the life that Leticia would have had for herself, if she hadn't had to burst through all the barriers that stood in the way of her people.

It was a symbolic moment in the family when Angela became a cheerleader at South San Antonio High, but that was just the first step of Leticia's audacious plan for her daughter's life. She believed that the opportunities Angela had were too precious to be spent on anything other than a historic existence, the hero child, the heir apparent. However, Angela was as determined and obstinate as Leticia, and her dreams didn't fit the bold design her mother had in mind. She said she wanted nothing to do with politics. True or not, she made it clear she didn't want her mother running her life. She saw plainly what a public life demanded: the privileging of causes, one after another, over intimacy and privacy, sacrifices Angela refused to make. She knew she was intelligent—*brilliant* was the word often thrown in her direction by the doting Mamas—but that didn't mean she had to give up her own ideas of a meaningful life in order to follow the path her mother had prepared for her.

Instead of going to Trinity, her mother's alma mater, Angela chose Peabody College at Vanderbilt University, in Nashville, because of its vaunted education program. She joined the highly competitive dance team, where she made most of her friends. In her senior year, she got engaged to a teaching assistant in the computer sciences department. Angela had not even bothered to introduce him to the family before making the announcement. The fact that Angela's intended was an Anglo from Connecticut with no link to Texas and no discernible political value was another slap in Leticia's face. Her entire life was a story of bending people to her implacable will, everyone except her oldest daughter, who refused to be bullied by her mother or the Mamas. It was made worse because Leticia knew she had no right to grab the levers of Angela's life. She just couldn't help herself.

The wedding was a disaster. Leticia came, but only on the day of the ceremony, and left immediately after. She dressed in black, as if she were attending a funeral. Her heart was broken and she wanted everyone to know it. Angela and her husband moved to New York, hoping the distance would eventually lessen the strain.

Then Leticia played a card that Angela didn't expect. She died.

Angela hadn't been home for three years. She had spoken to her mother only twice in that period, over the phone, once about a property settlement that had to have Angela's signature and another time when Angela, despairing because her marriage was cracking apart, made the mistake of turning to Leticia for consolation. Leticia couldn't suppress the glee in her voice. She had been longing for the day she could say *I told you so*. Angela decided she would never speak to her mother again. And she never did.

The funeral was held in the auditorium of the Central Library, playfully designed by a distinguished Mexican architect Leticia had lured into accepting the assignment. The auditorium was full, and the audience spilled over into the main reading room. One after another, people stood to offer testimonials, friends from Crystal City and power brokers from Washington. Julian Castro, another former mayor of San Antonio, spoke of Leticia's life as a beautiful tapestry, one that depicted struggle and sacrifice but also meaning and achievement. Will Hurd, a former U.S. representative from the west side of the city, recalled how she inspired him with her determination to lift people up. And of course, Las Mamas were there, telling stories about Leticia's humor, her compassion, her support—qualities so seldom experienced by Angela in her own relationship with her mother.

Angela asked the funeral director for a private viewing of her mother's body before the casket was sealed. Leticia had been laid out in the cerulean-blue dress embroidered with pink roses that she had worn to her middle child's wedding. The dress spoke of a mother's delight at another daughter's happiness. Angela choked back a sob, remembering the widow's weeds her mother had chosen to wear at her wedding. Leticia's face was cold to the touch, waxy and painted like a China doll. *Who were you?* Angela wondered, thinking of the thousands of lives Leticia had touched and improved and motivated. This was a city that was acknowledging its debt to her, to her big, meaningful life.

Angela realized at that moment that she would have to yield to Leticia. The life Angela had planned for herself might have been pleasant, but it wouldn't be transformative. Leticia had seen qualities in her older daughter that few people possessed, qualities that were the currency of politics—charisma, attractiveness, intelligence, and perhaps foremost, stubbornness, the quality they shared in such abundance that it had forced them apart, like powerful magnets face-to-face, but now Leticia was gone and the force field reversed. Angela fell to her knees, struck by revelation. She surrendered.

Within months she had moved back to San Antonio. She got a job teaching American history in a middle school and began to heal her relationship with her sisters. She became a wonderful aunt. She cooked once a week for her dad. But beneath the commotion of ordinary life, she was on the track Leticia had made for her. A year later she had taken Leticia's seat in Mi Tierra with Las Mamas. And the ladies began the task of realizing Leticia's dream.

Something about having a solitary kidney caused Sonny to be cold in the evening, usually between five and seven p.m. Like a reptile, he powered down during a chill, took a nap if possible or a light meal. Being damaged made him more cautious. He watched his blood pressure, avoided salt, and drank a gallon of water every day. High-protein foods were out, which meant that he hadn't had a steak since the war, and because avocados were filled with potassium, he had to give up guacamole, a loss that still pained him. No contact sports—he couldn't risk hurting his other kidney. He once peeked at a report on how people die when the kidneys go and decided he wasn't going to let that happen to him. But it meant that he was always on guard.

Once every five years he would go for a checkup at Walter Reed. While there, he would stop in at Arlington National Cemetery to visit Private Pinkerton's grave. It just seemed so odd and wrong that Sonny would be standing on the ground and Pinkerton would be underneath it. All those white crosses, as far as you could see, the finest people, slaughtered because of their best qualities, their courage, their loyalty, their patriotism, rolled over by merciless history. Like Pinkerton, their lives were plucked before they fully bloomed. Most days, there were no other visitors, or at least no one in immediate view. Sonny would be the only person standing upright in this vast horizontal congregation, and he wondered how that was allowed.

The doctors at Walter Reed seemed to think of the kidney in purely mechanical ways; it was all plumbing to them, and one kidney was enough to do the job of making pee. Sonny believed there was more to it. Once while he was in D.C., he visited an acupuncturist, who spoke to him about Chinese traditional medicine. She seemed very wise and not fringy. She said there's a reason we have two kidneys; one is the furnace and the other provides the fuel. Now the single kidney was having to do all the work. That's why Sonny got cold: his blood struggled to keep up with the kidney's demands, and by the end of the day it needed a rest. She told him he should paint the nail on his left big toe black, because that's where the kidney energy exits. He didn't understand the reasoning, but he also didn't question her suggestion. Since then, he'd always painted his toenail black.

★

Without cows to attend, Sonny's mornings began later, around six on weekdays when the House was in session. It was quiet just before dawn. He made coffee and read an account in the *Texas Tribune* about the governor's latest theatrics on the border. Sonny had lived all his life in proximity to Mexico. When he was a kid, he hunted rabbits in the desert with a Remington .22. The border then was marked with a single strand of wire, and if there were more rabbits on the other side Sonny dipped under the wire. Mexicans crossed all the time for work or school, nobody worried about it. Later, he and Lola would camp in Big Bend and take a rowboat across the river to Boquillas for dinner. Now you had to have a passport. The farther away people were from the border, the less they understood that it's a region, not a line drawn by a river called the Rio Grande on the American side and the Rio Bravo on the Mexican. The Americans needed the labor and the Mexicans needed the jobs, but practically the only people available to work the ranches were forced by immigration laws to become nominal criminals. They were the best workers Sonny ever saw.

When the narcos took over and the violence ramped up in Mexico and Central America, people started running north, not just for jobs but for safety. Immigration really did become a problem once thousands were crossing, or trying to, every day—more than two million arrested in a single year, most of them in Texas. A strand of wire wasn't going to stop them. Where to put them? How to adjudicate their claims? How to keep the drug lords from spreading their influence across the river? Lola's brother Buster, the border patrolman, saw awful sights. Once he stopped a truck with Mexican plates in the middle of July, a hundred degrees at least. In the back of the truck were eighty-seven people, and fifteen of them were dead from heat and dehydration. Several more died before they got to a hospital. Donald Trump's border wall was an attempt at a solution, but a fantastically expensive one, and it essentially ceded the river to Mexico. Moreover, most illegal migrants came with visas legally and then overstayed—no wall could keep them out. These days, many of them weren't even from Mexico or Central America; they came from Venezuela, Cuba, Haiti, Africa, all over the place.

Sonny knew Governor Abbott had spent several billion bucks of Texas taxpayers' money on the National Guard troops and Texas Rangers he sent to replicate the job the feds were already doing. They searched for drugs and contraband but found none. A bunch of heavily armed militia types suddenly appeared on the border claiming they'd build the wall themselves. They threatened landowners. Most of them had never been to the border. The governor welcomed them.

And now, here in the news, Sonny saw where a rancher in Candelaria had shot a migrant trying to cross his land. It wasn't surprising with all the rhetoric flying around that violence would follow, but instead of calming passions, the incident became a talking point on Fox News. The migrants were trespassing, the pundits pointed out. The land was posted in English and Spanish. In the past, there had been episodes where illegal immigrants had menaced ranchers or made off with valuables. Pantries had been raided, livestock stolen, fences torn down. No wonder this rancher felt threatened. Texans should stand by a property owner's rights. The fact that the rancher killed a twenty-year-old woman who was six months pregnant was unfortunate, but it was collateral damage, "the price of freedom," as the head of the NRA said on Tucker Carlson.

She had been shot with an AR-15, what the report called an

assault weapon. It was the semiautomatic cousin of the M16, the standard Army rifle, and the M4 carbine, the shortened version that Sonny had carried in Iraq with the Rangers. The AR-15 wasn't automatic, but in practice most warriors didn't use that function anyway, it was just a waste of ammunition. Sonny had seen what an M16 did to a person.

The rancher in Candelaria wasn't some eighteen-year-old school shooter. He was a cranky old hermit who hated the government and refused to pay taxes. He had been convicted of several misdemeanors in the past, and likely had mental health issues, but who would know? There were no questions asked about his many gun purchases, most of them at swap meets. He was just one data point in the mass of statistics on gun violence in America. People were sick of the carnage; most favored background checks and red-flag laws at the very least, along with raising the age at which one could purchase an assault weapon from eighteen to twenty-one. That sounded reasonable to Sonny, but the other members wouldn't even talk in public about such reforms. Guns had become a symbol of freedom, and even suggesting that owners should be responsible adults was an infringement of liberty. And yet they all knew they were making the state more dangerous. "You pick your battles," L.D. advised Sonny, and regulating guns in any fashion was a suicide mission.

As he was reading the news, Sonny had an unsettling realization: *It's up to me now.* He had been elected by his neighbors to solve problems, and these are the kinds of problems that desperately needed to be addressed. He finished his coffee and headed to work, determined to do—well, something.

It was only a couple miles to the Capitol, so he walked on mornings when it wasn't raining. He headed out the back gate of the trailer park to the municipal ball fields, and then to the hike-and-bike trail along Lady Bird Lake. The sun was not fully up, but runners were already out, slender as stilts, some wearing headlamps, like coal miners. The tops of the cypress trees caught the first rays, their bare branches ornamented with cormorants, their wings splayed out to dry. The trail passed through the dog park on Auditorium Shores, with pets frolicking about, catching frisbees, sniffing each other. The sight made Sonny miss Bandit. A few sculls were on the lake, following the implicit lanes, rowing west on the north side of the lake and east on the south. In the afternoon, you'd see the board people lazily paddling along like solitary gondoliers. Rowing teams would come down from wintry college towns to train in their tippy racing skiffs, flying along like the freight trains passing over them on the graffitied railroad trestle.

Traffic was waking up now, headlights and taillights still bright in the shadowy downtown streets. Sonny could sense the dynamism of the city, the newness, the incandescence as the sun crested the horizon and set Austin aflame. Building cranes, like titanic predatory insects, topped the ascending skyscrapers, adding more and more and higher and higher. The river lay below, a dark boundary, which the burgeoning city strained toward as if it would march right into the water and on and on to who knows where.

He climbed the stairs of the Ann Richards Bridge to Congress Avenue. There, eleven blocks away, on high ground, squarely in the middle of the avenue, even pinker in the slanting light of dawn, was the Capitol. Every time he saw it he took a breath. The building was perfectly balanced by the wings on either side and the soaring dome in the center, topped by the Goddess of Liberty holding up a golden star. As he walked across the bridge, it took a moment for him to notice the Mexican free-tailed bats—the same breed as on Sonny's ranch—returning from a night of foraging. They were early this year, people said, already beginning their return to Texas from caves in Mexico. Must be climate change. The sky was streaked with them, making long swirling smokey black clouds, the largest urban bat colony in the world, one and a half million of them, Sonny had read, capable of flying over a hundred miles an hour. They ended each night by plummeting out of the sky like regiments of dive bombers. Just as it seemed they were going to plunge into the lake they swooped under the bridge and went to sleep.

When Sonny showed up at his office, he was surprised to find that Wanda was already there, along with two new staffers she had hired.

One appeared to be a geeky teenager but was twenty-two years old, a tall African American with vitiligo on his hands and neck. He was also blind. "This is Ezer Prince," Wanda said. "Our intern. He's a graduate student at UT and a genius."

"What are you studying?" Sonny asked.

"Game theory, sir," Ezer said.

"Really? Like video games?" Sonny said, then realized what he'd said. "Sorry, I'm a dumbass. Explain to me what that is. Game theory."

"It's the science of logical decision making, using certain mathematical theories," Ezer said. "Basically, you can figure out what people are going to do based on their needs and past behavior."

"So you might be able to size up who would vote for my bills?"

"Mainly, how to motivate them to do so."

"That sounds useful." Then, for Wanda's benefit, "He could be useful!"

"There's a catch," Wanda warned.

"I'm only doing this for my doctorate," Ezer said. "I'm not really interested in politics, but there's little useful research on the utility of game theory in a dynamic political system. So I'll be studying you for my thesis. Whether you win or lose is up to you. I'll spell out the basics, but you'll have to find a way to employ the proper algorithms."

"Algorithms?" Sonny asked.

"I'll help you with that."

"And your name is?" Sonny asked a young woman dressed like a French schoolgirl in a turtleneck and beret. "Jane Stringfellow," she said.

Sonny looked at Wanda. "My granddaughter," Wanda said. "She's older than she looks."

"Well, thanks, Grandma!" Jane said, laughing.

"I know what you think, but she's the best researcher you're going to find," said Wanda. "And she was available."

"You've done this before, I guess," Sonny said.

"I studied political science at Harvard and got a PhD in American history at Yale," Jane said. "Research is my thing. I thought

I wanted to be a professor, but watching Wanda engage with real issues was inspiring."

Sonny could see a resemblance between Jane and Wanda. Jane was tall and had broader shoulders, but there was an echo in their eyes and noses and the shape of their faces. Except for Jane's more prominent jaw, Sonny could imagine Wanda at that age, wry and attractive, although somewhere along the line Wanda got to be formidable and Jane was softer—more academic, he supposed.

He asked her what area of American history she focused on. "Gender issues in the nineteenth century. The rise of women's suffrage and all that."

"Well, who knows, that may come in handy," said Sonny, totally uninterested in the topic.

Sonny noticed that Wanda's brow was knitted in some unspoken concern. "You'll have to decide where you stand on gender issues," she finally erupted. "That's one of the reasons I brought Jane on board. Several bills have already been filed that would criminalize parents and doctors who are dealing with children who want to transition. It's already passed the Senate twice but has never gotten through the House. You're sure to see it again this session."

"That's an easy one," said Sonny. "I don't believe that children should be allowed to make a choice like that."

Jane asked if he would be willing to hear the other side.

"Look, I'll listen to whatever, but there's no way I'll change my mind on this. When somebody becomes an adult it's a different matter, up to them, not the state. So what else?"

"Arming teachers," said Wanda.

"Good God, do we have to? Is it safe to put guns in the hands of elementary school teachers? I've got some real problems with this. And what if some kid in the classroom gets hold of the weapon? The liability issues."

"Many teachers are already armed," said Wanda. "Larger schools have their own police force. They're called resource officers, but they're really cops. This has been going on since Columbine. In the Uvalde massacre, you had nearly four hundred police officers show up, but they didn't do a darn thing, just stood around in the hallway for an hour while the killer did his work."

Jane explained that smaller schools could choose between the Guardian Plan or the Marshal Plan. Both were voluntary. The Marshal Plan, created by the legislature right after Sandy Hook in 2012, was far more rigorous, requiring eighty hours of firearm proficiency and active-shooter training in a police academy. The guns were locked in safes that could only be accessed with a code. "They modeled it on the air marshals who put an end to the aircraft hijacking craze back in the seventies," Jane said. "It might make a difference if teachers really wanted to sign up and the state would fully fund it, but neither is the case."

"So what's the Guardian Plan?"

"It's not actually a plan," said Jane. "It's essentially whatever the local superintendent says it is. Guardians have nominal training, there's no requirement that the guns be locked up, and nobody knows how many schools in the state have this policy. But it's a lot cheaper. Now there's a bill to make the Marshal Plan more like the Guardian Plan by lowering the amount of training. They say it's because the Marshal is too onerous for teachers."

"How much training?" Sonny asked.

"Eight hours."

"Oh, great, some teacher who had a day of training a year ago is going to whip out a Glock and start firing at who knows, maybe a fellow teacher with the same idea. And do either of these programs actually work?"

"There have only been a couple studies that look at schools with armed staff, and neither of them show a reduction in casualties. The problem is that a school shooter does most of his killing within a few seconds."

Wanda had listened to this dialogue with visible impatience. "This bill is going to pass," she said. "You'll only hurt yourself if you vote against it."

"How so?"

"Next time you go into the chamber, take a look up at the south gallery, you'll see a guy in a pearl-gray Open Road. He'll have a notebook in his hand. He works for an organization called Texas Scorecard. That's where bills like this come from. He's there to mark the names of anyone who votes against it."

"People vote against bills all the time."

"This is different. They'll put bills on the floor for the sole purpose of screwing you. They'll push some crazy amendment for free malted milk for shotgun owners, you'll vote against it, then they'll send mailers to every person in your district saying Sonny Lamb is against the Second Amendment. I guarantee it will happen on this bill. Understand, I don't agree with limiting the training, it's dangerous and absurd. But you'll be throwing away your career if you vote against it."

"What do you think, Ezer?" Sonny asked.

"Every bill is a game, but they're all a part of the bigger game, which is what can you do that's worth doing," he said. "Now if you don't plan to get reelected and feel you've got nothing to lose, you play it one way, but if you think you'd like to stick around, you'll have to choose which games you want to play."

"I just can't feature trusting teachers to turn into armed guards with so little preparation."

"Let's say that costs you reelection, would it be worth it?" Ezer asked. "Or another way to play the game, can you find a way to moderate the bill so that it becomes more acceptable? Bargaining is always a reasonable strategy."

"Like, propose an amendment that would be somewhere between six hours and eighty hours," Jane said. "Even then, you're likely to get mailers in your district."

This is what politics is really like, Sonny was thinking. He had always wondered why good people would make such awful choices, voting for bills they actually opposed, and now he was getting a lesson in his own moral limitations. It wasn't about doing good, it was about being less awful.

The longer this discussion went on, the more discouraged Sonny became. This was not the kind of legislation he expected to get buried in. "Okay, it's grim, I get the picture," he said. "Let's concentrate on getting my desalination bill in the hopper. This is our top priority. What can we do now? This very minute?"

Wanda had been around politics for decades, and she knew how to build a bill. Almost instantly she compiled a list of possible cosponsors among rural legislators whose districts were suffering from the drought. Coastal communities also had an interest in desalination that might map onto Sonny's plan. "The main thing is to put up a workable bill and start the process. Even with luck, it's going to take the whole session to steer this through."

Ezer proposed that they find other bills dealing with water rights. "That would be your best way of finding supporters." He had already developed a list.

"It would help if you could get on one of the committees that will deal with this bill," said Jane. "It could go to Land and Resource Management, Agriculture, Water and Rural Affairs, conceivably even State Affairs or Ways and Means."

Sonny asked how he could get on any of those committees.

"The speaker will interview you and ask you what you're interested in," Wanda said. "You'll fill out a card with your preferences, but he may not pay any attention to your priorities—that's especially true for newbies. They say he has some secret room where he covers the wall with sticky notes and comes out with the assignments. You don't want something like Cultural and Tourism, aka 'Bubbas and Ballet.' It's a signal you're dead meat as far as the speaker is concerned. The important ones are Calendars, Ways and Means, State Affairs, and Appropriations, but they're mostly reserved for the big shots."

It was just after eight in the morning, well before the usual start of business in the House, so no one was expecting L.D. to coast in as if he had been invited to join the meeting. He was wearing a blue-serge suit and Gucci loafers. There was always an air of heightened reality about L.D., like a TV star, or some guy you see on commercials. L.D. rolled one of the brand-new office chairs next to Sonny and helped himself to a donut. "The desalination bill, I presume," he said.

Sonny nodded. The others just stared at him.

"How are you going to pay for it?" L.D. asked.

"We haven't gotten to that yet," said Sonny.

"That's the only damn thing that matters. You come here, brand-new, offering a bill right out the gate, you gotta show you know what the score is."

There was silence until Wanda said, "He's right."

"Well, what do you suggest?" Sonny asked.

"What do I *suggest*?" L.D. said, meaning this wasn't exactly a suggestion. "I *suggest* you drop the whole thing. It's a huge waste of your time and that of the other members, who have to consider a bill that will never get out of committee, and if it gets out of committee, will never get passed in the House, and if it gets passed in the House, will never get through the Senate, and if it gets through the Senate, will be vetoed by the governor."

"How do you know any of that?" Sonny said, flushed with indignation.

L.D. turned to Wanda. "Tell me I'm wrong."

"I can't say one way or the other," she said, loyally enough.

"This is the whole reason I ran for office!" Sonny said.

"There are other worthy things we can concentrate on," L.D. said as soothingly as possible. "Look for bills to cosponsor, get your name on. Meantime, we'll line up support for your next term. Maybe there'll be a different governor. Maybe it'll rain."

"Excuse us," Sonny said to his team, "L.D. and I need to have a private conversation."

When his office cleared, Sonny asked what the hell was going on.

"I'm giving you good advice," L.D. said. "I'm sure Wanda already told you freshmen never get their bills passed."

"Yes, she did. But that doesn't mean I'm going to sit around and work on card tricks. I'm going to do what I intended to do in the first place."

"A noble stance. But political suicide."

By now, Sonny was really pissed. "What exactly did you expect when you brought me here, that I would just kneel down, take orders? I'm not your *hireling*"—to use a word that still burned. "I've got my own agenda. I intend to write the bill, and defend it, and pass it, and I'll get the governor to sign if I have to ram it up his ass. Just watch me."

L.D. chuckled. "Yeah, well. You can spend your time doing that. Or you can pitch in on some actual legislation that has a chance of passage. I'm here to help. Don't make me your enemy, Sonny. Many a member has made that mistake and learned to regret it. Ask anybody. Ask Wanda. You dance with the one who brung you."

★

The speaker's offices were behind the House chamber, as majestic as Sonny had imagined them to be. During the session, Big Bob lived in the quarters, which were elegantly outfitted with furniture appropriate to the construction of the Capitol in 1888. Unfortunately, that included the bed, narrow and short, a subject of frequent complaint going back two speakers before Big Bob. Apparently the real power in the Capitol resided with the State Preservation Board.

Sonny hadn't appreciated what a massive operation the speaker of the House ran. He employed hundreds of people, including forty or so on his personal staff, along with the clerks, the parliamentarian, the janitors, the business office, the legislative researchers, the librarians, and his own chef. Sonny was shown into the study, where the speaker was standing in an odd position, with his left hand outreached and his right held across his heart. Sonny started to shake his proffered left hand, but then he noticed the sculptor in the corner. "Don't mind him," Big Bob said. "He's an artiste and tells me not to move. Make yourself comfortable, we don't have to both be standing here like King Tut. We're gonna have a little chat about where you fit in here. Okay with you?"

"Yessir," Sonny said, still standing awkwardly because it just seemed wrong to sit while the speaker was posing.

Bob Bigbee was not so tall, maybe five-ten, nearly four inches shorter than Sonny. The impression of his bigness came from his awe-inspiring presence, like Obi-Wan Kenobi, not all knowing but all wise, not all powerful but all intentional. His eyes were heavy-lidded, serpent-like. Nothing escaped him. In his early seventies, his hair was implausibly still mostly black. He had a semicircular scar under his right eye from an elk hunt, when he got too close to the gun scope, which added a kind of monocular imperiousness, like an Austrian general from the Great War. Everybody knew Big Bob was a melancholic who refused his medication and carried a pistol, although he didn't carry it very well, as it occasionally fell out of his pocket, scaring the shit out of everybody. He kept his drinking mostly under control, but when he slipped, the Earth held its breath.

Above the speaker's desk was a portrait of Sam Rayburn—shiny bald, with dark mild eyes, an imperturbable visage reflecting absolute fearlessness. Mr. Sam, who was Lyndon Johnson's mentor, became speaker of the Texas House at the age of twenty-nine, and later speaker of the U.S. House, where he served until he died. He was often regarded as the finest man to ever serve either office. That painting said a lot about who Big Bob aspired to be. Under the portrait was a Rayburn quote, "Power's no good unless you have the guts to use it."

That had never been Bob Bigbee's problem. Like Mr. Sam, he was a graduate of UT Law; both men were from small East Texas towns. Rayburn was a Democrat at a time when Texas Dems were mostly conservatives, so his politics were not far from Big Bob's moderate Republican beliefs. Personally, however, the two men were opposites. Rayburn was a force, but a calm one, using his relationships with members and his reputation for integrity to guide legislation and subvert damaging bills. Respect was the emotion he summoned from the bodies he governed, whereas Big Bob was feared. Mr. Sam was married once and only for a few months, when the relationship ended for reasons never disclosed. Few knew anything about his personal affairs. Big Bob, on the other hand, was headline fodder, given his capacity for chaos. But he, too, had his secrets.

Bob Bigbee spent much of his childhood in Goliad, one of the oldest settlements in Texas, where in 1749 the Spanish built a mission on the San Antonio River with the goal of converting the Karankawa Indians. The first Texas Declaration of Independence from Mexico was signed in Goliad in 1835; four months later, a garrison of Texas rebels surrendered in the same little town, and the Mexican president, General Antonio López de Santa Anna, ordered that all the prisoners—more than three hundred—be executed. This history is known to every Texas schoolchild. It made a particular impression on Bob Bigbee; the historic sites were part of his growing up. He rode his bike past them nearly every day. The center of Goliad was the courthouse square, now a lively spot with shops and restaurants and even a yoga studio. When Bob was a child, the main attraction was an especially graceful live oak tree in front of the courthouse, with long, horizontal branches spread like octopus tentacles—the Hanging Tree. Even before the Civil War it was the site of numerous executions, usually right after a brief trial but occasionally without the benefit of the law.

His family didn't have the deep roots in the state so many in this part of Texas did. They haled from Shreveport, Louisiana, where Bob, the only child, was born and lived for the first five years of his life. His father, Keenan Bigbee, was an accountant with a gambling habit, which led to his being fired from the bank where he worked. He moved his family to Texas, a common story for people on the run from their reputations. They settled first in Beaumont, but by then Keenan had turned to drink and lost one job after another. The family drifted south to Wharton, then Goliad, never far enough to escape the habits of a man bent on ruin. Keenan ended his days as a farmer with a roadside vegetable stand and as an occasional reenactor of battle scenes of the Texas Revolution.

As a child, privation and shame were Bob's emotional companions, and they never really departed from his spirit. He was close to his mother, Pauline, and his demonstrations of affection increased as he gained standing—with his law degree, his election to office, his seemingly irresistible accumulation of power. He made sure Pauline was taken care of. Despite his entreaties, she refused to leave Goliad and move to Austin, where he promised to take even better care of her. She had her circle. Goliad remains a charming flyspeck of a town, fewer than two thousand people, but Pauline had taken root there, so Bob bought her a nice brick house with a spacious verandah, at the corner of Washington and Garden streets, near the historic St. Stephen's Episcopal Church. She seemed more at home there than anyplace else. In her last year, she remarried, to a very fine man, Patricio Alejo, who briefly brought her the peace and joy she had been robbed of.

Bob fought against the dissolution of his father's life, but something pulled him into the tempest, perhaps a genetic disposition toward loss and ruin, which would be diagnosed as manic depression; or perhaps it was a way of getting close to his broken father through his own self-inflicted wounds. The whipsaw tensions of destruction and accomplishment, power and abasement, were constantly working on Bob, who was never free to be wholly one thing or another. He was a paradox.

Before the meeting, Wanda had schooled Sonny on Big Bob, whom she had known for decades. "He's not a kind man, but he's not evil," she said. "He'll do what he must to get what he wants, and he doesn't mind leaving blood on the floor. His goals are noble, even if his methods sometimes border on Mafia tactics. Cross him and he'll never forget or forgive. You'll die of fright, believe me. He has one giant redeeming quality: he loves Texas. And if he sees that you do too—really do, intensely like he does—then you'll have a very powerful ally. There's never been anyone like him," she concluded, in a wistful tone that made Sonny consider the possibility that they had dated, back in the day.

"Sit the hell down. I thought I made myself clear the first time," Bob said. "Now tell me a little about your goals. I like to know all the members well enough to employ them effectively."

"Sir, you know I'm a rancher. Most of the people I represent are like me, struggling to make cows grow in what's turning into a desert. The country out there is all burnt up from grass fires. Lot of times you can't breathe because of the dust. Sometimes you can't even see. We're losing the battle."

"Climate change," the speaker said.

"Well, yeah. I didn't think you were supposed to say that."

"What we say in private is between us. We all know what's up.

TXOGA has us by the nuts," the speaker said, referencing the Texas Oil and Gas Association, the one lobby that had more influence than L. D. Sparks. "The question is what do *you*"—here he pointed at Sonny—"propose to do about it?"

"Hold still, please," the sculptor fussed.

"Desalination," Sonny said, expecting the usual eye roll. Instead, the speaker said, "Tell me about it."

Sonny took a breath, scarcely believing this astonishing opportunity to explain his dream to save the West. But he had barely gotten past the windmills and the very cool concept of reverse osmosis when the speaker cut him off. "I've got to scratch my ass," Big Bob said.

This was directed at the sculptor.

When he had relieved his itch, Big Bob resumed his position and asked, "How you gonna pay for this?"

"We're looking into that," said Sonny.

"Talking billions of bucks here."

"We're looking into it," Sonny repeated.

"And I'm supposing you want to be on, for instance, the Natural Resources Committee."

"Yessir. Or Land Resources Management."

"Hmm." Big Bob was quiet for such a long time that Sonny wondered if he was done with him. Finally the speaker said, "You were a singer, I understand."

"That was a while ago."

"But you served time in the juke joints and dance halls and the like."

"Many a night, yessir."

"You'd be a good fit on Culture and Tourism. Maybe break out your guitar on occasion."

★

Jane and Wanda started drawing up the bill. It was innocuously styled "A Bill Relating to the Development of Brackish Groundwater." They got some language from the Texas Water Development Board that would amend Subchapter D, Chapter 36, of the Water Code.

"And where's the money coming from?" Sonny asked.

"Fracking," said Wanda.

There was a hush in the room, as if someone had just suggested overthrowing the government.

"Do you know how much water it takes to frack a single well?" Jane asked. She had been digging into technical journals. "Up to ten million gallons! And that all comes out of the aquifer. They mix it with sand from Wisconsin and a lot of chemicals that are almost impossible to extract. By the time it comes out of the well and goes back in the ground, it's a whole lot more toxic, with all the random petroleum molecules and stuff like uranium and arsenic and other heavy metals that it picks up along the way."

"They're poisoning the future of Texas," Wanda concluded.

"So how's that gonna pay for my desalination bill?"

"You've heard of the severance tax?" said Jane. "Every bit of petroleum that comes out of the ground in Texas is taxed once it's 'severed' from the ground. In Texas, that tax is a fraction of what it is in other states, but never mind. It's still a shitload of money."

"Where does it go?"

"It's not dedicated, so it just migrates into the general fund. It's like karma, isn't it? Frackers are spoiling the water and they should pay for it."

"Allow me to interject," Ezer said. "The frackers may not care what the money is used for, as long as the tax doesn't increase."

"Yeah, but they see the aquifer as belonging to them," Jane said, "whereas in fact the water belongs to the landowner."

"Who *should* be on our side," said Ezer. "Poisoned water does nobody any good."

"But we would be taking money out of the general fund," Sonny observed. "Somebody's gonna have to make up the difference."

They sat with this for a moment.

"I guess we have to face up to the fact that it's going to cost money, and the fairest solution is to tap the severance tax," Wanda said.

"So what do we do next?" Sonny asked.

"We drop it in the hopper," said Wanda. "Tomorrow the clerk

will read out all the bills they have received so far. Then it gets a number and is assigned to a committee."

"And the game begins," Ezer said.

Sonny grabbed two bulging manila folders with the research Jane had put together. Nothing excited him more than laying out his vision. At last he had a wise and crafty team, experts who could thread the needle of the legislative process. He taped charts on the bare office walls illustrating the mechanics of high-salinity discharge. He was in a fit of exhilaration when he suddenly remembered.

★

Lola was waiting at Austin Fertility Sciences, in the medical complex near the university. The appointment was at 11 a.m. It was 11:15 and Sonny was nowhere to be seen. He wasn't answering his mobile. Finally she got a text: "on my way!!!"

Lola went in for the appointment alone.

"How long have you been off the pill?" Dr. Chaudhuri asked. She had a lilting, highly educated Indian accent.

"Five years," said Lola.

"Well, your tubes look normal and your FSH is fine. How often do you have sex?"

"At least twice a day during my fertility window," Lola said. "But it's really complicated with my husband here, and me on the ranch."

The door opened and Sonny peeked in, as sheepish as Lola had ever seen him. "You can see why it's hard to schedule appointments," she told the doctor, casting a warning glance in Sonny's direction, "even when he's only five minutes away. And don't say traffic."

Sonny kept his mouth shut while Lola and the doctor talked. All doctors' offices looked the same to him, overly bright and full of doom. Nor was it clear why he needed to be here. He turned his attention to the ceiling. Acoustic tiles, tidy white squares, but not perforated like the old-timey ones; they had a rigid arrangement of alternating horizontal and vertical incisions. A person could scream and not be heard in the outer office.

"Mmm," the doctor said, as she leafed through the test results that Lola had brought along. "I don't see anything in the file about a semen sample."

Sonny snapped out of his reverie.

"A lot of men think there's a connection between low sperm count and sexual potency," the doctor continued.

"Low sperm count?"

"Or mutations that make it impossible to achieve conception." The doctor pulled down a chart that displayed double-headed and pin-headed sperms, some riddled with holes, as if they were moth-eaten or machine-gunned. "It could be stress, antibiotics, hormone levels," the doctor continued.

"Sonny's been under a lot of stress," Lola said helpfully.

"There's nothing wrong with this old boy!"

"That will be easy to determine," the doctor said. "I'm going to make you an appointment at the lab."

"I've got a really busy schedule," Sonny said.

"How is next week?"

"Busy."

"The week following?"

"Really busy."

The doctor turned to Lola.

"Sonny has trouble masturbating," Lola explained.

"Does he?"

"Lola, for God's sake!"

"They told him in church camp it'd shrink him right up."

"You know that's not true, right?" the doctor asked.

"I'm not superstitious!" Sonny protested, although he was, on some things.

Lola looked at him evenly. "He still thinks he'll go to hell with hairy palms and a little bitty penis."

The doctor nodded. She had heard as much before. "I'm going to make an appointment for you three weeks from now. That'll give you plenty of time to clear your calendar. In the meantime, you might think about switching to boxer shorts. Also, stay out of the hot tub, the little critters don't like the heat. It helps to ice down the testicles twenty minutes a day."

The idea that his sperm might be grotesquely disfigured hit him hard. If he were shooting blanks that'd be one thing. This was worse. Something totally unexpected but which might explain everything. Bad sperm.

"You're not really mad at me, are you?" Lola asked, taking note of his silence as they drove to the airport.

"Why should I be mad? Everybody should know about my sex habits, even if I'm a little repressed, a little 'culturally out of step.'"

"Sonny! She's a doctor!"

"It's embarrassing is all," he said, and lapsed back into silence as he came to a traffic light. "Ice down the testicles," he grumbled.

"I know it sounds bad, but it might not be as big a deal as you're thinking."

"You sure you can't spend the night?"

"We're weening the calves in the south pasture," she said. "They'll be bawling all night."

Not in the fertility window is what she means, he thought. He dropped Lola at the airport and headed back to the office. On the way, he thought about sex. How it used to be fun. Lately he was just reporting for duty when Lola ovulated. Whatever happened to Little Miss Curious who let Sonny roam wherever his imagination took him? Then she would suddenly turn the tables and take charge, excitement building to crazy levels, never in history were there such glorious explosive couplings. Or the mornings when he woke up hard and they melted into each other dreamily, slowly, and when their bodies moved to the rhythm of "When a Man Loves a Woman," their wedding song. But lately when they made love Lola had been scratching him, clawing would be a better word, leaving bloody tracks on his back. There had been something exciting about it at first, but it began to feel like punishment and then more like despair.

★ 12 ★

The hounds were baying an hour before dawn on a cattle ranch in South Texas, where a select group of Texas legislators had gathered, bearing pistols. L.D. passed around sticks of beef jerky to keep the energy up. The lawmakers were hopping around in jeans and running shoes, trying to keep warm as they waited for the guides to conduct them to their blinds. Giant Jack Small led a group in calisthenics to get the blood flowing.

"It's as cold as a well digger's ass," L.D. remarked.

Big Bob chuckled at some private amusement. "What's so funny?" L.D. asked.

"Your boy is a sight more independent minded than I gave him credit for," Big Bob said.

"You heard about it."

"I did, indeed," Big Bob said gaily.

"He's green," said L.D. irritably. "Doesn't understand how this place works."

"He knows enough to find the honey pot first time out."

Carl strolled over and asked what they were discussing.

"That desalination bill Sonny filed," Big Bob said. "Or you could say anti-fracking bill."

Carl looked at L.D. "Mm-mmm, Daddy's gonna get the paddle out."

"It'll go to your committee, Carl," Big Bob said.

"Oh, well, then. Situation totally under control."

"I'll remember you in my prayers," L.D. promised.

"Are we just waiting on one person?" asked Carl, who was rocking on the balls of his feet and clapping his arms. "We oughta get this show on the road before we all die of frostbite."

Big Bob turned to one of the Mexican ranch hands. "¿Todavía esta dormiendo la señorita?"

"No, señor, se despertó muy temprano. Mira, viene ahora mismo."

And there was Angela coming out of the ranch house, perfectly turned out, wearing a Ralph Lauren belted safari suit and carrying a *New Yorker* canvas tote. She went straight for Carl, much to his delight, although he suspected her real intention. His feelings shuttled between lust and amusement but settled on condescension. "Hey, darlin', you remember to bring a *pistola*?"

"Why yes, I did, Carl," Angela said, reaching into her tote for the .44 Magnum she had just purchased. "You think this'll do the trick?"

"Whoa, lady! That's Dirty Harry's piece. It'll put the brakes on King Kong!"

"Yeah, they asked if I was going bear hunting."

Carl took a hit of Wild Turkey from his hip flask and waved it under Angela's nose.

"It's a little early, isn't it?"

"Nah."

"Well, it is awful cold," Angela said.

"As tits on a reindeer," Carl said automatically.

Did these people go to school on figures of speech, Angela wondered. If she heard another simile her head might pop. She took a sip from the flask, more than a little repelled by sharing germs with Carl, but she was not going to be good-ol'-boyed out of the action.

"L.D. tells me you're carrying a bill," Carl said.

"Health Protection for Texas Women."

"A pro-choice bill has about as much chance in the Texas Legislature as a kangaroo in a hockey rink."

Angela stared at him, her neurons popping like firecrackers. She took a deep breath. "It's not about abortion," she said patiently, reminding herself that she had trained for this moment, her chance to put her bill into play. "It's about maternal health. You're not opposed to mothers, are you, Carl?"

"No, ma'am!"

"When you guys blocked Planned Parenthood from delivering women's health services, you cut off access to health care for millions of Texas women. And you know what happened, Carl? Something terrible. Something I'm sure you didn't intend."

"What was that?"

"Texas jumped to the top of the list in maternal mortality. Mothers dying, Carl. The Health Protection for Texas Women bill is prolife, pro the mother's life—"

"Save your floor speech," Carl said. "I've heard it all before. First you gotta get it past the Texas Freedom Caucus. We hold a majority on the Select Committee on Health Reform, which is where your bill is headed. Our members run ice cold on abortion, as you may have heard. The powers that be have decided that the life or death of your bill was so important they left it up to me to decide if it would get a hearing before our group. Most bills never even come up, they die quiet deaths, nobody hears their cries." He passed the flask. "I'd hate to see that happen, yes indeed."

This time Angela took a deep swig. "We're talking about mothers, Carl."

"God love 'em."

"Okay. I get where you're coming from," Angela said. "What would it take to get my bill to the top of your agenda?"

Carl looked into the distance, as if he were giving the matter profound consideration. "Can you handle real life?" he asked.

"I think I can, Carl."

"I'll give you this one, because you ask me. But here's the deal. One day I'll come to you. I'll ask for something in return. And it'll be big."

"You're talking about a vote, right? I don't have to kill somebody."

"Sometimes you wish it was that easy. You wanna survive in the jungle, you gotta let the big cats eat. Just be sure they don't wind up eatin' you. You get what I'm sayin'?"

"I do."

"Then I think we can do business."

★

"That's a beautiful old Colt," L.D. said. "Can I see it?"

Sonny handed him his pistol. "Belonged to my granddad. Had it all my life."

"The Peacemaker," L.D. said in a worshipful tone. "Pre-war, single action, double-eagle grips, a work of art."

"Never a better sidearm."

"You know, Sonny, I'm disappointed in you," L.D. said as he stared down the barrel of the Peacemaker toward a chicken coop.

"That right, L.D.?"

"Smart, easy, got that Old West shit going for you." He twirled the pistol to make his point.

"Then I filed a bill you didn't like."

"An anti-fracking bill? You're pissing away your credibility. I feel responsible, letting you fly solo before you were ready. I did strongly suggest that you drop it and learn your way around before making a fool of yourself. But it's not too late to fix. Just pull that bill down. Rookie mistake. Happens to one and all. You'll live to fight again."

Sonny had known this day was coming. There would be a reckoning, a bill that L.D. objected to or demanded support for. L.D., the man who got him elected. L.D., who provided the hundred-thousand-dollar donor, check still uncashed. Why couldn't it have been a marginal call, something Sonny could have been talked into with a modest withdrawal from the moral account? Instead, it was the bill he had come to Austin for. L.D. had warned him it was a waste of time, but he didn't seem inclined to get in the way—until fracking got into the picture and everything changed. L.D. went nutso.

"You've created a disturbance in the force, my friend," L.D. said, still weighing the pistol. "Word has reached the penthouse. We're talking the pinnacle of the oil and gas world. All they really want is a dependable vote on energy matters. Sure, they have cultural issues they care about, but oil and gas, that's what brought you here. You owe them that."

"L.D., you're right. I owe you a lot," Sonny said. "I wouldn't be anywhere near here if it weren't for your help. I'm grateful, I really am. But I'd have to say we both miscalculated. You didn't bother to figure out who I am, you just saw that guy on the horse on the news and decided you could get me elected. I never bothered to ask you what the terms were, I guess I wanted it so much I closed my eyes to that. Now, here we are. My bill is not a mistake. It's my mission in life. You heard me talk about desalination all through the campaign, so don't act surprised and offended when I do what I said I was gonna do."

"It wouldn't matter so much if it didn't reflect on the people who invested in you," L.D. said, still toying with the pistol in a vaguely menacing manner. "People thought I was a good judge of character, that I could tell who could run with the ball, but apparently not." He scrunched up his mouth as if he had just eaten a persimmon. "This is ruining my reputation."

"Look, I didn't sign a pledge when you asked me to run," Sonny said heatedly. "I have my own reasons for doing this, and pleasing you or the people you represent is not why I'm here."

"You're taking an ax to the money tree. You just can't do that. It's political hari-kari."

"That's my business. Maybe I'm raw and don't know the ropes, but I do know why I decided to run. It was to make a difference, to change the course, not just drift in the breeze."

L.D. had listened to this with growing impatience, because Sonny was right but he was also wrong: right because they had both been captivated by fantasies of what the deal was, and wrong because he was too naive to understand how the game was played. "That bill is on a dead-end street," he said, adopting the tone of a disappointed schoolmarm explaining to a student why he got a D− on his paper. L.D. shook his head. "You're smarter than that."

"You puzzle me, L.D."

"How so?"

"I looked up your record. You were at one time a valuable and effective member. Tort law reform. Coastal waterways protection. You even offered bills to reform the lobby. Then you dropped out of the Lege and your pockets have been open ever since. I'd kinda like to know what happened."

"What happened is that I learned how the world really works. And that's something you're about to learn too, my friend."

"You're gonna teach me?"

"I got you elected and I can take you down just as quick. I say this with sadness in my heart: If you don't pull that bill, I'm gonna ruin you in this state. I'll kick your ass all the way to Tulsa. There won't be enough left of Sonny Lamb to stuff a taco. *Comprende?* It's nothing personal, understand."

"Politics."

"Politics."

"I'll have my gun back."

The guides were waiting on the porch steps when Big Bob motioned to them. "Vamonos," he said. "Get the dogs started. Sun's gonna catch us." To the lawmakers he said, "Be careful."

★

Harold waited in the blind. It was spooky. Rarely in his life had he sat outside in the dark, not even any streetlights, alone. No doubt there were snakes. Lots of them. Coyotes rustling in the salt grass, alligators in the marsh. Not to mention the feral hogs, which sounded fearsome. Harold never did Boy Scouts or enjoyed the wilderness adventures his white friends did. He was a creature of the inner city, having grown up in the South Bronx, the son of a pastor and a housekeeper. His dad, Harold Morton Sr., had once taken him and his little sister fishing in the Hudson River. The fish didn't bite, but the bugs did. At the last minute, Harold caught a bluefish. It was thrilling and unsettling, but when he reeled it in, the fish was monstrous, prehistoric, flailing around so desperately that Harold pleaded with his father to throw it back. It was an episode never repeated.

Harold was twelve at the time. He had an ominous awareness of his probable sexual orientation and the disruption it would cause. The fishing trip was an attempt by his father to nudge him into manly activities that would toughen him up. Being Black and gay in the Bronx was a challenge, and doubly so in the evangelical community where Pastor Morton held sway. Harold Sr. had been an activist in the Black Panther Party, aligned with another son of the Bronx, Stokely Carmichael; thus, Harold Jr. would be surrounded by icons of that era—Eldridge Cleaver, Diane Nash and James Bevel, Jesse Jackson—each of whom visited the Covenant Baptist Church when Pastor Morton was in the pulpit. Aretha Franklin sang "Precious Lord." The Staples Singers performed "Uncloudy Day." Unforgettable moments of spiritual transport. The congregation would exit the sanctuary radiated by the righteousness of their cause. Pastor Morton would be standing on the steps to greet them, with his wife, Clarice, and their children, Harold Jr. and Monique, the perfect family, as the congregants filed out into the elm-dappled shade of Morris Avenue, making the slowest possible exit as they rained praise on the pastor, who blessed them one after another and offered quick prayers for the bedridden and those who had passed. It took forever. Harold maintained his fixed church-boy smile as the women petted him, such a handsome young fellow, the men remarking on his height, sizing him up for the basketball team. But Harold didn't play sports or even care about them. This was a boy who lived within walking distance of Yankee Stadium when Reggie Jackson ruled the world, Black Power personified. There were heroes all around, who had fought for the liberation of Black people. Harold would often wonder why such fierce warriors for civil rights would turn out to be so hostile to the rights of their own children to claim their sexual identities.

The early civil rights movement was divided on many things, but it was united in opposition to homosexuals. The Martin Luther

King Jr. arm regarded gay African Americans as traitors because they prioritized their sexuality over their race. For King, scrupulous conformity—meaning heterosexuality—was key to gaining acceptance by the white world. The Panthers saw homosexuality as evidence of the emasculation of the Black male. They substituted hypermasculinity—muscles, guns, and attitude—for any trace of emotional availability. The Panthers would eventually find gay partners in their quest for social revolution, but many African American churches remained obdurate. Society moves on, but the word of God does not.

Harold was in the boys' choir when his voice changed, his vocal range dropping an octave and a half into a deep rich baritone, and he was promoted into the adult choir. His first intimation of romance was with a seventeen-year-old tenor. They touched hands while Pastor Morton quoted Leviticus about the "abomination" of homosexuality, although he didn't bother to finish the verse: "They shall surely be put to death." Harold knew the ancient injunction, and all the others. He competed in Bible Bees at a national level, filling his bedroom with trophies. His father assumed that his namesake would take over his pulpit one day, just as MLK had followed Daddy King.

Like Stokely, his father's mentor, Harold attended the Bronx High School of Science. It had produced eight Nobel Prize winners, more than any secondary school in the world. Harold had girlfriends, but they were always friends, not lovers. The girls instinctively knew. The boys were mostly eggheads, and Harold blended in. His height and his authoritative voice protected him against homophobes.

He knew he wouldn't be able to hide his sexuality from his parents forever; in fact, he suspected that his mother had known for years but never whispered a word, fearing the wrath of her husband. What would it look like if a fundamentalist preacher's own son was queer—an "abomination" in his own house? Harold and his mother fell into an unspoken conspiracy, which followed certain assumptions. To save his father from embarrassment, Harold would need to leave. He should be far enough away that visits were infrequent, in a community that would embrace both his Blackness and his gayness, and in a profession that would make him financially independent. With his test scores, he could have gone to any school, anywhere, but he required a scholarship. He and his mother put the puzzle together one piece at a time, and when it was finally assembled, the picture was clear. Rice University, in Houston, was one of the best schools in the country; it offered generous scholarships; the city was often described as the most diverse in America; and Rice was in the heart of the Montrose neighborhood, known as the gay capital of Texas. As soon as he arrived, Harold knew he was home.

Now he was in a long-term relationship with an acclaimed chef at a landmark Houston restaurant. Harold had a highly successful dental practice, with four partners, Harold himself being the orthodontist of choice for the children of Houston's elite. He was on the board of the Alley Theatre and the Houston Symphony. He and his partner, Julian Medrano, were reliable contributors to worthy causes and present at all the important galas and fund raisers. They were on the cover of *Houston* magazine, Julian at the stove turning chicken thighs and Harold pouring a glass of pinot grigio, both of them radiating confidence and bonhomie and casual wealth. It wasn't surprising when people began to speculate about Harold's possible political future. What was surprising was that he turned out to be a Republican.

Some of his supporters winked at this, telling themselves that Harold had made a canny choice. Republicans were so dominant in the state, he would be better positioned for a future in the GOP. His race and sexual orientation would make him a poster boy for diversity in a party that had little of it, but because his constituency was largely Democratic, he had to give them a reason to cross the partisan divide. "I'm conservative, but I'm not insane," he explained during the campaign. "I believe in the party of Abraham Lincoln, not the party of Trump." Harold was elected with a substantial mandate. Everything in his life was perfect. Except one thing.

Harold and his father had never reconciled. His parents were old now. Pastor Morton had long since become aware of Harold's sexual preference, but he refused to speak about it. He had an Old Testament intransigence that would brook no compromise, even if it shattered his family and broke his wife's heart. Clarice was showing signs of dementia. Harold Sr. suffered from diabetes, and already two toes had been amputated because of ulcers that wouldn't heal—a harbinger that death was zeroing in. He retired from full-time preaching and grudgingly accommodated the young woman who succeeded him in the pulpit. The history that Pastor Morton had lived meant little to her. She was modern, hip, accepting, and wildly popular. There was talk of building a new sanctuary because the congregation was growing so rapidly. All of these developments reflected Harold Sr.'s decline. As a young man, he had been angry, and that anger had propelled social change; as an old man, he was merely bitter. Holding on to his grudge against his wayward—once so beloved—son gave meaning to his declining years.

★

"Darn," said Angela. "I don't have any bars on my phone. I was hoping I could at least check my email." She was sitting on a camp stool, radiating frustration.

"It's about fifty miles to the nearest cell tower," Sonny said. "People in these parts aren't exactly up to date."

"Soooo," Angela said into the dark, "what do we do now? Just sit here? What's the usual procedure for hog hunting?"

"Well, if you were a hound, you could crawl around and sniff him out."

"Ha, ha. Very helpful information, thank you."

"Usually you just wait for the dogs to chase him out of the salt grass," Sonny said, wondering how long he would have to entertain her. "If we're half lucky, one of them will come chargin' right through here."

"Hmm." Angela rustled through her canvas tote and pulled out a laptop.

"Seriously?" Sonny asked.

"I'm working on a speech."

"Don't let me interrupt."

"You won't bother me," Angela said brightly. "I can do two things at once." She opened the laptop, which illuminated the blind like a searchlight. Her fingers clicked on the keys in rapid fire. *Can anybody think that fast?* Sonny wondered. She had a fine face, he could see, her forehead knotted in concentration, her eyes racing across the text. It would be wonderful to be so quick and alert. And inconsiderate, in his estimation. She was wasting a precious moment in nature, when the stars were out and the sun was soon to rise and the excitement of the hunt quickened the blood, all of which she was apparently immune to.

"What's that you're humming?" Angela asked.

Sonny was caught short. "I didn't even realize what I was doing. Sure didn't mean to disturb you."

"The song," Angela said impatiently.

Sonny sang softly:

> *They say we're young and we don't know*
> *We won't find out until we grow.*

Angela immediately joined in:

> *Well I don't know if all that's true*
> *'Cause you got me, and baby, I got you.*

Then, together, with harmony, louder:

> *Babe.*
> *I got you, babe.*
> *I got you, babe.*

"Oh my God, that was my favorite movie, *Groundhog Day*," Angela said.

"Exactly! I was just thinking about what if, you know—"

"Like we repeat this part of our lives again and again—"

"Every morning six a.m.—"

"On the alarm radio."

"And it starts all over again. The same day."

"But in our movie we'd be sitting on a log in the woods, repeating the same lines, like, 'I don't have any bars on my phone.'" Angela did this deadpan, making fun of herself in the voice of a whiny adolescent.

"People in these parts aren't exactly up to date," Sonny said, playing along, in a plausible Bill Murray imitation. They laughed.

"And you're named Sonny, too."

It took Sonny a moment to realize, "Oh, like Sonny and Cher."

"Yeah. And like Phil Conners had the same name as the groundhog."

"Punxsutawney Phil," Sonny said triumphantly.

"Bravo." Then: "People think it's just a comedy but—"

"I think it's profound."

"It's all connected."

"Layers upon layers."

Angela looked at Sonny with wide-eyed appreciation. "We're going to be friends," she concluded.

★

When the guides had settled everyone in their blinds, they set the hounds loose and beat the bushes with baseball bats. One of the guides, Modesto, accompanied Big Bob, who didn't appear much interested in the hunt. They walked along the edge of the marsh, dimly lit by the gibbous moon on the horizon like a lantern in a distant camp, casting a silvery sheen across the cattails on the shore of a narrow estuary. Big Bob gestured at a spot on the bank some fifty yards away. "Vete en la resaca," he told Modesto. "Quizás hay unos jabalís ayí."

"A sus órdenes, señor."

Modesto walked off with his bat resting on his shoulder. He was of the Tarahumara tribe in the Mexican state of Chihuahua. For centuries, his family had lived in the crevices and caves of Copper

Canyon, a sanctuary of peace set apart from history and urbanity, like another planet. Then came the *narcotrafficantes* who cut down the trees and forced the farmers to grow opium poppies. Modesto had an uncle, Isidro Baldenegro López, who had stood up to the drug lords, and they had murdered him. They killed anyone who spoke against them and many for no reason at all. People became too frightened to resist.

The Tarahumara were famous runners, able to run hundreds of miles at a time barefoot or in leather sandals. They could run down a deer. The narcos, seeing them as ideal drug mules, forced Modesto and some of the fastest young men, including his young cousin Arnulfo, to carry drugs to the border, five hundred miles north. The cartel provided blue jeans in place of their loincloths so they wouldn't be conspicuous beyond the mountains. Modesto and Arnulfo and several other mules would journey to Ojinaga and wade across the river, just above where the Río Conchos fills it again. They continued north, probably crossing Sonny and Lola's ranch, until they got to Marfa, where they dropped off their burlap packs filled with opium and bricks of marijuana at a hipster motel—El Cosmico, where guests stayed in tents and teepees. There they met a man playing guitar in a hammock, and he gave each of them eight hundred-dollar bills. But the last time they came they crossed the river west of Big Bend. It was a moonless night, the water was higher, and it was harder to find their footing in the starlight. There were five runners altogether, counting Modesto and Arnulfo. They wandered through a canyon wrought by a long-ago disappeared river, now a smuggling trail, shielded from the helicopters and airplanes of La Migra. They clambered over boulders, passing eroded towers of sandstone, and finally emerged onto a flat sandy plain, where floodlights burst upon them and they were trapped.

The runners shed their packs and scattered in different directions. Modesto was the only one who had the sense to run back into the canyon, into the dark and boulder-strewn path that the jeeps and motorcycles couldn't follow. Nor would any man on the face of the Earth be able to catch him on foot.

This time he didn't run back across the border. When he got to the river, he floated downstream, keeping his head low so the spotters on the banks wouldn't see him. For long stretches the river was dry, and Modesto could run, darting onto the Mexican shore if the American side was patrolled. He ate river walnuts and prickly pear and cooked a couple Rio Grande cooters in their shells. It took more than a week to reach Laredo, where he sat under the bridge until his clothes dried, then he walked to a church and a priest gave him a meal. His cousin and the other runners were sent to prison for five years, an extended sentence because in addition to opium they had carried fentanyl.

Modesto found work on this ranch, where the political people were now hunting. Each month he would send his pay home to his wife and three children, praying they would reunite one day. In the meantime, he made a study of the Texans, who were the only Americans he had ever met. He supposed they also had stories, as he did. Even the *jefe* they called Big Bob had a story, and in this moment they were all living a story together. Modesto could sense a deep place in this man, but something was wrong with him. There didn't seem to be any good reason why the hogs might be more numerous in the cattails along the marsh, but the *jefe* seemed to want to be alone.

Indeed, Big Bob was in a bleak frame of mind, as was common when the roller coaster of his personality went from manic to depressed. This was a black one. His mood had little to do with the facts of his life. Few public figures had contributed as much to the state of Texas, and few commanded so much power. Feared and beloved, often in the same instant, Big Bob was sure to leave an impressive legacy in the history of the state, and yet he regarded his existence as a colossal failure, marked by lovelessness and deceit. Once upon a time, he told himself, there had been a path to greatness, but he was too broken to follow it. He had set fire to manifold opportunities for happiness, destroying his most cherished relationships, rejecting the counsel of his friends. Eventually he would surface and claw back some measure of the affection he depended on, but there was always a reserve that his friends and loved ones had learned to employ where Big Bob was concerned. It kept them from getting too close, knowing that he couldn't be counted on not to lash out, to belittle, or worse—to turn that savage part of his personality on himself. He was the only resident of an island called Big Bob.

And so, standing in the dark, with a gun in his hand, looking at the Milky Way, newly apprised of the limits of his mortality, it did occur to him that this might be the moment to bring the curtain down.

★

Time passed. Harold heard the hounds and the occasional voices of other hunters, distant and spectral. He was alone with his anxious imagination. Branches moved, and suddenly a dark figure loomed in front of the blind. Harold jumped. Then he recognized Lurleen Klump. "Oh my God!" he cried, holding his heart. "You startled me, coming out of the dark like that. I thought you were some kind of giant hog! Of course, I was totally wrong!" he added quickly. And then he said, "Is that a sword?"

"I'm in it for the sport," Lurleen said, swishing the glistening blade through the air, much too close for comfort.

"Whoa, watch out! That's like ninja crazy!"

Lurleen placed the sword in its scabbard. "It's quaint, I know," she admitted. "It just seems like a fairer contest."

"That's an interesting perspective," Harold said, although he wondered if indeed a wild hog jumped out of the bushes and rushed toward them would a sword be an adequate response. His own marksmanship had never been put to the test, so where did that leave them? "Is there a lot of swordplay in your district?" he asked.

"Not as much as there used to be."

"Maybe that's a good thing."

"Now everybody has a gun," said Lurleen. "Which on the one hand is progress."

Lurleen sat down next to Harold on the wooden plank in the blind. They were quiet. It felt awkward. He had already sized up Lurleen as a MAGA fanatic, so there was little to do other than humor her. "Where do you get a sword like that?" he said, as if he were genuinely interested and not rattled by the absurdity.

"My father was in Japan during the occupation. Who knows how old it is. Maybe hundreds of years."

"How interesting."

"And now here I am. I think of the many samurai who wielded this blade and it humbles me."

"Did your father bring back anything else?"

"Oh, yes. Flags, knives, some wood prints. Some shrunken heads from the islands. He was quite the collector."

"I guess you're close to your dad."

"He passed ten years ago this May. I would say not especially close. When I found the Lord he dialed me out."

"Ah," said Harold, and then went quiet. This was delicate territory, given his history with his own father. Perhaps this was a moment to bond. "Religion can be very divisive," he said tentatively.

"That's the whole point, isn't it? We divide ourselves into the saved and the damned. It's very clear."

"You think so?"

"It's our duty to bring as many people into the light as possible before the Rapture. It does pain me a good deal to think that Daddy's in eternal torment."

Harold had plenty of experience with icy fundamentalists. Nothing he could say would sway them, he knew that, although it rankled him that Lurleen was so certain of her father's doom and her own salvation. But he also knew what it was like to be rejected. He anticipated Lurleen's next question.

"Harold, have you accepted Jesus Christ as your Lord and Savior?"

"Well, Lurleen, I do attend church."

"Baptist or Church of Christ?"

"I go to the Metropolitan Community Church."

It was Lurleen's time to be quiet. "I thought Metropolitan is for homosexuals," she finally said.

"We accept anyone in need," Harold said. "But yes, I am gay."

"But you're a Republican!"

"I can be gay and a Republican, there's no law against it. I can't be a Christian and a homophobic bigot. But that's just me."

No good was going to come from alienating a powerful colleague. It was pointless to pursue this conversation, but Harold felt compelled to continue the argument. "Do you really take everything in the Bible literally?"

"Who are we to say that the Bible is in error?" Lurleen said heatedly. "Are we God? Are we prophets of God?"

"And so if I violate the Sabbath by sleeping late that morning, I should be killed? If a girl marries and her husband discovers she's not a virgin, she should be stoned to death? Does everyone who has a tattoo go to hell? How far do you carry this?"

"The Bible is a stern document, clearer on some subjects than others," Lurleen said. "But on homosexuality, the prohibition is plain." She took a breath and added, "I don't even know why I'm wasting my time talking to a pervert."

"Funny," said Harold, "I was thinking the same thing."

★

"Oh, that's right, you weren't in orientation," Angela said. "That's what I thought, too, but they explained that it's a little more complicated. The bad news is that every day you're in office you're raising money for your reelection. And the people most likely to support you are lobbyists. So you need them, and they need you. It's a pathological mutually reinforcing dependency, and I'm kinda good at that."

Sonny didn't know how to respond to this disclosure, but he was certainly enjoying talking to her. He was attracted to women with wonderful posture, and Angela sat like a Marine, with her shoulders back, not tense but poised and totally natural. Physically confident. Sonny guessed that she must have been a dancer or a college athlete. Lola had a lot of the same physical qualities, although Lola was blond and fair and Angela had glistening black hair and eyes almost that dark and skin the color of cappuccino. Her teeth were also admirable.

"What else do you have in that bag?"

"Crackers and Brie. A couple apples. Toilet paper. First aid kit. A mirror."

"A mirror?"

"You wouldn't understand. You want an apple?"

"I'm good."

"Suit yourself." Angela closed her laptop and crunched into a Fuji. "Doesn't sound like much sport," she observed. "Shooting pigs."

"Well, this particular pig weighs about three hundred pounds, he's got tusks out to here, and he was born pissed off. If you shoot, you want to drop him, because he'll be really annoyed with you."

"I guess you do this a lot," she said, unfazed, between bites.

"I only shoot pests. Feral hogs can destroy a ranch. And they're taking over the state, them and the fire ants and cowbirds. Soon there won't be nothin' left but poison ivy and rattlesnakes."

"I never killed anything bigger than a cockroach."

"Why start now?"

"That's part of the deal, right? Gotta be one of the boys to get a seat at the table."

"It's highly overrated."

"Right, you try begging for basic services in a district with fifty percent of the constituents under the poverty line. It's about time that table got bigger."

"I mean the bein' one of the boys part."

"Hey, you get to freeze your ass off in the mud in the middle of the night in South Texas while waiting for a big-ass pig to rip your guts out."

"Yeah, that part is great." Sonny cocked his ear. "Hear the dogs? They're onto something."

Angela paid no attention to the baying hounds. "Can I ask you a question?" she asked in a tone of studied, academic neutrality. "Do you feel the times are moving away from people like you?"

"People like me?"

"Men. Of a certain type."

"Do you know me well enough to know my type?"

"Privileged, straight, Anglo, Republican, macho throwback-to-John-Wayne type."

Sonny took this in. She wasn't being mean about it, she was plainly curious. "I'm out of fashion, that's for sure. But I'm not so macho. The first day I got here, I walked onto the floor of the House and passed right out."

"Panic."

"That's what they told me. Some John Wayne. Who I admire greatly."

"He was sexy, if a bit fascistic."

"Is this conversation a condition of our future friendship, or do you grill all the guys like this?"

Angela smiled but didn't back off. "I just want to get a sense of what it's like to be on the other side," she said. "Start with being Republican. Does that mean you only care about guns and walling off the border and ending abortion even for women who have been raped?"

"Those are all big problems. To be honest, I hadn't thought deeply about these issues until I got into my race. I'm probably way more conservative than you. As for being privileged, my whole life I've felt I was half underwater."

"And now?"

"Maybe it's easier for me to make myself heard than it is for you, being who you are."

"And who do you think I am?" Angela asked.

"You're certainly full of questions, aren't you?"

"My phone is down and we've got nothing to do until we confront the apocalyptic pig."

Sonny could see there was no way out of this. "You're a teacher."

"That's in my bio. And I'm Latina, which you also know. What else?"

"You've got a king-sized chip on your shoulder."

"Oh, really?"

"This can't be news to you."

"A chip on my shoulder—is that what you would call ambition if I were a man?"

"Fair point. We've both got an agenda. We wouldn't be here if we didn't think we had something to offer the world."

"But my chip is bigger than your chip?"

"I'm guessing that you always had success in your life," Sonny said. "Homecoming queen. Valedictorian. Something like that."

"Both."

"So people had high expectations for you."

"You have no idea what a burden that is."

"See, that's where we differ. Nobody ever expected much of me. And that was its own kind of burden. I would never amount to anything because I never had. My wife, Lola, she's the real achiever in the family. This being elected thing has been a shock to just about everybody, me included."

"That rustling noise is getting louder," Angela observed.

Sonny stood up and listened. "You're right. There's definitely something headed our way. He could jump out just about anywhere."

"Eek," she said nonseriously.

"Not kidding. Draw your weapon," Sonny whispered. "You cover this direction and I'll take this one. Remember, you don't have to shoot, but if you do, don't miss." He thought a moment, then asked, "Have you ever actually fired a weapon?"

"Not actually."

"Is it loaded?"

"I had them do that at the store."

"You know about taking the safety off?"

"I did that already," she said indignantly.

"Okay, so if you see him coming at you, the best thing is to hold your weapon with both hands and wait till you have him in your sights before you squeeze the trigger."

"What are my sights?"

"Uh . . . just make sure you're pointed in the right direction."

★

L.D. was frantic. Big Bob hadn't shown up at their blind. He wasn't back in the ranch house. Modesto said he had left him on the bluff above the estuary, but when he returned, Big Bob was gone. Modesto observed that he was in a "*gran estado*," which L.D. understood to mean that Big Bob was in one of those states where anything might happen. He had seen it many times before.

By now the sun was beginning to lighten the sky, reflecting on the blood-red clouds on the eastern horizon. "Bob, where the hell are you?" L.D. asked in a theatrical whisper as he traipsed through the bush. "You know I don't like bein' out here by myself! I might get shot for a pig with all these pistol-packing amateurs!" The no-see-ums were swarming, adding to L.D.'s vexation.

He had known Big Bob since they'd been elected to the House the same year, decades before. Never was there a lawmaker so gifted, nor one who loved Texas more deeply. Bob pulled the public schools and hospitals in the state out of the discard pile where previous legislatures had left them. He passed production tax credits for renewable energy, which is why Texas led the nation in wind power. Year after year, session after session, Bob steered the ship of state as much as possible away from the fanatics who were always reaching for the wheel. Only those in the legislature knew how many times Bob had saved Texas from catastrophe. Everybody heard the worst about him, but only a few—maybe only L.D.—knew the agonies that this extraordinary man endured, how he suffered, how close he had come to cracking up, only to claw himself back from the grip of that isolating depression that Bob called Godzilla. It was in those moments that Bob might do something totally crazy. It had always been L.D. who rounded him up in the bar, paid the bail, forced the medications on him; L.D. who kept the news as quiet as possible; L.D. who mended the ruptured friendships, settled the lawsuits—and for what? For nothing, not a red cent, only for the love of the one person who made him feel there was a point to existence. Because if Big Bob Bigbee—the drunk, the philanderer, the barroom bully, the inconstant friend, a man given to lies if there was an advantage in them, this connoisseur of power who would willfully crush anyone he perceived as a threat to his position—if a man so flawed as he could add considerably to the good in the world, then there was some residue of hope for L. D. Sparks.

And there he was, Big Bob, on his knees under a mesquite tree, with the gun pointed under his chin.

"Bob . . ." L.D. said gently as he came up behind him.

"None of your business," Big Bob said. He was facing the majestic dawn. "Go away."

"Please, Bob. I know you're hurting, but this isn't the time or the place."

"You don't know diddly."

"That's true," L.D. said, improvising as he stalled for time. "But you can't go out of this world without settling your debts."

"What the Sam Hill are you talking about?"

"You owe me money."

Big Bob turned around, his face full of fury. "Get the fuck out of here!"

"I'm serious, Bob. Pay me what you owe me, then you can do whatever you have to do. I won't stand in your way."

Big Bob looked skyward, searching his memory. "You're just trying to trick me," he said. "I don't remember anything of the sort."

"The domino game, Bob! Think back! I spotted you eleven dollars and fifty cents. You said you'd pay me next time. Well, if there ain't gonna be a next time, just fork it over now."

"That is the silliest damn thing I ever heard."

"Gambling debts are debts of honor."

"Eleven bucks."

"Suppose it was eleven million, same thing. Big money, small money, it's still money. So here I am. I'll take a check if you don't have cash."

"To hell with you, L.D."

L.D. was just about to attempt to physically wrest the gun away when a shot was fired.

★

Amid the howling dogs and the calls of the beaters, the curious lawmakers streamed out of their blinds toward the sound of the shot. Now that the sun was up, certain mysteries vanished in the light. They could see where they had each been stationed, the hounds sniffing and baying in the salt grass, and the ranch house, which was not nearly so far away as they had guessed. Everything was slowly being revealed. But who fired the shot? Did they get something? The lawmakers came running toward the sound, waving their pistols.

"Holy moly, look at that beast!" Carl called out. He was standing next to Sonny and Angela's blind. The others gathered in the small clearing, each one slowing in the same cadence of excitement, recognition, and awe, forming a circle around the dead animal.

"That's a big pig," Big Bob observed.

"A really big pig," Harold confirmed.

"Look at the tusks on that sucker," said Gilbert. "I've seen bigger, but it's been awhile."

L.D. looked at Sonny. "That your shot?"

"Angela's."

Everyone turned their appraising eyes on her.

"Well, I'll be. She flat nailed that sucker," Carl said, more impressed than ever.

"You boys better watch out for this little lady," Big Bob said. "One day she'll have us all laid out like that ol' hog."

L.D. pulled out his hunting knife and said to Angela, "I'll get the head for you."

"Lemme do it!" Carl cried.

"Oh, please, no!" said Angela. "Can't we just bury it?"

The members were momentarily speechless.

"Lady," said L.D. quietly, "that head on your wall will get you more votes in the House than a month of barbeque suppers."

"At least let me gut it," Carl pleaded.

"It's my knife, goddammit," said L.D.

"You may want a more practiced hand," Harold offered. "I do the occasional oral surgery."

"Hell, I never get to gut nothin'," Carl said.

Suddenly, there was a banshee scream. Everyone froze in terror. L.D.'s knife was poised in the air as a much larger blade glinted in the morning sun, and a samurai sword accomplished the task in a single blow. Well, maybe not a single blow, as L.D. would tell the story, but no more than five.

Big Bob dipped a finger in the pig blood and painted a stripe on Angela's cheek. "Welcome," he said. "First kill."

★ **13** ★

A singular edifice overshadowed downtown Houston, seventy-nine stories high, shaped somewhat like an oil derrick, called Liberty Tower. It peeked over the forest of skyscrapers that defined the energy capital of the world. From the penthouse, a telescope allowed you to almost make out Beaumont, eighty miles away, and the spot where, in 1901, a gusher erupted a hundred and fifty feet into the air, ejecting more oil in a day than all the wells in America combined. When the well was finally capped, it was dubbed Spindletop. America's oil economy was born, and Houston became known as the Gateway to Beaumont.

That didn't last long. Within a few years, the Houston Ship Channel opened and the budding oil conglomerates migrated to a city that was as ambitious and greedy as they were. Houston itself was not an oil town, in the sense of being surrounded by pump jacks, but the petrochemical complex around it was the largest in the U.S., and Grand Central Station for the pipelines that radiated out to America. Tankers filled the ports along the Texas Gulf Coast, accounting for 80 percent of the shipments of crude oil that Texas exported to the rest of the world. Sometimes demand was so high that tankers were stacked up in the Gulf, waiting for days or weeks to get supplied. The banks of the channel were clogged with storage tanks and refineries that blotted the sky with smoke and dangerous chemicals. All of this you could see from Liberty Tower.

Many of the five thousand energy companies in Houston had offices there.

L.D. liked to think of it as his own private money tree. The penthouse belonged to Odell Peeples, who had made this building taller than any other in the city so he could look out windows on all sides and see his empire—petrochemicals, real estate, shipping, manufacturing—his fathomless wealth spreading across the Texas economy like a giant oil spill. Mr. Peeples was L.D.'s dream client, a man with so much money that he paid L.D. whatever he asked.

Odell Peeples began as a landman in the 1980s, when the price of oil collapsed to $7 a barrel, cheaper than a case of club soda. He was short and scrawny, with a smirk where his smile should be. His greatest asset was an invincible certitude, which he used to hypnotize the ranchers on whose land the mineral rights had expired. After the major oil companies had extracted all the easy stuff, leaving behind fields littered with abandoned equipment and rusted pump jacks—orphaned wells, they were called, good for nothing, even the stock ponds were contaminated so you couldn't run cattle—Odell Peeples would show up, persuading the landowners that enough leftovers remained to make a modest meal. Figuring their fields were played out, ranchers sold their rights for squat. They hadn't heard about a new technique called hydraulic fracturing, but Peeples saw that a revolution was coming, and the best way to find oil and gas was to look where it had been before, in the Permian Basin, America's Saudi Arabia. In 1998, with the first fracked well to turn a profit, the S.H. Griffin No. 4, in the Barnett Shale formation in North Texas, major oil companies returned to the Permian like old lovers, eager to squeeze petroleum molecules out of the ground with this powerful and nearly infallible technique, only to find Odell Peeples holding the mineral rights. He made so much money so quickly he got bored with it. All he had to do was follow the same formula of acquiring rights in abandoned fields, places such as Sprayberry and Eagleford, names that were legend in the oil business, and his portfolio ballooned from millions to hundreds of millions. He was just getting started.

In oil field parlance, Peeples was "working upstream," where the oil and gas were discovered and pumped. Midstream, the pipelines carried the product downstream, to the storage tanks, petrochemical plants, and refineries where crude oil was processed—2.6 million barrels a day. Different qualities of crude determined its use: The lighter, or less dense, variety was easily distilled into high-value products, mainly gasoline, jet fuel, and diesel; the heavier crudes, contaminated with sulfur and unwanted dangerous chemicals, required more expensive processing. What wasn't turned into fuels or asphalt was transformed into plastics, resins, dyes, rubbers, paints, coatings, fertilizers, pesticides. The manifold uses of petroleum and its by-products testified to the ingenuity of the engineers who learned how to turn petroleum molecules into the foundation of the industrialized world.

In December 1998, oil prices dropped again, to twenty dollars a barrel, and Peeples decided to move downstream. He picked up a refinery and a couple of petrochemical plants in Pasadena, just outside of Houston, the heart of the immense petroleum complex. Ten years later, oil prices reached $180 a barrel and Peeples was making serious money. He became a billionaire when that really meant something.

He also inherited a problem. Every day there were illegal releases of chemicals from the complex. Some were flared off like candles on a birthday cake; others were unseen but no less dangerous. A gray, noxious, stinking haze overlay the whole area, and the slightest wind fanned airborne chemicals into Houston and nearby communities, carrying what Mr. Peeples liked to call "the smell of money."

Thousands of people in Houston and surrounding Harris County died prematurely every year because of industrial pollution. One study, by the Episcopal Health Foundation, found a twenty-one-year gap in life span between residents of River Oaks, in the western part of Houston where Peeples had his mansion, and Galena Park, just across Buffalo Bayou from his main refinery. Harris County tried to impose regulations on the polluters, imposing significant fines, but one of Greg Abbott's first actions as governor, in 2015, was to sign a law limiting the ability of local governments to police the polluters. This was done, Abbott said, to reduce "the regulatory burden that drives up the cost of doing business." Meantime, the Texas Council on Environmental Quality had been defunded year after year to the point of being emasculated as a regulatory agency. The petroleum industry gratefully contributed millions to the governor every year.

A common affliction among billionaires is the belief that money equals wisdom. To share his abundant opinions, Mr. Peeples started his own radio station. You could scarcely escape his high-pitched nasal voice, with a residual Boston accent he never shook, denouncing all forms of government as infringements of liberty. He was easy to imitate and often mocked, but that was a homage to his ubiquity. In Mr. Peeples's ideal world, Texas would return to the days when women stayed at home, homosexuals were in hiding, Christianity was unquestioned, the income tax didn't exist, and titans like himself were unchained by law or regulation. With L.D.'s help, much of that agenda had already been enacted. Gun laws were abolished, along with abortion. School libraries were purged of controversial books and teachers were put on a leash. It was surprisingly easy to turn back the clock when there was so much money to spread around.

The waiting room in Mr. Peeples's office was filled with supplicants when L.D. arrived. He recognized Sister Minnie, the televangelist, who could always be counted on to deliver a sermon that blessed one of Mr. Peeples's enterprises, including hormone therapy and a vitamin supplement business. Among the items dispensed was colloidal silver, good for almost any ailment from constipation to cancer, although it had a tendency to turn the patient permanently blue. In fact, Sister Minnie's complexion faintly resembled a robin's egg.

Mr. Peeples's broadcast was being aired in the waiting room for everyone's benefit. It was a rant L.D. knew well—gay marriage: the work of the devil. L.D. had allowed himself to imagine that the culture wars in Texas were over. The fringe had won. Why couldn't they declare victory and relax? But as he listened to the broadcast, he realized the next battle was just over the horizon, and it was going to be ugly. "Where does it end?" Peeples cried. "First the liberals turn a blind eye to the bold depravity of the homofascists"—his word for members of the gay community—"then they appease them; then they change the laws to let men marry men and women marry women. But one law they can't change—they can't change God's law! Don't forget that, ladies and gentlemen. Nothing the U.S. government has done can change the fact that our country is in flight from the Lord. If these homofascists have their way, sodomy will not only be condoned, it will be mandatory! They won't rest until they gain control. Keep this in mind: homosexuals can't reproduce. They have to *recruit*. They have to *groom* . . ." And so on.

As the ads for Peeples Products ran at the end of the show, an assistant approached L.D. with the news that Mr. Peeples was ready to see him. The assistant led him through the Hall of Heroes, a vast and eccentric collection of memorabilia spanning oil, politics, and media, with a fascist slant. Suspended from the ceiling was the reconstructed airplane in which Charles Lindbergh accidently plowed into a hardware store in Camp Wood, Texas, in 1924. Lindbergh's visage was present in bronze, along with accounts of his adoration of Germany in the lead-up to World War II. Among the heroes in bronze were Torkild Rieber, the former head of Texaco, who secretly supplied the Nazis with oil; Pappy O'Daniel, the flour salesman who pioneered radio as a political medium, becoming one of the worst governors and, after that, worst senators Texas ever had; and of course, Rush Limbaugh, who had added considerably to Mr. Peeples's fortune when his show began running on the Peeples Network.

L.D. could tell that Mr. Peeples was in a sour mood. "*Fine young man*," he said, spitting out the syllables as L.D. came in. He was quoting L.D., who had described Sonny Lamb in those very words when he used Mr. Peeples's money to get Sonny elected. "You said he could be trusted."

"He made a mistake," L.D. admitted. "He wanted to show his

independence. It's nothing to worry about. The bill will never get to the floor, I've made sure."

"He's trying to rob my bank, Mr. Sparks. All of this"—Mr. Peeples gestured with his arms outspread, taking in not only the office and its precious artifacts but also, by implication, the entire Peeples empire that lay within and without—"that *fine young man* wants to get his hands on. Well, he can't have it! Does he understand that, Mr. Sparks?"

"Yessir. I'm sure he does."

"You make it clear to him. On one side—our side—lies profit and glory; on the other, disgrace and ruin. Put a noose around his neck, Mr. Sparks. Let him contemplate the alternatives. We paid for him! He belongs to us! A little gratitude is all we ask."

"I'll straighten him out. That's a promise."

Mr. Peeples stared at L.D. with his dark, beady eyes squinched as if he were trying to poke a hole into L.D.'s subconscious, where the real truth resided. Finally he sat back. "Very well. I expect you will. Let us pray together, Mr. Sparks."

Mr. Peeples took L.D.'s hand and closed his eyes. He prayed for wisdom and courage to fight the sinners and the heretics and the homofascists until the world the Lord created was purified. That, in essence, was the assignment that L.D. knew awaited him in a presentation folder Mr. Peeples slid across the desk. The Lord's battle was always being fought in the Texas Legislature.

★

"What's your dog's name?" Sonny asked Ezer, as they walked around the Capitol grounds. Ezer relied entirely on the dog to guide him. It reminded Sonny of his mare, Rosebud, who always seemed to know where he wanted to go.

"This is Honey." She was a Labrador retriever, leading the way down the sidewalk under the giant sycamores, which were just beginning to bud out. Honey's left ear twitched when she heard her name, but she didn't take her mind off her job. She was constantly patrolling, her head moving side to side, taking it all in. There was a tree limb down from a storm the night before, which Honey led them around before Sonny could race ahead to remove it.

"She's a hard worker, I can tell."

"Is this a good spot?" Ezer asked.

"Looks fine to me. Just grass for about ten yards on either side."

"Okay, Honey, poop time," Ezer said.

Understanding the command, Honey stepped off the sidewalk. No sniffing around, all business. Ezer traced the arc of Honey's backbone, so when she finished her business he was able to scoop up the dropping in a plastic bag. "Mission accomplished," he said. "Now, let's talk about your bill."

"Everybody says it's dead even before arrival," said Sonny. "People aren't just opposed to it, they're hostile."

"So why does it mean so much to you?"

"Because it makes sense and I don't see any alternatives."

"First principle of game theory is figuring out who the players are and what they want. There must be a reason people resist your idea."

"Money."

"That's all?"

"We estimate it's gonna cost like ten billion dollars over time."

"That's a strong move. So what's your counter?"

Honey led Ezer to a trash can, where he dropped the poop. This was an amazing dog.

"Well, I don't have ten billion dollars."

"But the state of Texas does, in its rainy-day fund."

"That's a good point."

"And there must be a cost of not desalinating the aquifer."

"Huge cost."

"More than ten billion?"

"Whole lot more. It's the end of the ranching industry in West Texas."

"So it's a cost-saving measure."

"Gosh, Ezer, I'm liking this game theory stuff."

"You need allies. People who would lose money if you don't do it, or make money if you do. Another thing. You gotta know the odds in order to figure your strategy. How many bills were introduced last session and how many passed?"

"Maybe eight thousand introduced in both chambers, and about fifteen hundred passed."

"Uh-huh, that means the chances for any bill getting passed is one in five point three. To put that in context, that's about the same odds as a man your age having genital herpes."

Sonny was impressed. "How do you keep those figures in your head?"

"I wrote a paper on romantic odds and the game of love. It's a way of understanding the real world versus the world we imagine we live in. For instance, the odds of a woman getting pregnant after having sex with a condom are one in a hundred and forty-two. That's the same as a major-league ballplayer hitting a triple on his next at bat."

"Eventually the odds will catch you."

"And the chances that a man didn't bother to use a condom on his last date are close to fifty percent. Probably higher in Texas, which leads the nation in teen pregnancies."

"Do you know anything about the odds of success for fertility treatment?" Sonny asked casually.

"What's the age of the woman?"

"Let's suppose thirty-five."

"A little less than forty percent conceive, and about thirty percent result in a live birth. It goes downhill quickly after that."

Sonny didn't say anything. The odds sure weren't in their favor.

★

When you drive into Huntsville on I-45, you pass the sixty-seven-foot-tall statue of Sam Houston, with a scarf at his neck, he was such a dandy, and a cane to compensate for his injuries during the Indian wars. Prisoners are tending cotton in the vast fields, watched by guards on horseback with shotguns, right out of *Cool Hand Luke*. There are seven prisons in Huntsville, and one of them, the redbrick

Walls Unit, occupies more than fifty acres in the middle of downtown, like a fortification from ancient times, formidable and frightening and meant to be so. It's where the executions take place. More people have been put to death inside Walls than in any other facility in the U.S., and yet even in Texas the number of executions has been dropping for years. Fashions change, but meanness of spirit remains. No more last meals for the condemned, or air conditioning in most of the prisons, where every summer a few inmates are executed inadvertently by heatstroke.

Despite its ghoulish history, Walls was a medium-security facility, housing robbers, gangsters, auto thieves, sex offenders, prisoners who were scheduled for near release—and Sonny's dad, who is part of a grand tradition: the first prisoner ever incarcerated inside those towering walls, in 1849, was William G. Sansom, also a cattle rustler.

Sonny was used to the procedure. He stood below one of the guard towers; a tin can hauled up his car keys and driver's license. After he was cleared, he entered the main door and was shown to a visitors' room that allowed contact. He had brought a hundred quarters, the maximum allowed, in a ziplock bag for his dad to use in vending machines. About a dozen families were sitting at round tables, many with children. At each table there was a man in stark white pajamas, the uniform worn by all Texas prisoners.

Jimbo Lamb was waiting. Against the bare white walls and prison pallor, his bright blue eyes appeared disembodied, like blueberries on unbaked pie crust, and you could tell he was thrilled; he'd been waiting three months for this, since the last visit before Sonny got elected. No doubt he had been boasting about it in the yard. Jimbo Lamb was not one to let an advantage go unpressed.

"Twenty-seven votes," his father said by way of greeting.

"How are you, Dad?"

"I coulda helped you with that," Jimbo said. "Got you into landslide territory."

"I'm sure you could. We were really short-handed in the campaign. But they don't ask about the size of your mandate when you walk into the Capitol."

"Well, they let you in, looks like. So tell me something I don't know."

"Pick your category, Dad. News, sports, family, weather, and whatever else." Sonny could tell that Jimbo was working up to something. His leg was jiggling and his blueberry eyes were wobbling in their sockets.

"I would say sex but I haven't had any in fifteen years. How are you in that department?"

"It's episodic."

"I thought you'd be mowing down the ladies in Austin, ain't that part of the deal?"

Sonny wondered what it was about his parents and their sexual fixations. "Doris is seeing the auctioneer in the sale barn," he said, as a kind of warning shot to keep a distance from the highly personal stuff.

"Oh, I know, she tells me everything."

Sonny was genuinely surprised by this. "She comes to see you?"

"Once a month. And it's a long damn drive, I can tell you. We got nothin' to hide anymore. I think she likes to visit 'cause I've got plenty of time and she still talks more than anybody I ever met." Jimbo signaled to one of the guards. "Hey, José, check it out—my son that I was tellin' you 'bout. Got elected senator."

José smiled and nodded at Sonny but did not leave his post.

"It's representative, Dad. Senators are the important ones."

"Yeah, well, doesn't hurt to promote yourself a little bit. Maybe one day you'll step up. I always told Doris you were political material."

This couldn't have been true.

The foreplay was coming to an end, as Jimbo wasn't interested in news of the world and Sonny was cautious about investing too much in this conversation. Jimbo was the kind of person that if he were drowning and you threw him a rope, he'd pull you in with him.

"Are you still making furniture?" Sonny asked. Jimbo had been in the woodshop for the last several years.

"Nope. Big news, they put me in the cemetery."

"How's that?"

Jimbo laughed. "I knew that'd get you. I'm working in the cemetery for prisoners, mowing and landscaping. It's not bad work. I like to prune. I guess you get older, they give you the choice jobs. Or maybe they just want me to get acquainted with my final resting spot. Gives a man a chance to think, I'll say that."

Jimbo began nodding like he was listening to music with a powerful beat. Sonny took it as a signal: Here it comes.

"Listen, Sonny, you gotta do me a favor. I wouldn't ask 'cept you're in a position to help, and Lord knows I need it."

"What do you want, Dad?"

"You don't need to use that tone. I'm just stating facts. The facts are I need help and you can help me."

"Okay, tell me what you want from me," Sonny said as evenly as he could.

"You gotta get me out of here."

Sonny nodded. This was a more ambitious ask than he expected but he wasn't really surprised. "And how do you see me doing that?"

"Tell the governor. Let him know I'm a new man. I've walked away from that old life. A good citizen now. I'd vote for him if I could."

Of course, Jimbo couldn't have any idea about how absurd his request was. He was asking a freshman House member to secure a pardon, which in Texas happened about as often as a summer snow in Houston.

"Dad, I don't know the governor, and more to the point, he doesn't know me. Or care."

"Just sayin', you meet him someday, and he asks if there's something he can do for you, all you do is say, 'Matter of fact, there is.' Isn't that politics?"

"I'll keep it in mind."

"There you go." Jimbo was nodding even more vigorously, until he suddenly stopped, as if the jambox in his head had run out of battery. "Here's the deal, Sonny. I don't want to die here. I've been here long enough. I was a cattle rustler, not a homicidal maniac. And some of them have walked out of here while I rot."

"Well, Dad, you'd have been out of here ten years ago if you hadn't pulled off that escape of yours. You had the authorities searching six counties. Helicopters, dogs, all that. It's expensive to track down escapees, and it scares people. No wonder they want you locked up."

"Fair point. I accept that. It was a mistake. But I've learned my lesson. I'll do anything. I'll behave. Just, you talk to the governor, okay?"

This was one of those moments where the truth had to be driven home. "Dad, I don't want you to think I'm ever going to do that. You'll spend day after day imagining I'm sitting in the Governor's Mansion, chewing the fat, and I'll talk him into letting you go. That is so far from reality. But I know you'll be fixed on it, and write me letters, and talk to the guards about how you're going to be out any day now. No. You've got two years left on your sentence. Don't try to escape. Just mow the grass and prune the roses and every day you'll get closer to release. False hope is worse than no hope. I'm not abandoning you, but I can't help you in the way you want. I'm not your ticket to freedom. All I can be is your son."

14

"Y'all certainly are prompt," Carl complained as he strolled in twenty minutes late for his own hearing, as chair of the Natural Resources Committee. "Polly, you can pass out the agenda," he said to the assistant clerk, a former hooker who had made herself indispensable.

Ten other members of the committee were seated on the horseshoe-shaped dais, tapping their pencils or making dinner plans for the rest of the week. The latter was a major task each day, as lobbyists let it be known which of Austin's finest restaurants might have an open credit card on file. The average poundage accumulated each session per member was a subject of constant complaint: not enough time to exercise; not enough willpower to pass up the pork chop.

The committee room exuded decorum and taste, despite being windowless and two floors underground. In the audience were lobbyists, along with tourists, retired folks, and homeless people, who came for the free entertainment, and several members whose bills, they hoped, would be under discussion. One of them was Sonny Lamb.

"As you can see, we've got a busy session ahead of us," Carl said as the members leafed through the agenda, "and we can speed things along by bringing noncontroversial items to the floor as soon as possible."

"Excuse me, Mr. Chairman?"

"Representative Lamb, I don't think I've asked for questions yet."

Sonny's jaw set and he got a look on his face that registered with Carl. "The chair recognizes the member from District 74," Carl sighed.

"Thank you, Mr. Chairman. I understand that H.B. 1341, Relating to the Development of Brackish Groundwater, has been referred to this committee."

"Yes, it has."

"I don't see it on the agenda."

"Well, it's not on the agenda."

"Well, where is it?"

"Well, you can find it in Appendix C."

Sonny turned to the back of the document and read the title for Appendix C. "'Bills for Future Consideration,'" he said. "What does that mean?"

"Why, Representative Lamb, I should think that would be evident."

"Yes, it is," Sonny agreed. "Evident as hell."

"If that little outburst is concluded, we will move to the first item of business," Carl said, "tax rebates for pipeline construction."

Sonny walked out of the committee room into his office and closed the door.

"Sonny?" Lola said as she stared into her phone. She was outside, on her horse, her cheeks glistening from perspiration, her eyes shadowed by her hat. A bandana snaked around her neck to mop the sweat. There's a reason cowhands dress like this. "Did you mean to FaceTime me?"

"I just needed to see you," he said.

"This isn't the best time. I can't believe I even got a signal out here."

"What are you doing?"

"We're cutting calves out of what remains of our herd."

"I sure miss you," he said.

"Is there something wrong or can this wait? We could FaceTime over dinner."

"I've got a thing tonight."

"You're keeping busy, then." When Sonny didn't respond, she asked, "What's wrong, Sonny?"

"My bill didn't even get a hearing in committee. It's dead and buried before it got out the gate. I feel like I just got here and I'm already done."

"Everybody told you that would happen."

"That's . . . true," he acknowledged. He had been hoping for some consolation. "I was fooling myself all along. I've been staying up half the night learning the rules—it's like a foreign language—trying to fit in, but most of these guys are lawyers, or multimillionaires, mayors, doctors, professional ballplayers, I'm just totally outclassed. What the hell was I thinking coming to this place? You were so right. I just wanted you to know. I should have listened to you. I'm sorry, that's the bottom line."

"Is that all?"

"Yeah, I guess."

"Now that you got that off your chest, you can quit feeling sorry for yourself. You belong there as much as anyone else."

Sonny had a hard time believing that. "I can't even remember why I ever thought I should do this," he said. "Or could."

"I want to show you something," Lola said. She held the phone up and slowly panned the view: the cows, the ranch hands, the rolling hills—the land, desolate and beautiful, a place both mythic and perishable, once so full of promise, now parched and troubled. The West was burning; a way of life was coming to an end.

Lola turned the phone on herself. "That's why you're there," she said.

★

Sonny hadn't followed the debate, nor had he, to his knowledge, ever met a transgender person, but one afternoon a delegation came by and sat in his office, along with Jane, who was taking notes. Sonny's signals were jammed, women being men and vice versa, it made him uncomfortable. He had no idea how to behave. He would never have taken the meeting if Wanda hadn't insisted.

"We fought the bathroom bill, and we won," said Dannika, a slender Black woman with braids and a diamond nose ring. She seemed to be the leader of the group. "But it's an unending war, believe me. Now they're trying to send our parents to prison."

Knowing that they were transgender made it somewhat easier to recognize them as such, but some were men with full beards and deep voices. The idea that they would walk into the ladies' room was crazy, he thought; and the women would set off a riot in the men's room.

"This is all new to me," Sonny admitted. "Can I ask you a question about the bathroom thing? Does anybody question you when you use a public bathroom?"

"Not after my breasts came in," said Dannika.

Another woman chimed in, "Before that, I'd just try to hold it."

"Or use diapers," said a man with chest hair poking through his shirt.

"The really funny thing is that I went to the men's room for nineteen years, and in all that time I never saw any genitals at all," Dannika said. "It's crazy, isn't it? And women are so much more discreet."

"What about locker rooms?" Sonny asked.

"As for me, I wouldn't go near one. I'm not sure I ever will. Right now, I'm nonbinary. There's really no place for me."

"The message we're trying to deliver, Representative Lamb, is that we're here," the bearded one said. "There are a million and a half trans people in America, and the numbers are increasing rapidly. Meantime, legislatures all over the country are picking on us in order to fire up the culture war."

"As I understand the proposed bill, it's designed to prevent children from transitioning before they are eighteen," said Sonny. "I can't see why that's a problem. Kids are too young to make such life-changing decisions."

"The attorney general charged my parents with child abuse when I started taking puberty blockers," said a Hispanic girl who looked to be in her late teens. "I mean, who's he? Does he know anything about me? Does he know how much my parents love me and have supported my decision?"

Dannika explained, "Puberty blockers essentially put the decision to transition on hold. It allows a person to grow up a bit and assess. We think it's a reasonable way to deal with a very confusing time of life for a lot of young people. It also prevents the onset of physical characteristics that can't be changed. I wish I had been allowed to do that."

"I gotta admit, this is hard for me," Sonny said. "Like, with those stories of men competing in women's sports. They've got to have an advantage."

"That may be true, and there's a lot of resentment on the part of cis women who feel they're being squeezed out of their sport," said Dannika. "Our feeling is that it shouldn't be a government decision. Leave it up to the schools or the leagues to arbitrate these things. Get it out of the political system. The opponents only want to demonize us."

The Hispanic girl said, "I don't want my parents to be punished for my decision. They shouldn't have to go to jail for loving me."

Then Dannika looked at Jane and asked, "How long have you been transitioning?"

"Two years," said Jane.

"Did you get the surgery?"

"Not yet. I'm still undecided."

Everyone in the group nodded. "It's a big step," said the guy with the chest hair.

"I'm taking it a day at a time," said Jane.

Sonny watched this exchange totally agog.

When the delegation left, Jane stayed seated and waited. "I should have told you," she said.

Sonny nodded. He was disoriented and uncertain of his ground. "Why didn't you?"

"I just figured you knew."

"How would I know?"

"Some people seem to be able to tell. Or maybe they knew me before. I always assume that people look at me and they still see John."

"John?"

"My birth name. But all my life I've had Jane inside me, and I finally decided to let her out."

"You sure fooled me."

Jane smiled. "I am a bit proud of that."

"I'm still confused about what I think. I don't want to dishonor your decision, or those people we just met with, but it really crosses wires with me."

"I'm not surprised," said Jane. "You're a conservative rancher from West Texas, just about the last person we'd expect to convert. All we're saying is, it's not your decision who we are or want to become. A lot of conservative members say they want to get government out of people's lives, but nobody feels that more than we do." Jane turned toward the shadowed light well. "I should resign. You didn't know what you were getting into. That was my fault, and I'm really sorry."

"That's the last thing I want," said Sonny. "But I do need you to be candid with me."

"Of course."

"We may not agree on everything, and I've got a lot of learning to do," Sonny said. "It's an adjustment, I gotta admit."

"You've got an open heart, that's the most important thing. It's a rare quality, I can tell you. When you make a choice like I did, windows open on everybody you meet, and it's not always a pretty sight. People feel free to say the most awful things, they would literally step off the sidewalk when they saw me coming—this was more in the past when I was just beginning to make the transition. Later on there was a lot of confusion about was I or was I not. Nowadays your reaction is more common. I'm beginning to be accepted as the woman I truly am. But this bill brings it all back up. I know we can't get your vote on this. I just wanted you to see that we're human beings, we've made decisions about our lives. Everybody is always talking about freedom, but when are they going to give us the freedom to be who we really are?"

★

That evening, the members attended Speaker's Night at the Broken Spoke, a cherished dance hall on South Lamar Boulevard, a relic of Old Austin now so eclipsed by towering condos that the sun rarely reached it. Asleep at the Wheel was singing "The Texas Hop," a new line dance that was sweeping through the honky-tonks:

> *Hidey ho, hidey ho*
> *Tip of the hat and say hello*
> *Kick up your heels and there you go*
> *That's how you do the Texas hop!*

Big Bob appeared to be in a fine mood. When the song was over, the speaker welcomed everyone. "Tonight's a time to just have fun and love on each other," he said. "We all know hard times are ahead of us, and a lot of tough choices. Sacrifices. Bitter losses. But let's not make it personal. Tonight, we're all friends. Remember, we're Texans, every last one of us, we're in this together, working to make our state better for one and all. So enjoy yourselves. Tomorrow we go back to the people's work."

When Big Bob came off the stage he walked right past L.D. without saying a word.

L.D. hadn't really expected a thank you, but he was chafed that he wasn't even acknowledged. Here was Big Bob having a high old time that he wouldn't be having if L.D. had left him alone to blow his brains out. It wasn't like Bob to dodge issues, no matter how personal. He waded right into them, headlong, thrashing out disagreements for as long as it took, that's what made him such a heroic legislator. To brush off an old friend who had saved your life was wildly out of character. Probably Big Bob had learned that L.D. had tried to get the speaker's troopers to secure his guns. Of course, a blast of wind from Big Bob and the troopers scattered like roaches when the lights come on. So much for that.

Sonny sat by himself at a table on the rail above the dance floor. There were some fair dancers out there, he observed. He missed the energy of being onstage, feeling the music course through him like electricity, watching as the beat commanded people to grab a partner and start to move. He missed it all. The joy. Nothing in his life had ever been as pure as that feeling. *How happy I might have been*, he thought.

Gilbert swung by Sonny's table to offer consolation. "That was rough going this morning in Carl's committee. We all have moments like that. Shake it off. You'll be back in the ring soon."

"Oh, that? It was only a temporary setback," Sonny said lightly. He didn't like people feeling sorry for him.

"*Setback?*" Gilbert exclaimed. "Carl just handed you your balls in a Happy Meal."

"If he thinks that's the end of it, he doesn't know who he's dealing with."

"You'll get another shot next session, champ." Gilbert patted him on the back and moved on, oozing pity. Nobody wanted to get too close to a loser.

At least when he was onstage, Sonny knew what he was doing. Music and politics did have some things in common, he reflected. The sorting process was brutal: only a few would ever rise to the top, and out of that number a precious handful were one-of-a-kind talents. The rest were lucky, pushy, or simply had enough money to hang in where others had to drop out to make a living. He could imagine a world in which the pols and the pickers changed places, where Nancy Pelosi was on the Grand Ole Opry and Dolly Parton was speaker of the House, or Lyle Lovett was a senator from Texas and Ted Cruz was a gospel singer for Joel Osteen. Ronald Reagan would have made a passable country music star in the Hank Williams mold. How much better the world might have been if Ray

Charles had been elected president and Donald Trump was an Elvis imitator in Vegas.

"Hey, cowboy," Angela said. She was done up in a pearl-button shirt arrayed with wildflowers, pressed jeans, and a pair of Luccheses. Every time he saw her she looked like she was headed to a photo shoot.

"The mighty hunter."

"That's me," she said. "I noticed you drinking alone and thought you might like some company."

"That's charitable of you."

Angela heard the bottom-of-the-well tone in his voice. "Tell me if you'd rather be by yourself."

"Am I that pathetic?"

"You do seem . . . not pathetic but . . . well, maybe a little."

The waitress came by and Sonny ordered another bourbon and branch. Angela was nursing a gin martini.

"What's got you so down?" she asked.

"It's too obvious to discuss."

He was so disconsolate that Angela put her hand on his and sat silent.

"I've gotta face the fact that I'm beat," he said. "It's like losing a game where you don't score any points at all."

"Sonny, you've got a lot more bills ahead of you."

"This is the one that got me into politics in the first place—my big, bright idea to conquer the drought and save West Texas. I still don't understand why people don't see that. It's hard not to take it personally."

"People respect you, Sonny. They're just scared of the enemies they'll make if they support any bill that stirs up the oil and gas lobby."

"Like Mr. Peeples."

"For example."

"Crops are dying, animals are dropping in the pastures, towns are drying up."

"I can see how much this means to you."

"But I'm getting no traction at all," he said, then gave her an appraising look. "Meantime, you really pulled off a hat trick with your bill. Sailed right through committee."

"Beginner's luck."

"People are noticing," he said. "You're making a mark. I don't know how you do it."

Angela laughed. "If you think this place is tough, you oughta try teaching middle school."

"Maybe you could give me a few tips."

"Maybe you could ask me to dance."

They took their place among the two-steppers circulating counterclockwise on the old wooden floor. It did not go unnoticed by L.D. Yes, other members were dancing together, but he sensed an absence of significance in those collegial encounters. Some were better dancers—women with their swirling skirts and men as confident as matadors, with a bottle of Dos Equis in their back jeans pocket—but Sonny and Angela caught your eye. They fit together. *Something could come of this*, L.D. thought. After all, the first rule of fucking a guy is to figure out his weak points and then let him fuck himself.

★

"There's something else we need to talk about," said Wanda, as Sonny came into the office the next morning. "Where do you stand on voting rights?"

"I'm in favor of voter ID," said Sonny. "Other than that, I think we should make it easy for everyone to vote."

"You know that's not the goal of the party."

"I suppose that's true, but I don't know where that's coming from. It's not democratic."

"Well, no, it's not, but that's the point," said Wanda.

"They want to bend the system in their direction," said Sonny. "That's part of the political process, as far as I can tell. Democrats do it too, right?" Jane started to say something but stopped. Sonny asked her to go on. "You said you didn't know where this was coming from, and I think you should realize that there's a secret agenda behind many Republican officeholders, especially in Texas. Have you ever heard of dominionism?"

"Dominionism?"

"It's a strain of theology preached by Rafael Cruz, the senator's father, although it's not original with him. At the end of days, Pastor Cruz prophesizes, there will be a transfer of wealth to the righteous, followed by the acquisition of cultural and political power that will lead them to take control of society and prepare for the return of Jesus. For this to happen, there's a checklist called the 'Seven Mountains Mandate'; that is, the seven areas of society that true believers must control to bring on the End of Days—family, religion, education, media, entertainment, business, and government. The abortion laws are seen as defense of the family. They hate the secular media; that's one reason Trump was so popular with them. So when they start restricting voting rights, their aim is to consolidate total control, not just over government, but all of society."

"That sounds a little whacko," said Sonny.

"Crazy ideas can turn into crazy public policy," said Wanda. "History is one long struggle for sanity."

"Especially in Texas," said Ezer.

"The biggest thing right now among the dominionists is their war on public education," Jane added. "That's why the leadership in the Senate is pushing bills to get school vouchers, that's why they threaten school librarians. They believe that public education is a tool of government to brainwash and corrupt schoolkids with secular humanism and Marxism. Their end goal is to replace public schools with private Christian ones. It's all a part of a plan to turn Texas into a theocracy."

"I don't think that'd go down well in my district or any rural area," said Sonny. "Our public schools are the center of our communities, by far the most important institutions we have in small towns."

"Just listen to Lieutenant Governor Patrick. He and many of our state leaders believe democracy is an impediment to achieving their goals. And who's going to stand in their way? Not the governor, that's for sure. A lot of the members fall in line because they're afraid of being primaried, even very conservative Republicans. I mentioned Texas Scorecard. It's backed by fracking billionaires—mainly, Tim Dunn and the Wilkes brothers—who will go to any lengths to bring lawmakers to heel. Then there's Mr. Peeples, who should be chained to a tree on a desert island. Instead, he's broadcasting his bigoted nonsense on the most powerful channel in the state. I could name a few more, but they all have the same goal: to impose fundamentalist Christian rule by seizing absolute control of the Republican Party."

"And the members stand for this?" Sonny asked.

Now Wanda spoke. "Sonny, you have to understand the one emotion that controls the Texas Legislature. It's fear. Yes, there have been courageous legislators who stood against these tyrannical forces, but they're gone. The best people. I'm not saying that the members who remain are cowards. They're working within the system. They test the limits. But they know if they cross the line, it's over for them."

"Why is this coming up now?" Sonny asked.

"The Freedom Caucus has filed a voucher bill, one of Carl Kimball's brainstorms. You're going to get a lot of pressure on this one. It could be a make-or-break vote."

Sonny asked Ezer what he thought. "The ultimate object of the game is to keep playing," he said.

★

The following evening L.D. invited Angela up to his office on Congress Avenue so she could behold the view. An unnervingly lifelike LBJ hologram greeted her when the elevator opened, like an emissary from the spirit world. "The presidency is like being a jackass in a hailstorm," Lyndon said. "You've got to just stand there and take it."

As L.D. stirred a pitcher of martinis, Angela examined the trophy wall, which was covered with photos of L.D. standing among the greats. Here he was with a tennis racket among the entire Bush clan at Kennebunkport. As a Boy Scout shaking hands with Ronald Reagan. Sharing a laugh with Karl Rove at the Gridiron dinner. No family pictures whatsoever, she noted, a life wiped clean of personal entanglements. Or merely hidden.

"So this is what real power looks like," Angela said.

"You do get a little jaded up here," L.D. said gaily.

"I can imagine."

"While you're saving your face, you're losing your ass." This was Lyndon again.

"Don't worry, he'll go to sleep in a bit," L.D. said as he handed Angela a drink. "Sapphire martini with a twist, I believe?"

"What are you, the KGB?"

"I keep my eyes open. Helps me know what people want. My business is to help them get it."

"Like a personal shopper," said Angela.

"I'm so pleased you see it that way. Cheers."

L.D. steered her to the wall of glass overlooking the Capitol. "Notice the nighthawks circling round the dome," he said. "They like to perch on the Goddess of Liberty. Always reminds me of buzzards circling over roadkill. Here"—he handed her a pair of binoculars—"take a look."

Angela stared at the statue with the upraised lone star. It was copiously covered in bird shit. "Kinda hideous when you see her up close like this."

"Her features are crude, are they not? Like a Neanderthal, in my opinion, but lovely if you're viewing her from the ground. Like many things in politics, she's best examined from afar."

Angela took a sip. It was a perfect martini, so rarely done well. She was playing it cool but buzzing with curiosity about what L.D. was up to. It crossed her mind that he might have slipped a date rape drug into her drink; there were dozens of men in the Lege she wouldn't put it past, but she never got that vibe from L.D. He seemed sexually antiseptic. It wouldn't have been entirely surprising if he was powered by artificial intelligence. But he clearly had an agenda.

"Things were a lot simpler back in the day," L.D. was saying. "A new generation is coming along—people like you. Different goals. Different constituencies. Some folks say it's time to recalibrate. Consider my options."

"You're thinking about stepping aside and letting younger people get a shot at your job?"

L.D. chuckled. "Don't get your hopes up. I'm gonna die with my spurs on."

"Still, it must be concerning. You get to an age. You see the world moving on." She paused and looked him boldly in the eye. "Without you."

L.D. smiled. He was not one to be thrown by a challenge. "I'll let you in on a little secret. The only thing harder than gaining power is letting it go. Every generation comes along with new ideas. First order of business is to push the old guard out of the way. I thought so when I was like you, green and hungry and ready to sweep away the past. But some things never change. The eternal verities. People go into politics because they want something. When I first came up, they used to say, 'There ain't but three reasons a man gets into politics: money, pussy, or power.' That's changed somewhat as women came along. The question is, what does Angela want?"

It was impressive how adroitly he turned the conversation to be about her. L.D. remained an enigma. "Isn't there a category for doing good?" she asked.

"Maybe at the Salvation Army."

Angela took another sip. She was feeling the need to be cautious, but uncertain of her ground. Who was this guy? Why did he take such an interest in her? "I think things are more complicated than that."

"Could be," L.D. said. "Money and sex are rather simple, if that's what you're after. But power—ah, power. That's the nectar of the gods. That makes you a lot more dangerous. A lot more like me."

"I know you mean that as a compliment."

"Let me ask you something. What percentage of your constitu-ents are on food stamps?"

"Thirty-two percent, highest in the state."

"Unemployed?"

"The census says 10.4 percent, but it's closer to 18, counting the ones who've stopped looking. Single-parent homes, 40 percent. Dropouts, 28.2 percent. Do I represent a lot of people who have been failed by the system? Yes, I do."

"And you want to change that."

"I am *going* to change that."

"How?"

"I'm glad you asked that question! I have a whole legislative platform—"

"A suitcase full of bills," L.D. interjected. "Year-round class-rooms. Day care. Homeless shelters. Not to mention your maternal health bill. And you know what's going to happen to all those bills? Not a goddamn thing."

He said it with such finality that Angela was shocked into silence. For an instant, L.D. had dropped his mask and allowed her to take the full measure of his power. The message was that her future was entirely in his hands. All of her defenses—her beauty, her youth, her mother's legacy—were beside the point. L.D. was stronger. She could accomplish nothing if he stood in her way. This was all con-veyed with a smile.

When she finally spoke, her voice squeaked. "I thought you were going to help—"

"The hunting trip was a favor, a little taste, just to show you how it's done. Anything else, you have to earn."

"You'd make a great drug dealer, you know that?"

"Remember, you and me, we're birds of a feather, like yonder nighthawks, beautiful birds of prey. You can fool your constituents, you can fool your colleagues, but you can't fool L. D. Sparks. There's a door you've been banging on your entire life, but you can't get in. Somebody holds the key. I have it. I have the key. I can let you in."

Angela was transfixed. "What do you want from me?"

"Turns out, I need a favor, too."

"Money, pussy, or power?"

L.D. smiled at the gibe. "I need a little help with Sonny Lamb."

"I hardly know him."

"Let's say it's an educated guess on my part. I think you can help me. I have a bill I want you to sponsor. It's sure to pass. You'll have your first victory."

"That's all?"

"It's a modest request, as I said. I'm betting that Sonny will vote for it if you speak on its behalf. I'm rounding up votes. Sonny's would be meaningful."

"A vote on . . ."

"Solid waste disposal."

That stopped her. Was this some kind of Tony Soprano thing? "I haven't read the bill," she said cautiously.

"No need to. One of those little bills nobody cares about."

"Apparently you do."

"I'm just running up the score. The bigger the win, the happier my clients are."

"I'll take a look at it."

"Just introduce the bill on the floor, no harm done, a good cause, in fact. You help me, I'll help Angela help her poor, unemployed, non-English-speaking constituents. Sound fair?"

★

"The House will consider H.B. 29, Highway Improvements," Big Bob said, gaveling to silence the side talk in the back of the room. "Representative Kimball will explain the bill."

Carl moved to the front mic. "Thank you, Mr. Speaker. Subsection b of the Transportation Code, as amended by House Bill 29, would be reenacted to redefine taking, as previously discussed in committee . . ."

Carl was an absolute genius at putting people to sleep. He cast a soporific fog throughout the chamber with his first mention of the Transportation Code. Angela caught herself yawning.

". . . payment and security of said bonds to be made under an agreement with the local transportation authority as provided for by Subchapter A, Chapter 362 concerning highway surfaces . . ."

You could hear eyelids slapping shut like a domino chain.

". . . and I believe that sums up the main elements of this routine maintenance bill, which was approved in committee in its entirety. Respectfully move passage."

"I want to thank the member of the committee for acting so swiftly," Big Bob said. "Questions and amendments from the floor, hearing none—" The speaker hadn't even taken a breath as he raised the gavel.

"Mr. Speaker?"

The question rose from the back of the room. That anyone would bother to speak on behalf of a road repair bill was practically unprecedented. With the gavel still poised to fall, Big Bob sought the source of the obstacle to the speedy flow of legislation. The bigger shock was that it came from a new member. Freshmen were firmly discouraged from approaching the back mic, where questions are posed and amendments suggested. You wouldn't get arrested, but it was poor form. "Mr. Lamb?" Big Bob said, puzzled at the breach of protocol. "For what purpose does the member rise?"

"Mr. Speaker, I offer an amendment to H.B. 29."

Eyelids cracked open. Carl looked at Sonny in disbelief. "Objection, Mr. Speaker! We've already closed discussion."

"I beg the chair's indulgence," Sonny said.

"We've had discussion," Big Bob said irritably. "We are now moving to a vote." The gavel fell. "Clerk will call for the vote."

"Point of order, Mr. Speaker!"

The chamber by now was fixated on the greenhorn at the back mic. "Once again, the chair recognizes the persistent member from District 74." It was clear from the tone of the speaker's voice that this impertinence better have a point.

"I refer to Section 22, Article 3, of the Texas Constitution concerning elected officials: 'Disclosure of private interest in any proposed measure—'"

There was a collective gasp in the chamber.

"Mr. Speaker, please!" Carl implored. "It sounds as if this member is making personal accusations."

"Mr. Speaker, I only wish to ensure that the legislation before us does not have the unintended consequence of bringing private gain to members who may be unaware that H.B. 29 limits construction bids to the counties wherein the work is done."

"The counties!" Big Bob said, awakening to the possible implications. "Please approach. You too, Carl."

Sonny and Carl met at the base of the rostrum, where they had a clear view of the enraged features of Big Bob Bigbee. "What's goin' on here?" he demanded.

Sonny explained. "Sir, I was reading the bill last night and wondered about that limitation. Was it possible that the bids might favor particular contractors? So I looked at the counties involved and I realized there was only one asphalt contractor in Corsicana, in Navarro County."

"Interesting point," said Big Bob, "but what does that have to do with private gain for the members?"

"The name of the contractor is Carl Kimball Jr."

Big Bob's nostrils flared. His eyebrows protruded, as if his reddened face was too hot to cling to. Such was the countenance that Carl had to deal with. "What are you tryin' to pull here, Carl?"

"Nothin', Big Bob! It was an oversight, that's all—"

"Oversight my flaming ass," the speaker said. "This is un-Texan."

Carl visibly wilted. There was no greater condemnation.

"How are we gonna fix this?" Big Bob demanded.

Sonny waved a piece of paper. "The amendment I was gonna offer expands the pool of bidders to—"

"Lemme see it."

Big Bob quickly scanned the document.

"If you let me propose—" Sonny said.

"Hell, no!" Big Bob thundered. "Here, Carl, you do it. You stick this in your own bill. Don't let somebody else clean up your damn mess."

A shaken Carl walked back to the front mic. It was as if his clothes were moving and dragging his reluctant body along. "If the speaker please," he said, scarcely audible, "I'd like to offer an amendment to H.B. 29 . . ."

Sonny passed Angela's desk on his way to his own. "Sonny!" she whispered. "What was that?"

"Payback," he said.

Angela wanted to hear more, but this moment presented an opportunity. "Listen, I'm about to present a bill on solid waste. Sure would like your support."

"Solid waste, no kidding. I didn't know you were interested."

"Passionate is the word," she said. "Can't get enough of it. Yum."

"Well, in that case, I got your back. I'm sure it's a worthy bill."

"Would you be willing to cosponsor?"

"You bet! We'll make it bipartisan."

"Thanks, Sonny. You made my dreams come true."

The clerk read out the next bill and Angela took to the front mic. "Mr. Speaker, members, House Bill 4216 approves a revenue-producing contract to move biosolid sludge from the city of New York to be safely deposited in a remote rural location. I ask the members' support."

"Would the gentle lady yield for a question?" Gilbert asked.

"I yield," she said to the leader of the Democratic caucus.

"Is it true that this is your first bill to come before the House?"

"Yes, it is, Representative Delgado."

"And further to the point, you bring before us a bill to carry sludge by train from the city of New York to the great state of Texas. Members, what shall we call this bill?"

In unison, the members cried, "The Poo-poo Choo-choo!" There were train whistles and lots of *choo-chooing*. The speaker indulged this horseplay. Angela knew that freshman legislators were often hazed when they introduced a bill, so she joined in, motioning like a train conductor pulling the whistle cord. She began to see the bargain she had made with L.D. as part of the fun. Why had she been so rocked by that experience? He was just setting her up for this raucous initiation.

The gavel finally fell. Gilbert concluded by saying, "You're a terrific new member. Welcome to the Texas House!"

"Mr. Speaker, I move passage!" Angela cried exultantly.

"All in favor signify by saying aye."

"AYE!"

"Opposed?"

"Nay." That was Lurleen, for reasons she did not disclose, but which had to do with unsanitary transport.

"The bill is approved," Big Bob said. "Congratulations, Representative Martinez, you just made your first law."

When Angela returned to her desk, she found Ernestine looking at her sideways. "What?" said Angela.

"I smell something. Mmm-hmm, it sure smells like something. Like a deal that just went down mighta had a little sludge on it."

"I have no idea what you're talking about."

"I've been here since God was a child. You just get a feeling when the room tilts. And something happened. That's how it smells to me."

15

Domino night, and Big Bob was still in a state. The usual players were there, but they were subdued, cautious, not making big moves, as if they were in a cage with a wild animal, let's say a cobra, ready to strike but undecided who would be the first to taste its fangs.

"Carl, you greedy son of a bitch," he began.

"It was Polly," Carl protested. "She's still getting the hang of the place. She'll learn to do her due diligence."

The other players stole glances at each other. They all knew what Polly was hired to do, and it wasn't writing legislation.

"That little greenhorn you were laughing about just took you apart," Big Bob said appreciatively. But he wasn't finished with Carl. "Now tell me you talked to Lurleen about her bill."

"I tried! Lurleen nearly bit me in half."

"Carl, you double-dealing weasel-brained catfish fucker! It's gonna take down the whole session."

"Anyway," said Carl in his defense, "it has Mr. Peeples behind it, so whaddaya gonna do."

Big Bob turned to L.D., who had been caught chuckling over the catfish fucker remark. "Are you responsible for this atrocity, L.D.?"

"Bob, it's nothing to worry about."

"A little errand Mr. Peeples put you up to," Big Bob concluded.

"It'll never get through the courts," L.D. assured him.

"The courts are changing, like everything else. Meantime, we're gonna make this damn homosexual bill the law in Texas."

"It hasn't passed yet."

"You know of a single Republican that'll vote against it? They can't be seen as being in favor. Can you envision the shitstorm that is gonna rain down on Texas?" When L.D. didn't respond, Big Bob thundered, "*Well, can you?*"

"It's gonna be bleak," L.D. conceded.

"Damn session is headed to hell and all you think about is Sonny's bill. That bill has about as much chance of passing as you takin' a dump on the moon."

"Carl," said L.D., seeking support wherever he could find it, "you have a coyote cross your pasture, what do you do?"

"Shoot him and hang him on the fence so the other coyotes get the message."

"Discipline," said L.D., "that's what this is about. Sonny has to learn a lesson."

Big Bob took a sip of ginger ale. "Gilbert," he said contemplatively, "you remember a sanctimonious little prick from Port Arthur who was gonna clean up the political process—till he got his ass vulcanized?"

"Hell, they come through here all the time."

"This ol' boy thought he was gonna be the next enchilada."

L.D. sighed. "Yes, Bob, you made your point. I know the fella you mean."

"Oh, you do? Whatever happened to that pig-headed SOB?"

"They say he got lucky. Once he learned the rules."

"That right? Maybe there are some rules he hasn't picked up on. Like the 'Don't fuck with Big Bob' rule. Ever heard of that one?"

"I know it well."

"Discipline," said Big Bob, "that's what this is about."

★

It was too late to put the brakes on Lurleen's bill. She stood at the front mic with an air of saintly certitude, like Joan of Arc arisen to block the slide of humanity into degradation and sin. This is the way her supporters on one side of the packed gallery saw her. On the other side were people who imagined Lurleen Klump as a rein-carnation of Hitler, or Stalin, or Joe McCarthy, or pick your right-wing villain. She was quickly becoming the most reviled figure in Texas politics, at least by the left, but this was a distinction sought and envied by their counterparts on the right. Texas had become a place where hatred was key to political advancement. The problem the Dems faced was that not a single one of them was enough of a threat to merit the hatred that would propel them into statewide office. And the GOP, after decades of dominance, their agenda long since enacted, was running out of issues. The energy was all on the fringe, where hatred needed to be continually refreshed and Queen Lurleen ruled.

She paused to take them in, her antagonists and supporters. No signs or placards were permitted in the chamber, but the way Americans currently adorned themselves politically conveyed their sentiments. Tongue studs, blue hair, pink bows, and men in drag on one side of the gallery, versus white supremacist haircuts, MAGA caps, Family Forum types, and evangelicals in suits or long dresses with Bibles in their laps. Some wore Texas flags draped around their shoulders. Tattoos were amply represented on both sides.

Lurleen was a tall woman but stood even taller in this charged moment. "Mr. Speaker, members, fellow Texans," she began. "Every God-fearing society faces forces of evil that wish to bring it down. House Bill 127 excludes sexual predators and agents of perversion from teaching in day cares, public schools, or schools chartered in the state of Texas; adopting children or supervising foster children; coaching or instructing music or other skills; participating in scout-ing activities, whether as scoutmaster, den mother, or scout; practic-ing medicine or dentistry on children, either as a doctor, dentist, nurse, orderly, or hygienist; and driving buses or taxis in which unsu-pervised children may be present. This bill will build a wall of law around our children so that the agents of perversion cannot twist their pliable young minds."

So far the gallery was relatively quiet, except for some groans and subdued applause. Nothing Lurleen had said was unexpected.

Sonny noticed his seatmate, Harold Morton, shaking his head and muttering under his breath. It wasn't entirely clear to Sonny what was so controversial. He and Harold hadn't talked about it, but who would want perverts dealing with children?

"Will the gentle lady yield for a comment?" Carl asked.

"I yield to the representative from Navarro County."

"I just want to congratulate you on this timely and important piece of legislation," Carl said, summoning his most sincere-sounding endorsement. "Every right-thinking Texan will surely support it. We will take back the state for families and for Christian values."

"Take back yourself, you Nazi creep!" someone yelled from the gallery, a lone voice in the restive audience.

Carl moved to stand beside Lurleen at the base of the rostrum, where other members were gathering in a show of support.

Sonny was surprised when Harold rose and slowly walked to the back mic.

"The chair recognizes the member from Montrose, Mr. Morton."

The audience was beginning to grumble. Harold waited until Big Bob gaveled them down. Then, instead of speaking, Harold applauded.

"Do you have a question, Representative Morton?" Lurleen asked.

"I'm just giving you credit, Lurleen. Behind a bill that pretends to protect children from pedophiles, you have crafted the most comprehensive piece of gay-bashing legislation that has come forward in any legislative body in the country."

This comment set off a roar throughout the gallery—cheers, boos, chants—the crowd had just been waiting to erupt. Big Bob pounded the gavel. "There will be order in the House!"

"Do you deny the intent of this bill?" Harold asked. "Why don't you spell it out plain and clear?"

Lurleen turned to Big Bob. "Mr. Speaker, the bill is what it says it is. Can we move to a vote?"

"There is a question on the floor," he replied.

Lurleen squared her shoulders and gripped the sides of the podium. She knew where this was headed. She was ready for it.

"Representative Morton, I will not deny a word of this bill. The moral fiber of the great state of Texas is under assault by a sophisticated and well-financed group of homosexuals—"

With this, the piñata of partisanship burst open and the design of the bill was revealed. People screamed curses and cheers, and few remained seated as Big Bob hammered the gavel again and again. Lurleen didn't even pause. "Homosexuals!" she shouted over the din, "whose lifestyle is an abomination in the eyes of the Lord!"

Amid cheers and boos a trooper dragged out of the gallery a protester who had ripped off his shirt to display the message painted on his chest: "FUCK THE FACISTS." Harold remained at the back mic, facing Lurleen, waiting for the pandemonium to subside. Despite the noise and the tumult, there was between the two of them a quiet recognition that this was an existential moment. This bill had the potential to define the future of the state. Everything about their backgrounds had brought them to this place. Harold saw the supporters crowding around Lurleen, and he imagined seeing his father among them. There was little question which side he would have been on.

More people were pulled from the gallery. Blows were exchanged. Several of the Family Forum types were loudly praying on their knees. Finally, the crowd subsided, mainly because they were dying to know what would happen next. Big Bob indicated that Harold still had the floor.

"Let me see if I understand the implications of this monstrosity," he said. "I'm an orthodontist. I straighten kids' teeth. Under this bill, every time I, as a gay man, treat a patient under the age of eighteen, I'm committing a Class B misdemeanor?"

"Correct."

"Lurleen, do you really want to put me in jail for being who I am?"

"What I want, Representative Morton, is to cause you to get some help."

"Well, then help me understand what I've done that deserves a ten-thousand-dollar fine and six months in jail for fixing buckteeth?"

"You have touched a child."

"With *these*?" Harold said, holding up his hands. "These hands? That have made thousands of children smile again?"

The gallery erupted again. Members stood at their desks shouting at each other, emotions hurtled around the room. It was impossible to hear the gavel, which finally broke under Big Bob's furious pounding. In all the commotion, Ernestine slipped over to Gilbert's desk and shouted in his ear, "Time to implement the plan! You think you can hold off the vote for twenty minutes?"

"Twenty minutes? No problemo."

Ernestine went around the well of the chamber, inconspicuously tapping certain members on the shoulder. One by one, they drifted nonchalantly out of the chamber, meeting up in the predetermined rally point, the patio rotunda called the Central Court, an enclosed outdoor area to which smokers often retreated or where conversations were held that might best remain unheard. Had the furtive lawmakers read the schedule of events, they would have found that the Central Court had been reserved by the Sweetwater Jaycees for their annual rattlesnake roundup promotion. The ground was asquirm with petulant snakes, irritated at having been rousted from hibernation. Jaycees in Kevlar boots wandered around poking the critters with poles trying to provoke a rattle. The snake handlers were thrilled to see such a surprising turnout of lawmakers.

"Get that disgusting thing out of my face!" Ernestine shouted at the Jaycee who had graciously offered to let her hold a five-footer. The lawmakers retreated to a far edge of the patio, which appeared to be snake free. "Here's the plan. Don't go home. Don't go anyplace familiar. Don't call your family, your call will be traced. Put your credit cards away. If you need money, stop at a cash machine."

As the lawmakers were tiptoeing through the rattlesnakes to make their escape, Gilbert remained in the chamber, standing at the back mic. "Will the gentle lady yield for a question?" he asked Lurleen. He seemed strikingly relaxed and immune to the hubbub. "I'm a car dealer in Three Rivers, so I hope you'll forgive me if this country boy finds your bill somewhat complicated, or not complicated but uh . . . intricate, I suppose, is the word. Finely tuned. Over my head, in any case. Would the gentle lady do me the favor of educating me on the biblical sources that you say underlie what is no doubt a historic piece of legislation?"

"I would be happy to do that, Representative Delgado, but we're trying to move to a vote."

"Please . . . humor me . . . Rep-re-sen-ta-tive Klump," Gilbert said, his stentorian voice slowing to present each syllable as a main course. "I must carry the message to my con-sti-tu-ents."

"Very well," said Lurleen, not really resisting the opportunity to preach this particular gospel. "We can begin with the Book of Leviticus."

Fifteen minutes later, she had arrived at I Corinthians, having crossed into the New Testament. Half the audience had drained from the gallery. "Here, Saint Paul specifically calls out the fornicators, the adulterers, and the homosexuals. In Timothy 1:8–11, Paul speaks of sodomites, whom he links to kidnappers, liars, and murderers."

Gilbert stole a glance at his watch. "Point of order, Mr. Speaker. I'm concerned that we may not have a quorum. Perhaps Representative Klump's brilliant exegesis has driven some of our less pious members from the chamber. I think we need a roll call."

Big Bob, who had been nodding off behind the rostrum, jumped to his feet and sized up the situation at once. "Quorum break!" he cried. "The sergeant-at-arms will summon the director of public safety and direct him to round up the absent members and present them to this chamber forthwith. Call! Call on the House! Lock the doors!"

Sonny saw what was happening and realized that he had to escape pronto. His desk happened to be near the back of the room, so he bolted through the door just before the trooper locked it shut.

★ 16 ★

"Sonny, it's your mother. Are you on your way to your appointment?"

"How did you know?"

"Lola and I talked about it."

"God, is there anything you don't talk about?"

"We're concerned about your state of mind."

"My state of mind is rattled. There's a quorum break and I had to make a getaway. Some folks prob'ly think I'm part of it. Meantime, I don't see that my appointment is any of your beeswax."

"There's where you're wrong," Doris said indignantly. "It is upmost on my list of concerns. I want a grandbaby. The only thing standing in the way is you doing your part."

"Let's not talk about this."

"You need to be in a relaxed state of mind when you go in there."

"You think getting into my business is going to help that?"

"Obviously, you're not doing such a hot job of it on your own," Doris said, adding, "I always thought there was something questionable about your level of sexual arousal."

"Mom! Who said that? I'm aroused all the damn time!"

"Well, how was I to know? We never talked about it."

"And we're never going to. Oh, shoot." A siren howled. "Darn it, Mom! You got me all riled up and now there's a cop on my tail."

"Blame me for everything, why don't you? I have sexual problems myself sometimes."

"I so much don't want to hear about it," Sonny said, hanging up. He pulled over and waited for the cop to knock on his window.

Officer Doolittle, shaped like a refrigerator, demanded license and registration. "I noticed your license plate," the trooper said. Sonny's plate number had an "SO" prefix, standing for "State Official," and then a number indicating the rank of the elected official, the governor being SO-1, the lieutenant governor SO-2, then the attorney general, the comptroller of public accounts, the state commissioners, the justices of the supreme court and the appeals courts (all of them elected, not appointed, in Texas), the 31 members of the Senate, and the 150 members of the House, at which list Sonny was the exact bottom, SO-208, the lowest-ranked elected state official in Texas. "Are you a member of the Texas House of Representatives?"

"I am."

"We've been ordered by the speaker to bring all escaped members back to the chamber."

"Honestly, officer, I know how it looks, but I'm not a part of this."

"You can tell that to the speaker. Sir, what's that you have in your lap?"

"What do you mean?"

"Sir, I see you hiding a bag," the trooper said, peering in the window to get a better look. "Do you mind if I ask what's in it?"

"I'm not hiding anything! It's just a bag of ice."

"Ice?"

Sonny held up the bag for inspection. Officer Doolittle stared at it. "That's really weird," he observed.

"It's a fertility thing," Sonny explained.

"No kidding. What's it do?"

"Cools off the sperm. You know, the Texas heat."

"Improves performance, that kind of thing?"

"That's what they tell me."

"Doesn't it shrink you up?"

"Yeah, I don't understand about that part."

"Learn something every day," said Officer Doolittle. "You're gonna follow me back to the Capitol, right? No funny business."

"Yessir."

As the trooper was walking back to his vehicle, Sonny's phone rang again. "Is he gone?" Doris asked.

"Yeah, he's gonna escort me—"

"Hit the gas."

"Mom!"

"You'll make it to the clinic before they find you. Go!"

"Mom!!"

"Go, go, go!" Doris cried.

Some irrational flashback to childhood seized control and Sonny hit the accelerator. His tires squealed as he raced off, leaving an incredulous Officer Doolittle watching him flee. He turned on his radio. "All units, escaped House member in red Ford 150 . . ."

★

The Alamo Courts in Lockhart was the designated hideout, chosen because of its proximity to a legendary barbeque joint, where Ernestine had stopped to pick up enough meat and fixings to satisfy fifty-one hungry members, the exact amount to prevent a quorum. Lloyd Johnson passed out the keys to the cabins. He was also in charge of the liquor, which meant that the representatives were well supplied. Overly so.

A spirit of gaiety arose from the picnic tables in the middle of the court, nursed along by the bottles of Mexican beer in a galvanized tub of ice and the extensive selection of spirits from Texas distilleries that Lloyd had curated. Despite the fun, Angela was agitated. The whole adventure seemed pointless to her. "Can I ask what we're supposed to be doing here?"

"Hiding," said Ernestine.

"I get that, but for how long?"

"Until the leadership is willing to force a deal on Lurleen's bill."

"And is that likely?"

"No."

"So we're basically just stalling."

"We're making a statement," Ernestine said. "Standing up for a principle."

"Stalling."

"If they catch a single one of us, they'll gain a quorum," said Lloyd, who had experienced several quorum breaks in his career, "but unless and until, they can't do a thing."

"And neither can we," Angela observed.

★

The sperm donation clinic was in an industrial zone in South Austin, amid a string of warehouses and shady storefronts, a part of town that had yet to give way to the tsunami of condos and office buildings that were obliterating everything that Austin used to be. The sign said "Conceivable Solutions." Apart from that clever hint there was no indication what was inside. Sonny parked some distance from the entrance in case someone, such as L.D., might have a private detective on his tail, or the state troopers would track him down and the location would be on his arrest form. Okay, neither of these things was likely, but Sonny wasn't taking a chance. He put on a pair of sunglasses, although it was overcast and threatening rain. He knew he was being irrational, but sanity was a little out of reach.

One other man was in the waiting room, also wearing sunglasses. They might have been blues artists. A receptionist sat behind what looked like a bulletproof sheet of plexiglass. There was a mousehole opening at the bottom. "Mr. Lamb?" she said too loudly. "You'll have to wait a moment till we get a room free."

Sonny sat down and tried to go through his email, but the signal was weak. The other guy was reading a *National Geographic* that must have come from the aughts. Eventually a surprisingly (considering the task at hand) elderly gentleman emerged with a proud smile on his face. He sported a natty driving cap and looked familiar. A nurse came to escort the guy reading the *National Geographic*. When the room was clear, Sonny asked the receptionist, "That fellow who just left, was that what's-his-name, the Nobel Prize winner?"

"I can't comment on that," she said.

"He seemed pretty pleased with himself."

The receptionist tittered. "You know we do accept donations for the sperm bank, and sometimes you get these celebrities who, like, sell their stuff," she said confidentially, but obviously bursting to talk about it. "They get paid a fortune! Our shoppers—the couples that are looking for the ideal donor sort of thing—they really go for the prestige. They visit our main office asking for lawyers or doctors, but when you show them, like, movie stars and prizewinners, they jump. Who wouldn't want Brad Pitt's stuff, you know? Not saying he's in our catalog. That's super confidential."

Sonny mulled this over. Was this where he and Lola were headed? Poring over a lineup of studs to see who would be the best replacement for him? If you were looking at such a catalog (assuming it existed), would you settle on a half-broke, half-assed rancher politician? It was too depressing to think about.

On the other hand, what if he had a son or daughter endowed with what's-his-name genius? Someone who could solve the mysteries of the universe. Cure cancer. Colonize Mars. Or maybe some great athlete, Kareem Abdul-Jabbar, say, and have a son seven feet tall, how would that feel? But how do you really know whose stuff it is, anyway? You just take their word for it. Or maybe what's-his-name is also a wife beater and general creep. Sonny wondered if there was a way of separating out the smart genes from what's-his-name and tall genes from Abdul-Jabbar and maybe Steve Jobs's business genes (possibly somewhere on file) into some kind of superstar package. That's gonna happen, he was sure. But when that day comes you can bet they won't be asking for my stuff. Not like there's a line forming now . . .

"Soooo," said the perky nurse as she opened the door to one of the deposit rooms, "we have some visual aids you might find useful. There's a stack of magazines. And you'll find a selection of videos on the computer with a wide range of options, depending on your predilections."

Sonny looked around. There was a desk with an office chair, a couch, and a plush La-Z-Boy recliner catty-corner to the desk. It was still partially reclined, probably from what's-his-name's rewarding experience. On an end table beside the La-Z-Boy was an old cassette tape player.

"That's a real antique," Sonny observed.

"I know!" the nurse said. "We keep thinking we'll throw it out, but many of our customers prefer it. Maybe it takes them back to adolescence. Maybe it frees up the imagination. Who knows what turns people on. Anyway, it's tried and true. You have several options to choose from. Each of them has been disinfected, in case you're worried about that."

Indeed, he could smell the Clorox wipes, the least erotic fragrance imaginable.

The nurse hesitated at the door. "You seem a little anxious."

"I'm fine."

"Keep the volume down so you don't disturb the other clients. The controls on the cassette player have gotten a little funky, but you'll get the hang of it. When you finish your business, make your deposit in the collection tube and set it in the cabinet outside my door. We'll send you the results."

As soon as the door closed, anxiety rushed in. Sonny leafed through the porn magazines, none of which he'd ever heard of, no *Playboy*s nor *Penthouse*s, these were hard core and funky. At the top of the pile was a magazine called *Dairy Queens*, which had a picture of a lactating woman shooting a jet of milk a remarkable distance. He tried the computer with its selection of videos, categorized by "predilections," as the nurse had accurately noted—anal, orgy, babysitter, there was even a channel for Mormon. It was depressing and ridiculous and not at all arousing.

Sonny could see why the cassette tape might be the better choice.

He locked the door and dropped his pants around his ankles. He set the collection tube on the end table, at the ready. The tape was already rewound. He leaned back in the La-Z-Boy and pushed Play.

"Hello, slugger," said a friendly, throaty voice. "Come on in and get comfortable. You look like you could use some relaxation, and I'm here to help. Just lean back and let me take control."

Sonny did as he was told. She seemed to know what she was doing.

"Oh, look at you! That's what I call a manly man! It makes me so excited. My lucky day when a big fella like you happens to drop in. Feel how strong you are! Oh, Daddy, it's so good, give it to me . . ."

Under the spell of this encouraging siren from the 1960s, who was probably dead now, Sonny began to relax. He closed his eyes and fantasized. He could envision her as a version of Lola, an unbuttoned cowgirl, teasing, pleasing, toying, pleading, so many images arose, fragmenting into erotic figments that were no longer Lola but portions of her, or others, pleasing female bits, nipples and calves and underarms, wisps of hair curling around a cute little ear, which he had noticed about the perky nurse, and then Angela burst in. Sonny had tried to keep her out of his fantasies, but she wouldn't be denied. There was so much to imagine. One could guess but never really know without seeing what was under those clothes, the smell of her—

Sonny's phone rang.

He fumbled with his pants to get the phone and accidently knocked the player off the table. "Hello?" Sonny said breathlessly.

"YES, DADDY, YES, DADDY, AHH, AHH, AHH . . . !"

That was the tape. Somehow the volume got turned up really high in the fall. "Just a minute," Sonny said loudly into the phone, trying to make himself heard. "I dropped something."

"YES, HARDER! HARDER! OH, YESSSS!"

"Sonny?" It was Harold. "Is this a good time?"

"OOOOHHH YEAH! POUND ME, DADDY!"

As he dove for the cassette player, Sonny tripped over the pants around his ankles. There was a vigorous knock on the door. "What's going on in there?" the formerly perky, now infuriated, nurse called out.

"GIVE IT TO ME, DA—"

Click. Sonny turned off the tape. "It's okay, it's okay," he said to the nurse, as calmly as possible. "It's all fixed now." He could hear her rustling outside the door, listening, then the sound of her walking away. He took a breath. "Sorry, Harold," he said. "You caught me at a bad time."

"Really? It sounded like fun to me."

"Can I call you back in a sec?"

"Okay, but it's important."

"Why? What's going on?"

"You know that waste disposal bill we voted on the other day? The preexisting agreement with the city of New York to transfer biosolid sludge?"

"The Poo-poo Choo-choo? What of it?"

"Do you know where they're disposing of it?"

"It was like some rural flatland two hundred miles from anyplace."

"Right. On a caliche substrate, minimal population density, less than ten inches of annual rainfall."

"Uh-oh."

"Afraid so."

"Presidio County."

"Your district."

"And I voted for it! I *sponsored* it! I am so screwed! I would never have done it if Angela—" He stopped himself. Just then, another call came in. "Harold, sorry, Lola's calling. I'll get back to you."

Lola's first words: "Sonny, do you know that there's an arrest warrant for you?"

"Man, it doesn't stop."

"Reporters have been calling."

"It's a crazy mix-up," Sonny said, not so reassuringly.

"They say you're involved with a bunch of escaped lawmakers. You better tell 'em what you been doing."

That would never happen.

"So, by the way, how did it go? Your appointment."

"Thumbs up," he said.

"Thanks, Sonny. I know it is hard for you, but it means so much to me."

The situation was, obviously, hopeless. Sonny pulled up his pants and reclined in the La-Z-Boy. His immediate problem was getting out of Conceivable Solutions without being totally humiliated. Was there, perhaps, a back door? He didn't remember one. A normal guy would be carrying his tube, brimming with his successful discharge—the fifty or a hundred million sperm swishing about like microscopic goldfish—and placing it in the cabinet outside the nurse's office like an Academy Award on the mantelpiece. But what do you do with an empty tube?

Sonny peeked out. There was nobody in the hall. There was no back door. It was now or never. He made his way as quietly as possible toward the nurse's office, terrified that she might suddenly pop out and observe his humiliating lack of production. He could hear the TV on in her office.

"PLACE YOUR TUBE INSIDE," said a sign on the cabinet door. Inside was one other tube, which must have been from the Nobel Prize winner. An impressive contribution, no wonder he was so pleased with himself. Sonny uncorked the tube and poured half of it into his own.

"Sir?" said the nurse. "Everything okay?"

Sonny jumped. "Yes!" he said too enthusiastically. "Just great!"

★

"More pizza, anyone?" Angela asked.

It was night, and time for the next meal. There was little else to do but eat and drink, especially the latter. All afternoon Lloyd had been concocting cocktails, which accounted for the giddy, out-of-focus conversations. Ernestine held up another slice of the pepperoni pizza. "I'm going to become a vegetarian as soon as I finish this."

Around this table of liberals many agreed that they had certainly overdone it on meat, and the way animals were treated was unjustifiable, especially factory farming, which was immoral, and what's more, grazing was a major contributor to global warming, because of farting. All these things they believed, but none would ever offer a single bill confronting any of these issues. The lure of pepperoni was too great. Nor would any of them ever become a vegetarian. But they endorsed the concept.

Suddenly, a pair of headlights turned off the highway and entered the Alamo Courts. The fugitives dove under the picnic tables or hid behind trees. The truck parked in the gravel lot. The headlights turned off. The door of the cab opened. Footsteps came toward them.

"Anybody here?"

"It's Sonny!" Angela whispered.

"Shhh!"

"Hello?" said Sonny.

"Maybe he wants to join us?" a voice from under the table muttered.

Finally Ernestine called out: "Sonny?"

"Where are you?" Sonny asked. "I can't see anybody."

"Can I ask why you're here?"

"There's a warrant out for me. Fleeing police custody."

That was an impressive excuse. Ernestine and several others caucused, then Ernestine demanded, "How did you find us?"

"Evidently somebody told Harold, and he let me know. He really appreciates what y'all are doin'."

"Did anybody follow you?"

"Pretty sure not."

There was another considered pause, then Lloyd said, "Welcome to sleepaway camp."

"You want a slice of pizza?" someone asked as lawmakers emerged from their hiding places. "I think we have an extra cabin or two." Candles were relit. Lloyd poured Sonny a healthy glass of Milam & Greene's single-barrel bourbon, 125 proof, which seemed, at the moment, to be just what the doctor ordered.

Sonny hadn't spent a lot of time around liberals, but they were behaving much as he expected—a lot more fun than the conservatives, who were so far gone into piety and indignation that there wasn't much room for playfulness. On the other hand, the libs complained a lot. Fenced dogs barking. They talked about issues with the same passion that Republicans talked about values, issues that would never get addressed and values that only pretended to be honored.

For the liberals, Sonny was an exotic, hard to get a fix on. Very traditional but not retrograde. A moderate, perhaps, if such a thing were possible in the lunatic Republican Party. He had voted against Carl Kimball's voucher bill, which took some nerve, although it still passed handily. Public education was being pushed over a fiscal cliff. No doubt Sonny would be shunned by the big-money boys who wanted absolute obedience. He would probably get primaried by one of the Nazi youth the dominionists were so capable of producing. The one thing the liberals agreed on was that Sonny wouldn't be around for a second term. The forces that had gotten him here were already turning on him. He would never pass for a Dem. Independents didn't exist. He had nowhere to run. He was a classic misfit. Poor fellow.

"Angela, can I have a word with you?" Sonny asked quietly.

"Sure!" she said brightly, her third martini having improved her mood immensely.

"Privately."

"Oh."

He guided her over to his truck. They leaned against the front fender. The crickets were making such a racket that their voices were safely drowned out. "That bill you sponsored, the Poo-poo Choo-choo, how was it that you came to introduce it?"

"L.D. asked me to."

"Do you know why he chose you?"

"He said he wanted your vote, and he thought if I introduced it, you'd support it."

Suspicions confirmed. "I guess he knows me better than I know myself."

"Oh, Sonny, did I make a horrible mistake?"

"No, no, not at all. I wasn't being professional. I should have read the bill more carefully."

"It'll be okay, right?"

"It's prob'ly the end of my career."

"Seriously?" Angela was aghast.

"When my constituents find out that I voted to dump New York City waste in Presidio County, they might hang me. And not just voted—*cosponsored* the dang thing."

"God, Sonny! And I did that to you?"

"I did it to myself. L.D. knew exactly which string to pull. I made it so easy for him. He knew I was soft on you. It must have been obvious to everyone."

Angela opened her mouth, but no words came out.

"Don't you feel bad about it," Sonny said. "I have a talent for screwing up."

"Not to me," Angela said, still absorbing his previous statement. "It wasn't obvious to me. I just saw you as a really cool guy and maybe my best friend here. I didn't know you had any kind of . . . feelings . . . like that."

There was a moment of quiet between them. The crickets were roaring and the liberals were laughing, but Sonny and Angela were in a separate universe. A universe of potential. A moment in time where everything could go one way or the other, but either way nothing would be the same. A moment with too much alcohol for clear thinking. A moment in which Reason was sleeping and Desire unfolded her wings. And in that pregnant moment, an aroma arose between the two of them, heady and primal, dizzying, mutual in origin. "I just feel awful, Sonny," Angela said, folding into him. "I wish I could make it up to you somehow."

★

Cinco, who was called that because she was Big Bob's fifth wife (really, she was fourth, as Mary Margaret was counted twice), summoned L.D. to the speaker's quarters. Carl was already there. It was late and Big Bob was out of control.

"Hey, L.D.!" he said with a big smile that looked completely unnatural on him, like a grinning jack-o'-lantern. "Have a drink!"

"He's been through a fifth of Macallan already," Carl said under his breath. Carl's slurred voice suggested that he hadn't done much to discourage the speaker from breaking his sobriety pledge.

"I'm trying to decide which of these lovely bottles to open next," Big Bob said. "Vodka or gin. Old friends. Haven't spent enough time with them lately."

"Bob, you might want to take a break," L.D. said. "You're gonna regret this."

"Because of regrets I'm a-drinkin' in the firss place." Big Bob flipped his ten-year sobriety chip on the domino table. "Gin wins. Gin it is. A win for gin." He poured a tumbler of Beefeater, not even bothering to add ice. "Here's to the crooks and phonies," he said, toasting the air.

"Who you talking about, Bob?"

"Talking 'bout myself, L.D. The biggest phony of them all."

"Bullshit. Everybody knows you're an honorable SOB."

"I'm a snot-slingin' drunk!"

"One night in ten years," Carl remarked. "I'd say you earned it."

"Ever' day I look out at a hunnert and fifty members and ask myself which one of you sorry bastards is gonna pick up the flag when I'm gone."

"Fortunately, that's not a pressin' question," said Carl, abjectly desperate to get back on Big Bob's good side.

"Carl, you keep lickin' my ass, I'm gonna slide right off my chair. You coulda saved the session if you'da talked some sense into Lurleen. But no. It's goin' up in flames."

"You know that woman, she won't budge for a Brinks truck."

"And you!" Big Bob wheeled on L.D. "I heard you really screwed Sonny. I guess you're proud of yourself."

"Yes, I am. His constituents are gonna tie him to the railroad track and let the Poo-poo Choo-choo roll over his ass."

Bob stared darts at L.D. and then suddenly deflated. Odd behavior. Troubling. He took a long, contemplative gulp of gin. "We're on a sleigh ride to hell, boys," he said out of nowhere.

"Not me," said Carl. "I've been saved."

"I've been thinkin' 'bout poor ol' Walter Dunne," Big Bob said.

"Have you now?" L.D. asked.

"He came to me in the night. Sat down, right at our domino table where he always sat. His eyes were on me, and his lips didn't move, but I could hear him speaking to me."

"This is real creepy," said Carl. "What'd he say?"

"He said, 'Bob, what's it all for?'"

"That was it?"

"I can't get it out of my mind."

"Let it go, Bob," L.D. said, "That was a dream."

"As real as lookin' at you right now. 'What's it all for?' Tell me, L.D., what's the answer?"

"There is no answer for that."

"Why would he make the trip if there wasn't an answer? You know what I think?"

"What's that, Bob?"

"Walter knows the answer. He just wanted me to ask the question. 'What's it all for?'"

L.D.'s phone tingled and he checked his texts. "Carl, you get him to bed, I got an errand to run," L.D. said. He was suddenly in a hurry.

"C'mon, Bob, time to go nighty-night, get your jammies on," Carl was saying as L.D. walked out the door. "You see Walter again, you tell him hello . . ."

★

Sonny was between worlds, not fully awake but snoozing, aware of Angela's presence and what it meant, but also distant from that reality. Dreams floated in and out, fiddling with his consciousness. Lola darted into mind but she was speaking French or something that Sonny couldn't understand. Then the body next to his stirred and his awareness partly returned, and he touched her.

"Sonny!" There was a pounding on the door. Sonny was startled. Was this part of the dream? Evidently not. He was awake and the pounding continued. "Sonny? Sonny? You're in there, I know it!"

"Jesus," said Angela, "who's that crazy person?"

"It's L.D."

"Open the dang door! I don't want to wake everybody in town. This is important!"

"Just a sec," Sonny said, struggling to get his jeans on.

"Hurry! Angela, you better come, too."

So he knew. Sonny and Angela exchanged a worried glance, each realizing that what was a drunken moment meant to be indulged and forgotten could be ruin for both of them.

"L.D., what the hell are you doin' here?" Sonny said as he cracked the door.

"Get dressed! Gotta split! The quorum break has been busted. The press is on its way here right now!"

"How in the world did you find us?" said Angela.

"I called in a favor from one of your colleagues."

By now, Sonny was fully awakened to the torpedo that had just collided with the hull of his life. "So what's this gonna cost us, L.D.?" he demanded.

"Don't worry about it. I'm happy to help you out."

"I bet you are."

"Suit yourself. Stay and take the heat. There's a news truck right behind me. A Republican member on the quorum break, juicy information. And a little bipartisan action on the side. Fine. Wait here and tell them the truth. Up to you. The truth doesn't do me any good. It's lies that matter. Take your pick."

Sonny and Angela traded a glance. "He's right, Sonny," Angela said. "Let's get out of here."

Just as they stepped out of the cabin, still buttoning up, Sonny saw L.D. videoing the two of them on his iPhone.

How stupid am I, Sonny thought. *L.D. has me right where he wants me.*

★

"Welcome to *An Hour of Power from the Man in the Tower*, Mr. Peeples!"

"Thank you, my friends," Mr. Peeples said. "Today I want to take you back in time, to the good old days, when America stood at the pinnacle of prestige and power. Happiness prevailed in the land. Yes, friends, I'm talking about the 1890s!

"People back then didn't bother about class or race. Everybody knew their place and got what they deserved. I'm not saying it was perfect, it wasn't perfect, did I say it was perfect? A lot of the same problems. Unions. Immigrants. But compare it to the world we live in today. Back then, men were free. And they were men! None of this crossing-over business. There were two sexes, like God made! Women were protected, worshipped you could say, none of the single mothers you see nowadays, except for war widows, there were plenty left over from the Civil War. But still, women had it great! Maybe they couldn't vote, but they were happy! Churches were strong! Faith was strong! Families were strong!

"And money! Money money money! It flowed, a river of money! Gushers! People got rich! And I mean filthy rich! What was the secret? Government didn't get in the way. Government didn't tell you what to do. Government didn't reach into your pocket and steal your well-earned pay. All this nasty talk you hear about plutocrats and robber barons. Who do you think made this country great? The titans of industry!

"Folks say, 'Mr. Peeples, you're so rich, you must be lucky.' No such thing. I'm rich because God wants me to be rich! There will always be the rich and the poor, it's part of the divine plan. Has it ever been otherwise? The more we as a state and a nation follow God's word, the wealthier we will be, all of us! That's why God empowers the righteous with vast financial resources, so that we can take dominion over his creation and return society to its God-fearing glory days.

"One thing you didn't see back then. Homosexuals. Yes, perverts have always existed, but they didn't rule the world like they do now. If we're going to make America great again, we have to return to the good old days, when the closet wasn't just where you kept your broom and mop. And that is what the Texas House of Representatives is about to do. Ladies and gentlemen, once again Texas leads the way. God bless the state!

"And don't forget to renew your pledge today. If you're new to this broadcast, call 1-800-733-7537. That's 1-800-PEEPLES. We take checks, credit cards, Bitcoin, and Venmo. If you send cash or valuable objects, please provide insurance . . ."

★

The quorum breakers straggled back into the chamber, singly or in bunches, jeered at by the raucous crowd in the gallery, who were behaving as if they were watching the Christians being fed to the lions. Most of them were on the side of the lions.

Sonny took his seat next to Harold, who was staring into space, his face blank. "I can't watch this," he said. "I guess there was never a chance this wasn't going to pass."

"What are you going to do if it does?" Sonny asked.

"Leave. Leave Texas. What else can I do? Even if the courts finally overturn it, who wants to live in a place where the haters rule? I've made my life here, Sonny. I love it. But I was fooling myself. There never was a place for me here. Maybe there's no place in this country that's safe."

In his life, Sonny had limited experience with homosexuals. It wasn't until he got into the "Don't ask, don't tell" Army that he spent time with men he knew to be gay. Mainly, he was thinking of Pinkerton, the Mississippi farm boy who saved his life. A brave kid who never made it back home.

Sometimes people are sent to you.

Big Bob stood on the rostrum, watching as the members checked in on the voting board. Finally, he announced, "There being a quorum present, debate will resume on H.B. 127," and gaveled the chamber back into session.

"Mr. Speaker, I believe we were moving to a vote," Lurleen said from the front mic. She was in her full glory, in a red dress, blue scarf, and the buzzard feather proudly erect in her white bun.

"Vote! Vote! Vote!" the lion contingent cheered.

Sonny looked at the faces in the gallery, inflamed and embold-ened, already celebrating victory. His own colleagues, many of them, were smiling—that particular smile that sometimes arises when a taboo is about to be broken or a crime committed. They knew what they were about to do was wrong. They knew that people—like Harold—would be harmed, maybe ruined. They didn't care. They could hide behind platitudes and scriptures, but fundamentally they were doing it because they were afraid not to. The crowd in the gal-lery demanded it. They were the boss here. The crowd represented the angry and resentful, narrow-minded constituents back home, the ones who would vote in the primaries. The majority of this House would support Lurleen's bill, even if they didn't agree with it, even if they knew it was harmful to the state and millions of citizens. It would pass to the Senate, where the same dynamic would play out. The governor would sign it. And Harold would leave.

"Final comments or questions before the vote?" Big Bob asked. He was pale and shaky, more wrecked than usual this morning after his binge the night before. He looked at the members who were about to take a vote that could only hurt their state, but he was unable to stand in the way. Then his eye caught a figure walking to the back mic.

"What purpose, Mr. Lamb?"

"Point of clarification, Mr. Speaker," Sonny said. "Representa-tive Klump, I think we all agree on the need to keep sexual predators away from our children, and there are plenty of laws that do exactly that. Let's focus on this term in your bill, 'agents of perversion.' Can you define that for me?"

There were a few more catcalls from the gallery demanding an immediate vote.

"The Bible lays that out very clearly."

"'Men who lie with other men,' for instance."

"I see you are familiar with the scripture," Lurleen said.

"So we're talking about homosexuals."

"The bill doesn't say that."

"No," said Sonny. "It leaves it up to interpretation. Now, you've got some awful stiff penalties in here, Representative Klump. How are you going to prove that a person is an 'agent of perversion'? If I'm a schoolteacher, for instance, you're gonna assign a couple detectives to follow me around, bug my bedroom, something like that?"

"I'm not a policeman."

"Okay, but let's just add it up. All the coaches, all the medical personnel, all the day care workers and foster parents and bus drivers—we're talking about a vast morality police force investigating hundreds of thousands of hardworking Texans. Is that what you're after here? Gonna cost a lot of money."

"Mr. Speaker! I protest!" Lurleen cried. "We're headed for a vote."

"Vote! Vote! Vote!" the crowd chanted. Someone began a rhythmic foot stamp, and soon the chamber was resonating to the deafening beat, drowning out Big Bob's gavel. He signaled to the DPS officers and they began clearing the galleries, which caused the uproar to slowly subside.

"I'm gonna allow this," the speaker said when he was able to make himself heard. "Anybody who makes a peep is gonna be hauled out immediately. Is that clear up there?" he said to the gallery, which subsided into sullen silence.

Lurleen resumed. "There is nothing in this bill that calls for expanded police powers."

"That's true," Sonny said. "The real goal here is to drive homosexuals back into the closet, to remove their presence from public life. But it's not just homosexuality you object to. I've been reading some of your literature, Representative Klump, and frankly, I don't think this bill goes far enough."

"What do you mean?"

"May I?" Sonny said, reaching into his jacket. "I happen to have one of your mailers right here. It says: 'Sexual relations should be limited to the purpose of procreation.' Do you believe that?"

"With all my heart."

"I guess that rules out any form of contraception, correct?"

"That is most certainly correct," Lurleen said defiantly.

"This document goes on to say that sexual pleasure is dangerous even in marriage and advises husbands and wives to practice sex with a sheet between them. Am I quoting you correctly?"

Lurleen nodded wordlessly amid hoots and gibes from the other side of the gallery, until Big Bob gave them the eye. Sonny's colleagues were rapt.

"I say let's put this plan into action!" he said, holding up Lurleen's brochure as if it were the Magna Carta. "I offer an amendment to House Bill 127. It should read, 'All sex in Texas must be done through a hole in the sheet!'"

There was no gaveling down the uproar that followed. The Family Forum types were on their feet—actually, everyone in the gallery was standing—some waving fists, some applauding and slapping each other on the back, but on the floor the expression on the faces of the members was mostly relief.

Lurleen's shrill voice cut through the hubbub. "Objection! Mr. Speaker, I object!"

"Overruled," said Big Bob, a grin on his face. "All those in favor of the amendment signify by crying 'Aye!'"

"AYE" thundered forth.

"Opposed?"

"Nay." This from Lurleen and Carl.

"The amendment passes. We will now proceed to vote on the bill—"

"Mr. Speaker?" Lurleen said, now visibly wilted, her broad shoulders slumping, "we will not watch this bill be turned into a laughingstock. I move H.B. 127 be withdrawn."

And with that, the legend of Sonny Lamb was born.

17

Alone, life on the ranch was more boring and more dangerous, and Lola felt considerably abandoned with Sonny gone so much of the time. She could count on seeing him only once a month, when she ovulated, and Sonny honored that. If he was really tied down, Lola would get her brother Buster, the Border Patrol officer, to spend a couple nights and keep an eye on the place while she was in Austin. Despite the solitary existence in what nearly everyone would describe as the middle of nowhere, Lola still connected with the stark majesty that surrounded her, especially in the late afternoon when the sky softened and a rosy glow lined the horizon. She had an early-evening ritual of walking the fence line with a margarita while taking in the Earth's majestic transition into night. Sometimes the sunsets were so glorious she had to catch her breath. It was in that magic moment when Venus clicked on in the eastern sky that Lola suddenly saw someone move behind a prickly pear.

She froze. It wasn't uncommon for migrants to cross their land. In the past, most of them were single men looking for work. More than once Sonny had hired them for odd jobs, paying enough to get them down the road a bit. In the last few years, the population wading across the river had shifted. Instead of single men, families were coming, fleeing political violence, part of a historic surge of despairing people looking for salvation, a vast human tide. Several times Sonny had come upon the carcasses of migrants who didn't make it. The county would come out and collect the remains.

Not everyone was looking for work. There were narcos. They were armed. Most migrants were just looking for food, but guns and jewelry had been taken. If the intruders determined that no one was around, they might stay for a few days, sleeping in the beds, showering, eating the food, stealing cars. Two weeks before, an elderly couple were killed in Valentine. Nobody was caught. Whoever shot them just kept on moving.

Lola retreated to the ranch house and took down the shotgun above the door, which had a red ribbon on the trigger guard indicating that it was loaded. She was well aware of how vulnerable she was if there was a confrontation. It was getting very dark outside. She turned off the den light and cracked a window, listening for any movement. In a moment, she heard voices, and then the sound of a child crying.

Don't get into it, she told herself. They are not your problem.

Someone was hushing the child. The cries subsided into hiccups.

Lola set down the shotgun and went onto the porch. She made out the figure of a young teenage girl and a child, a boy, maybe eight years old, his wet cheeks catching the light. As soon as the girl saw Lola, she lifted her hands as if she were surrendering to the police.

"¿Quien eres?" Lola said.

"No somos nadie," the girl said. We are nobody. She was maybe thirteen, too young to be the mother, so probably the older sister. It was a chilly evening. The girl wore a tattered print dress, torn in numerous places from the buckthorn and cactus. The boy was wearing shorts and a Dallas Cowboys T-shirt. His legs were scratched and bleeding. His lip was trembling. He was still hiccupping.

"¿Adónde vas?"

"Portland," said the girl.

"¿Que Portland?" Lola knew of at least three places with that name, in Maine, Oregon, and one in Texas near Corpus Christi.

Now the girl began to cry as well. She didn't know which Portland. She was a portrait of helplessness, but still trying to be strong for her brother. "Entra, niños," said Lola, knowing she was going to regret this. How would she explain it to Sonny?

★

"Brady left me."

"Oh, no! When did this happen?"

"Last night."

"Didn't I tell you it was going to turn out like this?"

It took Sonny a moment to absorb the fact that two horses were standing in his living room watching a soap opera on television.

"I don't think I can go on! I can't! I can't!"

Sonny took off his hat and shooed the horses out on the porch. "Ginger! For God's sake! Rosebud! C'mon now, git!"

And where was Lola in all this? He found her in the garden. "Lola! What'd I tell you 'bout letting the horses in the house?"

"Oh, they're just a couple of old maids watching *Days of Our Lives*."

"Lola, it's our house!"

"It's their favorite show!"

He could see there was no resolution at the end of this discussion. Also, he wasn't on solid ground. A ton of very awkward conversations awaited. "I guess folks in town are pretty stirred up. You think there'll be a crowd?"

"A crowd? Sonny, they're comin' in from Del Rio, Alpine, Fort Davis. I wouldn't be surprised if they sell T-shirts and corny dogs. What're you gonna say?"

"I dunno. I'm as jumpy as a grasshopper on a griddle."

"Well, they're all wondering what you meant by that vote on solid waste being dumped in Presidio County. My God, Sonny! From New York City!"

"It looks bad, I know. My mind wasn't in the game. I'll just have to go into Marfa and face the consequences."

Lola didn't say anything on the ride into town. Sonny needed to have a clear mind. She could see he was really on edge. Everything was on the line for him; it was no time for surprises, so no talk of little visitors.

Consequences awaited them, all right. L.D. looked approvingly at the banners on the storefronts and the placards scattered through the crowd, all professionally done to appear homemade. The streets around the courthouse were blocked to accommodate the people L.D. had bused in for the big show, which had cost more than a few pennies to pull off, but he wasn't cutting corners. A stage stood on the courthouse lawn so everyone could clearly see Sonny in his moment of pitiful rejection, weeping, begging for forgiveness, and being spurned for all that. It helped set the mood that the stage looked like a gallows. "NO MORE POO-POO CHOO-CHOO," read a banner draped across the courthouse.

Sonny and Lola heard the chants as they parked the truck. You never saw crowds like this in Marfa. They had to park three blocks away and shoulder a path through the food trucks and a multitude of unfamiliar faces. People looked at him as if he were an ax murderer. They hissed. They cursed. Lola shrank into Sonny's shadow. "Traitor!" someone cried, the nicest thing that was said. "Take your shit back to New York City!"

Sonny climbed the steps of the stage. Lola insisted on joining him, a gesture she didn't need to make and which moved Sonny immensely. When he came into view, the booing began in earnest. Normally, folks in far West Texas were so laconic they were practically mute, but the jeers and catcalls were Bronx-worthy. And there was Lola's family, the whole clan, children included, who had come to watch Sonny be torn to shreds by his constituents. Hadn't her family always wanted it to turn out this way? There was one other person Sonny searched for, as wave after wave of angry chants rolled over him—and there he was, L.D., standing under the portico of the Hotel Paisano, the happiest man in town. He tipped his hat in Sonny's direction. Just politics.

"Hidey, folks," Sonny said, as the PA system screamed. That at least had the effect of quieting them down. "If I could just—"

"Resign!"

"Sellout!"

There was a lot of this. Sonny called out, "If you want to throw tomatoes, at least let me have my say, okay?" Instead of quieting down, a new chant began: "Sludge, sludge, go away! Don't come back some other day!"

"You want me to quit?" Sonny yelled. That got the crowd's attention. "Okay!" Sonny said. "It's up to you. We'll vote on it today. Is that what you want to hear?"

The cheers gave him the answer, but now he at least had them under a modicum of control.

"Let me just say this. When you elected me, you trusted me to represent your interests. I worked hard to keep that trust. I filed a bill that could be the salvation of the West Texas way of life, a proposal to desalinate—"

"Sludge, sludge, go—"

"But that's not why you're here today," Sonny said, racing ahead of the chant. "You want to know about the waste disposal bill."

"Yeah! Keep your crap out of Presidio County!"

"I hear you!" Sonny said. "Let's talk about it. I'm gonna tell you the truth—"

" 'Bout time, loser!"

"Resign!"

"Sludge, sludge—"

Sonny felt he was physically wrestling the multitude, as if they were a single immense entity, and it took everything he had to keep from being overwhelmed and letting them rush over him and erase him and the memory of him from the face of the Earth. But then, amid the calls for blood, a surprising voice cried out, "C'mon, give him a chance. Let's hear what he has to say."

The crowd quieted down a bit. Sonny located the friendly source: it was Valerie Nightingale, his far more qualified former opponent, with an expression—well, it was not easy to read her.

"Thank you," he said in her direction, and then to the crowd, "When I voted for that bill, I had no idea what was in it. And that's inexcusable. But I have read it now"—hoots and jeers—"and I'm *glad* I voted for it! You wanna know why? Do you?"

"Tell us!" Valerie yelled.

"Not just for the jobs it will bring to our region, but because all that New York City waste you're complaining about will make some of the richest grazing range in the entire Southwest. Right now, the drought and the wind are stripping away our topsoil. Most places we can't grow grass, even in a good year. Sludge may be the answer. Imagine your pastures fertile again. Remember what it used to be like? It's always been hard to make it out here, we know that. But it wasn't impossible. This is what I'm fighting for, see? To give us a shot at making a real living once again. Lot of folks would say it's not worth it. The land out here is harsh, unforgiving. Yes, it is. But we know the beauty of the place. We live with a spirit of freedom and independence surrounding us that few people will ever get close to. That's who we are."

Sonny paused a moment. He knew a good number of these folks. Some he'd gone to school with, some he'd met campaigning, and some he'd been around his entire life. "Most of us have families that have been here for generations," he said. "Our ancestors are buried in this soil. They went through hard times, every single one of them. Now I look out at your faces and wonder, are you ready to surrender? Are you ready to give up on the land that our parents and grandparents and many before them sweated and bled into? That's what I'm in Austin to defend."

By now, the crowd was quiet. Not everyone was listening, but most were. He could see they all had the same fears. They were facing ruin sooner or later, and they knew it. His words reached places inside them that words had never found before, slowly but irresistibly transforming the mob into a community.

"Now that doesn't for a minute excuse the fact that I didn't realize the implications of this bill when it came up," Sonny said. "I don't blame you for being mad. Hell, I'd feel the same way. And if you want me to quit, I'll step down tonight. But if you let me stay, I'll make you folks a promise. If you give me another shot, I'll be the best representative District 74 has ever had. I'll read every bill. I'll be workin' for you, day and night."

"Sludge, sludge—" someone started to chant, but no one joined in, and the voice fell silent.

"All right, let's do it!" Sonny said. "Let's vote! All those in favor of havin' Sonny Lamb quit tonight, say 'Aye'!"

"Aye!" a hundred voices cried out.

"Opposed?"

"Nay!" Two hundred more.

Sonny felt Lola's hand grab his and raise his arm aloft. Amid the cheers, Lola asked him, "How'd you do that?"

That same question was in L.D.'s mind. He had never seen anything like it. Even people he had paid to be here had voted for Sonny. Reporters were trailing after him like baby chickens. It was going to be the very opposite of the story L.D. had planned to come out of this event—and a much bigger one, at that.

As Sonny and Lola made their way through the glad-handing crowd, Sonny sought out Valerie Nightingale. She gave him a crooked, ironic grin. "I know what you're going to say, but I have no idea why I did that," she told him.

"I never expected out of all these people that you'd be the one to stand up for me."

"Sonny, remember what I went through," she said. "I just don't think politics ought to be so nasty. Even for you."

"I know we don't agree on a lot, Valerie, but I wonder if you'd be interested in being my field director? I want somebody in the district with an ear to the ground, who knows what people need. I can't always be that person. I don't know of anyone else who could do a better job of that."

"Sonny, I'm still mad at you."

"You and everybody."

"But truth to tell, I really do need a job."

As L.D. headed back to Austin, he rehearsed his speech to Mr. Peeples. It was going to be rough, he knew. But he wasn't finished with Sonny Lamb. He had another card to play.

★

After they had talked about the speech and how people just want to hear the truth, Lola asked Sonny about his lab results. "You must have gotten them by now."

"Oh," he said, having forgotten all about it.

"Oh, what? You did go to the collection center, right? I mean, we talked. You said it was no problem."

"Yeah. I did."

"And?"

"Lola, it was a really hectic day."

"And now you're going to tell me the results."

"The thing is, they're not actually my results."

"God, Sonny, what is going on with you?"

"Lola, I'll make another appointment as soon as I get back to Austin."

"No, no, you're not getting out of this without telling me."

"You have to imagine the pressure I was under—" he began.

"You got results but they weren't your own, is what I'm hearing."

"Yes."

"And how would that happen? They mixed up the tubes or something? Like switching babies in the hospital?"

It was so tempting just to say yes to that. Sonny paused just long enough that Lola saw through that possible response. "Okay," he said. "I did something kinda stupid. You're not gonna believe it."

"Surprise me."

"I was rattled. The cops were after me. Everybody thought I was part of the quorum break. And right then was when I found out about the Poo-poo Choo-choo. Bottom line, I just couldn't, you know, perform, and I sure didn't want to let anybody know that, so I just snuck out of the room, they have these weird rooms where you—anyway, I took my empty tube and poured some other guy's stuff in it."

Lola stared at him in stark disbelief. "Sonny!" she cried, then started laughing. "You didn't!"

"No, I actually did," Sonny said, beginning to see the humor in it.

"That is so goofy."

"Wait, you haven't heard the end of it. The guy whose stuff I borrowed? He won the Nobel Prize."

"Really? What's his name?"

"I've been trying to remember that ever since I saw him."

All the way back to the ranch house, they laughed about it. He loved Lola's sense of humor, her appreciation of the absurd, but in the back of Sonny's mind, he knew that a reckoning was coming.

Lola also dreaded what would happen next.

Before dinner, Sonny ferried several bales of hay out to the pasture. The cattle saw him coming and rushed the gate. There was so little grass on the ground, they would jump into the bed of the truck if they could. These bales were precious; the price of hay was higher than Sonny had ever seen it, $300 for a large roll of alfalfa. He certainly wouldn't have been able to feed those fifteen heifers he'd auctioned off. As it was, the cows were getting awfully thin on the rations he was providing. He dropped off a small bale for Joaquin and fed him another peanut butter cookie. The majestic bull was still regal, but even he was dropping weight.

When Sonny came back into the house, he was stopped in his tracks by the sight of two children at the dinner table. "Whoa," he said. "Hello."

"They're from Honduras," Lola said. "They don't speak English."

"What are they doing here?"

"Visiting."

Sonny didn't know what to say.

"Just until we figure out what to do with them," Lola said, filling in the silence.

The children stared at Sonny, their eyes big and full of apprehension, knowing that their destiny rested in his hands. The girl was wearing one of Lola's old dresses that had been cut down to her size.

"Don't be mad," Lola said. "They got robbed and dumped by their coyote. They don't even know where they're going. The girl, her name is Carmelita, she told me they were headed to Portland, but it turns out there are places called Portland in nearly every state.

Like dozens of Portlands. Also," Lola said under her breath, "I think the coyote did something to her but I'm not sure."

"What's the boy's name?"

"Pedro."

The boy looked up anxiously at the mention of his name. He was swallowed up in one of Sonny's softball jerseys. He had the gorgeousness of childhood on him. Round face, full lips, eyes that promised to be merry. One day he might be a fat, bald old geezer but now he was perfect. And the girl was a Madonna, radiant, her hair braided into pigtails; that would have been Lola's work.

"Well, then," said Sonny, as he sat down. "Let's have dinner and talk about this." He turned to Pedro. "¿Listo para comer?"

Pedro grinned, showing a missing front tooth. "¡Sí, señor!"

Lola had made a huge bowl of spaghetti and meatballs, which the children plowed through like professional wrestlers, their table manners leaving something to be desired. Lola's Spanish was better than Sonny's, so she translated. These kids had traveled fifteen hundred miles as part of a smuggling caravan. Part of that way they rode on top of a train. That was fun but a little scary when they went over a bridge. When they reached the border, they were stashed in a house in Ojinaga for a week, and then another coyote took over and led them through a tunnel under Trump's wall. He drove them some distance up U.S. 67 and dumped them on the side of the road, in the middle of nowhere, taking everything the kids had.

The children were staying in the bunkhouse. After Lola got them to bed, she and Sonny sat in the porch rockers. "What are you planning to do?" Sonny asked.

"I don't know. They're children. They're lost. Carmelita doesn't even know her mother's phone number, it was on the phone the smuggler took. All I know is they come from San Pedro Sula, a city near the coast. That's where Pedro got his name. We could probably call the police there and see if they can get us in touch with any relatives. But it was the mother who sent the kids off, hoping they could get to Portland, Wherever, to be with her brother. I looked up San Pedro Sula. It's overrun with gangs. I mean, it's a mess. The murder capital of the world, says the internet. Just think about a mother sending her kids away like that, what she must be dealing with."

"Have you called Buster?" Sonny asked.

Lola shook her head. "Not sure I can trust him."

"If all you say about these kids is right, they'd have a good shot at asylum."

"Maybe . . ." Lola drifted into silence, her intentions suspended like motes in the air.

"Lola, I know how much you want kids, but these are somebody else's children."

"I know. But what kind of future do you think they have? Suppose they get sent back to Honduras? Wind up in a gang or abused or dead? God knows. I looked into adopting them, but unaccompanied migrant children are not eligible. It's against the law, can you believe that? If Buster gets hold of them, he'll put them in that giant detention center in El Paso. They'll just sit there for God knows how long and then get sent back. Or maybe they'll move through the asylum system and wind up getting placed in some foster home."

"Or else they get to live with their uncle, if they can find him. Buster might be able to help, you know."

"Possibly," Lola conceded.

"Let's play this out. If you just keep them here, you're gonna tell folks who they are? Put them in school? If they get sick, we'll have to pay the bills out of pocket. What about their own family, their mother, their uncle, who must be expecting them? They'll think the kids are dead, right?"

"Stop, Sonny. I know. I've been over these thoughts a zillion times."

"Let's do this. I've got to fly back to Austin in the morning. I don't see the harm in you taking care of these kids for a few more days before making any decisions. I know you'll get more attached to them, and that'll make it harder. They're adorable. They seem bright. God knows they're courageous. They're going to be all right. You'll know what to do."

Lola squeezed his hand. It didn't seem the right time for him to say anything about Angela. He didn't know what to say about that situation, in any case. He tried to put it out of his mind, but he was haunted by the inevitability of that moment arriving. Part of him wanted to get it out of the way; the confession was rising inside him; he would vomit it up and be purged and cleansed—at least that was how he imagined it, a great catharsis, followed by repentance, followed by life as it used to be. The other part of him knew this was nonsense and wanted to hide the affair forever. But that way L.D. stayed in control. The only way out was to confess everything. And lose everything.

The next morning, as he flew back to Austin, he had another panic attack. His breathing was shallow. It felt like the moment in the Capitol when he lost consciousness. It could probably happen again at any moment. He concentrated on taking a breath in for five seconds, holding it, then out for five.

His nerves had been shot since Iraq, but he had done a fair job of hiding it, even from himself. Sudden flashes of light that threw him off, the usual nightmares, a weight on his chest—there was nothing mysterious about his condition. Soldiers have lived with it since the beginnings of civilization. But it wasn't fear of dying that seized him now. It was the trap he had fallen into with L.D. The man was a genius of manipulation and totally unscrupulous. Sonny wasn't sure how much of his affair with Angela had been engineered by L.D., going back to the pig hunt when he'd placed Sonny in the same blind with her. Tendencies, that's what L.D. would have noticed, a tendency in Sonny to be interested, a tendency to give himself permission to act on his desire, tendencies—like the strings a puppet master pulls—and there must have been similar tendencies in Angela, although Sonny couldn't read her as clearly as L.D. did. Sonny didn't doubt that L.D. would throw the switch on his marriage if it advanced his agenda.

The brilliance of L.D.'s plan was that Sonny had walked into the trap willingly, led by longing and curiosity. He relished Angela's companionship. They were so different, but that difference fed the flames. If he weren't married to Lola, maybe he and Angela would have had a life together; but probably not. The differences that made their affair exciting would become barriers between them. Instead of teasing, they would argue. What was excitingly new about their relationship would become familiar and less intriguing. With Lola, that familiarity was the ground they stood on.

In the air, despairing thoughts raided his mind, climbing aboard like pirates. Down below, the unyielding earth awaited the moment—partly longed for—when he might black out again. The Cessna would bank hard, then go into a stall as the alarm horn screamed but failed to wake him. He would not feel a thing as the plane began to spiral, like water draining into a sink, tighter and tighter until the nose of the little craft found its way into the ground.

And his problems would be over.

18

"Mr. Speaker," Angela said from the front mic, "I rise today to speak on behalf of Texas women. Texas women who have been stripped of the health care they need and deserve. Health providers and clinics that formerly offered reduced-cost contraception and health screenings have dried up in this state. Yes, this is a national problem. The United States has a higher rate of maternal mortality than any other developed country, but in Texas the problem is particularly acute. Texas mothers of color die at twice the national rate. Our own Maternal Morbidity and Mortality Task Force has shown that most of these deaths are preventable. But they are not prevented. The number one recommendation of the task force is to increase access to care. That's exactly what this bill provides."

As she spoke, sympathetic female members, including several Republicans, joined her at the mic for support. This was the moment Angela had been aiming for. She had skillfully navigated her bill through committee and secured eleven cosponsors. A companion bill was under way in the Senate. But passage in either chamber was far from certain.

"Members, how can we talk about the right to life when we make it so hard for Texas women to survive the birth of a child? We have the highest rate of uninsured people in the country. Half the babies born in Texas are to mothers poor enough to qualify for Medicaid, but our leaders refuse to accept the federal funds that would expand coverage. The Health Protection for Texas Women bill doesn't solve all the problems, but it makes a start.

"I respectfully move passage."

"The motion has been made," Big Bob said. "Questions from members? Mr. Delgado."

"Will the gentle lady yield?" Gilbert said.

"I yield." Gilbert was a friend to the bill, she knew.

"This bill has been characterized as pro-choice," he said. "Right now under existing Texas law it is almost impossible for a woman to get an abortion for any reason at all. Is that correct?"

"That is correct."

"And you're saying that it can take up to six months for an indigent pregnant Texas woman to get an appointment with an ob/gyn?"

"Unfortunately, yes, that's also correct. This bill would offer Texas women a choice for medical care, which is currently unavailable for many of them."

The next questioner was Lurleen Klump.

"This bill is a stalking horse for the pro-choice liberals who want to murder babies," Lurleen asserted. "Clearly written into the bill are provisions for contraception and so-called emergency procedures that are a thin disguise for abortions."

"Representative Klump, I hope you realize that emergencies sometimes arise during pregnancies."

"Indeed, I know something about that," Lurleen said, her voice quavering, so uncharacteristic of her. "My mother had an unborn baby with an irregular heartbeat. The doctor told her there was little chance of survival, and he recommended aborting. Representative Martinez, that baby is standing in front of this body this very minute, with a strong heart, fiercely committed to stopping any other child's life from being snuffed out, as mine would have been, had my mother made the choice you advocate."

Angela hadn't expected such an affecting personal argument, especially from someone so formidable as Lurleen. Other members gathered around to support Lurleen, and now the pro-choice and pro-life partisans were facing off like rival gangs behind their leaders at the microphones on either end of the center aisle. Neither side could accept the arguments of the other because the issue wasn't about science or family values, it was about freedom, privacy, and death, the baby or the mother, and that's what made abortion the one political dispute that could split the nation into two camps, a house divided, just as this House was.

"Representative Klump, I'm glad you're here today. I say that with all sincerity," said Angela. "But there are thousands of Texas mothers who are not with us anymore because of the absence of health care and the lack of insurance—all because of the single-minded focus on the unborn at the expense of maternal health. How many mothers have to be sacrificed in the name of the right to life? Don't these mothers have a right to life as well?"

"Does Texas need to do a better job with maternal health?" Lurleen replied. "Yes, it does. But killing babies is not the way to save women's lives. Your bill provides a back door to abortions, even at later stages of development. We must draw a line in the sand, just like Colonel Travis at the Alamo. I urge everyone in this chamber to examine their conscience and vote against this godless bill."

Big Bob had witnessed the abortion wars for decades, and he didn't expect to see an end to them. Whenever one side gained a small advantage, the other side fought back with all the skill and dedication that intelligent, passionate people could bring to bear. Compromise was never in reach. It was total war.

"Thank you, Representative Klump," Big Bob said. "Seeing no more questions, Representative Martinez will close on the bill."

"Respectfully move passage," Angela said.

"The question occurs on H.B. 2104," said the speaker, adding, "This is a record vote."

The vote board began to light up, as a bell sounded each one cast. Big Bob called out the votes: "Marshall, aye; Adams, nay; Delgado, aye; Klump, nay," and so on through the roster until he came to, "Lamb, nay." Angela's head swung around to see him, then she turned back as Big Bob noted the tally. "All members voting, eighty-six opposed, fifty-eight in favor, six abstaining. The measure fails."

Angela strode out of the chamber before Sonny had a chance to say a word.

★

The ides of March brought change into the chamber. The pace picked up as bills began streaming out of the committees and the filing deadline arrived. Like a river nearing a falls, the flow became more concentrated as the true concerns of the session revealed themselves. Clearly, desalination wasn't going to be one of them, given that Carl refused to bring it forward for discussion in committee and nobody else was interested. Sonny's bill was a corpse awaiting burial. It was time to go to Barton Springs.

Sonny picked up Ezer at his apartment just north of the university. He was standing in front wearing swim trunks and a T-shirt. He got in the passenger side of the pickup and Honey hopped in the bed. Even though she was a service dog she sensed that an adventure awaited. She was panting and grinning, her tongue pulsing with excitement.

"You can swim, right?" Sonny asked.

"I'm actually a champion swimmer," said Ezer. "I got ribbons and shit."

Sonny had discovered the springs one Sunday morning when he went for a walk through Zilker Park, near where he was living in the Airstream. He was on the hike-and-bike trail when he diverted through a low-ceilinged tunnel, built for a miniature train that ran under Barton Springs Road, and followed the old tracks through a grove of towering pecans. He came to a little concession stand where he could buy a burger or a chicken sandwich. Nearby was a bronze statue of three tubby middle-aged men sitting on a rock in their swimsuits, one of the oddest memorials he had ever seen, but also endearing. Obviously, they were friends deeply engaged in brilliant conversation. The plaque described them as writers who used to hold court in the natural spring pool that erupted from the aquifer.

And it was glorious. The pool was nine hundred feet long, brilliantly blue, mottled green in the shallow end, clear, glinting in the sunshine, with swimmers crawling down the long aquatic corridor, dodging ducks along the way. Sunbathers lay on towels on grassy slopes lined with cottonwoods. Toddlers splashed in the shallows. A topless woman did the backstroke. Whatever Austin was, here you found its essence. It was like no place else in Texas.

Jane and Wanda met them at the clubhouse. Now that Sonny had been educated, he could see that Jane, in her bikini, was still transitioning. Her musculature was somewhat masculine, but if he hadn't known her backstory he would never have guessed. Wanda was a sight in a pink floral skirted swimsuit, a heavy old lady leaning on her walker, wearing heart-shaped sunglasses and flip-flops. "I haven't been swimming in Barton's in thirty years," she said.

"That's not true," said Jane. "You used to take me here when I was really little."

"Thirty years ago," said Wanda.

"Oops, I guess you're right."

They paid admission and spread their towels on the grass, then Sonny led them to the diving board. "Ezer, are you up for this?" he asked.

"Let's go, boss."

Ezer took off Honey's leash. He put his hand on Sonny's shoulder and they walked out on the diving board, with Honey trailing behind, tail wagging ecstatically. Sonny dove in first, Ezer did an impressive cannonball, then Honey leapt into the air, a picture of canine jubilation. Jane performed a dainty swan dive as Wanda lowered herself on a ladder into the frigid water—frigid for Texas, at sixty-eight degrees. They were each instantly shivering and filled with joy.

"I wanted you to see what we're fighting for," Sonny said, as they swam over to a limestone outcropping. Honey clambered out and shook water everywhere as the others pulled themselves onto the rock, except for Ezer, who paddled around on his back in a contemplative mood, his clouded eyes tilted toward the sun.

"Right here is where a branch of the Edwards Aquifer comes to an end," Sonny said. "It stretches from Del Rio through the Hill Country, rainfall seeping through the karst limestone, which is like a layer of Swiss cheese. San Antonio and San Marcos get almost all their water out of this aquifer." He didn't mean it to sound like a lecture but he couldn't help himself. "Humans have been living on the banks of this spot for ten thousand years," he continued. "Old folks say they used to see dinosaur footprints at the bottom of this pool. The Tonkawa Indians regarded it as sacred, and you can imagine why. I sorta feel that way myself. Ezer, you can't see the pebbles jumping around like popcorn on the bottom, but maybe you can feel the flow."

"Yes, I do," Ezer said from some distant interior place. "Hear them, too."

"We had artesian swimming holes like this in West Texas when I was a kid. They're practically all gone now, the water sucked dry by farmers or piped off to Midland for fracking. The question is, how do we save the water we have and use it in the best possible way? Right now, I'm stumped and I need your help."

"Take a hostage," Ezer suggested.

"He means not literally," Wanda interjected.

"Game theory says you need leverage to win, and right now you don't have any," Ezer explained. "If you can hold hostage something other members want, they'll have to deal with you."

Sonny couldn't think of any such leverage he might have, nor could the others. "More power would help," Wanda mused, "but you're at the bottom end of that pole."

"Believe me, I'm aware of how hopeless this whole idea is," Sonny said. The freshman on the Culture and Tourism Committee was about as far from real power as existed in the House. Leverage was a dream.

"Have you ever heard of the tragedy of the commons?" Ezer asked, as he hoisted himself onto the rock like a sea lion. The heat of the limestone felt comforting after the shock of the water. "It's a fundamental axiom in game theory. You're a rancher. Suppose there were no fences and all the land was open grazing. What would happen?"

Sonny thought it out. "Free land. Lowers your cost considerably. As long as everybody agrees not to overdo it."

"What if some people or big corporations decide to take advantage of the common grazing area and run a lot more cows than other ranchers do?"

"You'd overgraze and everybody else would pile on, just to get their share before it all goes *poof*."

"Same with fishing, right?" said Ezer. "Forestry. These are commons that can easily be destroyed by greed. That's what happened to those pools you swam in as a kid. It's a contest between self-interest and the good of society."

"How does that relate to aquifers?" Sonny asked. "In Texas, underground resources are private property. We have the rule of capture, which the oil business is built on. Anything under the surface belongs to the landowner or the mineral rights holder. Practically every other state operates on the principle of reasonable use. In Texas, it's grab all you can."

"Are you familiar with the catfish escapade in the nineties?" asked Jane.

"Did Carl have anything to do with it?"

"I wouldn't put it past him, but this involves a different catfish farmer, who owned some land on the Medina River above the Edwards Aquifer. It happens that his land was lower than the index well in Fort Stockton, so the pressure at that point in the aquifer was super high. When he tapped his first well, it blew rocks the size of basketballs twenty feet in the air. The flow measured thirty-five thousand gallons of water per minute! He had just created the largest free-flowing well in the world, this one catfish farmer. Fully opened, he could draw fifty million gallons of water a day, enough for a city of two hundred fifty thousand people. I mean, Barton Springs gets around ten million gallons a day."

"But the water didn't disappear," said Sonny. "Wouldn't it have been available for reuse?"

"Possibly. The farmer let it drain off into the river, but it could have been rerouted. San Antonio definitely needed the water, although many people argued that raising catfish for human consumption was a better use of the resource than watering the lawns in Alamo Heights."

"So what happened?"

"The water table plummeted, but there sure were a lot of catfish farmed. His crop was potentially worth twenty-five million dollars a year. Then the EPA found high levels of fecal coliform bacteria in the discharge from all the fish poop. The pollution threatened various endangered species, and it looked like the feds were going to take over management of the entire aquifer. That forced everybody to work together. San Antonio started paying farmers not to irrigate. Hydrologists proposed new ways of recharging the aquifer. San Antonio wound up buying out the catfish farmer for thirty million dollars and plugging the well."

"Sounds like everybody came out of it better by cooperating than they would have otherwise," Wanda observed.

"Like cigarette advertising," said Ezer. "A famous study in game theory. Back in the nineteen-seventies, you had tobacco companies spending boatloads of money on television ads, trying to gain market share. A classic win-lose scenario, because whenever R. J. Reynolds improved its sales, it came at the expense of Philip Morris. They were trapped, because if they didn't advertise, their market share would disappear, but they were barely making a profit. Then the federal government did them a huge favor. It banned cigarette ads on TV altogether. Sales went down, but profits shot up. Everybody won, just like with the catfish."

"In our case, we've got the ranchers versus the frackers, basically, and the frackers have more mojo," Sonny said.

"They're not the only stakeholders here," said Jane. "The big oil companies are going to fight it, but they're in constant conflict with the Texas Independent Producers and Royalty Owners

Association—TIPRO. They not only own the surface land, they also own the underground water. They have an interest in not depleting the aquifer."

"That's brilliant, Jane. Can you arrange a meeting?"

"I don't think that'll be a problem," Jane said. "When I was gay I dated a man who was an independent."

"Oil field services," Wanda added after a moment, her interest aroused.

"No kidding!" said Jane.

"What?" Sonny asked.

"All the equipment you need to drill and desalinate and send to market, the services have all that. A whole new business for them."

"Add pipelines to that," said Jane.

"So we might have some allies here," Sonny concluded. It was the first dollop of optimism for his bill he had tasted in quite a while.

"But you're going to have to find a way to get this bill before the members and convince them they're not going to be burned at the stake if they vote for it," Wanda pointed out.

Ezer had been off in some ruminative place, but he finally spoke up. "Why do you even have to drill for water? The frackers are already doing that. Couldn't you use the water when they're done fracking? All they do now is store it in deep injection disposal wells. Hundreds of billions of gallons every year. Where it causes earthquakes, by the way."

"Yeah, we had nearly three hundred earthquakes in Texas last year," said Jane.

"We felt them on our ranch," said Sonny.

"The pressure activates old fault lines," Ezer continued. "If you could take the fracking water and clean it up, you'd solve problems for a lot of people. You could make this a win-win."

★

A surprising invitation—essentially a command—came to Sonny from the speaker to meet in his quarters after dinner. "Don't take it personal," Big Bob said. "I try to keep tabs on all my members, especially when I think they're jumping off a bridge." He was sitting in his parlor wearing a red cardigan like a scary Mr. Rogers.

"You think I'm jumping off a bridge?" Sonny said, as Cinco brought a pitcher of ginger tea with a sprig of mint.

"I just want to give you a heads-up." Big Bob had an unsettling habit of staring directly into your eyes, daring you to look away—a tactic he had developed years ago, but one that came so naturally to him now that you felt the authorities had you chained to a chair with a light in your eyes and you weren't going to get out of the room until you confessed. "You had a bumpy start with that desal bill you floated," the speaker continued. "It pissed off a lot of important people. Now, that's okay. I don't mind seeing such folks get riled and put in their place. As long as it doesn't bounce back and wreck the session. I warned you the first time. A little birdy told me you were trying to breathe life back into that sucker."

"Yes, I am. Although we're making some modifications—"

"The time for submitting new bills has passed," Big Bob said with the understated authority that made him so compelling. "You keep this up and you'll stir up a shitstorm like you never dreamed of, and don't go expecting me to hold your umbrella. Now, you did us all a big favor by tanking Lurleen's homosexual bill. It did not go unnoticed. Nothing does. I'm advising you to take your time. Get your wings. Make some friends. You'll move up. And when you do, maybe you can get your desal bill passed. But remember, there are mighty forces arrayed against you. More powerful than you. Hell, more powerful than me."

"You're talking about L.D.?"

"L.D.? *Shiiit!* L.D. ain't got nothin' 'cept *clients,*" Big Bob said with unexpected scorn. "That certainly does give him entrée to members. He's welcome at parties so long as he pays for dinner. But he doesn't get to vote, not anymore. L.D. is the remains of what was once a great man."

Sonny couldn't stop himself, although he knew he was overstepping. "What happened? He sold out for money? There's some scandal or something like that?"

Big Bob shook his head. "I don't know the whole deal, and what I do I won't tell. I got a problem where L.D. is concerned. I still love that man, or at least the man he was. We're friends, even in his current incarnation. Politics makes it hard. Sometimes you feel like a hypocrite for caring about people who do things you don't approve of. Happens every day in the political life. It's a test of character, I believe, but I still don't know what the answer is. Is the right thing to turn away from any old soul who does wrong? Seems like our society has said you got to goddamn anybody who crosses a line you don't approve of. Maybe so. Maybe we've been too tolerant for too long and it's corrupted the whole damn society. Politics has been, for sure. Nobody talks to anybody who stands on the other side of the line, and that's why just about nothin' ever gets done. Nowadays the whole idea of the forgiveness of sins has been run out of town. I'm speaking of course as an old pol who has been forgiven more than he should have been, so I have an opinion about all this. I'm a Golden Rule man. Treat other folks the way you want to be treated yourself. 'Course, many would say that's horseshit, as it applies to me." He took a sip of ginger tea and gave a little laugh that was scarcely more than an exhalation. "I'd have to agree with that."

★

"I really got pushed off of my bill when I met with the speaker last night," Sonny said when he came into the office. "Something about mighty forces arrayed against me, an umbrella in a shitstorm. The message was real clear."

"It is rarely a good idea to steer against the prevailing wind," Wanda said.

Everyone was quiet until Jane said, "I saw my old flame last night. The independents would be totally on board."

"Shoot, this makes it hard again," said Sonny. "Big Bob will see it as a betrayal if I keep hammering on this."

"We should drop it," Wanda said. "Be pragmatic. There's not a path to a vote in any case."

"So, we're all agreed?" said Sonny.

Each of them nodded. And then Jane couldn't help herself. "When you brought up the bill in the first place, you were talking about reverse osmosis using selectively permeable membranes, which is a great idea. But Ezer and I were talking before you got here. There's a whole new process called forward osmosis."

"Never heard of it," Sonny admitted.

"Ezer, can you explain?"

Ezer typed in something on his screenless computer. He was able to navigate using voice feedback at a speed that was simply incomprehensible to everyone else in the room, rattling out syllables like raindrops in a typhoon. After less than a minute, Ezer had digested an entire scientific paper on the subject. "So what they're saying is that osmosis is a natural process, it's how plants and trees take up water from the soil. With reverse osmosis, you place your brackish water in one tank and the clean water in another, separated by the membrane, and then you apply pressure to the brackish water so that it is filtered and cleansed as it flows into the clean water."

"Yeah, that makes sense," said Sonny.

"The problem with reverse osmosis is the membrane gets fouled and has to be replaced frequently. With forward osmosis, you do the opposite, pushing clean water into brackish, so you dilute it, and the pressure causes reverse osmosis back into the clean water source, on and on, a circular process that doesn't foul the membrane. They're already experimenting with this process on frack water in Louisiana to make it reusable. The membrane is a cellulose triacetate polymer, easy to fabricate. But that's not what's interesting. They've already got an electrical plant in Norway that is using the energy of river water as it passes into the saltwater ocean through the process of natural osmosis."

"So what you're saying is . . ."

"Osmosis creates heat. Heat is energy. They're harvesting the energy of osmosis."

"It might even pay for itself," Sonny speculated.

★

That night he dreamed again of Angela. It was slow motion. He was tied to a chair watching her. She didn't see him. She was just out of the shower, preparing for bed, wearing an emerald nightgown with gold piping, her hair tied up in a towel, which she shook loose like spilling black ink, and she brushed it, slowly, slowly. She couldn't hear him calling to her, the membrane between them filtered out the sounds. Then she pulled up the sheets and turned out the bed-side light, and Sonny awakened and found himself lying beside her again. It wasn't a dream after all.

"I can't see you anymore," she said. "It's not just that you're married. I knew that from the get-go. I've wanted you ever since you shot that pig and gave me the credit. That was so cool. Sex seemed to be inevitable, so why torture ourselves? And I don't regret a minute of it. I loved being with you."

"Me, too."

"It was never going to go anywhere," she said. "I didn't expect it to. You wouldn't have divorced Lola and I wasn't interested in getting married again."

"What changed?"

Angela sat up. She was dimly illuminated by the streetlight leaking through the beige damask curtains in her apartment. "You voted against my bill, Sonny."

"It was bound to happen eventually. We're in different parties, we've got different ideas."

"I know it's naive, but I thought that because I care for you, you would care for what I believe in."

Sonny put his hand on her face, for the last time. He felt both loss and liberation. Their romance had been a parade of mixed feelings for him, guilt accompanied by delights he had only fantasized. He had never thought that he could love two women, or that two such different women would give themselves to him. His love for Lola was deep, unmasked, and lifelong; his love for Angela was electric, spontaneous, and secret. The women existed in separate universes. It was almost comical to think of Angela on the ranch; she was a creature of the city, of issues, of politics. *Urbane* was the word that came to mind, the opposite of rustic. In her company, Sonny learned about a world beyond his own experience. Lola didn't have much patience for city life, and although she often dreamed of travel, she had never been to New York or Washington, much less foreign capitals. Each of these appealing women claimed a part of him. He was trapped between desire and guilt, one emotion reinforcing the other, desire amping up the guilt and vice versa. He wanted to do the right thing, but as Angela spoke he knew he had been waiting for her to do it for him.

"I want to stay friends," he said.

"I want that, too, but Sonny, that bill is at the core of my being. I've been fighting this battle for years. I didn't expect some dazzling victory, just a small step away from the abyss that we've created in this state for women. A little something to make it easier to breathe, to crack open a window and let some hope in. And yet every year it gets worse. Doesn't anybody—any *man*—in this state care about women and the choices they are forced to make? They're trying to turn us into criminals!"

"I know how you feel."

"No, you don't! You'll never know! I just wish one man would get pregnant and everything would change. What makes it so bitter is that I got so close. I got the bill all the way to the floor. Nobody thought it would get to a vote. And then even you—you!—you voted against it!"

"You never asked for my support. I would have told you. We believe differently on this."

"Tell me. Exactly what is it you believe that made you vote against it."

"I believe in giving every baby a chance for life."

Angela pushed his hand away. "It's too hard, Sonny. It's too hard to hate a belief without hating the believer."

19

Lola called. "They're gone," she said.

"The kids?"

"I finally talked to Buster. He came and took them away." She paused, and then her emotions caved in. Sonny hadn't heard her cry like that for years.

"It's the right thing," he told her.

"That's what you say, but we don't know," she said, between sobs. "You should have seen their little faces when he put them in the Explorer. They were so lost. I had just enough time to buy some clothes and toys at the Dollar General. Now they're gone, Sonny! I'll never see them again."

He had to wait until Lola recovered. "Sweetheart, we don't know that. And I'm sure we can visit them in the shelter."

"Well, right now, he took them to jail."

"Good Lord, really?"

"They hold them for up to thirty-two hours, and then those little babies, they send them off to a refugee facility, boys and girls in separate centers. Can you imagine? They made this trip together but now they'll be pulled apart. Poor Pedro, without Carmelita to take care of him!"

"There'll be trained workers there to watch over them. They're strong kids. Look what they did already."

"Yeah, well." Lola was quiet. She was over her crying but not the remorse. "I couldn't keep them, you were right about that. And Buster really was sweet."

"He's handled tons of cases like this."

"He's just a patrol officer, Sonny. He doesn't have the clout to determine their future."

"He'll be able to locate the mother and the uncle. It's really up to them to decide what to do."

"Maybe."

"Those kids are going to be okay. You need to let the system take care of them, Lola. That's what it's set up for."

"Sonny, there's nobody in charge here! You live in some kind of make-believe. This is Texas! Nobody really cares about those kids. Buster says these centers are federally operated, but our own governor revoked the child care licenses of forty-two of these places all along the border."

"He can't do that," said Sonny.

"Maybe he can't, but he did. What kind of state are we, Sonny? Where's the compassion?"

"What about sending them to their uncle in Portland? Possible to find him?"

"We can hope for that. According to Buster, it can take years to sort out their asylum claim, and their uncle is probably illegal, too, so that it all gets to be a larger mess."

"I'm sorry, Lola. I should have been there to help you through this."

"It wouldn't have made any difference. I had to sort this out myself. I went a little crazy when these kids first showed up. It was like when L.D. appeared at our door and suddenly you went off into another world and I lost you."

"You haven't lost me—"

"And then it happened to me. Like a miracle. And I thought, this is what I've been waiting for, these adorable children. Who need me. And I needed them more. It was hard. Okay, they're not our children. But maybe they're not anybody's children. Who else cares about them? We don't know why their mother sent them away. We don't know who this uncle is or if he even wants them. All we know is they're caught in this heartless system that we created, with no road back into the world. We have a responsibility, don't we? To take care of the little creatures? Instead we treat them like criminals. What's wrong with us, Sonny?"

★

"The chair recognizes the representative from Three Rivers," said Big Bob.

Gilbert stood at the front mic. "Thank you, Mr. Speaker. Members, House Bill 2951, Water Resource Development."

It was one of those sleepy sessions where there was barely a quorum. Late afternoon, the gallery was empty. Past the time when new bills could be introduced, so everything was spewing out of committee, a firehose of bills, more or less preapproved so what's to talk about. Some of the members in the frat boy section were watching porn movies on their iPads. Sonny looked on as one representative, a former television sportscaster obsessively vain about his hair, surreptitiously pasted a strip of Scotch tape over the vent on the back of the cushioned leather chair in front of him, so when someone sat in it the little burst of air would not alter a strand of his coiffure. That kind of session.

Gilbert continued to drone on about his bill. "The bill provides revenue for water allocations, both from surface and subsurface points of origin. Moreover, this bill—"

Sonny suddenly snapped to and jumped to his feet as if he had been hit with 220 volts. "Will the member yield?"

Gilbert looked up in surprise, and when he recognized Sonny, he was clearly annoyed and on guard. "I yield to the impatient gentleman from Presidio County."

"Because this bill deals with water resources, I propose an amendment. I urge adoption of certain allowances pertaining to desalinating groundwater in this state for purposes of irrigation and household use—"

"Mr. Speaker!" Gilbert shouted. "I object. He's trying to unload his desalination bill onto my revenue bond."

"Because it's about water resources!" said Sonny, over a chorus of groans. "This amendment is appropriate and necessary. If the members would allow me to explain—"

But Gilbert wasn't giving way. "I move the previous question to end debate and proceed immediately to a vote on the revenue bond."

Everything went quiet while Big Bob conferred with the parliamentarian. When he emerged from the conversation, he ruled that the amendment was germane. "Representative Lamb, you may present your amendment."

"Thank you, Mr. Speaker, and Representative Delgado, I appreciate your indulgence. Members, so far what I've learned about politics is that it's all about choices. Every day in this chamber we make choices, and every choice we make leads to a different future.

"I'm a conservative in the old sense. I think we should conserve our natural resources. When we talk about those resources, we always think of oil. But there is a far more valuable resource. That's water. Right now we're squandering water as if we will never run out of it. If you want to see what happens to the state when we run dry, come visit us in West Texas, where the drought has just about extinguished our economy. We can run out of oil in Texas—and one day we will—and Texas will survive. But if we run out of water, the dream of Texas is dead.

"It's a choice. You're going to make that choice right now. My amendment will ensure the water future for our state for generations to come. If we do nothing, Texas will be pumped dry by the fracking interests. All that water we have stored in those deep injection wells is poisoned and useless. We have a chance to change that. I urge adoption."

"There's been a motion to vote on the amendment," Big Bob said. "All those in favor signify by saying 'Aye.'"

"Aye," said Sonny, looking around the chamber for at least one other voice.

"Opposed?"

"NAY!" It was resounding and deafening.

"Representative Lamb," said the speaker, "your amendment has failed. We move on to a vote about the revenue bond . . ."

Just like that, Sonny's bill was dead, one small moment in the session, unremarked by nearly everyone.

★

Sonny flew his Cessna back to the ranch. He had a lot of things to clear up.

When he had made that first trip in the other direction, only a few months before, he had been hopeful, full of promise, certain that he was on his way to a grand new career, one that his whole life implicitly had been pointing to, waiting to be discovered. These pretensions were rudely ripped away. He had talked himself into believing that he was another kind of man than he actually was. Which was, when you got right down to it, a nobody.

This thought occurred to him roughly over Junction, a little town named for being the junction of the North and South Llano Rivers and a number of highways, including I-10 where it arcs up from San Antonio and makes a beeline for El Paso and points west. Along the way were little no-count towns clinging to the interstate like ticks on a dog. Towns full of other nobodies. Cities differing from towns only in having a greater accumulation of nobodies. The vanity and pointlessness of existence, especially that of Sonny Lamb, were starkly revealed to him. When he got elected, there was a brief moment when he thought there might be a point to his being alive, that his existence had a direction, a purpose. But who was he fooling? The whole project of ambition was to become somebody rather than nobody. Some did it by pursuing money, or fame, or good works, or distinction in sports or the arts—or politics—but like it or not everybody starts out a baby nobody and winds up a dead nobody. The people who don't even try have it right.

He would crawl back to the life he thought he had escaped. It wasn't so bad. Maybe he had been onto something with the desalination scheme. Before, he only had routines, or what you might call repetitions, the same movements every day, from brushing his teeth in the morning to brushing them at night. Then, along came the Big Idea, which had awakened him to possibilities, which had awarded meaning and purpose to the nobody who had come up with it. New possibilities arose; new relationships. He fell under the spell of this exciting conception of himself: the man with Big Ideas. Ideas that went nowhere.

He had a stop to make. Just past the Pecos River was a little nowhere spot call Iraan, named after Ira and Ann Yates, where one of the first big oil fields was developed in the 1920s, a massive find. Once a real town grew up there. Texas was covered with places that mushroomed into existence with one oil boom or another, promising to be the next Dallas or San Antonio, and then drying up along with the exhausted wells. You could still see the pads laid out like egg cases emitted from the once-pregnant geology of Iraan. It was less orderly than in the heart of the Permian, where the oil fields looked from the air like graph paper, perfectly spaced to suck every molecule of petroleum from the clutch of the earth. The abandoned fields around Iraan stretched on and on, poisoning the earth with their methane breath, these marks of ruin and exploitation, enriching nobodies who thought they were somebodies, like Odell Peeples.

Sonny set his Cessna down at the ranch of one his constituents, Mamie Soderberg, an unmarried rancher who had inherited twenty-five thousand acres of played-out acreage on the edge of the Permian, just south of Iraan, on the northern edge of Sonny's district. She was a gruff old dame who had made a respectable fortune writing pornographic novels, which she published herself, under the name Dawn Delight. The heroine was a cowgirl who has tamed a few men in her time, meting out punishments they thoroughly deserved. Doris was addicted to them.

Mamie met him on the dirt strip in her Bronco. She was a bosomy woman in her seventies with sunbaked wrinkles and aviator shades, wearing a kind of French Foreign Legion hat with a flap to cover the back of her neck, and a flannel shirt with a pack of Virginia Slims in the pocket and the sleeves rolled up to display her erotic tattoos. She was on a tear.

"Sons of bitches ruined this place," she said by way of greeting.

The point of the visit was to let her air her complaints about abandoned oil wells on her ranch, some of which had been drilled nearly a century before, others fracked in the 1990s. Now they were returning in a grotesque afterlife. "Look at this," she said, as she guided her Bronco through the brush. Sonny could smell a gas leak at the center of a circle of dead acacias. "The other day we got us a geyser of radioactive brine from one of these supposedly sealed-up tubes, blew fifty feet in the air. Capping that fucker was a mess. I had to ferry one of my hands to the hospital in Fort Stockton for an MRI. He's alive, but Jesus on a Friday, what do we have to do to clean this shit up? We got pools of weird-colored liquids showing up like Yellowstone Park. And the cattle, it was a fucking massacre." She parked on a knoll that overlooked the remains of the old field, with maybe a hundred capped pipes spread across it. Black splotches of petroleum and other fluids bubbled up alongside the tarbrush and broomweed. About a hundred yards away was a pond, maybe two acres in size, the source of a powerful stench. "Look at it, will you?" Mamie said. "We don't want to get too close because it's not clear what's in there besides sulfur and salt. Heavy metals and arsenic for sure. It's weird because you see shore birds out here some days. Pelicans. I sometimes find their carcasses, so whatever's in there is dangerous as all get-out.

"When my grandparents owned this place, it was covered with grass. Waist high, they told me. Imagine how beautiful. And they overgrazed, like most everybody. Maybe they didn't appreciate what was at stake. There was still plenty enough good land here when the drillers came. I guess my kinfolk believed that the land was resilient, it was strong, it could come back from whatever. Or maybe they were just free-booters looking for the loot and out the door they go. But that didn't happen. They sold their mineral rights and made a tidy bundle, but it's not like they ever enjoyed their money. They didn't run off to Paris and kick up their heels. They just stayed in place. It was rare for them even to drive into Midland. My parents were the same way, although they got their education and saw some of the world. Yet something pulled them back here. I'm sure they could see what was happening. I'm the same goddamn way, really. Never broke free of this place. It casts a spell, even now, with all this"—she gestured at the apocalyptic landscape. "There's something going on underground, some terrible upset, who knows what got stirred up, but it's wreaking revenge. We take all this stuff out of the ground and then think we can close the door on it and just walk away."

She laughed despairingly. "Here's the deal, Sonny. This stuff is killing me. It did kill my folks, both dead before their middle sixties. The well water is the color of a storm cloud. I get rashes. I wake up coughing, although cigarettes, yeah. But these days stuff comes up out of me, kinda like what you see out there. And it pisses me off. Yes, I'm mad at the drillers who left this mess behind them, but I'm also mad at myself for letting it get worse and worse. So I got a favor to ask of you. I'd like to see this land repaired somehow. I've spent much of my fortune trying to breathe life back into it, but I don't have the wherewithal. It's gonna take a mighty force to bring back the Texas that we inherited. Will you help me? All of us?"

★

"This is our moment, Mr. Sparks. You've done splendid work this session," Mr. Peeples said. "Putting an end to the quorum break was a tidy bit of business. Are we sure that that little pest you brought on board has been dealt with?"

"I've taken care of that matter," said L.D. "I think you'll find that he'll be much more compliant in the future."

Mr. Peeples did a little war dance around the room, whooping and pounding his chest, spiking an imaginary ball. "I've got a little bonus for you," he said.

Such lovely words. Mr. Peeples pushed a button under his desk and the bookshelf opened to reveal a walk-in safe, something you would find in a bank downtown. He spun the dial and then turned a wheel and the massive door clicked open. "Come inside, Mr. Sparks, I'll give you a tour."

The first thing L.D. noticed were gold bars stacked like firewood, "like Fort Knox," he marveled.

"Oh, the gold, yeah," Mr. Peeples said dismissively. "The jewels, you get more bang for the ounce. Currencies of various denominations. A few historical artifacts. Confederate silver. On this wall you'll see some of Hitler's artwork, the better pieces. I just love to sit in here of an evening, buck naked, with a glass of chocolate milk. Sounds kinky, doesn't it?" He giggled. "But that's me!"

"It's stunning," said L.D. "Never seen anything like it, such a concentration of raw wealth." His fingers brushed across a tub of rubies.

"Go ahead, Mr. Sparks. Fill your pockets."

"Really?"

"Whatever your heart desires."

"Am I dreaming?" L.D. said, actually wondering.

"I'm getting rid of all this anyway. Moving into bitcoin." L.D. eyed the diamonds as Mr. Peeples talked. "We've almost achieved our goal of total domination. Texas is ours! Please, Mr. Sparks, help yourself! Do you want a bag?"

★

Sonny found Lola in the south pasture castrating bull calves. Along with Lencho, there were a half a dozen freelance cowboys roping calves and tending the branding fire. It took four of the hands to wrestle an animal into a squeeze chute, where it was ear-tagged and branded and vaccinated against blackleg. While this was going on, Lola made quick work with the knife. She knew Sonny was squeamish, but without even saying hello she directed him to hold the bucket for the testicles. She was so intent, pouring sweat, you couldn't help but be awed by her proficiency. There was rarely any blood, just a quick squeal from the calf and away he goes. Or what was formerly a he, having transitioned from bull to steer in a single instant.

Part of the ceremony, unfortunately, was that Lola would make a meal of the testicles—or mountain oysters, they were called, when sitting on a plate, like disembodied eyeballs staring at you, full of reproach. Lola never let anything go to waste. Lately her preferred technique was to string a dozen of them on skewers and put them on the grill, like shish kabob. Sonny forced them down. He wondered if eating testicles might magically help his sperm count, which turned out to be just ahead of marginal, according to a second trip to the depository. It proved easier to masturbate when the police weren't after you.

Sonny was reporting for ovulation duty, but Lola was in no hurry. She was probably worn out from the hard work, and no doubt she was still grieving for those Honduran children. He was cautious, giving her space to work out whatever was on her mind.

"I'm sorry about your bill," Lola said.

"I got spanked pretty hard."

"You'll recover. You always do."

He couldn't tell if that was a compliment. It made him sound superficial, as if events and emotions didn't penetrate very deeply, and yet here he was, full of despair and self-loathing, a whipped dog. "The whole session, I haven't accomplished a single thing."

"That's not true. And look how you handled that waste disposal bill. Folks are still talking about it, saying they were for it all along."

"Maybe I caught a few ground balls. That's sure not the session I wanted to have."

"It's not over. You've still got another six weeks."

As Sonny did the dishes, he imagined losing Lola. Their life was humble but happy enough. Why had he placed everything in the balance with Angela? His big secret. The morality of disclosing it was complicated. Thanks to Angela, it was over. But you never knew about those things, did you? What had once caught fire could again. And not telling meant that he kept the possibility alive. In that sense, he was still betraying Lola.

On the other hand, why inflict the truth on her when it could do so much harm? Was it really necessary to turn their lives inside out because of an affair so brief, of so little consequence when all was said and done? Would their marriage survive it? Would Lola ever trust him again? Why should she?

But could he live with this secret for their rest of their lives, hiding a part of himself from the person he was closest to in the world?

"There's something I've got to tell you." This was Lola. Sonny dried his hands. "On the porch," she said.

The moonless night sky was clear, the constellations utterly visible, their astrological secrets there to be deciphered if you could only read them. A satellite traced an arc about thirty degrees above the western horizon. The porch, where serious conversations took place, was two worn-down Amish rocking chairs on faded blue planks of cedar. Lola set a pair of tumblers with a bottle of añejo tequila on a repurposed avocado crate. "We need to talk," she said. "I got the new lab results."

"They sent them to you?"

"Sonny, I'm so sorry."

"That's all right, I'll deal with it. She said it was marginal."

"No, she didn't. She said it was hopeless."

"She did?"

"She said I'll never have children. It's a problem with my uterus. The endometrial walls don't thicken. There's nothin' we can do."

"You mean, there's something wrong with you?"

"God, Sonny, what did you think I was saying?"

"I thought we were talking about my test tube thing, which wasn't so hot either."

"Even if we got a conception, I wouldn't be able to carry it. Our child."

"We'll deal with it," he said.

"I'll never be able to provide that for you." Her voice was leaden and contrite, un-Lolalike.

"Listen, Lola, we'll deal with it!" he said again. "Really!"

But the consolation only pulled the emotional plug and her tears began to flow. "I'm so sorry," she kept repeating. She tried to stop crying, but she couldn't find the tap.

"Please, Lola, don't apologize. Honey, it's not your fault."

"Yes it is! It's all my fault!"

"Nothin' is all your fault. Biology, blame biology. But it doesn't have anything to do with who Lola Lamb is."

"Quit bein' a gentleman about it."

"We both wanted kids, but maybe that's not something that will be given to us. We've got each other, and that's more than enough for me."

Lola studied him. "You haven't told me how you feel, Sonny," she said, her voice steadied. "It's not just my loss."

"I'm . . ." He was going to say he was sad, but suddenly he felt a rush of emotion as he saw that part of his future had been erased, the future where there would have been children and a reason to live beyond your own life, someone little who would grow and become old and remember you. Someone who needed you, someone who would make Lola and Sonny into a family, not just a couple of lonely people in the dark with no future to look forward to. And no words came.

Lola took his hand. "I know," she said.

For a moment they just stared at the stars.

"So this is it," Lola said, as she sat back in her rocker and surveyed the dim landscape. "This is what we have." Then: "I don't deserve you."

Those words sank into him like a knife. He took a considerable sip of tequila. "Sweetheart, I've got something to tell you, too. It's kinda hard."

"Well, spit it out. Long as it's not another woman, I can take it." But when Sonny was quiet she gasped. "No!" she cried. "You can't be serious!"

As soon as she said it she realized she had always known this would happen. Their life together was headed for this from the start, but she had never allowed herself to look down the road of destiny, and now here they were.

"It's over. It was a mistake, a stupid and careless mistake," Sonny said to the air because Lola wasn't listening to this part.

"Who is she?"

"I don't know how it happened, but it's over," he repeated. "I swear to God!"

"Dammit, Sonny, who are you protecting?"

There was no way out once he had started. The thing about confessions was that you want to tell a part of it, but a part is never the whole and it's the whole that you have to spill. You can't just jump to the end. "Her name's Angela Martinez, she's a member from—"

"I know who she is," Lola snapped. "I always heard this is what went on in Austin. I don't know why I thought it would be any different with you."

"It was almost like an accident," Sonny said.

"I wish you could hear how that sounds."

Lola was quiet for a moment, but Sonny could hear the commotion in her brain, the dumping of drawers and the looking under mattresses until she found the thing that had kept him from saying anything at all, until now.

"There's something else, isn't there?" she asked. "Who knows about it?"

As much as he hated admitting it, he also admired Lola for figuring it out, for knowing him as deeply as she did. "L.D.," he said. "He knows the whole dang thing."

"Is he blackmailing you?"

"It doesn't work like that. It's the kind of deal, if I cross him, he'll put out the word."

"Are you saying he's got you in his pocket?"

"I owe him. It's a debt, and one day he'll collect." Sonny added, "I wouldn't want you to be embarrassed if this got out."

"*Me?* You're the one who can't keep his thing in his pants."

"Yeah, okay."

"I'm embarrassed for you, 'cause you're letting someone else control who you are. You already told me you're a cheater. Are you a quitter, too?"

"No, I'm not."

"Well, then, who are you? What happened to you? You went to Austin to do something good, remember?"

"Yeah, I do."

"Then you go back and fight 'em."

Sonny looked at Lola as if he'd never met this woman before, so powerful, so clear. "Damn, Lola. I love you so much."

"Well, you should have thought about that. 'Cause from now on, you're on your own."

$\star$ **20** $\star$

On the banks of Buffalo Bayou just west of downtown Houston the venerable River Oaks Country Club hosted an annual pro-am golf tournament. This year Jordan Spieth was there, along with Tiger Woods and some of the old timers, including Ben Crenshaw and Tom Kite. The celebrity cards were always filled with movie stars and country singers—Matthew McConaughey and George Strait were the go-tos—and a sprinkling of politicians who typically fudged their scores. Outdoor events in Houston were a risk, given the smothering humidity during eight months of the year, and the city's susceptibility to extreme weather events, including tornados, hail the size of softballs, floods, everything short of volcanos. The fact that the city was still inhabited was a testament to something or other.

"All these luminaries have turned out for a good cause, Chuck," said the blond reporter into the video camera. "The proceeds go to benefit the MD Anderson Cancer Center. Oh, here's Big Bob Bigbee, the speaker of the Texas House. Mr. Speaker, your observations?"

Big Bob was not in the mood. "Yes, honey," he said. "Them jeans you're wearing are mighty tight. You cut a fart and you'll blow your damn boots off."

"Back to you, Chuck."

"You sure are a sourpuss today," L.D. observed. He looked spiffy in his argyle sweater and knickers.

"Gonna have us a turd floater in about five minutes," Big Bob remarked. This event had been on the calendar for weeks, but a storm had arisen in the Gulf and thunder grumbled nearby. A club official scurried around, calling all the golfers into the clubhouse. "Chickenshit," the speaker said over his shoulder as the official passed by.

"Let's go, Bob, I'll stake you to a root beer," L.D. said, getting worried about the speaker's frame of mind.

"You thinkin' 'bout quittin'?"

"It's gonna storm, you said it yourself. Now let's go inside—"

Just as L.D. spoke, a bolt of lightning struck. L.D. counted eight seconds, so about a mile and a half away, he figured, but moving really fast.

"That was godawful close, Bob. C'mon, let's get into the clubhouse, work up a card game while this passes over." By now it was beginning to sprinkle. "All right, here comes the rain. We're gonna get pneumonia if the lightning doesn't get us first."

Big Bob toyed with his clubs as if he were planning to tee off. Another lightning strike. Six seconds.

"Bob. No shit. You're scaring me."

"Lee Trevino. Struck by lightning three times on the golf course. And lived to tell the tale."

"Yeah, well, he wasn't asking for it."

Big Bob took a couple practice swings. It might have been a mild summer day in Palm Springs. "I heard you really put Sonny Lamb in a fix," he said over his shoulder.

"Why, yes, I did, thank you. He was beginning to mess with the gods. Some kind of death wish."

"Everybody's gotta die, L.D. What's it all for?"

The rain began to come on full strength. "Let's go, Bob, this has stopped being amusing."

Big Bob turned to face the oncoming storm, his still-dark hair pressed back by the wind. He had a weird calm about him, as if he was living on the other side of reality, like there was a place where everything was the opposite of what you're used to and standing in a downpour was just what you do. "One day, L.D., I want you to do me a favor."

"You know I'll do anything for you, Bob. Let's go in the club-house and talk about it."

"I want you to do one decent thing for Texas."

"You cut me, Bob!" L.D. protested.

"One decent thing that nobody paid you for." As he said this, Big Bob stripped off his shirt and tossed it in the golf bag. Totally natural.

"What the hell are you doing? Put your damn shirt back on."

CRACK! Lightning struck with no seconds at all, illuminating the clubhouse through the rain like the noon sun.

"Jesus, Bob! No kidding! Let's get out of here! Run!"

But a confounding air of relaxation had settled on Big Bob as he kicked off his shoes and took off his pants. "C'mon, L.D.," he cajoled. "Strip 'em off, let's play."

"I'm goin' in, Bob."

"Existential golf. This is what the Lord intended."

"For Pete's sake, put your clothes back on. Somebody might get a picture."

"Man must face the elements, naked and alone!" Big Bob cried, his body now fully exposed: an old man's flab, scars from numerous operations, his mortality shockingly in evidence as lightning struck again. "C'mon, Lord!" Big Bob said, waving an iron toward the sky. "Bring it down! Show me what you got!"

L.D. might have been weeping, with the rain it was impossible to tell, but his voice was choking, and he could scarcely get words out. "Please, Bob! Don't tempt Him!" he begged. "Put down that seven iron!"

"Here I am! You gonna do me, do me now!" Big Bob roared.

L.D.'s hair rose off his neck, and at the same moment lightning struck their golf cart, for no special reason, the way lightning does, arbitrary and instant. The cart exploded.

"Missed!" Big Bob cried, laughing, doing a little jig. "I'm here! Over to the right about twenty feet."

There was only one thing to do. L.D. rushed Big Bob and tackled his wasted body to the ground. He fell with little resistance. "Give me that damn iron," L.D. said. "We're goin' in!"

They were nose to nose, L.D. lying on top of Big Bob to keep him pinned. They had never been so close. "What's wrong?" Big Bob said in an intimate and reasonable-sounding tone. "Are you scared, L.D.?"

"I'm scared shitless," L.D. responded in a similar intimate voice, as if they were worried about being overheard, although the rain closed them in like a curtain.

"You go on in, I'll be along in a while," Big Bob said.

"I'm not going without you."

"No need to be here if you don't wish to be."

"I don't want to die out here," said L.D. "You neither."

"You gotta die, L.D."

"What's wrong with you?" L.D. said, almost a whisper now.

"What's it all for?"

"Bob, what's goin' on with you? Tell me, please. I'm worried about you. Have been for weeks now."

"I got that shit," said Big Bob. "Cancer. I got cancer. And all the damn celebrity golfers in the world ain't gonna put Humpty Dumpty back together."

Lightning struck again.

"Now are we gonna play some golf?"

★

"Sonny, it's your mother."

"Mom, you always say that, and I always know who it is. I'm really busy." Sonny was sitting in his Airstream studying the aluminum parabola. He was intrigued by the absence of straight lines, the ambiguity of forms, like life.

"I talked to Lola."

"I'm sure you did."

"Marriage is complicated, Sonny."

"You're going to give me marriage advice? Didn't you and Dad divorce? I recollect blows being exchanged."

"You needn't be sarcastic."

"Mom, I'm going to say this with a lot of love: Butt out."

"I'm just giving you support. There you are, all by yourself in Sin City, no wonder you crossed the line. I did so myself, many a time."

"This is where I hang up, Mom."

"Tell me, Sonny, why do parents and children have to hide their true selves from each other? Don't you want to know the real me?"

"I've got a pretty good bead on that, actually."

"You have no idea."

"Goodbye, Mom."

"Don't you dare hang up on—Sonny? Hello?"

Sonny returned to contemplating the aluminum. He had done a thorough job of ruining his life, he had to admit. Going back to Angela had no future. It had stung when she voted against his bill, but, of course, everyone had, and after all he had voted against hers, so fair enough. Political differences were always going to stand between them.

He would need a new job. The ranch belonged to Lola. Not that it was providing much of a living for either of them. Moreover, he supposed his political career was over. So that was everything. A total wipeout.

Could he just let go of it all and start over? Was there even a choice?

He had felt alone and defeated before, after Iraq. Lola had mostly been supportive, but other times she was ready to wash her hands of him. He was broken and she couldn't glue the pieces together, especially when he got into drugs. Opioids make you feel like you up and walked away from the pain and the problems of the world, your own especially, despite the occasional nausea. But there was the gnawing need that followed, like you would tear down the house to get back to la la land. A lot of vets walked the same road. Some of them didn't come back. The suicides in Sonny's own unit were shocking. That might have been his destiny, but until now there was enough juice in life to keep him interested.

He called Valerie Nightingale. "I'm thinking of quitting," he told her. "I wanted you to be ready in case."

"That's nice, but why?"

He didn't know how much to confide in her. "I just kinda went off the rails," he said. "It all goes back to deciding to run for office. I made some poor decisions in my personal life. I doubt the voters will forgive me."

"Really? 'Cause I've been spending a lot of time setting up your district office, and from my perspective right now you're pretty much unbeatable."

Sonny weighed this. Sometimes people outside yourself know better than you do, so he paid attention. "I'm trying to decide what's more important, my career or my marriage," he admitted.

"I can't judge that. Nobody but you can do that. But do you really think that sacrificing your career will save your marriage?"

"Maybe. I don't know what else would."

"Was your marriage in such great shape before you got elected?"

"I'd have to say no. But that was because of me. I couldn't accept the life I had. So I had to go out and get a new one."

"And you don't know if the old one is still available."

"That's right."

"I'm not the best person to ask, Sonny. I'd love for you to quit and give me the chance to run again. I doubt I'd get elected, after what you did to me in that last campaign. But I'd hate to see you go. You stirred things up, that's for sure, more than Walter Dunne did in his thousand years of office. It'd be hard for me to believe you behaved any worse than that old scoundrel. Think about all the harm that man did, those gun laws he sponsored, making it practically mandatory for teenagers to carry assault weapons. Those attacks on gay marriage. His scarcely disguised racism. And he was a Democrat. Or called himself one. Sonny, Walter was a bad man. He was bad for Texas. He hurt the state, and yet folks here kept reelecting him like they were hypnotized. You're the first good thing to come out of this district in a long, long time. Promise me you'll think carefully before you throw it away on something that may not be worth going back to."

★

The only law the biennial legislature of Texas is required to pass is the General Appropriations Act—the budget. It must be submitted by the 90th day of the 140-day session and be large enough to fund the nearly sixteen hundred bills passed by the two chambers. None of those bills are safe from the hundreds of amendments already filed that are fighting for salvation. It all happens on Budget Night, the climax of the session, an all-night Walpurgisnacht, when deeds are done and blood is spilled and dead bills rise from their graves.

On the afternoon before Sonny's first Budget Night, members and staffers began to wander the hallways searching out the margarita machines in various offices. By midnight, the level of drunkenness was such that few could legally drive. If they were too drunk to stand, the troopers would escort them out. And the night was just getting started.

Big Bob ruthlessly ran through more than four hundred amendments as rapidly as possible, but many had yet to be debated on the floor. By design, the chamber was freezing cold, to keep members alert, but the shivering made it hard to concentrate. More experienced members wore long johns or brought a blanket. To fight off sleep, five-hour energy shots were available, which some members downed every hour. The horse trading was frantic. Clusters formed around the speaker's rostrum, an ongoing agitated churning fueled by desperation and exhaustion. Under the rules, proposed amendments couldn't add to the budget's bottom line, so any increase meant a decrease somewhere in the proposed expenditure. After all the maneuvering to get their bills passed, members who had already taken a victory lap watched their bills get defunded at the last moment, their efforts counting for nothing. Many hearts would be broken on Budget Night.

Sonny offered two amendments. One was his desalination bill, a last hopeless attempt to smuggle it into Gilbert's revenue bond. The speaker assigned that amendment to Title XI, otherwise known as the wish list, the very last thing voted on, which it never is. Nothing makes its way off the wish list; it's a death sentence.

Sonny's other amendment was to H.B. 2781, sponsored by Royce

Drummond, a Republican member from Garland, pertaining to the oil field cleanup fund, which had been established in 1991 to address the problem of orphan wells, such as the ones on Mamie Soderberg's ranch. In the decades since that bill was passed, little had been accomplished. Drummond's bill sought to clarify the uses of that cleanup fund before it could be raided for other purposes. Around two in the morning, the speaker called for Sonny's amendment to be read.

Wanda, Jane, and Ezer were watching from the gallery. They had been working on this for the past week. Money was the problem, as it always is on Budget Night, but Jane had been researching the dark alleys of dedicated accounts from prior legislative sessions. Often money is allocated but never spent, in which case it resides in a state bank account, a zombie, neither dead nor alive. Budget writers like to have unspent money on tap; it's like a savings account that will cover the overage of a check that doesn't clear; however, the money has to be replaced or spent for the purposes for which it was allocated. Jane's eye had fallen on Account 5071, titled Emissions Reduction Plan, which had a balance of more than $2 billion. There was another $150 million appropriated but never spent for a law titled Oil and Gas Regulation and Cleanup. Those two accounts represented less than half the unspent money in the state treasury.

"This amendment puts into action the intentions of lawmakers from previous years to repair the damage to our air and water that industry has left behind after profiting from the petroleum resources of our state," Sonny said, when called upon to explain his amendment. "Again and again, lawmakers have attempted to hold the polluters to account. Bills have come forward only to be shot down or relegated to the wish list. Those that have been placed into law have had their pockets picked for purposes that fail to serve the original intention. The amendment before you directs that funds already in the general account be used to restore Texas to its natural state."

"Will the gentleman from Presidio County yield for a question?" This from Kent Maxwell, an oil and gas lawyer from Houston, who spoke with ease and disdain reflecting his long experience in the House. "You're talking about using taxpayer money to pay land-owners who already profited from the sale of their mineral rights. Why should the people of Texas pay them again? If a tornado rips off the roof of your house, you don't demand payment from the state. It's an act of God."

"Representative Maxwell, I don't think God bears any responsi-bility for the poorly capped wells that are despoiling our land. We've been drilling holes in this state since the turn of the twentieth cen-tury. Dry wells, water wells, test wells, gushers—we're talking about millions of holes in the ground. Over time, they become corroded. Some were never capped in the first place. Many of the companies that did the drilling are long gone, as are those original landowners who may have profited. But the problem hasn't gone away. These wells have been described as ticking time bombs, poisoning our air, our aquifers, and our surface waters. What kind of stewards are we if we don't even spend the money that we've already set aside to address the issue?"

"There may be other and better uses for those funds," Maxwell said. "I've been given to understand by one of our colleagues in the Other Place that the lieutenant governor has placed a claim on those same accounts for purposes of S.B. 1433, pertaining to reimburse-ment of oil companies for cleanup for existing wells."

That woke up the chamber. The speaker didn't like being sur-prised. He turned off the mic and signaled to Sonny and Maxwell to approach the rostrum. "When did this happen?" he demanded.

"I just now heard about it, Mr. Speaker," Maxwell said. "The lieutenant governor specifically targeted those same funds."

"To pay the oil companies for doing what they're required by law to do?"

"Sir, it may seem that way—"

"That son of a bitch." The speaker's feelings about the lieuten-ant governor were well known. "Well, let's vote on the amendment. If it passes, we'll work this out in conference."

Sonny called for the vote. The fact that the Senate bill was clearly a raid on taxpayer money to profit the oil companies raised the ire of a sufficient number of members to pass the amendment. The speaker stunned everyone when the bell of the last vote had rung, saying, "Show the speaker as voting aye." He was sending a message.

★

The conference took place at six in the morning when the House briefly adjourned, having passed a $260 billion budget that was supposed to carry Texas through the next two years. The speaker wanted the House budget reconciled with the Senate's as quickly as possible because the deadline was approaching. "Get this over with," he commanded the House conferees. "Be nice, give them a snack, but don't let them have a full meal. Keep in mind this is all complete horseshit and we can't let them get away with it."

Sonny had just enough time to meet with his staff. Ezer was ecstatic because he saw the negotiation as a perfect opportunity to employ game theory. "Each delegation has five members, and a resolution requires a majority vote from both sides. So nobody wins unless three members on each side agree. It's a beautiful game."

"So how do we play it?"

"Start with what you know about the other team's goals. Suppose you're in a foreign country and you're buying a rug. Hard to put a value on that, it's not like buying a car, where you have comparables. The actual value is how much you want it. That's something the seller doesn't know. If he guesses you'll have it at any price, he won't negotiate. So, I'm the seller, ask me what the price is."

"What's the price?"

"Ten thousand dollars."

"I'll give you five."

"See, that's your first mistake," said Ezer. "The seller knows that's what you're going to offer. He deals with tourists every day and they always go to half. You're starting at different places. You think he wants ten, but he really expects five because that's the price you're going to name. Maybe he can bargain you up from there. He'll sure try. But five is his bottom line and you've already agreed to that."

"What would you offer him?"

"Nothing," said Ezer. "The best strategy is to walk out of the store. Chances are, he'll go to five as soon as you reach the door, and then you can bargain down from there."

"In this case, we've got five buyers and sellers on each side."

"That's the game within the game. You have to court a majority of the other side without surrendering your own, finding strategies that will break up the resistance and allow you to pick up susceptible members on the other side. If you know what they want, you've got a chance. Otherwise, they'll push you aside and game over."

"Gotta go," said Sonny. "I'll let you know."

The House delegation was chaired by Joe Tran, from Galveston, who headed the House Appropriations Committee. Royce Drummond was there because it was his bill, and Sonny, because his amendment triggered the conference. The two remaining House members were Ernestine Smallwood and Lurleen Klump. They met in a handsome Senate conference room behind the lieutenant governor's office, enemy territory. It was certainly a signal of the leader's interest. A plate of breakfast tacos lay before them, along with a pot of coffee. The cups were cobalt blue and emblazoned with the seal of the Senate.

The senators introduced themselves. They were led by Doc Holland, head of the Senate Finance Committee, a skillful legislator and Dan Patrick's attack dog. The author of the Senate bill was Irene Petri, who worked at Exxon headquarters, in Irving. It wasn't against the law to carry a bill that would benefit her employer, but it was dangerously close to an ethics violation. The other three senators were all very senior and firmly embedded in the lieutenant governor's camp. His picture adorned the wall that the House members faced.

Doc Holland, a former federal prosecutor in Dallas, was in his mid-fifties, with a deceptively genial manner. In contrast to everyone else he was fresh and on top of his game, looking as if he had just awakened from a two-hour nap. He began by reviewing the conference rules. "We can only negotiate on matters we don't agree upon. Both bills deal with oil field cleanup and both target the same money. Our position is that these monies are better used by private industry, which has the experience and know-how, as well as the legal responsibility, to maintain the oil fields, now and in the future. The cleanup provision has proved onerous to many of these companies, which are of course foundational to the Texas economy. Our object here is to find a middle ground. I'm going to turn now to my House counterpart, Mr. Tran, for his opening remarks."

Joe was a fortunate choice to lead the committee, Sonny believed. He was a sharp poker player in the informal House game, smooth of manner, unrevealing and cool-headed; he had sat in with pros in Vegas on occasion. "The main difference in our bills is that we are targeting abandoned wells. Your bill would raid those accounts to reimburse the industry for working wells that they currently lease or those recently out of service. Any money you take out of our bill will go to reward the industry for shirking its responsibilities. It's a form of corporate theft."

"I didn't hear an offer in there," said Doc.

"This wasn't my bill," Joe said. "I'm going to let Representative Drummond speak."

Shoot, thought Sonny, our best negotiator just handed off the ball. Nor did Royce seem ready. Sonny prepared himself to hear that they would split the pot, everybody comes out with something, who can complain, the tourist in the rug shop. And Royce had only asked for $150 million to start with. He'd be ecstatic.

"Our proposal is ninety-ten," said Royce. "You get the ten."

That was surprising, equivalent to walking out the door, Sonny thought. Now was the place where Doc counters with halfsies and we go home.

"I'm sorry, Representative Drummond, but we don't have the authority to negotiate the money," said Doc.

"Ten percent. It's still a lot of money," Royce said, not quite understanding what he just heard.

"When we walk out of here, we'll have to have the entire $2 billion already dedicated for emissions," Doc said, reaching for a second taco, as casual as can be, "plus the $150 million in the cleanup account."

"This is the middle path you're talking about?" Royce said, dumbfounded, as were all the House members. He turned to Irene, the Exxon employee. "You're thinking about giving your employer billions of dollars of our tax money?" Royce delivered this with an edge. Everyone on the House side thought her bill crossed a line.

"Well, there are other companies—a number of them—that would benefit," Irene said. "Not just Exxon. We have a strong interest in a clean environment, but we shouldn't be left with the entire responsibility. It's perfectly reasonable to ask the state to pitch in."

"I'd like to see your Christmas bonus," said Lurleen.

"That's not fair," said Irene, fingering the gold cross on her necklace.

"I've seen this before from the Senate side," Lurleen said. She was plainly furious. "You're robbing the people of this state. Our citizens have previously expressed their interest in cleaning up the mess your industry left behind. That's what we're here for, not to further enrich a company for whom two billion dollars is a rounding error." She stared at the other senators. "I know what she gets out of it"—gesturing to Irene—"but I expect all of you have been well rewarded by industry contributions. That's the only reason you're in this room."

Sonny watched this outburst in total shock. Until now, he had only seen Lurleen the culture warrior, the religious zealot, and he had allowed himself to think that was all there was to her. But seeing her defend her state so righteously, he realized that she was much more complicated than he imagined. She reminded him of so many of his own constituents, people he cared about despite choices they had made that he didn't agree with. A lesson, he thought, about categorizing people you haven't really gotten to know.

"Look, let's cool down," said Doc. "We are all aware this is personal on the part of leadership. Inside this room, we need to be cordial to each other, no matter how great the differences between us. The leaders asked us to work this out. On our side, we've made ourselves clear. We're willing to negotiate on certain matters. Such as oversight. Such as certification. We can give on the management of the resource, but the money is nonnegotiable."

"Then we can't make a deal," said Joe Tran.

"We'll have to go out of bounds," said Doc.

★

"What does that mean, 'out of bounds'?" Sonny asked Wanda, as the delegations took a break to consult with their leaders and their staffs. "I can't find it in the rules."

"It's not in the rules, at least by that name," she told him. "It's like a secret codicil where anything goes. You'll find it in Rule 13, Section 9. Here," she said, opening a spiral-bound rulebook, "page 232: 'Limitations imposed on certain conference committees by the provisions of this section may be suspended in part by permission of the House to allow consideration of and action on a specific matter or matters which otherwise would be prohibited.'"

"When you say it out loud, you realize what powerful words those are," Sonny marveled. "So, no limits? Anything goes?"

"Most members don't even know it exists," said Wanda. "And it almost never gets invoked. Usually the leaders will just call another conference, but we're on such a tight deadline, there's not much choice."

"They're playing a different game," Ezer warned. "I don't think this has anything to do with oil field cleanup."

Big Bob met with the House delegation in his quarters. The exhaustion of Budget Night was apparent in his features, and when he spoke his voice was hoarse. "They think they can bully us into agreeing to steal taxpayers' money. It's a game of chicken. We gotta finish the budget today. Everybody's worn out. They waited to spring this on us so we'd be watching the clock. Well, they've got the same problem. Representative Tran, you put the resolution on the floor to go to Section 9. You'll have to be careful, there's no guidelines when you get in that spot, no rules. It's like zero gravity. Everything's up for grabs and you're on your own."

The members straggled back to the chamber, some hungover, some still drinking, some sleeping at their desks. They awakened long enough to approve a resolution for the conferees to go out of bounds. Few of them knew what they were voting for.

This time the delegations met in neutral territory, a tiny conference room in the basement of the extension. No tacos, no table, just a bunch of school chairs with tablet arms. No portraits on the walls. A mop and a bucket had been left in the corner by the janitorial staff, which had colonized the space.

Joe Tran began the meeting. "You asked to go out of bounds, and here we are. Now why don't you tell us what you really want."

"We want the two billion, but we're willing to make a trade," said Doc. "Royce's original bill asked for $150 million. We won't contest that. He gets what he wants. We'll even double it. But leave the rest of the two billion in the general fund. Our leader wants to repurpose those monies."

"Oh, let me guess," said Lurleen. "The wall."

"It's the top priority, not just for the lieutenant governor but for the majority of our voters."

"There's just no way in hell we're gonna make a deal like that," said Sonny.

Doc's eyeglasses had been resting on top of his head, but they plopped onto his nose. He examined Sonny as if he were a germ under a microscope, intrigued and a little amused by the impertinence. On the other hand, Doc could see that he had lost Lurleen and now another member of the House committee. In the game within the game, he couldn't afford to lose a third vote.

"What's your name again?" he said.

"Lamb," said Sonny, "Sonny Lamb."

"You're new, right? You've never been in conference before, I'm guessing. Much less out of bounds. Here the real deals are made.

This will be the most popular item the legislature has accomplished this session."

Joe weighed in. "I know we're in an imaginary space where rules don't apply, but whatever we decide has to be related to natural resources." He sounded persuadable.

"We can make it work," said Doc. "The Rio Grande is a natural resource. There are lakes and parks where the wall will be. Wildlife refuges. That's the least of our worries."

"It'll never slip through," Royce said. "The parliamentarian will call a foul. Some member might stand up with a point of order and bring the whole budget down."

That gave everyone pause. Wanda had warned Sonny that the only way being out of bounds worked was when members were too sleepy or indolent or hungover to notice a small change in the thousand pages of the General Appropriations Act, or, if they did notice, they didn't want the wrath of their colleagues to fall on them when the budget failed.

"I guess it's time to take a vote," said Joe.

Sonny figured that Royce was on board with the deal. Joe as well. He thought Lurleen might be on his side. That left Ernestine, who had been uncharacteristically silent during these negotiations.

"We have a proposal on the table," said Doc. "Those in favor raise your hand."

Seven hands went up, five senators and two representatives.

"Well, then," said Doc, looking at Ernestine. "What do we have to do to get that other vote? How about a state park in South Oak Cliff?"

"I figured you'd come after me, try to buy me off with something like this. And yes, we need parks in our community," said Ernestine. "But it galls me something terrible that you'd take money meant for clean air and water and throw it into building a wall, which God knows is a federal responsibility, all for some bit of theater to excite your base. My people are the first to suffer from environmental degradation. Bottom line, I'm not taking the bait. Maybe I'll come to you one day when you want something that means life itself for your people, and I'll say, 'Remember that park?' But now is not the time. Now is the time to live up to the pledge we made to our citizens to repair the damage the industry has done in the past and continues to do until this very minute."

Doc sat back. He put his glasses back on top of his head. He suddenly looked as tired as everybody else. "Other ideas?" he asked.

Tracy Hinojosa, a senator from San Angelo, said, "Let's be honest about this or we'll never get anywhere. We've got clear orders from our leader to get the money. The wall thing is a long shot. Some of us don't believe it has any business being in a natural resources bill. If you had agreed to our terms about reimbursing the industry, rather than extending the wall, he'd be okay with that. He just wants credit for making it work."

Doc gave her an irritated look but didn't contradict a word she said.

"I can see a way out of this," said Sonny. "It's called desalination."

Joe looked at him impatiently, having been through several cycles of Sonny's bill. "What does that have to do with oil field cleanup?"

"It's something new we've been working on in my office." He looked at Irene. "I'm not a bomb thrower. I believe that the industry wants to leave behind a different legacy than it has in the past. But every day you're extracting hundreds of millions of gallons of water from our aquifers for fracking, and then burying them in deep injection wells that are causing all kinds of damage. Like earthquakes. That's getting to be a huge problem. I'm sure you worry about the liability. You've had earthquakes right under your headquarters in Irving. Have you ever felt them?"

Irene nodded.

"Maybe you feel it at three or four on the Richter scale. How 'bout if it hits seven and brings your building down? Cowboys stadium? Do you guys ever talk about this?"

Once again, she nodded wordlessly.

"What if, instead of burying poisoned water, we were able to clean it up and put it to use?"

"How would we do that?" Irene asked.

"There's a natural process called osmosis. You take your treated water, which is practically black with petroleum molecules and full of heavy metals, thick as molasses, then push it through a membrane that filters out the noxious particles. It's not drinking-water level, they haven't got there yet. But the EPA has said that it's good enough to irrigate crops. They've allowed discharges into the Allegheny River. Imagine, instead of burying the water, we can reuse it. We can fill our rivers with it."

Senator Hinojosa looked intrigued. "When I was a kid, I used to swim in the Middle Concho River. It doesn't exist now. Right now, we're using wastewater, discharging it into the main channel of the Concho, and then recapturing it downstream. By that time, much of it has been purified by natural processes."

"Water is a renewable resource," said Sonny, "or can be."

"Is there a motion in there, Representative Lamb?" asked Joe Tran.

"I propose that Royce Drummond gets the hundred and fifty million he asked for, plus the hundred and fifty million the senators offered to add. The remainder of the two billion dollars will go to industry leaders to establish a desalination program to cleanse the water they use and return it into nature."

21

Word of the speaker's condition spread like measles through the chamber. It was sad about Big Bob, members said; he was a legend and all that, but who was going to succeed him? Some of the old bulls were out of the blocks and hunting for pledges while trying not to appear unseemly. Still, that's how the game is played. Where there was grief there was also opportunity.

Two days after the speaker's operation, Sonny flew his Cessna to Houston Hobby and Ubered over to MD Anderson. "I'm here to see Bob Bigbee," he told the receptionist. "Can you tell me what room he's in?"

The receptionist checked her computer. "He's on restricted access."

"I think I'm on the list," Sonny said. "He asked to see me."

The receptionist confirmed his name. "Speaker Bigbee is in our James E. Ferguson Jr. critical care suite, room 1101. Turn right off the elevator and go to the end of the hall."

The elevator was brightly lit, smelling of disinfectant, and deep enough to accommodate a hospital gurney. Sonny rode up alone. There was a time, when he got back from the war, that he couldn't stand to be on an elevator, by himself, penned in, trapped. It didn't matter that he knew he was safe. Nobody dies in elevators anymore. You never hear about them plummeting like they used to. He had never gotten stuck in one. But something about the elevator experience invoked death.

Many doors on the eleventh floor were open. As he walked down the hall, Sonny cast furtive glances at the sallow faces of the patients, the anxious loved ones, the official caregivers—doctors, nurses, interns, orderlies—all dressed in the same drab blue egalitarian scrubs, no medals or signals of rank on them, just their embroidered names, the heroic guardians at the portal between life and the end of life. Room 1101 was directly at the end of the hall, neither left nor right. Sonny knocked softly then cracked open the door. "Mr. Speaker?" he said quietly.

Big Bob was sitting in a cushioned armchair. He opened his eyes as Sonny came in. "Oh, hello, Sonny. I must have nodded off." His skin was as pale and thin as skim milk. An IV ran from a tube hanging on a rack and he was breathing oxygen from a nasal cannula. Sonny could see how weak his pulse was as it traced a red track on the beeping monitor. Big Bob Bigbee, the terror of the House, one of the most memorable figures of Texas history, was a frail old man approaching the end. Sonny was struck by the democracy of death. *It all comes down to this*, he thought. *It always does.*

"Do you want to lie down?" Sonny asked.

"No, they tell me to sit up. I don't know why." Big Bob's breath was heavy and labored.

"They want you to get better."

"Hell, they just sewed me back up. Too far gone to fuck with."

Sonny didn't know how to respond. He just said, "I'm so sorry," knowing how inadequate that sounded.

"We all have to face the final moments. I thought it would take courage, but the truth is you just sit around and wait. Like being in the bus station. And you wonder, 'What's it all for?'"

"I heard they're naming the new airport after you."

"You know, I'da greatly enjoyed that when I was alive. Now I'd trade that for a week on the Frio, watchin' the monarchs and the painted buntings." He thought for a moment. "And one more blow job." He was lost in a moment of reverie. "I wanted to tell you something, Sonny, and I ain't got a lot of time. I'm not gonna be around to clean up the mess some of these lunatics are gonna create. Texas needs you, Sonny."

"Me?"

"You're a real screw-up, but you've got talent. And you care. We don't have enough of that combination 'round here. I've had my eye on you from the start. I wish we'd had gotten to know each other better, but along came the Grim Reaper and here we are."

Sonny was practically struck dumb. This, coming from Big Bob, who before had only threatened him, who had essentially killed his bill, first by assigning it to Carl's committee and then by sabotaging Sonny's amendment to Gilbert's revenue bond. And yet, at the end of his life, the speaker had asked Sonny to come all the way to Houston to give him this benediction.

"Thanks, Mr. Speaker, but I'm getting out of politics."

Big Bob took a deeper inhalation through the oxygen tubes and let out a sigh. "I thought you might say that. Public life and personal life have a hard time mixing."

"So I've learned."

"Secrets don't keep in politics, Sonny. I know all about your situation. Everybody does."

"Everybody?"

"I can see you're torn up about this. I know your marriage is under pressure. I can imagine what you're dealing with." He added wistfully, "I was a lot like you when I was a younger man. Only worse."

"Oh, I doubt that."

"Five wives."

"Well, okay."

"And I survived. At a cost, a great cost. Part of being a public servant is you sometimes have to put your most precious relationships on hold. You gotta learn to balance 'em. I never could."

"This whole experience has made me realize what's important to me," Sonny said. "And it's not politics."

Sonny knelt beside the chair to be face-to-face with the speaker, who put his hand on Sonny's. "Many a time I wished I had made the same decision," Big Bob admitted. "Lot of heartache along the way. I was never a saint. Many, many regrets. But I learned a lesson. Something about what keeps a good man from being a good politician." He took another gulp of air. "A good man wants to win clean. But you never win clean, Sonny. You always give up something. You just gotta make sure it ain't more important than what you win."

"Compromise."

"Hard word to say," Big Bob said. "Harder to do. Compromise on the issues but don't compromise on yourself. Advice I wish I had taken long ago. Now, I wouldn't tell you this if I thought I was gonna stick around and deal with all the lunacy. That's on you and others. Texas is in trouble. There's a lot of good in it. Wonderful people. But it's like a family with a bad gene. A crazy-making gene that turns some folks into fanatics. You can't reach them, but if you let them take over we're sunk. God knows how far they'd go, with the guns, the heartlessness around health care and gays and stuff. The way we treat kids in our custody. A whole lot of people in high positions know the danger we're in but they're afraid to step up. Afraid of being targeted. Hell, it's the same all over the country. Texas has spread everywhere. We'll always have scoundrels and cowards in politics. I don't get that from you. You're crazy in a different way, maybe crazy enough to make a difference."

This speech exhausted him. Big Bob leaned back in his chair and closed his eyes. "I wasn't strong enough," he muttered, almost silently.

"Thank you, Mr. Speaker," Sonny said. His voice was clouded with emotion, knowing he would never see this great man again. "I'll let you get some rest." Sonny rose and started for the door.

"Don't go yet." Big Bob opened his eyes and gestured wanly for Sonny to come closer. "I got a favor to ask but there's no payback on this one."

"You name it, Mr. Speaker."

"I want you to say some words at my service."

"Me? What do you want me to say?"

"Make up some bullshit."

"Okay."

"Say, 'He loved Texas from the Red River Valley to the muddy waters of the Rio Grande.' You know the kind of nonsense. Just don't forget the love part."

★

Big Bob lay in state in the Capitol Rotunda for two days, guarded by the same troopers who had attended him in life. His body was taken to the First United Methodist Church, on the west side of the capital, where he was nominally a member. The pews filled with friends formed through the ages. Arrayed on the front row were his weeping wives, Cinco and the exes. Many humorous stories were told about his failings, but most of the speeches were lamentations about Texas without Big Bob. A former senator remarked, "I never saw a person more ill-suited for public office, nor did I ever meet a man or woman who served the state with such devotion." Democrats who had worked beside Big Bob as far back as the Ann Richards administration recalled his openness to bipartisanship. One after another, the mourners tolled the loss of something that was bigger than Big Bob.

"He asked me to help him do his twelve steps," Jose Garza, who supervised parking at the Capitol, said. "I don't know why he turned to me. He knew I loved him, and respected him, and sure as hell feared him. He tore through those steps with passion. I couldn't count how many people he saved—that's the twelfth step. But there was one step he never got past. The fourth step. Making a list of your good points and your bad points. Speaker Bigbee could never find a single good thing to say about himself. He had the biggest heart of anyone I ever met, and maybe the softest, but he couldn't see that. Many a time I watched him weep because of the problems of others. I never met a better man. I only wish he knew that."

Sonny also gave a eulogy. Few of the mourners knew who he was and practically no one understood why he had been chosen. He wasn't sure himself, except that Big Bob had singled him out to deliver a message.

"The speaker was a hard man," Sonny began. "Our bills, our political futures, were in his hands. He made sure we knew that. We also knew that however much we loved the state, he loved it more. However hard we worked, he worked harder. Sure, we knew the legends, the stories we all liked to tell about him. If you ever saw Bob Bigbee get mad, you'd never forget it. I've had that experience. It took me a few days to get my breath back.

"We can't talk about Speaker Bigbee without acknowledging that this great man, who seemed to fear nothing, had one great fear. It was that Texas—the state he knew as well as anyone in our history—was in trouble. Texas, a place as full of mythology as ancient Greece or Rome, a land of freedom lovers and heroes, where creativity is honored and enterprise respected, is at risk."

Sonny looked out at the mourners. Much of the Texas congressional delegation was there. The governor and lieutenant governor; the attorney general; the supreme court justices; on and on, it would be hard to find a state official who was absent. Some of them, like the governor, stared at Sonny in stark puzzlement, visibly asking themselves why he had been asked to speak and not them. Sonny's colleagues were scattered about. Harold gave him a nod of support. Lurleen, Carl, oh and there was Angela, sitting with Gilbert. She avoided his glance. He spotted L.D. in the back pew, looking lost and stricken. The only person absent from this tableau was Lola.

"Big Bob wanted me to share his concerns with you. Our Texas hearts have hardened against each other. Our politics have turned into culture wars, me against you, wars that are nominally about values but really are about identity. The truth is, in Texas, conservatives and liberals, Republicans and Democrats, have pretty much the same values. We love our families. We're proud of the economic dynamism of the state, the jobs we create, the opportunities we provide. We want the best for our children—the best education, the best future—but we're continually fighting over things that don't really matter. You know this. We're sick of the hatred of immigrants, the school shootings, the attacks on people who are different in one way or another from who we are, all the carnage caused by a political culture that is reeling out of control. These are the very problems that we've been elected to resolve. Instead, our political leaders exploit these differences and lead the state further away from the Texas we all love.

"At the end of his life, these were the concerns that preoccupied Speaker Bigbee. But he won't be here to shape the future. That's up to us. If we want to honor the legacy of Bob Bigbee, we need to keep him in our hearts and cherish the state as he did. That's a tall order. But as the speaker would say, to do otherwise would be un-Texan.

"Big Bob wanted you to know that he loved Texas, 'from the Red River Valley to the muddy waters of the Rio Grande.' He wanted to be sure we didn't forget the love part."

★

Lola heard the Cessna as it buzzed over the mountain. She figured Sonny would be back to settle things, so she had packed a bag of his clothes and boots and his military medals, just about anything he would have asked for. When all was said and done, it wasn't a lot. She wanted to make this as surgical as possible. No spending the night. Just goodbye.

Sonny walked from the airstrip past the pasture where Joaquin still ruled. Sonny had a peanut butter cookie for him. It was odd to think that a bull could be a person's friend, close to being a best friend. Sonny felt Joaquin's soft pink tongue on his palm as he scooped up the cookie. "Hey, buddy," Sonny said as he kissed the curly white space between Joaquin's eyes, "you bring me luck, okay?"

Lola stood on the porch, alongside two suitcases and a cardboard box, which represented much of Sonny's investment in their life together. It was clear he wasn't invited inside.

"Can we at least talk?" he asked.

"What do you have to say?" No sitting in the rockers, sipping tequila. Lola stood there, arms akimbo, waiting for him to spit it out. It pained him to see her so angry and hurt.

"I want to come home," Sonny said.

"I packed up your stuff," she said without even acknowledging his plea. "Anything else I can put on the Greyhound."

"Do we have to do this?"

"Quicker the better."

Bandit came out on the porch and sat beside her. No rushing over to Sonny, tail wagging, demanding to be petted as per usual. Clearly he was taking sides.

"I'm gonna step down. Resign. Just let me come home."

"I don't think you got politics out of your system. I don't think you ever will."

"Lola, baby, I made some real stupid moves. One thing I learned for sure is that you're the only thing that really matters to me."

Lola nodded, but it wasn't assent. "What about Angela?" she said, spitting out the name.

"I'm so sorry. It happened. But that's not the life I want to live."

"Maybe she's better for you."

"No," he said. "No, she's not. She was different but she wasn't better."

"Did you love her?" she asked. Then: "*Do* you?"

Sonny looked around at the ranch, at the barn, the cattle in the pastures, the mountains, the scrub, all the familiar sights he had grown weary of that now seemed so precious, perhaps the last time he would ever see any of it. And Lola. "Yes, I suppose I did love her. I don't know what that word means except as some kind of pledge. Or maybe it's like the volume on a stereo, it goes up so high you can hardly bear it or down to where you barely hear it, but if you hear it at all, you can call it love. But it never matched what I felt for you. And still do."

"You turned your back on the life we had. Evidently it wasn't enough."

"I did, yes. That life wasn't so bad. I don't know why I thought I had to change it." The vast and overly familiar sky offered no help. "I guess there's nothing I can say that will change things. You're angry and disappointed, and I am, too. I let you down. I let myself down. I let everybody down."

"You're right," Lola said evenly. "Words don't matter."

"I have to believe that if you knew how much I love you, how sorry I am—"

"Actions speak louder."

"Then let me show you! I want to spend the rest of my life proving how much I love you. Lola, please. Let me come home."

Lola nodded, so slightly, a gesture that had more to do with some internal observation, something that had been confirmed in her mind. She gave him a look that was at last full of compassion and possibility, at least that's how he read it. But he was wrong.

"Goodbye, Sonny."

She went inside. Bandit roused himself and followed.

★

When Sonny went back to the chamber the next day, there was a shift in perception where he was concerned. He had been anointed to speak for Big Bob, and his words had lodged in the minds of many members. It was as if they had heard the speaker himself imploring them from the grave. Gilbert nodded when Sonny came in. Ernestine came by and put her hand on his, wordlessly. Angela cast a conflicted glance at him.

"Sonny, I've got to tell you what happened last night after the service," Harold said. "What you said really affected me. And I did something I never thought I'd do. I called my father."

Sonny knew about their estranged relationship, how Reverend Morton could never forgive Harold's homosexuality. "We had our first real talk in such a long time—for years! I told him I loved him. I was thinking of what Big Bob said about not forgetting the love part. And then, oh—!" Harold caught his breath. "He said he loved me! He'd just been waiting. We both had. For the other to say it first. So stubborn, it runs in the family. I told him that Julian and I are planning to marry in November—at our place in Santa Fe—and Sonny." Harold swallowed, scarcely able to speak. "He asked if he could perform the service!"

"That's wonderful, Harold."

"I'm telling you this because it wouldn't have happened if you hadn't made me think about what I was missing because of my pride. This is a long way of asking if you'd consider being my best man."

While they were talking, a page delivered a note to Sonny. He hugged Harold and then walked out to the lobby, where L.D. was waiting.

"Funny how it worked out, isn't it," said L.D. An odd grin played unconvincingly across his lips. "I guess neither of us had a clue when I first dropped in on you that we'd wind up in this place, with so much on the line. It wasn't even six months ago and look at how the world has changed."

"L.D., I'm not in the mood," Sonny said.

L.D. quickly switched tactics as Sonny started to walk away. "Those were beautiful words you spoke at Big Bob's service," he said, then wandered into reverie. "All those folks in the church, the multitude who came to pay their respects while Big Bob lay in state. Thousands. Maybe tens of thousands. The lives he touched. Sometimes we forget they're the reason we're here in the first place."

Sonny wheeled around. "What do you mean 'we,' L.D.? I know why I'm here. I know why Big Bob was here. But you don't represent the people. Those folks came to honor Big Bob because he always kept the people of Texas in his heart. When you die, who's gonna be there for you? Big Oil? The payday lenders? Mr. Peeples? Isn't there some little shred of humanity left in you? Some regret for the life you wasted?"

"Are you done?" L.D. was still grinning in a most annoying manner.

"Hell, no, you sorry pervert. You really think you can take down Sonny Lamb? I may be low, but I'm comin' back, and I'm gonna ride your sorry ass like a bareback pony. You won't—"

"I want you to run for speaker."

"Jesus," Sonny said, reeling back, "I'm gonna have to drive a stake in your heart."

"It's a long shot. I mean crazy long."

"What makes you think I'd want to do that?"

"'Cause you're ambitious—"

"I'm gettin' out of politics."

"—'Cause you got the skills. 'Cause you care about the people. 'Cause without my help you're just another dead armadillo on the side of the road with his paws in the air."

"And the game would go on, wouldn't it?" Sonny said. "You'd get me elected speaker, and then you really got me. A big trophy on your wall. Or would that be Mr. Peeples's wall? I can't tell the difference with you."

"That's good, that's good," L.D. said, hopping and nodding like a madman. "I was afraid you weren't cynical enough for this job."

"I'm not going to sell out, forget it!"

"You stubborn son of a bitch," L.D. said. "You think I don't care about this place? Jesus Christ, Sonny! It's the only thing I do care about! You want to walk away and let Carl take over?"

"They'll never pick Carl."

"He's out there on the floor right now, suckin' heads and peelin' tails."

Sonny considered this. L.D. would know. It made sense that Carl would be Mr. Peeples's choice.

"What's in it for you?"

"Let's just say I'm doin' a favor for a friend."

"I'm not your friend."

"No," said L.D. "Bob was."

★

L.D. was back in his Lincoln on I-10, going ninety, trusting in Waze to alert him to the radar traps. Sonora and Ozona flew by. Fort Stockton. Take the turnoff at Balmorhea, then south on State Highway 17 to Fort Davis and Marfa, another ten miles on U.S. 67, then left on Farm and Ranch Road 169, which runs between the Cuesta del Burro and the Del Norte Mountains. Turn right at the second mailbox on a little caliche road that snaked over a mesa and dropped into a valley to a ranch house surrounded by desert willows where it had all started.

"You!" Lola yelled. L.D. hadn't even gotten out of the Lincoln. "What do you think you're doing here?"

"Commiserating."

"Of all people! You got no business here now."

"That worthless son of a bitch," L.D. said.

"I have no interest in hearing anything further."

"That miserable curl of sheep shit."

"Stop it and get off my land."

"That unfaithful slime-slobbering maggot—"

"STOP!" Lola screamed. "You've got no right getting into our business! You never did."

"You're absolutely correct." L.D. stood at the foot of the porch steps looking up at Lola. He was glad she wasn't armed. "But we got one thing in common, you and I. Sonny. He's at a crossroads, and what he decides to do is gonna change everything about our lives, you and me."

"What's it to you?"

"I got a bad habit of telling people what they oughta do. Thing is, cowgirl, sometimes you only get one chance to make things right."

"You had that chance, and look what came of it."

"Well, yes. Indeed so. More than anyone could have hoped, I dare say."

"I have no idea what you're talking about."

"I see a young man on TV, riding a horse out of a barn, hugging a little girl. Let's face it, I'm in the market for a useful idiot, and he's hunky and has that big goofy grin. So voilà, there he is, the ideal candidate. He doesn't have the brains of a plate of spaghetti, or seems not to. A cipher even to himself. Never even voted, can you believe it. Perfect, absolutely perfect. I'll create him. I'll be his Henry Higgins. And he'll repay me with votes." L.D. chuckled. "I had no idea what I was in for. Listen, Lola, maybe you don't realize it, although I bet in the back of your mind you've always known. Sonny, he could be one of the great ones. I've seen 'em all, from Lyndon on down. He could go the distance. All depends on you."

"From now on, what Sonny Lamb does is his own affair."

"Fair enough. Fair enough." He paused and kicked the dirt with his ostrich-leather boot. "I guess I'll head on back. I was gonna tell you a story that might have changed your mind. Something I never told anybody before. But I see it's pointless. Sorry to bother you. Sorry for all the upset I brought into your life." He walked back toward the Lincoln. Slowly.

"What story?"

L.D. gave her a look. He seemed strangely nervous, unsettled, not the legendary L.D. of lore. "I'm not proud of this," he said. "But there's something I'd like you to know. I was in the Texas Legislature myself, once upon a time."

"Sonny said as much."

"I doubt he knows why I left. I had a career ahead of me, stretching all the way down the road. Great things, everybody said. Golden boy. That kind of talk. Went to my head. I thought I could do anything, get away with anything. Got to where I thought I deserved it. And so I siphoned off some campaign money for a condo in South Padre. Not as if it's never been done before. In the beloved scheme of things, it wasn't the worst offense, but it was stupid and unnecessary. I rarely went to the place. Tell the truth, I don't even care for the beach. Probably if I had gotten away with this one little peccadillo I would have done something grander, a yacht or some such. But I got caught. The man who figured it out was Big Bob Bigbee, at the time head of the House investigating committee. I was headed for a vote of censure. Public humiliation. Thrown out on my ass. Which I deserved. But Bob did me a favor, allowing me to pay back the money and quietly resign."

Lola listened to this with little sympathy. She had never pictured L.D. as a beacon of virtue. She crossed her arms impatiently.

"Oh, I kept my reputation, all right, but I lost my honor," L.D. said, reading her thoughts. "Turned out, that was the only thing that mattered. Other losses followed. My marriage, many friends, self-respect. Out the window. I might should have gone off to Washington or gotten into business, but I couldn't break away from the Lege. I built up my lobby practice, which flourished in part because members knew I was shady and they were hoping for money. And I was there with bags of it. Maybe revenge on my part, trying to show that everybody was corrupt, they weren't any better than me. And you know what? All that time I was actually on a quest. I was searching, looking for one righteous individual who didn't care about the money or the power, who only wanted to do the best for the state. I thought if I could find that person, I wouldn't need to buy off the Texas Legislature, proving my point one member after another. I think I was looking for myself, the person I could have been. And then I sat on your porch and found that man, and his name is Sonny Lamb."

Lola was quiet for a moment. "That's a real nice sales pitch," she said, "but I'm not buyin'."

L.D. nodded. She was a tough one. "If that's the way you feel . . ."

"That's the way I feel!"

"Then do him a favor. If you're gonna close that door, slam it so hard he'll never want to see you again. 'Cause he's crazy for you. He's mad like a moonstruck dog. It's killing him. You gotta put him out of his misery. Set him free. Here," he said, finding a business card in his wallet, "take this. It's the name of the best divorce lawyer in the state of Texas. He'll cut out Sonny's heart and serve it to you for breakfast, I guaran-damn-tee it."

Lola took the card. She looked like a pigeon that couldn't get the air under its wings. "I don't want to talk anymore."

22

Speaker races typically take place at the beginning of the session and are no surprise. The pledges have been lined up and everybody knows the outcome. The game is played cautiously because betting on the wrong candidate can doom a member's session. No committee chair assignments, your bills die pitiless deaths, you can even get busted on your parking spot. Vengeance is not the least of the privileges of office. On the other side are the favors, the bills you get to pass, the contributions you rake in. Everything is on the table in the speaker vote. Therefore, early indications of victory can be—usually are—definitive as stragglers pile on, the favorite emerges, and everybody says they were with you all along.

The race to succeed Big Bob was unlike any before, taking place near the end of the session, rather than at the start, with little time for candidates to canvas and no time at all to organize. Chaos, in other words. Half a dozen members had pledges in hand, although they wouldn't say how many. Carl had the advantage, being so far to the right that he practically stepped off the flat Earth. Oh, yes, the power brokers sneered at Carl's undisguised cupidity, his phony piety, and his awe-inspiring ignorance, but when they sized up the voters they concluded that Carl Kimball was just what the times called for.

Ezer operated Sonny's command center, such as it was. "I can give you the rules of the game, but they only make sense if people make rational choices. That's the flaw in game theory. Sometimes people don't recognize their best choice. Sometimes their minds are clouded with prejudice or superstition."

Wanda was calculating what promises Sonny could make to woo the uncommitted. She suggested that Sonny start with the Dems. "You were with them on the quorum break, even if you voted against them on most bills. There are sixty-three Dems altogether. If you can corral fifty of them, you'll be in the race."

Ezer agreed. "From their point of view, you're the lesser evil. That's not much of a campaign pitch, but it's something."

"Carl will have at least fifty votes to start, so you're essentially starting from the same place," said Jane. "After that, it gets a lot harder. Every single vote will be a victory."

Sonny went to the chamber. It was like a disturbed beehive, buzzing and frantic. He paused a moment to appreciate the weirdness of his task. His whole life had been transformed—as he had so longed for—but also ruined. Here he was, just a few months into this new career, and he was bidding to become one of the most powerful figures in the state. It was crazy. On the other hand, he had sized up many of the leaders and realized that they weren't gods. Power only clarified who they were at the core, weak and greedy and coldhearted.

One thing he had learned about the leaders of Texas was that they didn't really represent the wishes of the majority of Texans. Most citizens wanted reasonable gun laws—red flags and background checks and no assault weapons in the hands of teenagers. Most Texans wanted immigration laws that controlled the flow of people into the country but didn't demonize those who came here—after all, the economy of the state depended on immigrants. Most Texans wanted affordable health care and good public schools. They wanted clean air and water. They supported the oil and gas industry, but not at the expense of renewable alternatives. They wanted fair elections. The leaders were turning the state away from the direction the people wanted to go. All this was true, but it was also true that Texans had it in their power to make a change, and they simply didn't do it.

Sonny had come to care about his fellow members. He could

see now that there was nothing perfect about them, or about their politics, and because of their shortcomings they needed leadership. Perhaps there were more skilled, more diverse, certainly more experienced candidates, but were there better leaders? Was he really the one?

"Gilbert, if I was to run for speaker, would the members support me?"

Gilbert was surprisingly not surprised. "A lot of them respect what you're tryin' to do, Sonny, even when you're a king-sized pain in the ass."

"What about you?"

"Carl already asked for my pledge."

"Oh."

"I told him I'd think about it." Gilbert paused and studied the giant chandelier for three seconds. "Now that I've thought about it, you're gonna need some lieutenants out there. Carl's got his people all over the place."

"I gotta warn you, Gilbert. This could cost you a spot at the table. Carl has the money behind him."

"Mr. Peeples, right? I guess L.D. is milking the herd."

"Actually, L.D. is on our side."

Gilbert whistled. "Boy, that domino game will never be the same. ¡Adalante, compadre!"

"¡Que nos vaya bien!"

★

"By all rights, it should be you," Sonny told Ernestine. "You've been here the longest. You've got the respect of all the members."

"Me? Speaker of the House?" Ernestine chuckled. "I do hope to see the day when a Democrat can stand on the rostrum again, much less a woman; much, much less a person of color. You tell me how many strikes there are against me. Let's be real. This is not a fairy tale. We're a long way from that day. What I want is power now."

"What would that look like?"

"Chair of Appropriations. If the budget was in my hands I'd

deliver the entire Black caucus. I doubt you'll see any Dems walk away."

"You know the rules. I can't make any promises. But I've got your interests in mind. The difference between me and my opponent is that he wants to shut the door behind him. I want it wide open. I think you want that too."

Ernestine nodded. "Sonny, your problem isn't with me and my folk. You gotta deal with the math. It's not in your favor."

Sonny knew Carl had a lock on the majority of the Republicans, although there was a key vote that could change that.

★

"Respect," said Lurleen.

"I'll certainly give you that," said Sonny.

"If Carl wins, we'd expect to chair Higher Education or Judicial Affairs."

"I'll be straight with you, Lurleen. I can't have education and judicial appointments becoming a battleground for religious fundamentalists."

"Then you lose."

"I'd rather lose and keep my principles intact."

"Oh, honey," said Lurleen, "we do that all the time." She gave him a pitying look. "What you did in conference was impressive. Nobody else could have pulled that off. I've got no doubt you'll fight hard for your causes. But your causes aren't mine."

Sonny admired the woman. She waged a lonely battle most of the time, in the vanguard of forces that Sonny believed were taking the state in a dangerous direction. But he didn't doubt her sincerity. "Representative Klump, you and I differ on most things, but we have one big thing in common. We both want to do right by Texas. Carl may be able to offer you something I can't. If your heart tells you that will make Texas a better state, then you should vote for Carl. If you vote for me, I'll be fair with you. You'll have a seat at the table. But more than that, I promise to treat the people of Texas with compassion and love. You've got a chance to decide how we're gonna run our government, whether it's gonna be for the people or the cronies and insiders. It's in your hands, Lurleen."

"Sonny," she said coolly, "that's about the shittiest offer I ever had."

★

He found Angela in her office. She had been expecting him.

"Everybody else is out on the floor, trading votes," said Sonny.

"I wasn't feeling so great," she said.

She did look a little frayed. Instead of her usual upright posture, she was slumped and deflated. "Sorry to hear that," Sonny said. He added, "I heard a rumor that you're leaving."

"I've been offered a position in the administration," Angela said. "Assistant secretary for community development at HUD." She drummed her fingers on her desk impatiently.

"That didn't take long. You were always too big for these parts."

Angela smiled wanly. "I hope that's a compliment."

"It's an observation."

"God, I'm going to miss this place," Angela said. "It brings out the worst in everybody."

"You'll be missed, too," he said, a statement that was about as far as he could go in expressing the lingering desire and disappointment and unsettled state of their relationship, as well as the favor he had in mind. "You and I come from very different places," he said. "The experience of working in this chamber has taught me a lot. Good people can have different beliefs. I know you'll never agree with me on everything, that wouldn't be possible, given who we are."

"Cut to the chase, Sonny."

"I'm asking for your vote. I hope you'll support me for speaker."

"I gave my pledge to Carl."

"Huh," said Sonny. "I guess I should have expected that."

"It happened at the beginning of the session. It had nothing to do with whatever happened to us. It was a deal. He said it would cost me, but I never knew how much. Now listen, Sonny, I don't mean to be rude, but I'm gonna have to ask you to leave. I'm really not feeling well."

"You want the nurse?"

"I don't need the nurse."

"If you're sick—"

"Damn it, Sonny! I'm not sick. I'm pregnant."

The word was hurled in the air, and hung there, floating on a cloud of disbelief and astonishment.

"I'm sorry I said that. It was mean. You really didn't need to know."

Sonny sat down. "Pregnant?" The word seemed strange on his tongue, like a foreign language. "How could that happen?"

"I thought we were careful," Angela said. "What are the odds, right?"

"One in a hundred forty-two," Sonny said, almost to himself. "Just like hitting a triple."

"I had a home test last week. I couldn't believe it, so I went to a doctor this morning, and it's true. I saw it."

"You're pregnant?" he said again, as the reality sank in. "With my child?"

"It's my child, Sonny. And it's my choice what to do with it. I'm not going to let a mistake get in the way of my future."

So many powerful emotions collided in Sonny's head, but the words that came out of his mouth were, "Please, don't do that."

"Or what?" Angela said furiously. "You're going to turn me in? Call out the vigilantes? This is my decision, Sonny."

★

On the floor, the candidates were giving their speeches. Carl had the wind at his back. He ticked off his priorities, which mirrored exactly the platform of the state GOP: arming teachers; bringing Christianity back to the classroom; eliminating gay marriage; abolishing the Federal Reserve and the Department of Education; protecting Confederate monuments; withdrawing from the United Nations and the World Health Organization; and voting on whether Texas should secede from the union. "I love God and God loves Texas," Carl said in summation. "He has a plan for this great state, and I plan to follow the plan that He planned. A vote for Carl Kimball is a vote for God's will. Y'all keep that in mind as you cast your votes this afternoon."

When it was his turn, Sonny approached the front mic. He hadn't had a moment to compose his thoughts, and he was so rattled by Angela's news he wasn't sure he could go through with his speech. Just before he opened his mouth, he caught sight of Lola in the gallery. Everything was happening at once.

"Members, I stand here, humbled by the opportunity to ask for your vote. I know a choice like this is hard for all of you. Each of the other candidates has more experience than I. Each of us has a different vision for the state. The choice you make will determine what kind of Texas we—and our children—will live in.

"Texas is growing. Within a few short decades, we'll be the largest state in the union, larger than California and New York combined. The choice we make this very moment will determine not just the future of Texas, but the future of America. And America will shape the future of the world. That's the burden we carry.

"I'll be frank. If you vote for me, Texas will turn in a new direction. I've sat through this session. I've watched the bills that come to the floor. Many of them are helpful and necessary. But—members, you know this—many a bill has come to the floor and been enacted into a law that will harm our state, that will turn Texans against each other. Much of this is the result of a handful of billionaires who think they can buy the political system in our state. Instead of supporting the education of our kids, they're talking about prosecuting teachers who honestly acquaint students with the world they're going to live in, whether it is sexuality or racial issues. Certainly, parents should have influence over what their children learn. But these campaigns are not about education. They are political issues that keep our citizens fighting each other rather than assuming the responsibilities Texas must take on in order to lead the nation.

"We often talk about being the most pro-life state in the country, but when it comes to the health of our citizens, and particularly young mothers, we fail the test. We turn away federal money that would contribute to our citizens' health. We have to recognize that in our zeal to save unborn children, we have placed thousands of women's lives in danger. We have forced them to have babies that are the product of rape and incest. We have made doctors afraid to do procedures that would save the lives of mothers, even with babies that will never be born alive. There are moral claims on both sides, and we need to acknowledge them.

"A month ago, two kids from Central America wandered across our property. Adorable, abandoned kids. They shouldn't have come here. It's against the law. But they're children. They came from a violent environment, so violent that their mother chose to send them alone into America in hopes of finding a family member. Now they're in custody. Separated. Caught in the jaws of the American justice system. Who knows how long they'll be held there, future uncertain, lives on pause. As Texans, don't we have the responsibility to see that they are cared for and dealt with as rapidly and compassionately as possible? Our country and our economy depend on immigration. Yes, we need to guard our borders, but we also need to streamline legal immigration, so that asylum seekers like these children can enjoy the benefits of our culture and we can gain from their contributions to our society.

"All of these are political problems—infrastructure, education, health, abortion, immigration—and they're problems we can solve. We should solve. I don't have all the answers. But if you vote for me, I can tell you that we're going to work the real problems, not the ones we make up to fan the flames of partisan hatred. That day will be over in Texas."

★

Sonny looked for Lola, but she was gone. Then he got a text saying she would meet him at Starbucks. She was waiting there with a Frappuccino. Her hair was combed out and she was wearing a black dress that Sonny had always admired. He couldn't believe how beautiful she was. "I wanted to see what you do, to really try to understand you. You belong here, Sonny. I see that now. You deserve the chance to work on all those problems you spoke about."

"I'm not going to win. I don't have the votes. And I don't think Texas is ready for the change. Anyway, I'm getting used to losing. Just about everything."

"Except me."

Sonny choked back a sob that nearly leapt out of his mouth. Lola took his hand. "We had a good life together," she said. "I don't want to lose that."

"I can't tell you how much that means to me. Lola, Lola, Lola, I just don't want to live my life without you."

"We don't have to. I'm not saying we'll forget the past, but we don't need to throw everything overboard out of wounded pride."

"I'm not making myself clear," Sonny said. "What I mean is, you're making a mistake. It's best you go back to the ranch and we'll settle up stakes. We'll work out something."

Lola jerked back in her chair. "What's going on with you, Sonny? You said you wanted to come home! You begged me! And now—what? I feel like such a fool, coming here, forgiving you, what was I thinking?"

"Everything I say or do makes it worse. It's hopeless," Sonny said, mostly to himself.

"It's politics, isn't it? The big show. This is the life you really wanted. We never had a chance after you got here."

"I'd walk away from this in a minute if I thought I could make up with you."

"But what?"

"Angela's pregnant."

Lola's jaw hung slack for a considerable time. "You got her *pregnant*?" she said in a voice Sonny had never heard.

"There's no end to how dumb I am."

"She's got your baby inside her? The baby I can never have? It's like a curse! Every time I get close to forgiving you, it's a whole new disaster."

"Lola, I am so sorry."

"Stop. Stop talking. There's nothing you can say." Lola walked out of Starbucks, leaving behind their life together.

★

"As speaker pro tem, I call the vote," Lurleen said from the rostrum. The candidates had come down to two, Carl and Sonny, with the three other candidates freeing their pledges. The dinging of the votes was irregular, *ding! ding ding ding! ding . . . ding*, a strange rhythm that spoke of indecision, misgivings, and buried fears.

Angela couldn't watch. She went back to her office without casting her vote.

Lola was waiting for her. "You're Angela, right?" she said icily. "I'm Sonny's—"

"I know who you are," Angela said, glancing at her staff. "Can we talk in my office?"

Angela sat at her desk, the trophy hog head on the wall behind her. Lola walked around a bit, trying to settle. She finally took a seat.

"If it's any consolation, I'm leaving Texas," Angela said. "You needn't worry about me anymore."

Lola nodded impatiently. "You think you can break into people's lives and run off like some kind of thief?" she said, her eyes like weapons. Angela was afraid to look at her.

"I owe you an explanation, but I don't know what to say. God knows, it would be too much to ask for your forgiveness. This whole experience has knocked me down to a place I never imagined I'd be. I thought it was enough to be on the right side of the issues, but now I know that being right is not the same as being good."

"I'm really not interested in your philosophy."

"No. Of course not."

Despite the humiliation, Angela had to admire Lola. She was strong in ways Angela was not. Rooted in who she was, not plagued with the kind of ambition that pulls you off center, away from your core. Angela wanted that. And that made her more ashamed. And the shame made her angry. "Why are you here?" she asked curtly.

"I wanted to see if there was anything about you that was redeemable. If you had any good qualities. Like remorse."

"If you're asking if I feel guilty, yes. I wish this had never happened. I can't go undo it. We weren't in love, if that matters to you."

"Maybe not you, but Sonny was."

"I don't think I was in contention," Angela said. "Or would ever be. I can clearly see that now."

"Sonny says you've got a good heart."

"Sonny said that?"

"He said one day you'd know yourself well enough to make a real contribution."

"God, I hope that's true!"

"Frankly, I don't think people change that much," Lola said briskly.

"Why would you care?"

Lola took a sheet from Angela's memo pad and wrote out a name. "This is an adoption agency in Fort Worth. Our name's on the list. They'll know exactly the baby we're looking for."

★

"Members, the votes are counted," Lurleen said. "With 148 votes cast and one abstention, we have a tie. It falls to me to cast the deciding ballot. As always, a vote for this office is a vote of conscience. Sometimes our heart tells us to do things that our head does not agree with. In this case, we have decided to vote with our head."

And Lurleen Klump cast the deciding vote about the future of Texas—and America.

That evening, Sonny and Lola went over to the Texas State Cemetery to put yellow roses on Big Bob's grave. One day Sonny and Lola will lie in this same hallowed earth, where Stephen F. Austin, the founder of the Texas Republic, reposes, along with governors and senators and musicians and writers. They were all somebodies once, now faded into the anonymizing fabric of history. They too made choices, some of them catastrophic. There are a whole lot of Confederates in this graveyard. Stephen Austin, whose statue gestures toward them, allowed slavery to take root in the Texas Republic. A fair number of crooks are scattered among the stones. Heroes lie here as well. Soldiers and astronauts and explorers, people whose choices made the world better.

With Lurleen's vote, the course of history was determined. One day, historians will tell the story.

ACKNOWLEDGMENTS
AND NOTES ON SOURCES

I have long been enchanted by the politics of Texas and the vivid characters who inhabit the marbled halls of our legislature. Longtime Texans will no doubt note the resemblance of some of those figures to the characters inhabiting these pages. Although this is a work of imagination, not of history, it entailed considerable research and comes encumbered with debts of gratitude that have accumulated as the work has evolved over four decades.

Story ideas come to me dressed in the garments of an article, or a book, or a screenplay, or a movie, but the same story can be told in different forms as it struggles to find its truest expression. *Mr. Texas* began as an unproduced movie script, titled "Sonny's Last Shot." This was decades ago, when Ann Richards was governor. Molly Ivins was the resident wit, living down the street from us. You had the feeling that women really ran the place.

Texas was in its last incarnation as a Democratic stronghold. Pete Laney, a cotton farmer from the Panhandle, and a Democrat, was speaker of the House. He proved to be a candid and delightful guide to the intricacies of his office. He loved the idea of telling the story of the Texas House and gave me inspiring and invaluable tips. I'll never forget the afternoon when I asked him if the members ever went on hunts. He got his buddy John Sharp, then the state comptroller (now chancellor the Texas A&M system), on the phone, and they regaled me with tales of pig hunting, much as I have recorded here.

Pete's counterpart in the Senate, Bob Bullock, was also a Democrat. However flamboyant you may think my portrait of Big Bob Bigbee may be, I assure you that Bob Bullock exceeded him in every particular. There's no doubt I treated his memory too kindly, but his personal journey through Texas politics was a spectacle that captivated the state. His many marriages and his struggles with alcohol were always in full view. He survived scandals that should have ruined him. But in his last years in office, finally sober, he redeemed himself. He often counseled other alcoholics, sometimes by saying that if things were really so bleak for them they may as well end it all now. Then he would pull out one of the guns he kept in his briefcase and offer to let them do it right there in his office. It was a form, I suppose, of shock therapy. No one ever pulled the trigger, and many have testified that Bob Bullock brought them back from the land of despair.

In 1994, George W. Bush became governor. In 2003, the Texas House turned over, and Tom Craddick became the first Republican speaker since Reconstruction. The state changed, and so did my story. Sonny Lamb, my hero, evolved into a Republican. That year, Marco Perella, an actor and director, suggested that I rewrite "Sonny's Last Shot" as a play. Marco already had a theater lined up a few months later. That first production could scarcely be described as a success. One night I counted twenty-seven people in the audience. Marco confided that only six of them had actually paid for their tickets, everyone else was comped. I realized that I had paid for those six tickets myself.

A number of legislators eventually came to see it, and a few actually made guest appearances because we were so desperate for an audience. A representative from El Paso, Pat Haggerty, paid for the privilege by hosting a dozen of his colleagues with the proviso that he would get to speak a line in the play. The line he delivered was, "The only thing I know for sure is the first time I jacked off, I knew I was going to do it again." It is hard to write about Texas without straining credulity.

A young rancher and assistant district attorney named Dan Gattis played Sonny in that first production. He was an inexperienced actor but embodied the character's forthrightness and long Texas lineage. He must have seen himself in the role in real life, as he then got elected to the Texas House and served four terms. We were fortunate to have the great comic actor G. W. Bailey play L.D. I learned a lot from watching him in that production and the next. G.W. wanted to meet a real lobbyist and so I arranged a lunch with Bill Miller, one of the titans of the field, who educated G.W. on the hardball politics of the state. I could see G.W. taking notes as the stories spilled out, told with relish and humor.

In 2005, we had a revival of the play, with full houses in one of the respectable theaters downtown. I was rewarded by hearing Molly Ivins's distinctive guffaw. I wanted to cast her as Lurleen, but cancer had got her and she begged off. A Broadway producer, Margo Lion, best known for *Hairspray* and *Angels in America,* came to Austin to see it. She said it should be a musical, and who was I to argue with one of the great figures of American theater. So I recruited my friend Marcia Ball, a terrific singer and songwriter and hellacious piano player, to join me in writing tunes.

Margo did us the immense favor of introducing us to Jack Viertel, then senior vice president of Jujamcyn Theaters and author of *The Secret Life of the American Musical,* one of the most useful books I ever read. He schooled us on the dramatic formulas that undergird the architecture of this peculiarly American artform. It was thrilling to be tutored by this great master. We believed we were on a glide path to Broadway.

But then our Broadway producer suddenly changed her mind. "It should be a television series," she said. I sold a pilot to HBO. Margo paired us with Lauren Donner, one of the powerhouses of Hollywood and a great story guide. The studio was thrilled, they said, but then they fired the executive on the series and dumped his projects. So no musical and no television series.

I wasn't done with Texas politics, however. In 2009, Joe Straus, a centrist Republican, took over the speaker's gavel. I wrote about him in a 2017 *New Yorker* article, "America's Future Is Texas," and subsequently in my 2018 book, *God Save Texas*. I was struck by the fact that when I began "Sonny's Last Shot," Texas was solidly blue, and now it was bright red. That transition only made the story more intriguing and relevant.

Thwarted on television and the stage, I turned to another medium. Together with my son, Gordon, and Marcia Ball, we decided to create a musical podcast. We believed that we were creating an entirely new medium. I wrote eight episodes and together we produced more than fifty songs. I never had more fun in a creative endeavor. We soon learned that podcasts are meant to be cheap productions, and here we had a large cast and enough songs to fill three or four musicals. The estimated cost to arrange and produce it was a bit absurd. It was as if we'd built a ship in the basement and then couldn't get it up the stairs. I'm determined that it will one day be realized, either as a musical podcast or a television series.

All of this led to the writing of the novel. Each step along the way has deepened my understanding of politics and my engagement with the characters, who changed with the times and with my endless rewrites. It's a saga that perhaps other young writers might benefit from as they try to get their stories through the door. It turns out that there are other doors. Movie script, play, musical, TV series, podcast—they're all forms of storytelling, each with particular challenges and opportunities. Maybe this tale should have been a novel from the start, but I believe, having explored nearly every alternative, that it has been enriched by the journey. I certainly have been.

As I was writing this book, I had the assistance of many thoughtful people. Donna Howard, who is the representative from my district, and members of her staff, schooled me on the intricacies of legislating. Ursula Parks, who served on the legislative budget board, led me through the arcane intricacies of legislative magic. Lyle Larson, a former Republican member from San Antonio, was a great source of inside knowledge. Lyle was a champion of water issues and actually passed legislation much like Sonny's desalination bill. Glenn Rogers, a member from Palo Pinto County, is a veterinarian and sixth-generation rancher—in many senses a dead ringer for

Sonny. He filled me in on dominionism and the chicanery of certain billionaires. I know many readers will view the character of Odell Peeples as crossing the line into farce, but some of the big money men who pull the strings on the legislature are too exotic to lampoon.

Chris Tomlinson, a business columnist for the *Houston Chronicle,* consulted with me on oil and gas. Evan Smith, the founder and CEO of the *Texas Tribune,* and Ross Ramsey, its executive editor and co-founder, were especially generous with their time and capacious knowledge. Ross read through a draft and offered many helpful suggestions. Dan Okrent, Stephen Harrigan, Ali Selim, and Philip Bobbitt also read all or portions of the manuscript and saved me from embarrassment in a number of instances. Stan Olano at the Texas School for the Blind and Visually Impaired educated me on a world I knew little about. So many others, unmentioned here, have guided and befriended me, and I hope they know how grateful I am.

Andrew Wylie, my agent, has been my steadfast advisor. I've been fortunate to have a long history with Knopf and all the wonderful people there. But this book also marks a farewell with my editor, Ann Close, who is retiring. This is number eleven, our final venture together, a bittersweet moment for both of us. Thanks, Ann, you've been a delightful partner.

A NOTE ABOUT THE AUTHOR

LAWRENCE WRIGHT is a staff writer for *The New Yorker*, a playwright, and a screenwriter. He is the author of two novels, including the best-selling *The End of October*, and eleven books of nonfiction, including *Going Clear*, *God Save Texas*, and *The Looming Tower*, winner of the Pulitzer Prize. He and his wife are longtime residents of Austin, Texas.

A NOTE ON THE TYPE

The text of this book was set in Sabon, a typeface designed by Jan Tschichold (1902–1974), the well-known German typographer. Based loosely on the original designs by Claude Garamond (ca. 1480–1561), Sabon is unique in that it was explicitly designed for hot-metal composition on both the Monotype and Linotype machines as well as for filmsetting. Designed in 1966 in Frankfurt, Sabon was named for the famous Lyons punch cutter Jacques Sabon, who is thought to have brought some of Garamond's matrices to Frankfurt.

Typeset by Scribe,
Philadelphia, Pennsylvania

Printed and bound by Berryville Graphics,
Berryville, Virginia

Designed by Cassandra J. Pappas